The Mother I Never Had

a novel

Gary Goldstein

The Mother I Never Had. Copyright © 2022, by Gary Goldstein.
This is a work of fiction. Characters, places, events and organizations are fictitious or products of the author's imagination. Any similarity to actual persons, events or locations are coincidental.

Hadleigh House Publishing
Minneapolis, MN
www.hadleighhouse.com

All rights reserved.

No part of this book may be reproduced or transmitted in any form or by any means, electronic or mechanical, including photocopying, recording, or by any information storage or retrieval system, permitted by law. For information contact Hadleigh House Publishing, Minneapolis, MN.

Cover design by Alisha Perkins

ISBN-979-8-9850576-1-4
ISBN-979-8-9850576-2-1 (ebook)
LCCN: 2022908696

PRAISE FOR *THE MOTHER I NEVER HAD*

"There are so many surprises and joys in this beautiful, human, well-told, emotionally rich story, that you won't want it to end." – Iris Rainer Dart, bestselling author of *Beaches*

"A highly pleasurable read with a lovable main character at its center … Goldstein expertly captures Nate's essence with sharp dialogue and a relatable interior monologue. The author also gives us a fine-tuned exploration of what family means … in this TREASURE OF A NOVEL. I highly recommend it to anyone who has ever been at a crossroads in life—which is everyone!"
– Elyssa Friedland, author of *Last Summer at the Golden Hotel*

"Goldstein has crafted a 'what if?' tale that's as poignant and profound as it is propulsive. An evocative journey of love, loss, and discovery." – Darin Strauss, award-winning author of *Half a Life* and *The Queen of Tuesday*

"Gary Goldstein's sensitive, wonderfully detailed imagining of what would happen if you found a mother you never knew you had, is deeply emotional and filled with complex, but ultimately lovable characters—in other words, just like a real family."
– Bruce Cameron, #1 *New York Times* bestselling author of *A Dog's Purpose*

"Can a mother's love ever come too late? A poignant and powerful story about loss and love, and the lie that sent two lives on trajectories of regret. You'll think about *The Mother I Never Had* long after you put it down." – Ken Pisani, *Los Angeles Times* bestselling author of *AMP'D.*

"Goldstein is a skilled storyteller and his latest book is a real page-turner. His vividly crafted characters draw you in and the plot has twists and turns about family dynamics that keep you guessing right up to the end. I couldn't put the book down—and neither will you." – Andrea Cagan, *New York Times* bestselling author of *Diana Ross: Secrets of a Sparrow* and *Grace Slick: Somebody to Love?*

Also from Hadleigh House Publishing

PRAISE FOR GARY GOLDSTEIN'S
THE LAST BIRTHDAY PARTY

Winner of a 2022 IBPA Benjamin Franklin Award for Excellence in Fiction.

"With wry humor and compassion, Gary Goldstein has written a vividly drawn portrait of a year in the life of a 50-year-old man navigating the ups and downs of midlife romance, family dynamics, and professional challenges. A great read."
– Peter Lefcourt, author of *The Dreyfus Affair: A Love Story*

"Goldstein's crackling wit makes his debut novel an absolute joy. His characters are wonderfully drawn; by the end, they feel like old friends. Come for the frothy plot and zippy writing, stay for the heartfelt storytelling and deliciously satisfying ending. A refreshing and uplifting read, highly recommend!
– Susan Walter, author of *Good as Dead*

"Brisk, funny, and wise, with a keen eye for the absurdities of L.A. living, in a city of constant reinvention, Gary Goldstein has written a warm, appealing, and heartfelt coming-of-middle-age story." – Mark Sarvas, American Book Award-winning author of *Memento Park*

"A wonderful read: fun, insightful, and surprising right up to the last page. I found the inner life of our protagonist not only entertaining but thought-provoking. Do not miss this party!" – Robin Riker, author, *A Survivor's Guide to Hollywood*

"The adjectives 'hilarious' and 'painful' have never been so seamlessly married as they are in the pages of Gary Goldstein's new novel, *The Last Birthday Party*, an achingly funny love letter to 'midlife' in all its anxiety, anguish, and awe. I loved it."
– David Dean Bottrell, author of *Working Actor*

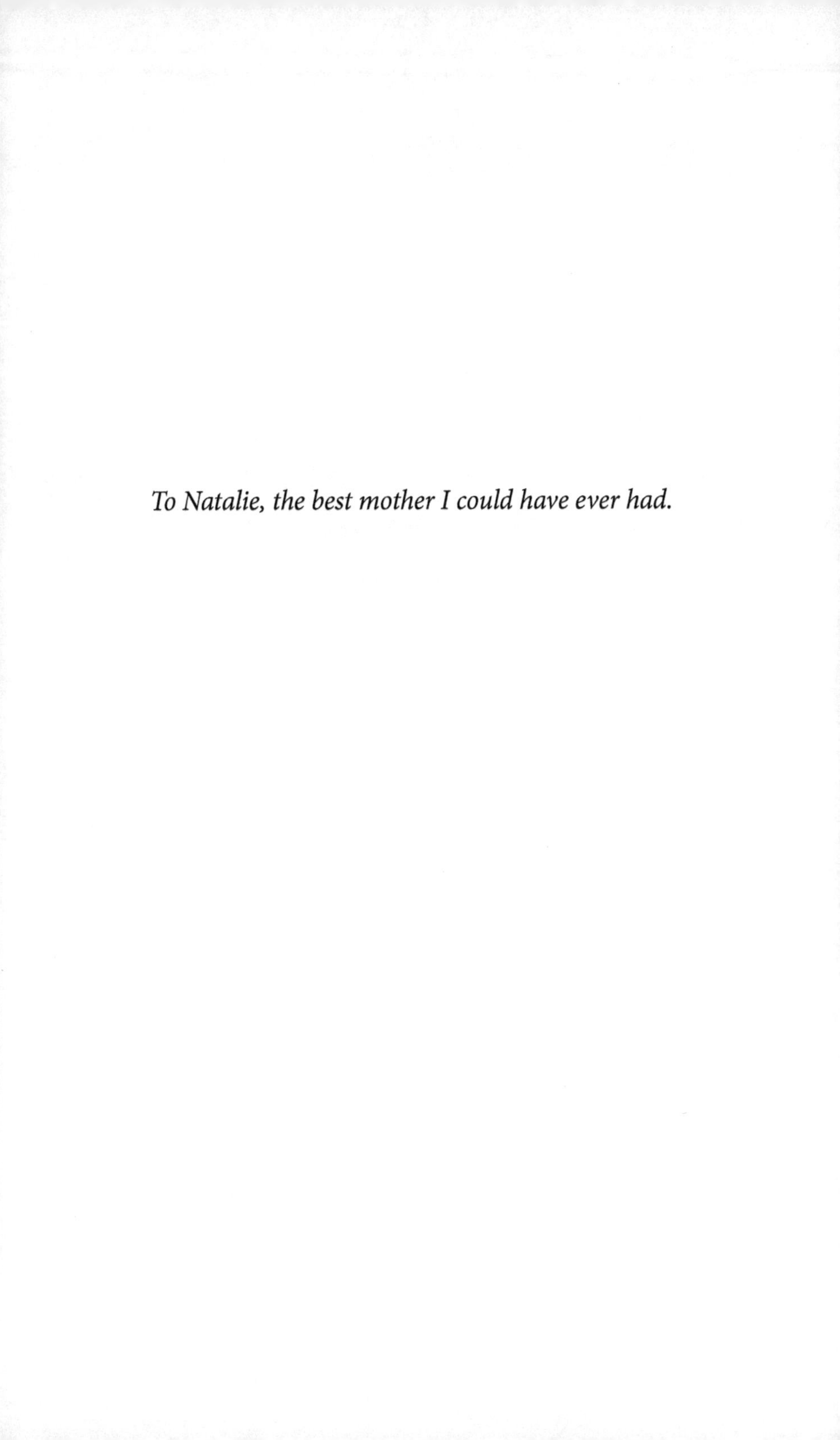

To Natalie, the best mother I could have ever had.

"Life changes in the instant. The ordinary instant."
-Joan Didion, *The Year of Magical Thinking*

ONE

NATE'S MORNING BEGAN like any other. So how could he possibly know that, well before the day was over, his life would never be the same? Who would have guessed that something that was laid to rest for him some thirty years ago would soon return to upend everything he'd ever thought and known and alter his entire worldview? All that, just as another major part of his life was about to disappear?

He'd often swing by Occidental College to visit his dad, who had taught American Literature there for the past twenty or so years. Nate loved to linger in the back of a lecture hall listening to the cool, accessibly erudite Jim Cronin theorize on one great author or another, one great novel or another, always making it sound like the first time he'd ever held forth about either. Jim had a wondrous view of books, of the written word, and this enthusiasm made the professor seem far younger than his sixty-two years. That and his longish, still more pepper-than-salt hair; vintage T-shirts; athletic build (strange, because Jim's idea of exercise was pacing in front of a lecture hall); and warm, melodious voice that made the potentially dull seem captivating.

Nate would spot the occasional coed—and even a few so-inclined male students—eying his dad like they would readily jump his bones if the opportunity knocked, age difference be damned. Jim acted oblivious to all that, and looked at Nate like his son had three heads the one time he mentioned that his dad's students seemed "hot for teacher."

"I could be their grandfather, for God's sake," Jim said. But Nate knew the thought tickled his unaffected dad, even if he would never act upon it. He was more of a straight arrow than he looked, which may have added to his appeal.

"I can't believe you still teach *The Great Gatsby*," Nate said as he and Jim exited stately Fowler Hall that pivotal morning and made their way across Occidental's lush, bucolic grounds. Jim's lecture on the famed, if oft-trod, novel was his usual mix of inspiring and insightful, positing that the reader's trust in narrator Nick Carraway is the key to believing that Gatsby is, in fact, great. "I mean, it never gets old for you, does it?"

"'It is a lucky man who succeeds at that which he loves,'" quoted Jim with professorial authority.

Nate assessed his father as they turned onto the lovely Academic Quad, where students gathered, studied, sat, and ate under its towering old oak and eucalyptus trees. It made Nate's heart ache for his college days, its freedoms and possibilities. "Don't tell me," Nate guessed about the source of his dad's bookish quote. "Albert Camus."

He flashed Nate a devious twinkle. "Jim Cronin," he answered, tapping his chest. Camus clearly had nothing on Cronin.

"I should've known," Nate joked. He wished he had half his dad's *joie de vivre*, his puckishness, his intellect. But Nate, earnest and orderly, sometimes felt more like the parent than the child, especially as he was growing up motherless, Jim filling the role of both mom and dad. Their differences somehow worked for them; Nate adored his father and the feeling was mutual. "How about that cup of coffee you promised me?" Nate asked, worried he'd be late for the noon estimate he had to give on a new landscaping job.

Jim hesitated. "I need to talk to you about something first."

The sound in his father's voice, so serious and troubled, gave Nate pause. He saw something fearful in his deep blue eyes. "What is it, Dad?"

"Let's sit down, okay, son?" Jim said, indicating a quiet area toward the edge of the campus. Nate's head and heart began to race. His father quickened his pace; Nate silently followed. Jim waved at a few passing students, though never turned to meet their gaze.

They reached a bench perched on a bluff overlooking downtown Los Angeles, its familiar structures and towers shimmering in the hazy spring sun. It was an especially beautiful day in contrast to the kind of news Nate was expecting to receive. He and his father sat side by side and faced out at the city skyline and the dense residential areas that lay before it.

Jim told Nate his painful story in an uncharacteristically careful, plainspoken manner, struggling to reach the finish line without shedding a tear. Somehow, Nate saw his own life flash before his eyes as if it were he and not his beloved dad who had the inoperable tumor.

"You've known for six months and you haven't told me?"

Jim absorbed his son's anger while formulating the most honest answer he could. "It's bad enough I had to know," he finally said. "Besides, there's nothing you or anyone else could have done."

"Except be there for you," Nate said quietly, his fury morphing into something more desperate, more helpless. He could barely remember his father being sick a day in his life. What kind of cruel joke was this?

"You've been there for me, pal," said Jim, unable to contain his tears any longer, "you just didn't know it." He wiped his eyes with the back of his hands, swallowing hard. "I promised myself I wouldn't do this." But that didn't stop his tears.

Nate only had one more question. Not that he wanted the answer. "Did the doctors say how long … how … much time?"

"A month, maybe two," Jim answered, his voice muffled.

Nate stared at the distant skyline, strained to remember the name of that iconic white tower with its rounded sides. It used to be the tallest building in Los Angeles but now it was number two or three. What a strange thing to be thinking about at such a dire moment. The mind works in mysterious ways, especially when one needed protection.

"Pretty shitty, huh?" Jim's eyebrows arched in a kind of wry disbelief. For a flash, he looked like the old Jim: charismatic Jim, raconteur Jim, the Jim who would live forever. But all Nate could see was the Jim whose body had betrayed him, the father he couldn't picture a life without.

Nate knew the answer to the question he was about to ask but asked it anyway. "And there's absolutely nothing that can be done?" Jim shook his head. Nate nodded just as faintly. It hit him: The U.S. Bank building. *So fucking what?*

Jim turned to Nate. "Look, I don't have a lot saved up, but I'm leaving you the house. Live there, sell it, whatever you decide. It's yours." Nate couldn't quite process what his father was saying. Jim cracked a small smile and added, "Hey, you'll finally be able to landscape the place the way you want."

"Jesus, Dad." It was all Nate could muster. Maybe that said it all. He wanted to ask, "How can you joke at a time like this? How can you even think straight? Get up in the morning? Get dressed? Keep teaching the fucking *Great Gatsby*?"

Instead, Nate thought about Jim's house, that small, weathered Craftsman just a few blocks away on Eagle Rock's winding Escarpa Drive. How it cried out for a shot of new paint and, yes, a new front garden and a serious tree trim. How the place was not unlike Jim himself: charming, casual, deceptively solid. How Nate had lived there with his dad for a decade before college, moving from their modest rental in Valley Village about a mile from where Jim had once taught high school English.

A door shut on Nate's fleeting memory and suddenly he found the right words to say—and the heart to say them. "I'm so, *so* sorry, Dad."

"No, Nate. *I'm* sorry." They were four short words but filled with unspeakable sorrow. "And just know that whatever I've done as a father, it's always been with your best interest at heart."

Nate studied his dad, still so effortlessly handsome despite the destruction unfolding within him. "Why would I ever think anything else?"

Jim returned his son's gaze with an enigmatic stare. It would take a while for Nate to receive his answer.

TWO

Jim didn't want a funeral, so he didn't have one. He had an unexpected request instead. Or maybe not so unexpected given Jim's love of the literary: He wanted to be cremated and his ashes scattered in the waters off Portuguese Bend, a remote area on the Palos Verdes Peninsula south of L.A. where one of Jim's favorite authors, Joan Didion, lived with her family during the 1960s. Nate had been to the scenic spot a few times with Jim over the years, though never quite understood his father's fascination with Didion, whose writing Nate found too stark and gloomy. Jim would say Nate was missing the point, to which Nate would ask "What *is* the point?"

So a week after Jim's death, Nate and Cody, his lovably galumphing, six-year-old Shepherd Lab mix, piled into Nate's Chevy Silverado ("Nathaniel Cronin—Landscape Design" graced its driver's side door panel), and drove down to Portuguese Bend, the classic rock of Jim's Central California youth blaring in memoriam from the truck's Bose sound system. Nate grew up listening to the Stones, the Steve Miller Band, Fleetwood Mac, Steely Dan, Bruce Springsteen, and all his dad's other favorites, making these "moldy oldies," as he'd jokingly call them, his own as part of their many bonding rituals.

It was easier than reading Joan Didion—or even Fitzgerald, for that matter.

Nate sang along, that appropriately overcast summer morning, to "My Old School" and "Second Hand News" and "Rosalita" as he and Cody wound their way down Pacific Coast Highway past Manhattan Beach and Redondo Beach, then swung into more upscale Palos Verdes. When Nate saw the sign for Inspiration Point, an iconic hiking spot with awesome views of the Pacific, he knew Portuguese Bend wasn't far behind—and there it was. He parked on the grassy bluffs above the rustic beach and leaned across the passenger seat to open the door for Cody, who leaped out and instantly peed on a patch of weeds. Nate reached beneath his seat, grabbed the small bronze urn that held Jim's ashes, and joined Cody, who was now urgently sniffing at a thicket of Pride of Madeira. He was clearly not the only dog who'd staked its claim up there lately.

Jim's doctor had lied. Nate's dad lived beyond the "month, maybe two" that had been predicted. By two weeks and three days. Hardly an eternity but precious bonus time to help Nate settle into the crushing blow that was on its inevitable way. Jim managed to finish the semester just as the exhaustion and pain began to overtake him. He spent his last month laying low on Escarpa Drive, rereading old books, smoking dope and popping edibles (not always for medicinal purposes), and saying his goodbyes to friends, students, and colleagues. Nate spent as much time at Jim's as he could, sleeping over with Cody as needed until a hospice nurse had to step in. Jim stayed mostly upbeat, more for Nate than for himself, even if the wistful resignation in his ever-weakening voice was hard to miss. It was sad and profound and strangely civilized, and Nate held his father's surprisingly warm hand when he finally slipped away.

Portuguese Bend Beach was thankfully empty that Sunday morning. Maybe the clouds were keeping folks away or maybe it was just the early hour—it was barely nine—but it gave Nate a wider berth to scatter Jim's ashes into the choppy ocean. Though he had gotten a permit to do so—Jim had looked into that in plenty of time— Nate didn't want weird looks or hassles from any proprietary locals.

"It's so crazy," Nate noted during one of his many marathon talks with his dad those last two months, "it's not illegal to take a dump off the coast but a little ash is some kind of federal offense!" Jim laughed, as much at the irony of the statement as the fact that, of the two of them, Nate was the one more prone to play by the rules. Maybe the kid was loosening up in his "old age."

Nate had played this scene over in his mind many times, but it felt different once he was standing at the edge of the Pacific, about to fling a gob of his father's ashes into the hissing cobalt waves. He had thought about what he'd say before letting go of those eerily finite remains, imagining something that was not quite a prayer—think: more literary than liturgical—yet had its own sort of eternal gravity. Still, when the time came, words escaped Nate. So he relied instead on memories of his dad, a kind of greatest hits-worth of images from Nate's childhood to last week, as the ashes swirled and flew through the salty breeze. Cody romped and barked as Nate threw handfuls of dust out to sea until the urn was as empty as Nate's heart.

Nate felt exhausted, as if he'd just raced from one end of the beach to the other. He sat down on the rocky sand—it was more like sandy rock—Cody panting at his side, and gazed out at the horizon, envisioning the slow and steady voyage of Jim's remains. As if on cue, the sun peeked out from behind the clouds and reflected against the waves. Nate lifted his face to the sky, closed his eyes, and took in the emerging warmth. He hoped his dad would have approved of that morning's ritual; it was, after all, his idea. "At least you'll know where to find me," Jim had told Nate, with a sly smile, after choosing Portuguese Bend for his seaside sendoff. It was a far more comforting thought now than it was at the time.

That night, Nate downloaded a copy of Joan Didion's *Blue Nights* and stayed up till three—while Cody sawed logs beside him—reading about Didion's days as a resident of Portuguese Bend. He finally understood what his dad saw in the iconic author.

THREE

JENNIFER HAD WANTED to accompany Nate to scatter Jim's ashes, but Nate respectfully declined. He actually used those words: "Thanks, Jen, I appreciate it but … I respectfully decline." They may have sounded like they were coming out of someone else's mouth, someone a bit more arch than Nate, but they seemed appropriate and, well, respectful. He never wanted to offend Jen—nor she, him—even though they did plenty of that when they broke up shortly after New Year's. They'd both said things then that they now regretted—probably regretted them at the time—but they'd made the mistake of holding back so much for so long that when it finally came out it was excessive and wrongheaded.

At the heart of their problem was that, after almost two years together, Nate had been unable to commit to the next step with her. It was something she'd been aiming for once she realized they were truly good together. That if they weren't madly in love, they did seriously love each other, felt safe and protected around each other, two things neither could unequivocally say about their exes. But Jennifer was too prideful—or maybe insecure—to simply lay out a plan for her boyfriend, expecting he would eventually make some kind of offer: if not marriage, then at least cohabitation.

But Nate wasn't ready: emotionally, financially and, he feared, romantically. What if there was someone better out there for him—or he for them—and he was being held back from finding that person? Then again, he would ask himself in his quietest moments, what more did he want from a woman? Who did he think he was to even ask that? He was crazy lucky that Jen said yes to that first date to begin with, after their chance meeting at a popular Silver Lake dive bar. Not to mention that she kept saying yes to him until they woke up together one morning a month or so in, made coffee and smoothies and avocado toast, and realized they were a couple. Nate remembered thinking during that breakfast how he wanted to freeze the moment, never leave it; it was so idyllic. And in a way that's what he did. It soon became a matter of "If it ain't broke, why break it?" and, for a while, it seemed—at least to Nate—as if Jennifer was on that same wavelength. It was easy, comforting, sexy, and Nate felt better about himself than he had in ages.

That was certainly because of Jennifer, but also because his landscaping business was taking off after building it up to the point that, thanks to great word-of-mouth, jobs not only came to him but he was always booked out at least one or two gigs ahead. He was able to bring on a full-time co-worker, the talented, resourceful, and eternally chipper Danny Soto, who was magically able to round up a work crew anytime, anywhere. Danny's adorable wife, Alicia, a quick-witted accountant, managed Nate's billing and helped keep his finances and taxes in order. That is, when she wasn't busy tending to her and Danny's rambunctious two-year-old, Raffi. Danny had become as much a partner as a best friend. Nate felt almost fraternal toward him, like a not-much-older brother—even if the younger Danny, already a dad, husband, and homeowner, was in some ways the more stabilizing influence.

Jennifer did, however, convince Nate to hold a small lunch gathering in Jim's honor that Sunday, the day after the ash scattering, and Nate hesitantly agreed. (And there was their dynamic in a nutshell: when he held back, she pushed forward—and vice versa. It was an inspiring, often empowering balancing act, until all movement stalled.)

Jim had specifically said "no parties or memorials," perhaps because he didn't want to burden Nate with any more emotional—or financial—expenditure. But Nate knew that so many of Jim's Occidental friends, students, and fellow profs wanted to pay their respects, so it seemed like a fitting coda. Nate lined up a reasonable caterer (Jen forbid him to go the Costco route), sent a mass email invite to Jim's contacts, and, the morning of the memorial, after not much sleep the night before (thanks, Joan Didion!), went and straightened up his father's home to make it presentable.

It was the first time Nate had been alone in the house for more than a few minutes since Jim died and it felt weird, even invasive, to be organizing or discarding so much of his dad's belongings, things that suddenly belonged to, well, no one. Sure, in truth, Jim's stuff was now Nate's to do with as he pleased—whatever made the most sense. Even stranger, the whole house was now Nate's, at least after Jim's lawyer drew up the deed transfer and whatever else would make it legal and binding. It hit Nate that, not only would he be moving back into the house where he lived as a kid for so many years—where he kissed his first girl, where his father had died—but that he hadn't yet made plans to move out of the boxy one-bedroom apartment he'd been renting in North Hollywood for longer than he ever expected. He'd been on automatic pilot these last weeks without even realizing it.

For a guy who had a definite style, a certain *je ne sais quoi*, Jim was never much in the decorating department. So, Nate realized, as he vacuumed faded rugs, plumped shrunken pillows, and dusted scratched tabletops and bookshelves, that he owed it to his dad—and to himself—to get the old house, with its good bones and deep history (built in 1923!), back up to speed. Not that Nate was so great either in the indoor aesthetics department—unlike his landscaper's measured eye for outdoor beauty, his apartment had remained largely utilitarian, more dedicated to Cody's comfort than to his own. In any case, Nate had his work cut out for him, on so many fronts.

"**THANKS FOR BEING** here," said Nate to Jennifer after she wound her way through the guest-packed living room to reach him. They shared a gentle, awkward hug. It was the first time they'd seen each other in a month, since Jennifer had stopped by one Saturday to visit Jim. Since then, their interactions were all by phone or text—and all related to Jim. Nate wasn't quite prepared to see her even though he knew she'd be there. After all, the lunch was her idea. She wore a sleeveless print summer dress that showed off her toned arms and dancer's legs.

"Nate, I thought the world of your father, you know that," Jennifer said, sweeping a few stray strands of longish, chestnut brown hair off her face. In the past, Nate might have been the one to do that for her—as he would lean in for a kiss. But not anymore.

Nate said, "I meant, thanks for being here for *me*." Jennifer nodded, half-smiling. Just as Nate was about to fill in the silence, a trio of Occidental profs converged on him, plates of braised mustard chicken and Caesar salad in hand.

"Your father was a wonderful teacher and a truly fine man," said the first. Nate thought her name was Penny but realized he might have been confusing her with someone else.

"Occidental's lost a great one. The English department won't be the same without him," added the second. This was India, a trans woman who Nate hadn't seen since she was Ian.

"He talked about you all the time, Nate, you meant everything to him," said the third prof, resting a hand on Nate's shoulder. "I hope you know that."

"I do, Tomás, thank you," answered Nate. Tomás taught creative writing and Medieval Lit. He and Jim were occasional drinking buddies. Nate had joined them once or twice what seemed like a lifetime ago.

The three gazed at Nate with empathy but it read like pity and made Nate squirm. "Thanks so much for coming," he finally told the well-meaning educators and gestured in the direction of the backyard. "I have to go check on my dog, I think I hear him barking at something."

"I'll go with you," Jennifer offered, knowing that barking or not, Nate needed to escape. She turned to the professors. "I'm Jennifer, by the way, Nate's … friend. Jim's too." They all exchanged solemn nods. Jennifer followed Nate to the kitchen and out to the quiet yard where Cody was sprawled on what was left of the grass, happily gnawing on a grungy rawhide bone. He bolted up to greet them, tail thwacking away.

Jennifer eyed Nate. "You okay?"

"Yeah. I guess. Not really, I don't know." He chucked the old bone across the yard and Cody raced after it. "Anyway," Nate continued, "it's nothing to worry about."

Nate vacantly watched Cody snap the bone up off the ground and hustle it back to them. "Y'know, just because we're not together anymore doesn't mean I don't still care about you," Jennifer said as Cody dropped the slobbery toy at her feet.

It wasn't that Nate didn't believe her, but hearing it out loud like that fucked him up a little. He let the comment go, indicating Cody's bone instead. "He wants you to throw it," Nate said, a small grin spreading across his face. He knew how she felt about drool. She was a bit of a clean freak.

"Yeah, I know the drill," she said, gingerly reaching for the bone and tossing the gloppy thing a few feet. It was so endearing Nate had to look away. Cody dove for it like she'd thrown it a mile.

"Of anyone I ever dated, Dad liked you the best," Nate told her. "Always joked that if I didn't marry you, he would." As soon as the words were out of his mouth Nate wanted to cram them back in. *The "m" word. Jesus!* He could feel the sweat begin to pool beneath his light blue button-down.

Jennifer let the awkward moment slide and sat on a rickety teak bench that looked like it might collapse under her. "It's too bad he never remarried," she said. "Your dad was a catch."

"He never got over my mom. Said he was a one-woman man." Nate thought about sitting next to Jen—he was suddenly so tired—but kept standing. Cody had lost interest in the bone and was sacked out in some weeds.

"She was the love of his life. I get it," said Jennifer, looking away from Nate at a pomegranate tree that still, remarkably, bore fruit. It was big and ancient and thrived on neglect.

Nate gave in and sat next to Jennifer, daring the bench to hold together for two adult bodies. It did. "And yet, to be honest," he said, "Dad never talked much about her. Their life together, how he felt when she died. In his way, he was kind of a private guy."

"Like father, like son." Jennifer turned to Nate, shoulders slumped, an unmistakable look of contrition on her face. "I'm sorry … I didn't mean it that way."

But Nate knew that she did and he deserved it. Maybe not at this very moment, but still. He looked back at his ex-girlfriend, at her gentle, uncomplicated beauty, and chose to say nothing.

FOUR

MOVING OUT OF his apartment and into Jim's house took a lot less time than Nate expected, largely because he took so little of his own stuff with him. So little that he was able to fit it all in the Silverado's cargo bed and the compact U-Haul trailer he hitched to the back. He chose to donate most of his furniture to Habitat for Humanity and just live with Jim's old pieces which, even if they were hardly in mint condition, had a sentimental value that Nate's IKEA collection (plus a few entries from Pottery Barn and Wayfair) decidedly did not. His clothes, books, an LG flat screen, year-old Dreamcloud mattress (the memory foam was killer), Cody's worldly possessions (the mutt had three huge beds), a few items that were Jim's to begin with—a cool mid-century wall clock, a hammered brass coffee table, an impressively framed Miró print—and Nate's pride: a rangy quartet of thriving potted plants, all made their way to Escarpa Drive.

Jennifer had called the night before to see if Nate needed any help moving; they hadn't spoken since Jim's memorial gathering the previous week. He was happy to hear her voice and appreciated her offer but told her Danny was going to help him with the heavier pieces and that the rest would be a snap. Both of those things were a lie—Danny had, in fact, offered to help, but Nate needed him on their current landscaping job, which was running behind—and little about moving was ever a "snap." But seeing Jennifer last time was painful and, as much as Nate missed what they once had, he thought some time apart would be best. Apparently, so did she.

"Nate, I'm going to start dating again," she said after they got past the moving day talk. "I need to get on with things."

All things considered, Nate should have felt relieved, a little anyway, but he didn't. He clearly didn't know what the fuck he wanted. "Good. That's good," he answered. What was one more lie?

"I can't wait for you anymore," she continued. "Not if we're not going somewhere." Her voice sounded clear, maybe practiced. Nate respected her resolve.

"I understand. I do," he said as he packed the last of his linens in a Hefty bag.

Jennifer was silent, perhaps expecting a different answer, maybe some fight. "What are you so afraid of?" she finally asked. Nate could tell she was still in the dance studio, probably after teaching class; there was a familiar hollowness on the line.

He sealed the linens bag with a plastic tie and set it aside. "I'm not afraid of anything. But Jen, we've been through this. I'm just not there."

"Just don't resent me because I am. Okay?"

There was a catch in Nate's throat. "I could never resent you." He sat on the dusty floor and leaned against the wall. The seconds ticked by.

"Look, I'll call you," she said with sudden finality. "Good luck with the move."

Nate wanted to tell her how if she could just wait, just give him time, he'd come around, and they could be together. Forever. But he knew that wasn't fair to her and that he couldn't promise that—or much of anything right now. This was Jennifer's call and Nate was making a conscious (some might say ridiculous) choice.

He thought about this last conversation with Jennifer throughout the day that he moved into Jim's house and wondered what it would have been like to share the place with her, share a life with her. And yet, as Nate took the first steps in the long and arduous process of making his old home his new home, while still keeping the spirit of his father alive, he found himself embracing his independence in a way he hadn't in the past. He was starting over.

Nate decided, as part of the "new him," he would give as much attention to the inside of the Escarpa house as he was planning for the outside, or at least as much as his time and his budget would allow. It turned out that, despite years of regular gainful employment, Jim did not, as he'd told Nate that day on the bench looking out at L.A., have much money put away. There were always clothes on Jim's back, food in his refrigerator, and a roof—leaky though it may have been—over his head, so he never pried about his dad's financial state. It was enough that Nate was trying to keep his own propped up as he grew his landscaping business. Still, he decided to use the small chunk of savings Jim had left behind in a zero-interest checking account to fix up the old house. And if he eventually had to dip into his own funds, so be it.

NATE RESERVED SUNDAYS for re-landscaping his house (*his house*: that still blew him away), paying Danny and the crew above their usual rate—plus breakfast, lunch, and four o'clock beer—for their help. Danny hadn't wanted to take money for something so personal, but Nate insisted, pulling whatever rank still existed between them. "You think I'm gonna take you away from the fam on your day off for free?" he asked rhetorically.

"Who says you're not doing me a favor?" Danny shot back with a grin, but Nate knew he was full of shit: Danny was crazy about Alicia and Raffi.

"Better call HGTV," Danny said as they began work on the needy front yard. "We're talking 'before and after' to the max!"

"I begged my dad to let me spruce the place up, but he liked it just the way it was: low-maintenance," said Nate.

"I think you mean *no*-maintenance," Danny joked as he dug out a tall pyracantha bush that had turned wraith-like. "Did your pops, like, not know you're actually supposed to *water* a yard?" He stopped himself. "All due respect."

"Oh, he knew," answered Nate as he unearthed another crumbled shrub that was, by all rights, unkillable. "But watering was like a game between us: Whenever I'd stop by I'd set the sprinkler timer and then as soon as I'd leave he'd turn it off. He was always convinced it was going to rain."

"In L.A.? Dude was an optimist."

"Super laid-back was more like it. But not about his classes—or his books. About those, the guy was laser-focused." Nate stood back and surveyed the sad-looking planters that flanked the short driveway. At least the few jade plants in them were still alive; they were tough little buggers.

Danny started hacking back what was once a lush lantana bush, hoping to revive the normally hearty plant. "Must be weird, living in the same house you grew up in all over again."

"It was for the first week or so, but I'm getting used to it. There's something kinda … healing about it, I guess," Nate explained. "Even if my dad is still everywhere."

"But that's a good thing, yeah?" Danny grunted between hacks. "Gone, but not forgotten. It's like when my grandma passed last year. Thought about her every day—dreamed about her at night." He put down the pruning saw and recalled, "And you know what? She was always happy and healthy in those dreams, wanted to know why I hadn't called her in so long. I could never tell her the truth: 'Because you're dead, *Abuela*. No phones where you are!'" Danny flashed a faraway smile. It unnerved Nate.

"Okay, that's enough therapy for one day," said Nate, forcing an upbeat tone. "Pretty soon you'll be charging me shrink fees!"

"On the house, dude," Danny said with a wink and went back to work on the pyracantha.

A few Sundays into the front yard renovation—Nate planned to replant the back too, but curb appeal took priority—he and Danny were digging a hole for a gorgeous Japanese maple Nate had splurged on, when a small white sedan stopped diagonally across from the house. Nate looked up from his shovel and spotted the driver, an attractive brunette, gazing at the garden in progress. He didn't think much of it; people were always driving past, checking out his work, and sometimes copying his phone number off the "Nathaniel Cronin Landscape Design" placard he proudly displayed at his jobs. (He wondered if sticking one in his own front yard was tacky until Danny said "Bro, that's why it's called 'your house.'")

But this woman seemed to be staring right at Nate—not the work, not the sign—as if she were trying to place him. Nate wondered if he wasn't just being paranoid or self-conscious and went back to digging. A few moments later, the white car glided past them and down the road. Nate looked up again as it disappeared and found Danny eyeballing him.

"What?" Nate asked, a tad defensively.

"That pretty lady was scoping you out, son." Danny's grin was wider than usual.

"How do you know? Maybe she's a potential client."

"Yeah, sex client. 'Ooh, Nate, plant your big, fat hoe *right here.*'" Danny made a lewd gesture with his own, actual hoe, which was conveniently at hand.

Nate couldn't help but laugh at his good-natured sidekick, even if there *was* something a bit unsettling about that driver's gaze. He thought it best to change the subject. "Hey, so I'm also thinking of widening the path and lining it with lavender," Nate said, pointing at the trail of slate slabs leading to the front door. "What do you think?"

"I think you haven't had a bad idea since I've been working for you," said Danny. "At least about landscaping."

Nate leaned on his shovel, staring at Danny, who couldn't hold back a grin if it killed him. "Want to finish that thought, D.?" Nate asked, though he could have finished it for him.

"Well, dropping Jen wasn't exactly the move of the century." Danny stopped what he was doing, fixed his deep brown eyes on Nate.

All traces of a smile were gone—he meant business.

"She dropped *me*, remember?"

"Yeah, okay," Danny said flatly. "Do me a favor, though, bro, never say never, okay?"

"I never do," Nate answered unconvincingly and went back to work.

FIVE

After Danny and the guys left, Nate sat on the front porch and downed a couple of the leftover Tecates he'd bought for them. He wasn't that thirsty, despite the long day's work and lingering July heat, but needed something to douse the gloom he was feeling since Danny's comment about Jennifer. Nate had tried to play it off the rest of the afternoon but Danny seemed to know he'd overstepped and largely stayed out of Nate's way.

Nate looked out at the yard, pleased with its progress (that Japanese maple was totally worth the bucks), as Cody lolled at his side snapping in vain at a halo of gnats. The beers had provided a welcome buzz and Nate was now feeling a bit lighter and more hopeful. His timing with Jennifer had simply been off and he needed to trust that, trust himself—something that was not exactly his greatest strength. He wondered if he would have talked more about her with his dad had he not been sick; romantic issues seemed so trivial compared to what Jim was going through. This isn't to say Jim didn't weigh in on Nate and Jennifer's split ("Just because she's the perfect woman doesn't mean she's perfect for you," he'd offered.) Then again, Jim's successful track record with relationships began and ended with Nate's mom, so even he knew he was hardly an oracle in that arena.

Cody paced around the small porch as the sun dipped out of sight for the day, reminding the zoned-out Nate that it was past a certain four-legged someone's feeding time. "No rest for the weary, huh, doggo?" Nate asked as he hauled himself up out of the webbed patio chair and made for the front door.

Nate gazed around the kitchen as Cody inhaled his turkey-and-sweet-potato kibble, which Nate had mixed, as he often did, with a splotch of sugar-free applesauce. He tried to feed the dog as healthily as he could, though, in truth, Cody would eat a bowl of rocks if that's what was put in front of him. Or at least try his damndest. After nearly a month living in the house, it struck Nate that the shiny new stainless fridge he'd bought—the old one wheezed like an asthmatic—had made the kitchen, with its faded walls and mottled woodwork, look even drabber in comparison. It was nothing a quart of paint and some cabinet stain couldn't help, though Nate wanted to get more done outside before starting on the inside.

His renovation reverie was interrupted by his ringing phone. He didn't recognize the number, but he answered anyway. It was someone inquiring about an estimate for a full yard makeover—front and back. It sounded like it could be a big job with a big payday and the more of those the merrier, especially now. The caller, Amy, seemed friendly, with a warm, curious voice. They made a plan for him to stop by her house in Toluca Lake, an upscale town near the Disney and Warner Bros. studios (and not far from his old apartment), first thing Tuesday morning, before she would have to leave for work.

It wasn't until after they hung up that Nate realized he hadn't asked how the woman had heard of him or his business, usually one of his first questions of any prospective client. Maybe those three Tecates were the culprit, but, whatever: they'd been worth it. Washing out Cody's dinner dish and refilling it with water, Nate flashed on the mysterious driver who'd passed by the house that afternoon and wondered if there was any connection.

AFTER TAKING THE freeway exit for Toluca Lake, Nate rechecked the address and found himself driving north into an adjacent area known as Toluca Woods, whose homes were charming but mostly smaller and less pricey than most of those off the village's main street to the south. (Nate had once shopped next to Steve Carell at the Toluca Lake Trader Joe's; the surrounding neighborhood was filled with celebrities.) Amy's house was a modest, well-kept, stucco ranch and, as soon as Nate laid eyes on its neat, if minimally landscaped, front yard, he had a flurry of ideas on how to transform it. (When he couldn't fall asleep at night, which was often these days, he'd redesign gardens in his head; it had become second nature to him.)

The front door opened just as Nate was about to knock, and standing there was the same woman who'd driven by his house on Sunday. Or was it? As Nate eyed the attractive homeowner he realized he had no recollection of what that lady in the white car really looked like. *She had dark brown hair, didn't she?* he wondered. Amy's was more auburn. And wasn't she wearing sunglasses at the time? Or maybe Nate was, and everything had looked a few shades off to him. And wait, was her car even white? He glanced around for it, but the front curb and driveway were empty. Was it parked in the garage?

"Hi, you must be Nate," she said. He straightened up and shook her extended hand. Its soft but confident grip made an instant impression on him.

"Amy?" Who else would it be? But it seemed like the appropriate question. She was looking less and less like the woman he now barely recalled from Sunday but he had to ask anyway. "This is weird, but have we met before?"

She studied him a moment as if checking to be sure herself. "No, I don't believe we have. But I must have one of those familiar looks because people are always asking me that." Amy smiled, revealing a few encroaching lines around her eyes and mouth. Her skin was otherwise smooth and her hair fell to her shoulders, where it landed with a slight flip. Nate pegged her for early forties, though he was admittedly bad with ages. "Who's that big guy?" she asked, pointing beyond Nate to his truck parked across the street. Cody's blocky head stuck out the driver's side window.

"That's Cody. My assistant."

"Would he like some water? Coffee? Or I have tea." Her grin betrayed her little joke. Nate was charmed. He liked anyone who liked Cody.

"Wanna meet him?"

"I thought you'd never ask."

Cody trailed Nate and Amy as they toured the front and rear yards. The back was flat, scrubby, untended. In some ways, it was in worse shape than Jim's, which at least had the pomegranate tree and some decent flowering vines.

"How long have you and your husband lived here?" Nate asked. The question sounded blunter coming out than it did in his head, but his curiosity was strangely piqued.

"About a year," she answered. "And it's only me. I haven't been a 'Mrs.' in a long time." Nate nodded, left it there. What business was it of his, anyway? Amy knelt to pet Cody, who immediately gave her a tongue bath.

"Cody, no!" Nate commanded, though he secretly enjoyed seeing the big galoot showing his unbridled affection to anyone who was even remotely interested. To Amy's credit, she didn't pull away but instead leaned into the dog's soggy kisses. "I'm sorry," Nate told her, realizing that she was dressed and coiffed for work.

"Don't be, he's a love," Amy said between giggles. "Aren't you just a love?" she asked Cody as he got in his last licks. She patted her face with a tissue and smiled again. "A minute in the mirror and I'll be good to go."

Nate was duly impressed. Now for the task at hand: "So what exactly did you have in mind?" he asked Amy. She looked momentarily unsure, so he added, with a sweep of his hand, "For your yard."

"You're the professional, what would you do? And let's start here in the back, which is in worse condition than the front."

Nate had immediate ideas for replanting her backyard. But he usually waited for the homeowner to announce what they wanted and then built on it from there. When he started landscaping for a living, he discovered how the feeling of partnership—or even the illusion of it—could make all the difference in a client's happiness with Nate's work; everyone likes to feel listened to. Except maybe for Amy, who was awaiting Nate's response.

"Well, for starters, I'd rip out whatever's left of this Bermuda grass, replace it with a few small, individual gardens. Maybe connect them with crushed rock or brick paths—used brick, not the new stuff. Looks so much more classic." Nate could hear the momentum in his voice and apparently so could Amy.

"Please, go on. I love watching an artist at work," she said.

Nate could feel his face flush. "Oh, I'm not an artist. Just a landscaper." He didn't know why he felt the need to be humble, but he did.

Amy studied Nate, narrowed her gaze. "You sell yourself short."

He shifted into cockier gear. "Wouldn't want to get your hopes up too high."

"You already have."

Nate, buoyed by the compliment, went full bore around the yard, recommending she plant a few shade trees—a ficus or a sycamore or a crepe myrtle or any combination thereof —plant colorful vines to mask the ugly old grape-stake fencing, line either end of the yard with a variety of succulents, add a cluster of large terracotta pots filled with roses, vincas, and snapdragons, and on and on. Then, with Cody trotting alongside them, they returned to the front yard and Nate eagerly knocked out a second design.

Nate sat in his truck writing up an estimate while Amy neatened up for work. When he handed her the rough contract she glanced at it, didn't blink an eye, and said, "When can you start?" Nate was stunned—his clients usually offered him half then haggled their way up until he took at least twenty percent off. For some reason, he told Amy that.

"You seem like a hard-working guy," she said. "You can't feed your family on 'half.'"

"Oh, it's just me—and Cody. No family." It was the first time since Jim's death that Nate expressed those words aloud and it sent a sad surge through him. Amy watched as if she wanted more from him. It didn't come.

"Girlfriend? … Boyfriend?" she finally asked with care. Nate was amused by her equitability but overwhelmed by the question. He decided to wrap it up.

"I have two other jobs to finish, then we can start here. Say, two weeks?"

Amy smiled and extended a hand. "I'll be counting the days," she said brightly.

"By the way," Nate said, "I never did ask: How did you hear about my company?"

Amy paused. "You have some lovely reviews on Yelp. Though I'm sure you already know that."

He did know that, even if he hadn't gotten much business yet off the popular website. Still, he was satisfied by her answer; it made as much sense as anything.

As Nate shook her hand goodbye, Amy held on a tick longer than he would have expected. Was she coming on to him? *No*, he decided, *it wasn't that*. He was as bad as Danny. Still, it made him a bit skittish. He withdrew his hand and signaled Cody. "Let's hit it, guy."

They crossed the street, hopped in the truck, and drove off. Nate glanced in the rearview mirror and saw Amy watching them go.

SIX

NATE HAD LEFT Jim's office-den for last in his increasingly inspired mission to clean up, clear out, organize, and personalize every room in the house. The real renovation work would have to wait, but this was a great start and helped Nate prioritize the swelling list of indoor projects he would eventually have to attack. (He realized the kitchen would take a lot more than new paint and wood stain.) Yet he remained committed to preserving what mattered to his father. That mainly involved the spare room that Jim disappeared to most nights of Nate's tween and teen years to read, think, and prepare for his next day's classes while Nate holed away in his own room doing homework, watching TV, playing video games, or hanging out with the occasional friend.

Nate rarely used those times to do what Jim hoped his son would: read a book. A real book—a novel, something enlightening, transporting, motivating, and not just something foisted upon him by a teacher following a perfunctory syllabus. "And no," Jim would remind Nate, "comic books, graphic novels, and the Internet do not count as literature."

Then there was the newspaper. Jim had the *L.A. Times* delivered every day until he died. (Nate still hadn't canceled the subscription; didn't yet have the heart.) Jim somehow managed to read the paper every day, even if it only meant scanning the bigger national stories and editorials and a sweep through the Calendar section. He would also never read it online; like his love of physical books, he was a purist about the press. Nate's entire contact with the newspaper growing up was bringing it in off the front porch—or wherever the delivery guy's haphazard aim landed it that morning—and depositing it on his father's desk. Unlike with books, Jim never even tried to persuade his boy to read the newspaper. He knew it was a generational thing—a rapidly vanishing one at that—and a lost cause. Still, Nate would randomly zip through the sports section to see what the Dodgers or the Clippers were up to. And for a while, during his middle school days, he'd sneak a look at the horoscopes to maybe learn something—anything—about a girl he was liking, get a leg up so to speak. He eventually realized those forecasts were confusing and interchangeable and the girl wasn't going to like him anyway.

So it was a shock to Jim, as well as to Nate, when, in his second year at Cal State LA, he decided to study to become a teacher. "Since when did you want to get into education?" Jim asked Nate when he heard the news.

"I thought you'd be happy," Nate answered.

"I want *you* to be happy," his father said in response.

Nate took that to heart and became something else.

As for books, the adult Nate did start to read them, took lots of recommendations from Jim, liked some, struggled with others, found his type, then found some more he liked until he was no longer wary or intimidated about what might lie between any two hard or softbound covers. Now *that* made his father happy. Nate would never read another book again without thinking of his dad and wanting to talk with him about it after.

When Nate finally did ensconce himself in the office-den one night to assess how to maintain the place, he found it as emotionally daunting a task as he expected, which was why he'd waited so long to deal with it. (Before that evening, every time Nate had to go in there, he made a bee-line for what he needed and acted as if he had no peripheral vision.) He was in the room until after midnight doing the memory lane thing, reliving, reappraising, and revisiting everything about the cozy space.

A gallery of framed photos of Nate and Jim throughout the years filled an entire wall, as did his dad's diplomas, teaching certificates, and other honors (Nate had forgotten about the Distinguished Faculty Award Occidental gave him five years ago). There was an ancient, overstuffed couch covered in a faded floral print fabric that couldn't have been less Jim's style if he'd bought it blindfolded, which maybe he had. It was always less comfortable than it looked—still, his father napped on the couch every Saturday and Sunday after lunch and sometimes between classes. He wouldn't get rid of it for all the coffee in Brazil, not that anyone had offered. Nate sat on it, for the first time in ages, and reconfirmed its scratchy, springy lumpiness, yet could swear he got a faint whiff of Jim's aftershave off one of the flattened back pillows. And just when Nate had decided to dump it.

There was a solid oak desk with two file drawers that was not as old as the couch but Nate couldn't remember a time there without it. It was neater than it should have been but only because Jim, while he still had the strength, had emptied and organized much of it so his son wouldn't have to. He'd handed Nate all his important papers so they wouldn't disappear, but Nate had put them back in the desk drawer—so they wouldn't disappear.

And of course, there were the books, stacked around the room on bookcases of various heights and widths as well as on shelves in the office's narrow walk-in closet that also held a collection of Jim's clothes Nate swore went as far back as college.

He pulled a leather-bound volume off a shelf: *The Great Gatsby*. Of course. It stood next to a quartet of other Fitzgerald works, each one also nestled between beautifully etched red leather covers. They were far from collector's items; Jim had bought the set about ten years ago in a used bookstore they'd stumbled into on a road trip to Carmel. Jim always liked the richness of those deep red covers: "Worthy of Fitzgerald," he said when he first gave them a place of honor on that very same shelf. (Jim had about six other copies of *Gatsby* strewn around the bookcases—from paperbacks to hardcovers to even a Dutch translation because why not?)

Flipping through the volume in his hands, Nate thought back on his dad's lecture that day about Nick Carraway and quickly slipped the slim book back in its place before he got weepy. *Fuck you, Nick Carraway!* Nate took a deep breath and went back to scanning the shelves that were filled with so many other familiar titles and authors—John Steinbeck, Philip Roth, Toni Morrison, Kurt Vonnegut, and, of course, Joan Didion—who had become like veritable family members to Jim over all these years. There were also obscure works by obscure writers (not that Nate was the best judge of who was who) and a surprising number of "beach read"-type books—crime novels and thrillers and celebrity memoirs —that Jim certainly never taught but still knew how to enjoy.

Nate then picked up the one framed photo Jim had kept out on a shelf of himself and Nate's mom, Eileen, taken sometime before they got married. They were posed in front of the Tower Theatre in the arts district of Fresno, the city in which they both were born and still lived at the time, about to go into a classical concert. They were each in their late twenties; Eileen was about six months younger than Jim. He was teaching at Fresno High, she was working as a dental assistant, and they were living together in a small house not far from where the photo was shot. She was on the tall side—almost as tall as Jim—and what one might call willowy, with long, medium-brown hair, light eyes, and, Nate always thought, a kind of faraway smile. Jim said she was an amazing cook, read as voraciously as he did (though they agreed on few books), and never forgot a face or a name. She died bringing Nate into the world.

He never saw her grave; like Jim, Eileen was cremated, her remains pitched into the ocean at Big Sur, where she and Jim had honeymooned. Nate spent much of his life missing someone he never met and knew only what his father had told him about her, which was less and less as the years went on. Jim apparently took Eileen's loss quite badly, though never—ever—equated Nate's existence to her demise. Once his son was born, Jim had a job to do and he threw himself into it fully, moving past the pain and regret, and loving Nate enough for two.

Nate scanned the room and decided he would thin out the bookshelves and wall photos, replace the fraying area rug, hang the Miró poster he'd brought over from his apartment, and clear out a corner for one of his tall indoor plants; the fiddle leaf fig would look great and the light was right. Neaten it all up and keep it the relaxed, unfussy spot it always was. Oh, and be sure to spend a lot of time in there.

SEVEN

FOR SOME REASON he couldn't quite put his finger on, Nate found himself thinking a lot about Amy over the two weeks he spent finishing up his other jobs—including his own home landscaping, which came out superbly if he had to say so himself. Danny, who had fallen right back into jabbing Nate about his love life—or lack thereof—was convinced, without even meeting Amy, that she was the woman who drove past them in the white car that day.

"Yelp, my hot brown ass," Danny said with a toothy grin as he helped Nate pick up a truckful of trees and shrubs and flowers at the vast Starlight Nursery on the way to Amy's house.

"Well, whoever she is, she's nice and seems easy to work for and I think you'll like her," said Nate, deciding between two equally lush Meyer lemon trees.

"But do *you* like her? That's the question." Danny pointed to one of the two lemon trees and Nate listened because the guy was kind of a plant whisperer; he had a sixth sense about these things.

"She's our client, dude. Long as her checks cash, I'll like her. A lot. The rest: Really, can we not go there? Because honestly, it's a little weird," Nate said, moving on to a row of fragrant rosemary pots and grabbing a pair.

Danny's lively face turned serious. "Just looking out for you, pal, that's it." He paused. "Know why?" His infectious smile returned. "'Cause I love you, man." He clapped his big hand onto Nate's head and pulled him in, as if for a kiss, but stopped short and let him go with a cackle and a wink. "Maybe next life, huh?"

"Right now, I'm having enough trouble with this one, but, sure—why not?" They shared a fraternal grin.

When Nate and Danny arrived at Amy's, along with their crew of two (Butch and Luis were Danny's newest finds: prompt, hard-working, and funny as hell), she was waiting for them out back with donuts, juice, and coffee, all laid out on a small patio table. "Help yourselves, guys," Amy said with a welcoming smile. She raised her coffee cup in a toast: "Here's to a great first day!"

Danny gave Nate an impressed look and Amy warmly shook hands with the guys and repeated their names to make sure she had them right. She was dressed more casually than Nate would have expected given it was a work day: jeans, sleeveless top, flats. Amy seemed to notice him noticing.

"Oh, I thought I'd go in late today, stick around here this morning in case you had any questions or needed anything. Is that okay?"

"Your garden, your choice," said Nate. Some clients liked to hang out and watch the process, dull as it could often be. Others didn't care how the sausage was made, just wanted to know when the job was finished.

"I won't be in the way, promise," Amy said, flashing a Scout's Honor sign.

"No worries, it's all good," he assured her. "I'm going to have the guys start the removals, so any last thoughts? Requests? Warnings?"

Amy considered that for a second. "Nope, have at it!"

Danny, who'd been uncharacteristically quiet, swept his hands around the yard and said, "Okay, but take a good look 'cause nothing's ever gonna be the same again!" He tipped his ball cap to Amy and moved off with the crew.

"He's a little prone to hyperbole," said Nate, a bit unnerved by Danny's comment.

Amy glanced around her yard, perhaps imagining its imminent transformation. "Oh, I don't know. Something tells me he knows what he's talking about." She returned her gaze to Nate as if she was about to say something more. When she didn't, he started for his truck.

"See you in a bit," Nate said, then joined the others who had begun to unload the tools and plants they'd need to get this garden party started.

At the Silverado, Danny shot him a grin and a wicked eyebrow raise. "What?" Nate wanted to know, as if he didn't already know.

"Okay, Miss Amy, with the snug jeans and coffee and juice and shit? Definitely the one checking you out that day on Escarpa, *jefe*." Danny reached over the open tailgate and hauled out one of two ten-gallon ficus trees. Nate grabbed the other one.

"What makes you so sure? And you know it bugs me when you call me *jefe*."

"White boy guilt got the better of you?" He set the ficus on the ground and climbed up into the truck cab.

Nate cringed. "What? No, you're my friend, *mi hermano*, not my employee. I'm not your *jefe*. Not really."

"Who pays who at the end of every week?" Danny asked as he started tossing bags of mulch off the truck.

Nate couldn't argue with that. Danny was the king of verbal checkmate.

Later that morning, Amy, who'd been observing the first stages of the makeover, asked Nate if he wanted to join her inside for a quick iced tea. He rarely took a break unless Danny and the day's crew did. But when Danny overheard Amy's offer he eye-nudged Nate and firmly whispered, "Do what the nice lady says, *jefe*." He was relentless and annoying and, for some reason, Nate listened to him.

As he took off with Amy, Nate pointed out two brimming pots of white gardenias they'd soon be planting. "You're gonna love those. You'll think you're living in Hawaii."

"Compared to where I used to live, this *is* Hawaii," she said, a crinkle in her gray-green eyes as she led him through the back door and into the kitchen.

"Oh, so you're new to L.A.?" Nate asked as they sat at a round butcher block dining table.

Amy poured two glasses of iced tea from a tall pitcher, handed one to Nate. She raised her tumbler in a toast. "To … beginnings," she announced.

Nate, a bit self-conscious, touched his glass to hers. They each took a swig of the iced tea like it was the Long Island kind, discreetly watching each other as they drank.

"So, where did you say you moved from?" Nate asked, glancing around the neat kitchen, slightly more updated than his but still in need of refreshing.

"I didn't, but … up north." She squeezed a slice of lemon into her tea, took another sip. Finally: "Do you know Fresno?"

Nate nearly coughed up his drink, even if a tiny part of him was not entirely shocked by the coincidence. It reminded him of the times he'd asked someone their birthday and somehow knew they were going to say September 2: the same as his. Nate cleared his throat, swallowed.

Amy put her glass down. "Are you okay?"

"Yeah, I'm fine. Tea must've gone down the wrong pipe. Anyway—Fresno, seriously? "My father was from Fresno. I was born there!"

She looked surprised. "Wow, that makes two of us."

He felt a bit lightheaded. "Maybe you knew my dad—Jim Cronin? Taught English at Fresno High? Late '80s, early '90s?" Nate asked as if there was one high school in the entire city—or one teacher.

Amy drained her iced tea glass and considered her landscaper a moment. "No, I don't think I knew him." She looked away. "Anyhow, I went to Roosevelt."

"Well, if you had my father, you would have remembered." Nate felt such a sharp pang of loss for his dad just then that it caught him short.

"I'm sorry, did I say something wrong?" Amy leaned in as if she were going to take his hand, which she didn't—just waited respectfully for him to respond.

Maybe because she seemed easy to talk to or because he felt the need to open up—not his usual go-to reaction—Nate ended up telling Amy about Jim: his death, his work at Occidental, his great love of literature, and the kind of emotional legacy he left behind for his son. It uplifted him in a way he hadn't realized he needed. Amy listened intently; at one point, Nate thought he could see a tear form in her eye, but it vanished as quickly as it had appeared. He spoke for all of a few minutes but it felt far longer.

They were silent a moment after Nate finished until Amy asked, "If you don't mind my asking, was he disappointed you didn't follow in his footsteps?"

"Actually, I started working toward a teaching degree but realized I'd rather spend my days outdoors, less tied-down. My dad just wanted me to take my own path—like he did, I guess." Nate took another slug of iced tea and stood, ready to move on. "Thanks for the tea, but I'd better get back out there. Those guys plant something in the wrong place and I'll have one angry client on my hands." He smiled for the first time since he'd sat down.

"Don't worry, I can keep her in line," said Amy, matching his smile.

When Nate returned to the backyard, he tried to avoid Danny's wily grin, which was like trying to avoid the sun. "Fly's open," said Danny matter-of-factly as he passed, electric pole saw in hand. Nate reflexively looked down to check, then realized it was a joke. But not before Danny shouted, "Made you look!" without even turning around.

EIGHT

NATE HADN'T HEARD from Jennifer since her last call, which was now more than a month ago. Not that Nate had reached out either. There wasn't much to discuss, it seemed; they were both getting on with their lives. Nate at least hoped that Jennifer thought about Nate as much as he thought about her, which was to say often. But even if she was in his mind, she wasn't in his heart, at least not the way she once was. Still, it didn't take a psych degree to know he was being self-protective and, if he was being totally honest with himself—which he tried not to be—was largely in avoidance mode. He hoped Jennifer was happy because, well, one of them deserved to be.

He could have gotten out there, tried to start dating again, even if only to get laid. But in the scheme of things that felt like something less than a priority. (The cashier at Starlight Nursery, an adorably punkish brunette with a yin-yang tattoo on her arm, gave him a me-ga-watt smile the other day but he let it ride.) Nate had driven by Jennifer's dance studio several times in the last few weeks, thinking maybe he'd catch a glimpse of her going in or coming out—to what end, he wasn't sure. It felt weak and stalkery yet it didn't stop him.

He also never saw her, so it was a safe—if futile—exercise. Nate didn't want to believe he was floundering but, lately, the word had an inescapable ring to it.

One night, after he'd had a couple of post-workday beers followed by two bonus shots of tequila (the Patrón bottle was such an inviting shape), a fortified Nate found himself wearing one of Jim's old Springsteen T-shirts—*The River* tour 1981—under his dad's gray tweed sport coat, hustling Cody into the Silverado, and driving south into Hollywood to pay Jennifer a surprise visit. He was soon parking on a tree-lined side street off a quiet, residential part of Hollywood Boulevard east of Fairfax and knocking on the door of the quaint little guest house she rented from a film editor and her optometrist husband.

Jennifer—in pink sweats and a sports top, hair up in a scrunchy—opened the door, and looked startled to see Nate standing there with his tail-thwacking dog. That she answered the door to begin with was a good sign, thought Nate, even if he still wasn't sure why he was there.

"Nate? What are you doing here so late?" she asked. From the slightly unnerved look on her face, it hit Nate: *What if she's with someone?*

He wanted to turn and go, escape this ill-considered pop-in, but Cody had already pushed past Jennifer and was nosing around her living room. "I'm sorry, I … was in the neighborhood and I thought I'd—"

"You were in the neighborhood?" she asked with the suspicion it most certainly called for. But instead of waiting for a response, she said, "I kind of wish you'd texted or called," then waved him in with a resigned look.

"I should have asked, are you … alone?" Nate grabbed Cody by his scruff as he was about to stick his snout into a basket of yarn and knitting needles next to the fireplace.

"Not anymore," Jennifer joked, and sat on one of two upholstered loveseats the color of black cherry sherbet. She tucked one leg under the other and stared at Nate as he sat on the opposite loveseat.

Cody rested his big head next to Jennifer for some immediate attention, which she happily gave him. "Is that your dad's jacket?" she asked as she rubbed the dog's soft, floppy ears.

"And T-shirt," Nate said, opening the jacket to fully reveal Springsteen's then-youthful face. "I gave away a lot of his clothes to a homeless shelter, but somehow ended up keeping more than I expected. I never thought much of this thing when he used to wear it," he continued, studying the sport coat, "but, I don't know, I kind of like the way it feels."

"Y'mean, familiar?"

"I guess."

Cody decided to switch allegiances and turned to Nate for the next round of love. He scratched the dog under his neck, which always caused a euphoric reaction in the big guy. Nate was glad to be making Cody feel good; he sure wasn't having that effect on Jennifer, if her impassive gaze was any indication. What did he expect? Their rift was his doing, not hers. Even if no harsh words had been spoken, the meaning was there: *I don't love you enough to commit to you for the rest of our lives.* And even if that wasn't quite how Nate felt, how could Jennifer interpret it otherwise?

"He never gets enough, this one," Nate said as he pulled his hand away from Cody, who, on cue, pawed at him for more.

"I miss seeing him," Jennifer admitted. "Dogs are so consistent, so reliable."

"Unlike people?"

"Unlike some people. Most people," she said, adding with a shrug, "I don't know." She unlocked her leg and readjusted herself. Cody lost interest and wandered off, presumably in search of dropped food.

Nate was at a loss for conversation. "Had any interesting dates lately?" The question hung there.

"You really don't want to talk about that, do you?" She clearly didn't want to—and why should she? Why should he, for that matter? What were they, BFFs?

"Not really, no," Nate said, looking away. He knew that dropping by was a mistake and told her exactly that, adding, "I'm sorry. I'll let you get to sleep." Nate rose, hoping she would stop him—but she didn't.

Instead, Jennifer stood and took his arm. "Look, I know these last months have been really tough on you. And I'm here if you need me—as a friend. But more than that, I can't do." Fortunately, Cody trotted in with a huge ear of corn—husk and all—lodged between his teeth, the image causing the humans in the room to laugh, breaking the awkwardness.

Nate wrestled the corn out of the dog's mouth and, with an apologetic smile, presented the soggy, tooth-marked thing to Jennifer. "Sorry, you still want it?"

"That's okay," she answered, lips still curled into a smile. "I bought a bunch more at the farmer's market this morning. You can take it for the road."

"Next time, he'll ask. I promise," Nate joked, but realized he could have been talking about himself and his impromptu visit. "Anyway, take care, okay?" he said, turning serious again, then directing Cody out the door with a whack on his rump.

Nate didn't wait for Jennifer to say goodbye, good luck, or good riddance. He exited the cottage and crossed through the well-kept yard that led back onto the street. He drove off, Cody seated alertly at his side, and thought about his brief stop-by. What if some other guy *had* been there? Was that what Nate subconsciously—or not so subconsciously—showed up to find out? Was that why he'd passed by her dance studio those few times? Jennifer said she could only be his friend, and understandably so. But did he really need another friend? (He did, especially since Jim died, but not the way Jennifer meant it.)

There were no real answers, only questions, so Nate decided to let it go for now and trust the decisions they'd both made.

NINE

NATE HADN'T SEEN Amy for several days. She left for work before he and his crew arrived and returned after they'd left. The backyard was progressing well: They'd been uprooting, planting, seeding, reconfiguring. It was one of Nate's better team efforts and he was feeling good about the results. Each morning Amy left snacks for Nate and the guys with notes that read "Keep up the great work!" or "Have the best day!" which was weirdly inspiring. A part of Nate was sorry she wasn't there to observe them—she seemed to appreciate what they were doing—although another side of him was a bit relieved he could work without distraction. Amy seemed more interested in him than the average client and that last talk over iced tea had put him in a strange mood for the rest of the day.

Danny was still sure she was their mystery drive-by that Saturday on Escarpa, but they'd yet to see her car to help confirm his suspicion. Not that it mattered one way or the other, as Nate repeatedly reminded him. "Some detective you'd make," Danny retorted.

One morning, after their first week or so at Amy's, she appeared in the backyard in a sleek, navy business suit and black pumps, attaché over her shoulder, a tray of muffins in hand.

"Morning, all!" Amy said brightly as she set the tray on a small teak table. The guys all swung around from their work spots and eyed their well-dressed employer. "I tried a new muffin recipe last night. Let me know how I did, okay?"

"You're gonna spoil us, y'know," said Danny with a smile as he went for a muffin.

"They're just carrot muffins, not lobster tails," Amy joked, eyes crinkling, as she watched him savor the pastry. Butch and Luis came up for a taste as well.

"Hey, I want to show you something," Nate said. "Do you have a second?" Amy, intrigued, followed him across the yard to a newly dug garden filled with a row of bright, crimson-colored bushes. "See, we tore out those boxy old hedges and replaced them with these great hydrangeas. It's going to be all about the color back here."

Amy studied the hearty plants. "They're beautiful. It's looking much more … 'artistic' than before," she noted. He smiled, proud and a bit self-conscious. Amy checked her watch. "I'm running late, I'd better be going," she said, "but I'll see you soon."

Nate didn't want her to go. "Where do you work, by the way?" he asked to stall her but also because he honestly had no idea—and it seemed like something he should know.

"I freelance at a law firm downtown."

"You're a lawyer?" Nate wondered, as much a question as a statement.

"Para-lawyer. Paralegal," she explained.

"Well, you look nice," said Nate, surprising himself. Danny shot him a discreet—for Danny—eyebrow raise.

Amy looked Nate up and down attentively, and said, "You look nice today, too. Very handsome." And, before Nate could respond, she shifted gears. "Have a good day, everyone!" She made an appreciative scan of her garden, then walked off to the garage adjacent to the backyard.

Before Amy was fully out of earshot, Danny lurched up to Nate. "She wants it, dude. And don't even try to say she doesn't!" Butch and Luis, overhearing, traded grins.

Nate, his face flushed as red as those hydrangeas, kept his voice down. "You don't know that." He grabbed a shovel and started digging a trench. Amy's garage door groaned open beyond them.

"Oh, yeah? I've got two eyes—and obviously, so does she."

Nate considered Danny. "Look, if she likes me, I'm flattered, okay? But she's old enough to be my … well, I don't know how old she is." His digging sped up. "Besides, I'm not dating *anyone* right now."

Danny got in his face. "Yeah—exactly! And what the fuck are you digging there, bro? A hole to jump into and hide?"

"Ha-ha, you should do standup. It's for the herb garden, if you must know." He stopped digging and faced Danny, who was still looming over him. "And you know what *I* think?" Nate asked, shoulders back, chest puffed. "I think you want to live vicariously through me, you old married man." He grinned like he had just scored the winning touchdown.

Danny devilishly assembled his retort. "If I'm gonna live 'vicariously' through anyone, it's gonna be, like, LeBron James or the gazillionaire from Amazon, not you, son." Before Nate could volley back, Danny looked toward the garage, his eyes widening. "Oh, shit!"

Nate followed Danny's gaze. Amy's car was backing out of the driveway. It was a Toyota Camry—like that small white sedan from that day on Escarpa. Without a word, Danny raced out of the yard and into the driveway. Nate, shovel still in hand, went after him. They landed at the head of the driveway and watched Amy's Camry vanish into the distance. The guys said nothing until the car was out of sight.

Finally, Danny's face twisted into a shit-eating grin. "You're just lucky I'm not the kind of guy who'd say 'I told you so.'"

"Oh, yeah, you'd *never* do that," Nate shot back.

At the end of the day, as Nate was about to get into his truck, he spotted a note stuck under his windshield wiper. He unfolded the sheet of paper, which had been torn from a realtor's promotional pad ("Hallie Dell knows how to sell!") and read the flowery script:

Looking for a landscaper. Could you stop by for an estimate? - The Russos, 4648 Fortuna.

It was already well past five and Nate needed to get home to feed Cody. He had stayed on after the others left, as he sometimes did, to assess the day's work alone and unwind before he got on the road and faced the inevitable rush-hour crush. But the Russos, whomever they were, lived only a block from Amy and, rather than chance them finding another landscaper, Nate hopped in the Silverado and sped around the corner.

Their house was a ranch like Amy's though slightly larger, as was their decently manicured front garden. Nate assumed they had backyard issues—most folks did—and he was proven correct when he met Corey and Brooke Russo, an attractive couple he guessed to be in their mid-30s. They greeted him holding full glasses of cocktail hour rosé which, based on their cheery looseness, might have been refills. *These two clearly don't have kids,* Nate mused.

Corey and Brooke yakked away with Nate like old college pals as they took him into their backyard. The place was a mishmash of rickety shrubs and abandoned gardening projects strewn amid blotches of dirt and grass. A gleaming, high-end stainless-steel grill stood proudly on a square of concrete beneath an awning; the Russos' priorities were evident.

As if reading Nate's mind, Corey said, "As you can probably guess, we're bigger cooks than gardeners." Corey and Brooke shared a quick peck on the lips. Brooke turned back to Nate.

"Sure you don't want a drink?" she asked, tilting her glass at him. "We have beer, too."

Nate passed on the offer and launched into an impromptu redesign. First, he recommended they go heavy on drought-tolerant plants (from its position and exposure, Nate could tell the spot got a ton of sun), stressing their eco-friendly nature. He went on to suggest a variety of trees, vines, and flowers—some of which he was using at Amy's, others that would work better at the Russos'. They nodded happily in agreement.

"You might consider building a small gazebo over there,"

Nate added, indicating a wide, barren corner. "It'd break up the yard and look really stylish."

"I dig your ideas, Nate," Corey said, adding, "No pun intended." Nate laughed politely as if he hadn't heard that joke before. Corey reminded him of one of those popular jocks who peaked in high school yet still relied on their charm and good looks to get by. Meantime, Brooke seemed like someone who didn't bloom until college and still couldn't believe she nabbed the prom king. Nate felt a twinge of envy at what they had (he even fleetingly wondered if their parents were all still alive) and it made him angry—at himself.

He slapped a smile back on his face and finished tossing out his ideas for their yard. Corey said they'd discuss it and be back in touch, which was good because Nate didn't want to take the time then to rough out an estimate.

"How's it going at the house around the corner?" Brooke asked as she and Corey walked Nate to his truck, now-empty wine glasses in hand.

"The place is really taking shape," he answered. "You should stop by and check it out, see what you think."

"It's none of our business," said Corey, turning serious, "but do you find it a little strange that she's putting that much work into a rental? I mean, you're redoing the front *and* back, right?"

Nate stopped a few feet before they reached the Silverado. "A rental? Amy owns the house," he said, quickly replaying his and Amy's first conversation in his head. *That was what she said, wasn't it?*

"No, a woman named Jane Tanaka owns it. She retired to Monterey, keeps it as income property," explained Brooke.

"I'm pretty sure Amy said she bought it last year," Nate said, unlocking the truck door with a chirp. "Or maybe she said she moved in last year." He stared at the key fob in his hand as if for clarity.

The Russos looked at each other. "I don't know," Corey said with a shrug, "I could swear she just moved in a few months ago—if that."

Nate thought about that curious discrepancy all the way home, so much so that the 134 Freeway's crawling traffic barely registered.

The Russos may not have been the most reliable of narrators, at least not at that particular wine o'clock, but their words were jarring—especially after seeing Amy's car again (*was* it again?) that morning. Taken individually, each item may not have meant much, if anything at all. But together they made him wonder.

TEN

AMY HAD ALREADY left by the time Nate and the guys arrived on Friday morning. He'd spent last night's remaining hours of light working off his nervous energy by prepping the outside of his own house for its much-needed paint job. It was a huge undertaking—he knew he should really hire a crew to do it or at least to help—but Nate figured the long-term project would help keep his mind and body gainfully busy and distracted. (Jim would have said, "Forget the paint, read the entire works of John Dos Passos;" Danny would have said—and not for the first time—"Get with that cutie from Starlight Nursery!" Nate chose an electric sander instead.)

The day at Amy's was productive—they were almost finished with the back and it was looking awesome—if uneventful, that is, in terms of any further revelations about the lady of the house. Danny felt like he was coming down with the cold that Raffi had the week before, and only brought up Amy and her phantom car once.

"You gonna ask her if she was snooping on us that day, or what?" he probed as they filled a line of terracotta pots with bursts of yellow, peach, and purple snapdragons.

"Or what," Nate answered and ended it there.

Nate hung around again after Danny and the crew made their exit. He told himself it was to inspect the day's work and determine what was left to do before they could start on the front. But he also knew that, despite trying to keep his curiosity about Amy at bay, it was getting the better of him. What he expected to learn, however, he hadn't a clue.

"Have you been abandoned?" Startled, he turned and faced Amy, who was standing there in another sleek business suit and pair of spiky heels, hair pulled up in a messy, end-of-the-day half-bun.

"Oh, hi! Sorry, I didn't hear your car pull in," Nate said as if he was caught stealing quarters from a change jar.

"Ah. I parked in front. I have to go out again, just wanted to change first."

Was it Nate's imagination or were those last few words tinged with a bit of spice? He bent down to pluck a yellowing leaf from one of the new gardenia bushes. "To answer your question: No, not abandoned. Sometimes I like to spend some alone time after the guys leave."

Amy studied him tending the shrub. "Your answer to therapy?"

"Gives me a chance to think, that's all," he answered, eyes still averted.

"What are you thinking about?"

"This and that." Nate stood, brushing some dirt off his jeans. He wasn't trying to sound evasive.

"Sorry, I didn't mean to pry." Amy looked contrite, her voice softening.

Neither of them moved nor spoke for a few moments. Nate broke the silence. "Can I ask you a personal question?"

Amy's warm smile reappeared. "Turnabout is fair play."

"Do you own this house?" he asked. Amy's smile faded; her posture stiffened. Nate was instantly sorry he'd gone there. In a flash, Amy seemed to recover, her expression relaxing.

"You're right, these gardenias are fabulous," she said, sweeping a hand toward the bright flowers.

He nodded in agreement. "Look, it's really none of my business,"

Nate stumbled. "Anyway, I should get going." He made a move to exit but Amy put a hand out to stop him. He froze; they watched each other for a few awkward seconds. Amy swallowed, an unmistakable look of anticipation crossing her face.

"Nate, would you go inside with me?"

And there it was: what Nate had tried not to see and Danny saw plain as day. Nate's pulse quickened; his throat went dry. He knew that the choice he made in that split second could alter his universe. "Amy, I'm flattered but … Well, you *are* my client and I don't think I should—"

His clunky rejection was cut short by a burst of laughter from Amy so loud and unbridled he may just have been telling the world's funniest joke. Nate was thrown, unsure if he should hoot along with her or leave before whatever quicksand he'd stepped into took irrevocable hold. But before he could do either, Amy's guffaws morphed into tears: the kind of loud, wracking sobs usually reserved for the grimmest moments. How could standing amid Amy's lovingly designed new garden on this balmy summer day even remotely qualify?

"Amy, what is it? What's wrong?" Nate asked with urgency. "I'm so sorry, I didn't mean to offend you in any way." But she was too overwhelmed to respond and before Nate realized it, he was holding Amy in his arms, taking in the heat of her tears and flushed skin, trying to calm her down. She clutched his shoulder as if it were a life preserver on a sinking ship and they stood like that until her eyes dried and her breathing steadied and Nate's heartbeat regained its normal rhythm.

Nate and Amy remained silent as they sat at the kitchen table where they'd last chatted over iced teas. Amy, suit jacket off, make-up smudged from her tears, hair set free and grazing her shoulders, looked spent and embarrassed. She traced imaginary shapes on the wooden tabletop with a manicured nail as Nate tried to figure out what to say or do.

"Do you want to talk about it or would you rather be alone?" Nate finally asked. He tried to sound gentle and respectful but was still at a loss.

Amy gazed at Nate through glassy eyes. She sighed. "Nate, how much do you know about your mother?"

Nate had no idea what to expect, but a question about his long-dead mother was about the last thing on the list. "My mother? What does she have to do with anything?"

"Please, just answer me." Her stare grew urgent, implacable.

He was officially creeped out now. "My mother died thirty years ago. She died giving birth to me. There were complications."

"And how do you know this?" Amy wondered. She sat up straighter, her composure returning.

Nate stood, his heart starting to hammer again. *What the fuck was happening here?* "What do you mean, 'how do I know this'?" he practically spat. "My father told me. Why are we even talking about this?" He paced the length of the long, narrow kitchen. Call it a premonition, but it felt as if an *Indiana Jones*-sized boulder was hurtling toward him and he was powerless to get out of its way.

Amy rose from the table, crossed to the sink, stared out the window. "It's not true," she said in a voice so low, Nate could barely hear her. She turned to him and repeated, more forcefully, "It's not true."

"What's not true?" Amy turned away, speechless. "What's not true, Amy? What do you mean?"

She spun around, eyes wide. "Nate, your mother didn't die in childbirth."

"What? How the hell do you know?" He could feel the blood rise in his face, his head beginning to pound.

Amy spoke quickly now, anxiously, with the force of a dam being unplugged. "She was very young when she had you. She had to give you up. You can't possibly imagine how difficult it was for her." Amy studied her hands as Nate stood frozen by the window.

When he finally responded, he sounded calm and firm. "I don't know where this is going, but I think you've got me mixed up with someone else."

"I'm sorry, Nate, but no, I don't." She looked up at him, the tears welling in her eyes.

Nate moved through the adjacent dining room and into the living room. He gazed at the formal, ivory-white couch and two brocade wingback chairs that sat opposite. A vintage-style Persian rug covered most of the hardwood flooring and a caramel-colored spinet piano stood against the picture window that faced out to the street. Nate might as well have been standing in a hall of mirrors for as disoriented as he felt. *Why didn't I go home when I had the chance?*

"Nate, for the last thirty years, your father has led you to believe a lie."

He refused to turn around and dignify her wild assertion. His eyes remained fixed on the pristine couch.

"My father? How do *you* know?" he finally asked the air.

Amy appeared in front of Nate and took a breath. "Because I've been a part of it. I'm as guilty as he was." Her face was a map of pain. She looked as if she'd aged ten years since they were in the kitchen.

Nate asked, "A part of what?" Amy tried to take his hand. He flinched, backing into a small side table he didn't realize was there. He whirled around and tried to grab the spindly thing before it fell to the floor, which it did regardless. Nate swung back around and lashed out at Amy. "Who are you, anyway?"

They both froze, mere inches from each other, their heartbeats nearly audible. Amy's silence spoke volumes. Nate gazed at Amy, stunned, incredulous. He suddenly understood everything—and nothing.

ELEVEN

AMY LUCAS THOUGHT her eleventh-grade English teacher was the most handsome man she'd ever seen. Not that she was such an expert on men, much less men over, say, seventeen. Still, she'd had her share of silly crushes on famous older actors and musicians and even a few local newscasters, so she had some frames of reference. (She used to get butterflies in her stomach whenever she passed her neighbor, Pete, a farm team jock who in summer would wash his car in the driveway without a shirt.)

To Amy, Mr. Cronin was not only good-looking—there was something about his ropy forearms and rolled-up shirtsleeves that made Amy's heart stop—but kind and patient and so incredibly smart. He seemed to know about everything and not just books, though he certainly made an avid reader out of Amy that year. But she was not alone: All the girls had crushes on Mr. Cronin. They knew his clothing by heart, could anticipate when he would get a haircut, would laugh almost in unison at his witty remarks. They would hang around him after class, hoping for a compliment about their book report or an answer they'd given that period. They would wonder in private and in pairs about his marriage. Had anyone ever met his wife? Seen a picture? Was she pretty? Did she know how lucky she was?

It was all fantasyland though. Jim Cronin may have been sexy and charming and brainy and generous, but he never, ever acted flirtatiously. He never "accidentally" touched any of the girls' hands, talked to them up close, allowed his eyes to meet theirs for that extra second, made an even remotely off-color remark. In truth, he never seemed at all aware of the rapt attention he received from his female students. He was known as a stand-up guy, a talented teacher, and unerringly likable.

So it couldn't have come as more of a shock when one day after everyone else had filed out of the classroom, he asked Amy, who was absent-mindedly still at her desk immersed in that day's chapter, if she might want to have a cup of coffee with him sometime. Just like that: no preamble, no guile, no leering stare, no words of warning or explanation. She didn't drink coffee—not yet, anyway—but that was beside the point. Who even knew if coffee would really be involved? Still, as polite and unforced as Mr. Cronin was at that moment, his intentions were unambiguous. Even to someone with as little sexual experience as Amy.

What was not obvious was: why her? She was pretty enough, but far from the most attractive or brightest or most popular girl around. She was mostly quiet and studious; friendly but unassuming. She hardly jumped out as teen-mistress material, especially for someone as dreamy as Mr. Cronin. No matter, she found herself saying yes to his offer with a confidence and resolve she barely knew she possessed. In retrospect, she realized she had no idea what she was doing.

They never did have that coffee. Instead, Amy and Jim met up the following Saturday at Woodward Park, which despite its popularity, was an easy place to go unseen—if that was your intention. At first, Jim didn't act as if there was anything to hide: He suggested they take a walk around the park's enormous, winding lake, which was scenic but conveniently deserted that cool and overcast December day.

They talked about books and poetry; Amy mentioned she'd written some poems but they weren't very good, and Jim urged her to keep at it. He praised her work in class and she told him what an inspiring teacher he was. When Amy asked what they'd be reading next, he said *Invisible Man* by Ralph Ellison. He asked about her other classes, and she described a chemistry project she was struggling with. If either of them was nervous, it didn't outwardly show. Amy found Jim as mellow and engaging in "real life" as he was in school; Jim would later tell Amy he found her as soulful and mature as she was in class. He never brought up why he'd asked her to join him that day—nor did she. It felt like two new friends taking a stroll in the park.

Until it didn't.

They made love on a small, secluded grassy stretch beneath an immense canopy of magnolia trees. It didn't just "happen"—one thing did, in fact, lead to another—though Amy, alarmingly in control of her senses, was given the power to stop it at any time: Jim asked her permission every step of the way. He was no more aggressive or demanding than he was in class, but still a wholly captivating presence. Amy fought not to ponder the implications of what they were doing—it was undeniably dangerous, wrong, and stupid—and, for once in her circumspect life, simply gave into the moment. It was a thrilling combination of pain and pleasure, freedom and validation. That she lied and told Jim she was on the pill when he revealed he hadn't brought a condom (*Was he careless or was this truly not premeditated?* she wondered) was debatably her biggest mistake. Still, she would have been lying if she didn't admit, at least to herself, that she'd dreamt about this happening since she first stepped into Jim's classroom.

Through it all, she still called him Mr. Cronin.

He told her about his wife. How they were trying to have a baby, but couldn't. How it was taking a toll on their marriage. Amy didn't know what to say but it didn't matter—he just wanted someone to listen.

They saw each other for a few weeks until they knew they couldn't continue. Jim was afraid for himself—and Amy. It had gone too far. He confessed that he'd never done anything like that before—had never even considered it—and never would again. He hoped she'd understand. She said she did. It was the truth. Amy cherished the sweet moments they'd shared and tucked them away to think about whenever she felt lonely or sad or unloved. She and Mr. Cronin resumed their student-teacher relationship as if nothing had happened. She finished the class with an A, but only because she truly earned it.

Except for telling her parents, Amy remained a sphinx about her affair with Nate's father for the rest of her life. Until now.

TWELVE

NATE SAT ON the stiff white couch thinking about how he had to get home to Cody; the poor guy had to be hungry. Thank God for the doggie door; at least he could get out to take care of business. Nate realized he should probably invest in one of those Wi-Fi-controlled pet feeder contraptions for when he was running late; wouldn't hurt for them both to have a bit more freedom. But these were just a few of the random, deflective thoughts rattling around Nate's head while Amy recounted the unthinkable tale of her high school fling with his father. He seethed as he heard each absurd detail as if he was supposed to believe what she'd been trying so desperately to tell him. Why in the world would he? His mother was his mother—not Amy Shields, if that was even her real name. After all, she lied about how long she'd lived in this house, about not knowing her father when he first asked, about going to a different high school. What else would she lie about? He would finish up the last few things in her backyard tomorrow and call it quits. Nate thought she had seemed like such a fine, considerate person, and now this. What a terrible judge of character he turned out to be. He couldn't listen to her story any longer, felt like his head might explode if he did. He didn't know why he'd sat down in the first place.

"This is all bullshit," Nate said as he leaped up from the couch. "I don't want to hear anymore. Whatever it is you want, I can't give it to you."

Amy rose, meeting his cold stare. "Nate, you need to know the truth."

"What? That you got pregnant and you gave up your son?" Nate moved toward the front door; Amy stopped him.

"My parents convinced me having a baby would ruin my life. I loved my parents and didn't want them to disown me. I was young and impressionable and incredibly confused."

Nate tried to reach the door again and Amy grabbed his arm.

"Then my parents threatened to expose your father. The last thing I wanted was for him to get hurt. But by that point, I had decided to have the baby." Her eyes filled up again. "Decided to have you." She swallowed. "The option … was never an option."

Nate pulled away from Amy's grip. But as he grabbed the front doorknob, something stopped him. He stood facing the door, his heart pounding.

Amy continued, the urgency building in her voice: "Your father wanted a child more than anything. Wanted *you*. But had one request: that for as long as he lived, I'd never come after you. What happened between us had to be forgotten. We made a pact I promised never to break. I wanted the best for you. No matter the price."

Nate glared at Amy and wrenched open the door. "Y'know what? I'm outta here." And he was.

Amy yelled from the doorway as he jumped into his truck. "Nate, please. Wait!" She ran out after him, but it was too late.

Nate sped out of Toluca Woods, onto Cahuenga Boulevard, and toward the freeway that would take him back to the safety of his home in Eagle Rock. His hands were trembling as he gripped the steering wheel so tightly his knuckles turned white. He drove in a trance, so stunned by what he'd just heard that he could barely see straight. A block before the entrance to the 134, an elderly man pushing a shopping cart appeared just yards in front of the Silverado, causing Nate to slam on the brakes. The old guy trundled across the busy street as if nothing had happened. Nate pressed on the gas pedal again and slowly made his way to the freeway.

The 134 was its usual early evening parking lot, which only added to Nate's frazzled nerves. Sitting in traffic he replayed Amy's story in his head, trying to make sense of what she said in the context of the father he knew so intimately. There was no way Jim would have lied to him all those years about his mother—his real mother—which made Nate wonder why Amy would concoct such a detailed account of her alleged affair. Did she want something from Nate? Did she want money? What did she think she was entitled to? Was she really who she said she was?

As the traffic slowly opened up after the Buena Vista Street exit, Nate could feel himself calming down, his stomach unknotting, and his thoughts settling. He switched on Pandora's classic rock station in honor of Jim—the Jim he knew and trusted—and let the music his father loved fill his truck and soothe his brain. Playing was the Eagles' "Take It Easy." *Don't let the sound of your own wheels make you crazy*, those California rockers sang. It seemed like especially sound advice at that moment—and Nate tried to heed it.

And he succeeded, for the rest of the ride home, accompanied by Electric Light Orchestra, Styx, Blondie, and The Kinks, allowing the tunes from these classic bands to block out Amy's disturbing disclosure. But once Nate had arrived home and fed the antsy Cody, who gobbled his dinner like it was his first meal in a week; checked his few pieces of snail mail (all of which were still addressed to Jim); and downed a beer at the kitchen table, he was stewing again over information he simply could not process. It was like he'd been told he wasn't who he thought he was but rather a completely different person with a completely different life.

As if Cody could read his mind—and who said he couldn't?—he plopped his head in Nate's lap for a mutually comforting scratch behind his floppy ears.

"Are you really my dog?" Nate asked him, sticking his nose into Cody's snout. "Or are you someone else's and my real pooch lives somewhere else?" He gave a rueful half-laugh and kissed

Cody atop his blocky dome. The dog responded with his two-bark signal: *Gotta go!* Nate grabbed Cody's leash, snapped it on, and took him out for a walk.

The mild evening breeze sent the fragrance of pine and rosemary and jasmine up and down the curvy road. It reminded Nate of childhood summer nights when he and Jim would roam the darkened Occidental campus, playing silly word games and repeating godawful jokes that made them crack up anyway. Jim would bring along some messy dessert that they'd share sitting on a brightly lit bench along the Quad; someone in the sprinkling of traversing students would always offer Jim a hearty wave or hello. Nate would feel like a little celebrity.

So it was no surprise that he and Cody ended up back at Occidental that evening, following the handful of streets that led from Escarpa to one of the campus's many entrances. Cody was in full-on exploring mode, nose plastered to the ground, as a near-gravitational pull led Nate to the bench he'd shared with Jim just over three months ago. He sat, Cody sprawled at his feet, and gazed out at the city, now a canvas of twinkling lights, shiny towers, and crisscrossing roadways. Jim's sad, stoic voice from that day echoed in Nate's head as he recalled his dad's words: "Just know that whatever I've done as a father, it's always been with your best interest at heart."

Nate didn't think much of that at the time, didn't ask for elaboration. It just seemed like the sort of eternal and encapsulating thing someone whose days were numbered might say. Besides, as far as Nate was concerned, Jim had always acted in his son's best interest; he'd never been given reason to think otherwise. But there's a first time for everything and perhaps the unthinkable scenario Amy had painted earlier was the "whatever" Jim had been referring to. But, if true—and Nate was still far from accepting that it was—how could hiding such a monumental truth have been to his benefit?

The more Nate pondered this, the more his thoughts moved in dizzying circles until he was back where he started: Amy, whoever she was, was lying or crazy or cruel—or maybe all of the above. As Cody sat up on his haunches expectantly, it struck Nate that he wanted to talk to Jennifer. He wanted to lay out the pieces of this astonishing puzzle for her and get what he knew would be a fair and objective opinion. Whereas Nate could sometimes miss the forest for the trees, Jennifer was all forest. She was great at seeing the big picture, which may explain her pointed, 10,000-foot view of her and Nate's relationship and where it was—or, more crucially, was not—going.

Nate eyed Cody for guidance and when there was none—the dog was itching to finish their walk—he started to dial his ex-girlfriend, but stopped. He realized he didn't want to seem desperate or needy, two things he was undeniably feeling at the moment. She said she'd be there for Nate as a friend, and isn't that what friends were for: to listen, weigh in, tell you that you weren't crazy, that everything would make sense in the morning? Maybe—and maybe Jennifer would be willing to be his sounding board. But right now, Nate didn't feel he deserved whatever it was she may have to offer. Fuck, no wonder he was alone.

Suddenly, Nate knew what he had to do.

Before he could talk himself out of it, Nate dropped Cody off at home, barreled back onto the freeway, and sped, music-free this time, to where his baffling day began. He pulled into Amy's driveway and, without even locking his truck, knocked on her front door. It was late, but not that late: a few minutes before ten o'clock. Nate stood under the porch light—heart racing, throat dry—and listened for Amy's footsteps. Unlike his surprise visit to Jennifer's house the week before, his intent now was purposeful, even if he couldn't predict the outcome. Amy opened the door, still wearing parts of the business suit from before—teal silk blouse, charcoal pencil skirt— and gray quilted scuff slippers. If she was surprised, she didn't let on.

"Would you like to come in?" Amy asked, backing into the foyer to make way.

Nate entered, marching past Amy and into the living room. She followed and he whirled around to face her.

"Okay, who are you really, and why are you doing this?"

He regained his vigor—and his voice.

Amy considered her words carefully. "It was time," she answered, as if that explained everything.

"Time for what? To fuck with the lonely landscaper's head?"

Nate paced the room, past the couch and wing chairs till he reached the fireplace—a real, wood-burning kind that he hadn't even noticed before—then swung back to face Amy. She stood there, tears in her eyes, shoulders hunched, cradling her elbows. She looked more vulnerable than Nate had yet seen her and it gave him pause. He found himself studying her eyes, her nose, the contours of her mouth, the jut of her cheekbones, wondering if he bore any likeness to her. People had always said he looked just like Jim—similar six-foot frame, oblong face, squarish jaw, crinkly smile. He rarely examined his favorite photos of Eileen for any resemblance, always more curious about who she'd been on the inside, how emotionally alike they may have been (because, in that sense, he didn't much take after Jim). Still, if Nate saw any of himself in Amy at that loaded moment, he was incapable of acknowledging it.

"My father told me my mother's name was Eileen and that she died in childbirth," Nate finally said. His words hung in the air as Amy swallowed back her tears.

She sat on the couch, nestled into a cushioned corner. Nate loomed over her, awaiting a response. He wasn't trying to rattle her, exactly, but he could tell she was struggling to find the best way to explain herself out of the hole she had dug for them both. After a few strained moments, she sat up straighter, smoothed out her skirt, and took a breath.

"Eileen was his wife. She tried to forgive Jim for the affair, tried to pretend you were her child. But she just couldn't. When you were a few months old, she left Fresno. Right after, at the end of that semester, Jim moved down here with you." Amy tried to meet Nate's eyes but they were unavailable to her, hooded with anger and doubt.

"Why should I believe you?" he finally asked. "Why should I believe any of this?"

"Because it's the truth."

Nate tried to absorb Amy's words, make sense of their possible place in his history, but he came up short. He stared at the rug beneath his feet, mesmerized by its swirls of saffron and scarlet thread. "My father was the most honest man in the world," Nate said, looking up at Amy. "He never did anything wrong. Ask anyone—he was perfect." But even as he said this Nate knew it wasn't true: There were cracks in everyone's pedestal.

Amy paused, and then eerily echoed Nate's thoughts: "With all due respect to your father's memory, no one is perfect."

Okay, then. Nate rose calmly. "I've got to go."

Amy leaped off the couch, blocking his path. He didn't fight her, not this time. For a moment it seemed as if there was nothing left to say until, with quiet force and startling conviction, she said, "Nate, for better or worse—I'm your mother."

He searched her pained face for any sign of hypocrisy or deceit but saw only resignation and need. Her expression threw him. It was like watching an actor who'd been playing a role suddenly become that role. It was more than he could bear.

THIRTEEN

NATE **WAS SO** worn out by the time he returned home he didn't even undress before collapsing into bed. He fell into a dead sleep so quickly he didn't hear Cody plop onto his own bed on the floor next to Nate. And then, just as quickly as he'd conked out, Nate was awake again—wide awake. He checked his phone: *1:33 a.m.* Exhausted as he felt, his mind raced, his pulse keeping time. Images of a younger Jim and a teenage Amy spread out together on the grass flickered across his brain. Nate imagined Amy giving birth and then handing his swaddled self over to Jim and Eileen, leaving Amy in a pool of tears. Or maybe she was relieved, wracked by guilt, or just angry. What had she said? *I was young and impressionable and incredibly confused.* How could she not have been? If it were true.

The one person who *could* verify all this was, obviously, no longer among the living—which was how this whole twisty tale had reared its head to begin with. Then again, what about Eileen? If she didn't die thirty years ago, as Nate had been told, where was she now? There was a good chance she was still alive, wasn't there? Yet who's to say she would tell Nate the truth either? If he could even find her, which seemed like a ridiculously gargantuan task.

As Nate's thoughts turned kaleidoscopic, he pulled himself out of bed, tiptoed around the snoring Cody, and made his way to the garage. He felt around the right-side wall, turned on the glary overhead light. It threw streaks of white against Jim's twelve-year-old black Mazda hatchback, which, Nate remembered for the umpteenth time, he still needed to sell.

But he was there for the cartons. They were piled six-high in a corner, a totemic cache of history. They'd been in that exact spot for as long as Nate could remember and had served as a catch-all for anything small that Jim had wanted to save but didn't know where to keep. He never subtracted from the boxes, only added, until each container was ready to burst. Nate was pretty sure his dad never revisited anything once it was stored.

Nate didn't quite know what he was looking for so late that night—or so early that Saturday morning, to be exact. But when he found the envelope of fading color photos buried under a stack of Jim's childhood 45 RPM records (Who the heck was Norman Greenbaum?), Nate wondered if he'd stumbled upon something useful. He rifled wide-eyed through the random shots that he hadn't seen in ages. There was an array of poses of Jim and Eileen—posing in front of a bookstore, sitting on a low wall with the ocean behind them, dancing at an outdoor party—along with pictures of Jim and baby Nate, a six-year-old Nate on his first two-wheeler, and college-age Jim with an unflattering handlebar mustache. Then there was one of Eileen that Nate couldn't recall ever seeing: She was at the kitchen counter, standing over a tall, newly baked chocolate cake. Her long hair was pulled back and she wore a Fresno High T-shirt, likely one of Jim's, based on its baggy fit. She looked lovely, yet thinner than in other shots, maybe even fragile. Nate sensed a kind of sadness beneath her half-smile. Or was he channeling the melancholy the pictures made him feel?

Nate studied her likeness, searched it for a sign, yet found nothing. She was a woman who'd made a nice dessert. Maybe Nate looked like her, maybe he didn't. Maybe he looked like Amy, maybe he didn't. What would it prove, anyway?

He stuffed the photos back in the envelope, returned it to its place beneath the archaic 45s, put the carton atop the stack, and left the garage ready to go back to sleep.

When Nate woke up later that morning, he realized he did learn something from his little snapshot sojourn: He didn't want to go through this alone. He would call Jennifer, talk to her about Amy's claims. He decided it didn't matter how needy or desperate he came off: she would understand. He would do the same for her.

A few hours later, he texted Jennifer and invited her to lunch between classes. He lied and said he had to be nearby. Quickly realizing she didn't buy that excuse the last time, he added that he needed to pick up some plants at his favorite specialty nursery, a few blocks from her house. It could have been true, right?

Except it didn't turn out the way he'd planned.

Nate met her at Marco's—a casual, brick-walled Italian place where they'd eaten their share of meals together—instead of picking her up at home or the studio like he once would have. She was already waiting at one of the trattoria's narrow window tables when Nate arrived. It seemed formal and awkward, like a blind date—or a last date. Nate hugged Jennifer hello, but she felt stiff, resistant. He didn't know what he was expecting but was hardly surprised by her reticence.

Chris, a Chicago transplant and aspiring actor, who'd been Nate and Jennifer's frequent server there, arrived with menus, a basket of hot focaccia, and a welcoming smile. They exchanged hellos, listened to him recite the lunch specials, and ordered beverages: a Moretti for Nate, an Arnold Palmer for Jennifer. When Chris left to get their drinks, silence fell over the table and Nate promptly buried his nose in the menu. Jennifer opened hers as well, though kept her eyes trained on Nate.

"Is everything okay?" she finally asked.

Nate looked up from the menu, unprepared to answer what might have otherwise been a simple question. He studied Jennifer's concerned expression, Nate's resolve to bring her into his burgeoning drama fading by the second.

"Yeah, I'm just really hungry all of a sudden, so …" He trailed off, realizing how unconvincing he sounded.

Jennifer, still eying him, shrugged and returned to her menu. They decided to split a small cheese pizza and a large beet salad. It wasn't the first time they'd shared that combo, maybe even at that very table. But from the cool vibe Nate felt coursing off Jennifer, he suspected they wouldn't be doing it again.

"What did you buy at Mickey Hargitay's?" she asked, referring to the popular nursery Nate had mentioned in his text. She'd actually been there with him many times, hoping they'd catch a glimpse of the owner's sister, TV actress Mariska Hargitay from the "Law & Order" series. They never did.

Nate had completely forgotten he'd concocted that excuse to see Jennifer, so he stumbled a half-second until he pulled "A dwarf Cara Cara orange tree" out of thin air. He covered his tracks by tacking on "But I'm going there after lunch" on the off-chance she ended up back at his truck and wanted a look. That was the problem with making shit up: once you started, you had to keep it going, detail by detail. It was so much easier to tell the truth—so why didn't he?

They caromed from topic to topic—her dance classes, Nate's house, a few world news items—as they waited for their food to arrive. They tread lightly on anything too personal, which to Nate felt so hugely impersonal after how close they had once been. Still, he understood how and why their dynamic had shifted and that it was largely his own doing.

Their uninspired chat continued through the lunch and only confirmed Nate's earlier inclination: to not mention the Amy situation for now; he'd barely processed the fantastical tale himself. And, between bites of pizza that could have been cardboard for all he could focus on it, Nate realized he'd simply wanted a reason to see Jennifer. But there he was, feeling foolish that he had disappointed someone so special. And that he continued to.

"Nate, why did you ask me to lunch?" Jennifer finally asked, a slight edge to her voice, after Chris cleared their plates.

"Why did you come?" he volleyed back.

She looked out the window as a couple, maybe a few years younger than her and Nate, walked past hand in hand, laughing like one of them had just told the greatest joke. "I don't know," she answered, turning back to him. "I thought you had something to tell me."

"I … just wanted to see you," Nate found himself backtracking. "As a friend."

She considered that and shook her head. "This probably wasn't the best idea."

"Why?" he asked, as if he didn't know the answer.

"Because you obviously have something on your mind that you can't talk to me about. And if it's about me—about us—then I deserve to hear it." Jennifer's soft features hardened; her jaw tightened. It was a look Nate had rarely seen—and it was unnerving.

"It's not about us," he said. "It's about …" Nate stopped. He could have continued, should have continued, but didn't. "Look, forget it. I'm sorry I invited you." He put up his hands defensively. He didn't know who he was at the moment and it was clear: Jennifer no longer wanted to find out.

"Nate, let's not do this again. Not like this." She didn't sound angry, but rather direct and composed. And maybe a little resigned.

Nate nodded in agreement—what else could he do? He considered fixing the mess he'd made by telling Jennifer what he had initially planned to, but let go of the thought as quickly as it had returned to mind.

Their waiter returned with dessert menus but Nate asked for the check instead. It was time to leave.

FOURTEEN

IT WAS LATE afternoon by the time Nate returned home from West Hollywood. He'd stopped by Mickey Hargitay Plants after all, needing to decompress after that unnerving meal and before jumping back onto the freeway. Nurseries were Nate's happy place and it was the rare visit to one that didn't lift his spirits. There was always something new and intriguing or exotic to behold, everything at various states of growth and bloom; every time a different visual and tactile experience. And the smells: so many fresh, heady scents that deepened and spread in the sun and the heat and the breeze.

He was usually in a rush on those early work mornings when he'd stop at a nursery or garden center to pick up his supplies for the day's landscaping project. Yet even then, when it was more about satisfying a list than his soul, he'd still soak up the aromas and shapes and colors and be inspired to seize his day. But it was when he was off the clock that Nate most enjoyed perusing the flats of flowers and vegetables, pots of herbs, clusters of cactus and succulents, and jagged rows of sprouts and saplings and dwarf fruit trees. He'd take photos and notes and sketch out garden designs on drawing pads and in his mind. He'd get lost in the beauty of it all.

Jim used to feel the same way about bookstores: not the big chain stores, even when they were in vogue, but the cozier indie booksellers that dotted the map in and around L.A. and somehow managed to survive—and even thrive—despite their endangered species status. He used to drag young Nate with him on endless visits to bookstores that smelled musty and papery, intoxicating Jim and boring the heck out of Nate. But Nate, good soldier that he was (and, to be fair, he persuaded his dad to take him to his share of toy stores, arcades, and sporting goods shops), would pretend to be interested in books about animals or science or wizards while Jim would vanish into the alphabetized shelves of classic and contemporary fiction. He'd never leave a bookstore without buying something, even if it was some three-dollar potboiler from the remainder bin. "Browsing shouldn't be free," Jim would say. "They've got rent to pay, too."

Maybe it was a holdover from his dad, but Nate always picked up at least a container of herbs or a tray of flowers whenever he'd drop by a nursery and today was no different. He set aside a pot of burgeoning red salvias and a small Boston fern to purchase on the way out. At least now, as a homeowner, he had somewhere to immediately plant things—front yard, back yard, in the clay urns on the porch—unlike when he lived in the apartment and most everything would end up either lining his terrace, struggling on the kitchen counter, or donated to his current design job.

As Nate continued through the twists and turns of Mickey Hargitay's nursery, he ended up in the rear of the garden where the taller trees and fuller-grown plants were on display. He spotted a Cara Cara orange tree perched in a corner and remembered that was what he'd impulsively told Jennifer he was stopping in for. Maybe he should buy the tree after all, just because. The thought quickly passed when he saw the price tag—the tree's unique pink-fleshed fruit made it expensive—and continued browsing until he had sufficiently chilled out from his ill-fated time with Jennifer.

Nate and Jennifer had shared a brief hug goodbye outside Marco's—despite their strained lunch, it would have been more awkward not to—and made no mention of seeing each other again.

That still left the specter of Amy's story to haunt his thoughts, but Nate knew it would take a lot more than a nursery tour to purge that.

NATE HAD FINALLY finished all the prep work on the outside of the Escarpa house and was now ready to start painting. Like all these kinds of projects, it had taken much more work than he'd expected. But it kept him busy during the odd times at night and on weekends when he would do all the sanding, scraping, and patching needed to get the place ready for its facelift. Danny lent a hand now and then, even brought his carpenter brother, Mateo, with him a few times to speed things along. Nate enjoyed the company—as well as the help—and paid them in beer and pizza because they wouldn't take a nickel. (This time, Danny won that battle.)

"You'd do it for me," Danny repeatedly told Nate.

"How do you know?" Nate would joke in return.

"I just know, that's how I know," Danny would answer, and he was right.

Next-door neighbors Max and Carter and other fellow Escarpans would stop by and chat with Nate while he worked, visibly happy he was getting the place up to speed. Their subtext: "Your father kind of let the place go, so while we're so sorry he's gone, it's good that someone more ... proactive is living here now."

That Sunday, the morning after the crash-and-burn with Jennifer, as he started to apply paint primer to the house's capably sanded trim, he heard a car pull up and park. Cody, who'd been lolling on the front porch, jumped up. Nate, on the top step of an eight-foot ladder, turned around and was startled to see the familiar white Toyota Camry sitting at the curb. He could feel his skin flush and his pulse pound as he spun back to face the house. The car door slammed and Nate tensed, though he resumed his work as if he were still alone.

"All work, no play, Nate?" Amy called up to him. She leaned down to pet Cody, who'd run over to greet her. *Traitor*, Nate thought darkly.

He stayed focused on his paintbrush. "Yep, I guess so."

Amy stood in the shadow of the ladder waiting for Nate to turn and face her. But when she was only met with more silence she moved in closer. Amy shielded her eyes from the sun as she looked up and gently asked, "How are you doing?"

"Couldn't be better," he snarled at a now-glossy section of the eave. Nate kept working, his rhythm increasing with his discomfort. He knew he couldn't ignore her forever, but he could sure as hell try.

"Could we talk for a minute?" It was part plea, part request, but with enough steel in her voice to imply that she was not going anywhere.

Nate reluctantly climbed off the ladder. Amy looked pretty and relaxed in a pair of linen pants, a sleeveless cotton blouse, and strappy sandals.

"Hi," she said with a note of caution as if starting her arrival over again. When Nate didn't respond, she pointed at the house. "What color are you going to paint it?"

"Green," he said tersely. "What are you doing here?"

She considered Nate's stony, unrelenting face and dug her heels into a soft mound of grass. "I wanted to know if I'd see you and the guys at the house tomorrow. If you'd be finishing up."

"You could have just texted," he said so dismissively he barely recognized himself.

Amy studied her feet. "I wanted to see you."

Nate was unmoved. "I'll pay you back whatever I owe you, I won't rip you off." He made for the ladder again, though stopped at the base. His legs felt stiff, uncooperative.

"I don't want my money back, I want you to finish. You've done such a wonderful job."

Nate's legs found their purpose again and, as he climbed back up the ladder: "You got what you needed—to get next to me. I think my job is done."

"That's not fair."

"Let's not get into 'fair,' okay?" He grabbed the paintbrush, plunged it in the can of primer, and smeared it on a new stretch of the trim. Nate could hear Amy expel a world-weary sigh behind him. Which didn't mean she was leaving.

She crossed to the ladder. "Is this the house your father bought when he moved down from Fresno?"

Now it was Nate's turn to sigh. "I really don't want to talk about my father," he said, eyes still facing front.

"Well, I do. I'd like to know more about him. And I'd like to know more about you."

Amy's arms crossed stubbornly across her chest. For a fleeting second, Nate thought he recognized himself in the set of her jaw, her brooding stare. He pushed the notion out of mind. "I'll drop off a check for the unfinished work sometime this week."

An unmistakable mix of anger and frustration washed across her face. "Don't bother. I'll text you my Venmo address," she said, then pivoted away from the ladder and toward her car.

Nate was startled by her flat, snappish retort. It left him speechless, stock-still. He thought about responding in kind, getting off the ladder—and in her face—and having it out with her. But he simply gazed out from his perch as Amy got into the Toyota and sped off.

FIFTEEN

NATE DIDN'T PLAN to return to Amy's on Monday, even though there was much work left to be done. Her backyard was essentially completed but Nate and Danny had a way to go in the front of the house, even if, with Butch and Luis's help, they'd made a lot of progress. No matter, Nate had been ready to turn the page on Amy's property, return any advance payments, and start on the Russos' place.

But it occurred to Nate that, his and Amy's "situation" aside, it would be totally unprofessional to bail on the project midstream. (What would the Russos think if they passed by?) Plus, Nate, the gardening control freak that he was, would hate to see anyone other than himself and his team complete the yard as he'd mapped it out. In his mind, no one would ever do quite as detailed a job—would never put in the time and care—and it would pain Nate to see his vision monkeyed around with. Or at least that's what he told himself.

Then there was Danny. Nate wasn't ready to bring him in on the secret—or whatever it was. And the tale he'd have to concoct to justify bailing on Amy would never pass Danny's finely tuned bullshit meter.

So that's why, when Amy exited her front door that morning ready to leave for work, she found herself facing Nate, a fragrant tub of heliotrope in hand, about to plant the purple, white, and baby blue clusters in a newly dug flower bed beneath her living room window. If she was surprised, she didn't let on.

"I'm glad you decided to finish," she said evenly, Danny and the others out of earshot.

"Yeah, wouldn't want to leave any loose ends," Nate mustered, not realizing the dual meaning of his testy response. But Amy did.

"Loose ends?" She moved in closer to Nate, lowered her voice, and looked him squarely in the eye. "I moved my life to be near you, Nate."

He was not prepared to have this conversation with Amy—or any conversation for that matter—but there they were, face to face. For the son of a man who spent so much of his life devoted to words—reading them, pondering them, discussing them—Nate had picked up few of his father's crack oral skills. Maybe it was all those years in front of a classroom or lecture hall, but Jim could get to the heart of an issue in such a pithy, forceful, and persuasive way, it either opened the door to further rational discussion or closed it for good. Whichever way, Jim would win, yet he never made the person he debated feel as if they'd lost. That was an art. Fortunately, Jim rarely played those kinds of word games with his son, never tried to one-up him or engage in the rhetorical chess he reserved for his students and colleagues. That may have kept their relationship equitable and even-keeled but it didn't prepare Nate for the type of deft verbal sparring that was sometimes needed. Now, for example.

Nate glanced across the yard where Danny and the guys were busy trimming an unruly jacaranda tree. Nate knew he had time: they'd be occupied for a while.

"And how's that working out for you so far?" Nate, still holding the pot of heliotrope, asked Amy with an uncharacteristic smirk. He wondered how Jim would have handled a situation like this—that is, if he wasn't the cause of said situation.

Amy studied him, her stance softening a bit. "Look, I can only imagine how hard this must be for you," she answered, not taking the bait he'd tossed. "But it's hard for me, too."

"Well, if it's that hard, you can always move back to Fresno. I mean, can't you?" The impatience in his voice was undeniable yet Nate also realized it was a real question, one he truly had no answer to. It was hard to know what he did and didn't know about Amy, how much to believe and how much to question. All he knew for sure was that he couldn't take everything—or anything—she'd told him for granted.

"I'm not moving anywhere. I have a job here. And a son."

Nate was startled by the assurance of her words, so much so that he had no immediate reply. Instead, he placed the pot of heliotrope on the ground and dug a hole for it in the flower bed. Amy loomed behind him, watching him work, apparently prepared to wait for as long as it took for Nate to pick up the conversation. Which, from the looks of it, wasn't happening anytime soon.

Suddenly, Danny crossed toward them. But he stopped short at what could have been construed—if you had a mind like Danny's—as Amy standing there, checking Nate out, as he kneeled to plant the colorful flowers. Without turning around, Nate could feel Danny's presence and froze, imagining how this must appear to his wily partner. Amy, still waiting for Nate's response, was so silent she might as well have vanished.

"Am I interrupting something?" Danny asked with forced sincerity, as if trying to square how he could razz Nate yet stay respectful to Amy while getting both of their attention.

"Oh, Nate and I were going over a few things before I left for work," Amy answered.

Danny asked to borrow Nate's shovel, then left, carefully tossing a jokey leer at Nate, should he care to catch it. He didn't and went on with his planting.

"Do you know what the name Nathaniel means?" Amy asked when it was clear that Nate still wasn't talking.

"I don't know, 'fool'?" he shot back as he packed the soil tightly around the heliotrope with his hands.

Amy let several seconds pass before dignifying that with an answer. "It means 'Gift of God.'" She allowed that to sink in, then added, "*I* named you that."

Nate finished with the plant, then rose to face Amy, his look inscrutable. Even he seemed unsure what was going to come out of his mouth next. Would he finally take the high road and listen—really listen—to what the woman had to say? Or would he recoil once again, in fear of the possible truth—and its possible consequences?

The latter won out. "Do you always return your 'gifts'?" he heard himself say.

Amy's skin tightened, her eyes dark. They stared each other down for as long as they could bear it until Amy gave in and broke the spell. "I think today should be your last day here," she said with near-frightening resolve. "You can refund me a thousand dollars. That should cover what you'll owe me." And without another look, she turned and walked off to the garage, leaving Nate stunned by the taste of his own medicine.

Before Nate could process what just happened, Danny was in his face. "Dude, what the fuck just happened? She did not look happy." Nate considered how he could answer, but honesty seemed too crushingly complicated.

"Today's our last day here," he punted. "It's a long story."

"I got time," Danny said, crossing his arms and narrowing his gaze at Nate. Butch and Luis, who were finishing up the jacaranda tree, looked across at their bosses as if they were in trouble. Danny called over something in Spanish that seemed to calm the guys.

"So you gonna tell me or play all mystery man like you always do?"

Nate could feel his hackles rise and his stomach sink. Danny was his friend, his partner, and he owed him the truth. But it was not forthcoming. Not yet. "I'll see if we can start at the Russos' house tomorrow," Nate finally said. "If not, take the day off, okay?"

"With pay?" Danny asked, a hint of his trademark twinkle resurfacing.

"Don't be a dumbass. Yeah, with pay." Nate gave Danny's

shoulder a playful shove; Danny returned it, grinned. Yet behind his smile was a well of concern. He'd have to leave it there for now.

They worked till four and called it quits. After the others left, Nate stood alone and glumly looked around at the half-finished yard. He felt like a failure. So much left undone—and even more unsaid.

85

SIXTEEN

NATE HAD ENERGY. So much energy he didn't know what to do with it. So, he ran. Ran like the wind. He shocked himself with the stamina he still had after a full day's work as he pounded along the paths of Heidelberg Park, a transporting expanse of grass, trees, and trails in Mount Washington, one town over from Eagle Rock. Like the Occidental Campus, the lofty park had its share of sweeping views of Los Angeles and beyond. But Nate barely saw anything but the air three feet in front of him as he swooshed along like a real-time Nike commercial. That Cody kept up with him for as long as he did was the second marvel of this early evening lung-buster. Or maybe it was Nate who was keeping up with his indefatigable dog.

Either way, the running cleared Nate's mind and expanded his heart, which was feeling small and cold and hard—a development that was more disturbing than Nate would allow himself to admit. And he couldn't even pawn it off on his father's death. If he was honest, it had started in tiny, imperceptible ways well before that, before he even knew about Jim's condition. It was in the months before the split with Jennifer, as he began to sense both her encroaching need for a deeper commitment and his own desire for more sustained freedom. And not the freedom to sleep with other women or go on a bender at will or zigzag the map in an RV or any of the other lies guys told themselves to justify dismantling a perfectly good and healthy relationship.

And what of Amy's bewildering appearance in his life? Had that brought out an even deeper, chillier side of him? Had he become more confined to life's probabilities than to its possibilities? Nate considered himself to have a creative spirit, at least where his work was concerned, so why not emotionally? The answers continued to elude him.

So, for that magically lit hour in Heidelberg Park, Nate was decidedly—literally—running from his confusion instead of toward it and the obvious metaphor of it all was hardly lost on him. Nor was what happened when a mother and her young son, maybe out on their own late-day escape, found themselves in Nate and Cody's path, and the four almost collided in a regrettable heap. Fortunately, the mother yanked the boy out of Nate's way just in time to avoid a crash, with Cody stopping short before Nate snapped out of his trance.

"Oh, my God, I'm so sorry!" Nate exclaimed when he realized he'd nearly flattened this hiker and her kid, whose impish grin implied he'd enjoyed this unexpected bit of action. His mom, on the other hand, looked rattled as she gripped her child. The boy calmly gazed beyond her clutches at Cody, who was desperate to investigate the little stranger. Nate held him back, in case his mom wasn't a dog person. They exist.

"You should really be more careful," she told Nate.

The boy reached for Cody, who sprang loose from Nate and made a new friend. The mother, calmer now, stayed put—she apparently felt the dog was safer than Nate.

Nate watched the woman watching her son. He was struck by her protective stance, her tiger-mother instincts, and thought how blessed this boy was to have that kind of love in his life. Did he have any idea how lucky he was? Did he ever think how his world would be without a mom? Of course not, he was too young, too unformed. Besides, she was always there; why should he think otherwise? Unlike Nate's mother who was never there—a ghost, a shadow, a rumor. What would having a mom have been like? What would it *be* like?

It haunted Nate all the way home. And through dinner, which he pulled together from three nights of leftovers. And as he sat in his dad's former office and tried to read Jim's dog-eared copy of Jerzy Kosinski's *Being There*, intrigued that the main character's name was Chauncey Gardiner—even if he was not exactly Nate's kind of gardener.

The words began to blur. Nate flashed back on the mother and son in the park. That look in her eyes: I'd lay down my life for this boy. Nate shut the book and grabbed his laptop. He Googled: "Fresno, CA High School Yearbook." What did he think he was looking for? What did he hope to find? He clicked. Clicked again. A page appeared on the screen: "Fresno High: Find Alumni." Nate paused, knew whatever he saw, he couldn't unsee. But he was seeking the truth: her truth, his truth. He entered Amy's name and there she was, in her senior class photo. Nate's breath caught; his heart skipped a beat. How had she described herself back then? That she was "pretty enough?" If other girls were, in fact, more attractive, Nate couldn't picture it. Yeah, maybe some were more overtly sexy, more striking, or more seemingly mature. But Amy had a fresh-faced, unstudied, accessible beauty that was still evident so many years later; a depth and soulfulness to her eyes that held both mystery and magic.

As Nate studied the photo, he tried to imagine how Jim saw her, what he saw *in* her. What had made him take such a precarious, some might say unconscionable, leap at that exact moment in time? And suddenly Nate realized: He was asking questions as if he believed Jim and Amy's affair was real. That without knowing it or expecting it, Nate had turned a corner and stopped resisting the potential facts. And with that, the prospect that Amy could be his mother.

"I WANT YOU to see this," Nate said as he handed Amy a laser printout of her high school yearbook picture. They were sitting across from each other on the patio at Patys, a cozy, reliable diner that had been a Toluca Lake institution for more than sixty years. Last night, after his epiphanous shift in thinking, Nate impulsively texted Amy to ask if she'd meet him for breakfast the next morning on her way to work. At first, she said no. Five minutes later, she texted him back a yes.

Amy stared at her teenage photo.

"This is you, right?" Nate asked, as if there was anyone else it could be.

"My God, how young I looked," she said, eyes fixed on the old picture. "Where'd you find this?"

Nate didn't answer, just pulled a second, larger photo from the manila envelope he'd brought along. "Do you know these people?" he asked, as he handed her Jim and Eileen's wedding picture. It was another obvious question, of course, but it was all Nate could think of to say. The truth was: he was more nervous than he expected to be.

Amy studied the slightly faded photograph. She swallowed hard and then gazed up at Nate. "I can't believe how much you resemble him," she said, her eyes filling at their corners.

The waitress, a sixtyish redhead with a pixie haircut, arrived with their scrambled eggs and toast. "Anything else I can get you folks for now?" she asked. Amy and Nate shook their heads tightly and, message received, the waitress left to take an adjacent table's order.

"He always said I looked just like my mother," said Nate, the aroma of the fried eggs both enticing and overpowering. He leaned across and tapped his index finger on the wedding-gowned Eileen.

Amy straightened up in her seat and locked eyes with him, as if daring him to see the similarity, not to Eileen—but to her. Nate knew what she was doing, knew that no matter what Jim may have said, that he looked like Eileen in, at best, coincidental ways. And now, staring at Amy with more compliant eyes, he noted flashes of resemblance: their full eyebrows, straight noses, small chin clefts.

He turned away, had seen enough, and gazed out at the morning traffic on Riverside Drive.

But Amy was just getting started. "What do *you* think?" she asked, a challenge in her voice.

Nate looked back at her, then slid the last photo out of the envelope and passed it over. "I don't know," he said, "you tell me." It felt fitting, if somehow cruel, to bring out his baby picture just then—a kind of visual coup de grâce. He didn't mean it that way, but it didn't stop him.

Amy seemed gobsmacked by the snapshot, struck in a way that, unlike with the other photos, was too much to take. She set the picture on the table and began to cry: quietly, regretfully. Nate wished he hadn't done this, hadn't done any of this, had left bad enough alone. But the damage had been done—long ago, it seemed.

"You were so tiny," Amy finally said in a soft, mournful voice. "When I held you in my arms, I was afraid you might break."

"What did you tell people? After I was born," Nate asked, realizing as he did so that he was admitting Amy might be who she said she was. It noticeably registered: Nate could see her shoulders relax, her eyes clear, her chin lift.

Amy took a sip from her coffee cup, her hand lightly trembling. "Nothing," she answered. "No one ever knew, except Jim—and my parents. I managed to cover up the pregnancy through the end of eleventh grade, hid away that summer, gave birth in September." Amy paused purposefully and added, "September second."

There were, of course, many ways she could have learned Nate's birthday: a few minutes online, a tossed-off question to Danny, a visit to the city clerk's office. But her words felt authentic, authoritative; the words of someone who was there. Nate nodded in a kind of tacit confirmation, a signal that she could—should—continue.

"I started senior year a few weeks late. We said I had viral pneumonia. It was going around so ..." Amy drifted off, looking sapped by the memory. She picked up a fork, vacantly poking at her eggs.

Nate eyed her, feeling a twinge of empathy. It passed. "Oh, what a tangled web you wove," he said evenly, channeling his literary-minded dad. He took a big bite of his wheat toast.

"Your father and his wife told everyone they'd adopted a baby. All I could think about was how I gave you away. I didn't eat, couldn't sleep, nearly flunked out of school."

Nate tried to picture that, how terrible it must have been for Amy at such a young age. And yet, he wasn't objectively moved. "You really screwed up, didn't you?"

Amy took that in—the attitude, the message—and looked squarely, unapologetically at Nate. "Seeing you sitting here right now, that's the last thing I could ever think."

SEVENTEEN

THERE WAS, OF course, the matter of Nate finishing the work on Amy's front yard, which, like so much else, was not even broached during their awkward breakfast. Nate had decided to take the day off altogether, hoping that meeting with Amy might give him the clarity and direction he needed to get back on track—whatever that track was supposed to be. But despite what he may have learned that morning on the diner patio, the jury was still out for Nate on the veracity of Amy's tale, not to mention his acceptance of it.

If true, he had the right to be just as angry at his father as he was at Amy—angrier, maybe, if he was really being fair. After all, Jim had been the adult in the room back then. He was the one who'd abused his power and cheated on his wife. Plus, he'd had thirty years to tell Nate the truth, yet chose not to. He simply couldn't imagine Jim deceiving him all those years. Not his dad. And yet.

Nate drove home after breakfast, sat out in the back garden with Cody, and tinkered with his design for the Russos' yard. He never did contact the couple to see if he could begin their job a week early. In truth, the Russos told Nate a while ago they'd be ready whenever he was—but Nate was clearly not ready. He hated unfinished business and that seemed to comprise most of Nate's life these days. As for Danny, he answered a jovial "Sweet!" when Nate reconfirmed his paid vacation day, no further questions asked—for now.

The Escarpa house paint job was hanging over Nate's head, so he figured he'd put in some time on it while he had a free afternoon. But twenty minutes into painting the front trim, Nate was feeling antsy, guilty, like he should be somewhere else. He checked the time: *1:25 p.m.* He could get to Toluca Woods by two and, even working alone, get a decent amount of planting done at Amy's before she returned from her office. No one was asking him to do this; Amy had, in fact, asked him not to. But something was pulling him back there and he preferred, for once, not to think too deeply about what he was doing.

Nate stashed the painting gear, hustled Cody—who was giving him the "don't even think about leaving me" look—into the Silverado and hopped back on the freeway.

He hoped to finish up before Amy arrived home but lost track of time after he decided to jettison the planting and start digging a trench for a dry creek bed. This "river" of rocks was something he was planning for the Russos and thought it might work here as well. He knew there was a chance Amy wouldn't want it—it wasn't in the original design—but once he got creatively inspired in the garden, he could be like a man possessed. Still, he knew even as he was doing it that he wasn't thinking clearly: it was a big job that would need Danny's help.

He barely heard Amy's car door slam. Cody did and ran to her.

"Nate? What is all this?" Amy asked, a bag of groceries in each hand. Her attaché was slung over her shoulder.

"I'm building a dry creek bed," he said, rising to face her.

"Is that so?" She put down her groceries and assessed Nate—and the S-shaped trench he'd started digging. Cody stuck his snout in the market bags, sniffing loudly.

"Cody, leave it!" Nate called and, amazingly, the dog trotted away and plopped down on the lawn. Meanwhile, Amy's eyes never left Nate. He knew an explanation was in order. "Look, I know we didn't talk this morning about me finishing up here. But I can't afford to give you back your money, so you're stuck with me."

They both knew that was a lie, that even if he couldn't return the balance he'd find a way. But Amy had her pride, too, and, apparently, her own breaking point.

"You can keep the damn money," she answered impatiently, then grabbed the groceries and made for the front door.

Nate watched as Amy fumbled for her keys. He was such a jumble of emotions, felt such contradictions, it was like two of him were there at once.

Cody leaped up and started doing laps around the yard, kicking up dirt and grass as he went. It jarred Nate back into action and he grabbed the dog, stopping him in his tracks. "Hey! Relax!" Nate yelled, with enough force that Cody cowered, something the eager, happy dog rarely did. It made Nate feel like a jerk. Before he could feel any worse, something came over him and he marched toward the front door just as Amy was about to enter.

"Are you really my mother?" Nate half-shouted. It was a plain and painful question.

Amy stopped cold. She looked older than she did at breakfast, wearier, worry lines etching her forehead. Her entire body practically sighed. "Nate, tell me: What possible reason would I have to lie?"

Her question was as direct as his and he couldn't formulate a rational rebuttal. It made Amy's lips curl into the faintest smile: not one of satisfaction but vindication, of release. Standing in that doorway, Nate and Amy could feel an invisible curtain lift—and a floodgate open.

"So you really never spoke to my father again?" Nate asked, with a sincerity that made Amy's eyes mist up.

"Not even that last semester at Fresno High. When we'd pass in the halls, I couldn't even look at him, it hurt so much. And then he was gone. No forwarding address, no nothing."

Cody loped up and butted Nate's leg for a pet. He leaned down and stroked the dog's thick coat as Amy stood over them both. Nate looked up at her, flashed on his dad's rakishly handsome face, and said, "It's strange how you can know someone so well, yet not know them at all."

Amy watched him nuzzling his beloved dog. "No matter what," she said, petting Cody's haunches, "I guarantee your father loved you very much. Isn't that what's most important?"

Nate thought about that as he gazed out at the unfinished front garden. "I don't know, is it?"

"I'd like to think so," Amy answered. Nate wondered if she was talking entirely about Jim.

He pointed to the trench he'd dug. "I got a little ahead of myself. I can stop if you want."

"That depends," she said, narrowing her gaze at the curvy ditch bisecting a patch of her lawn. "What's a … what did you call it? A dry creek bed?"

Nate laughed and explained how he envisioned it would tie in with the rest of his design, and even offered to throw it in for free. His mood had lightened so dramatically he was giving shit away.

"Okay," Amy answered, "but on one condition."

"What's that?"

"You let me cook you dinner tonight. I bought all this good stuff at the market and I have no one to share it with." But as soon as the suggestion was out of her mouth it was clear it was too much, too soon.

"Maybe another time," Nate responded, eyes on Cody, who was nosing around the creek bed ditch. Nate turned to Amy and they shared a long, knowing look: no further words were needed.

EIGHTEEN

DRIVING AWAY FROM Amy's house that early summer evening, Nate felt more buoyant—or at the very least guardedly optimistic—than he had in a while. He cranked up the Killers on his Pandora radio, which catapulted him back to his high school days when he'd discovered the retro-rock band and dove into their catchy sound. He introduced his first real girlfriend, Kayla, to their music and they nervously lost their virginity together while the band's "When You Were Young"—how on the nose was that?—roared on his bedroom CD player. Jim liked that particular tune, too; said it reminded him of Springsteen, a mighty compliment indeed.

The music reminded Nate of Jennifer, who was also a Killers fan, though not because of Nate; she was a devotee long before they met.

Jennifer.

Nate glanced at the clock and realized, unless her schedule had changed, she would be leaving work in around thirty minutes. He estimated that, if traffic cooperated, he could make it over Laurel Canyon and to the Melrose Avenue dance studio in time to catch her before she took off for the night. It had only been a few days since their strained lunch at Marco's but it seemed like weeks.

He'd messed up so badly with her, had kept her at such arm's length, that he couldn't fault her if she never wanted to see him again. She deserved someone better than him—or certainly a far better version of the Nate she once cared for. But could he be that person? Did he even know who that person was anymore? He had no idea, just felt—knew—that he'd veered ridiculously off-path and that his life wasn't working too well without her. But would it work with her? And did he even have control over that anymore?

He decided to find out, made a swift, illegal U-turn, and sped south to Ventura Boulevard. Nate found himself singing along and pounding the steering wheel in time to the rousing music as he hurtled toward his destination. Cody turned to him with, Nate could swear, a puzzled look that said "Who *are* you?"

He found a parking space in front of the dance studio, with three minutes to spare before Jennifer's class ended—if she was, in fact, there. Nate felt awfully conspicuous perched in the huge Silverado, Cody's head stuck out the window, his goggly eyes trained on Jennifer's workplace. There was something almost invasive about it, but, hey, it was a public street! And before Nate could talk himself out of what he was doing (what *was* he doing?), the studio doors swung open. A dozen or so lithe young women—and a few wiry men—in leotards, tights, and dance pants, streamed out, breaking off left and right in singles and pairs.

A few moments later, Jennifer appeared in the doorway, wearing a shoulder bag and the form-fitting dancewear that accentuated all her best angles and curves. She stopped short at the sight of Nate and seemed unsure how to proceed. Nate, realizing this could be a bigger misstep than he had imagined, hustled out of the truck and made a beeline for Jennifer, who had yet to move from the doorway, studio keys dangling in her hand.

"Is everything okay?" she asked.

"Hi. Yeah, I'm fine," he said, joining her on the sidewalk. "I didn't mean to just show up, but—"

"But you just did. Again." She locked the studio door, tried the handle to be sure.

Nate tried to read Jennifer's level of annoyance. She nodded in Cody's direction.

"How's he doing?"

"Oh, Cody's great. Man's best friend. Y'know." Okay, that was stupid. This was getting him nowhere. "Look, I wanted to talk to you about something. For real this time."

Jennifer shot him a dubious, impatient look. "Nate ..." She glanced at the eagerly panting Cody, his huge pink tongue flopping this way and that.

"I'm serious," he told Jennifer. And when she was still silent, Nate added, "How about a grande half-caf latte, extra foam, shot of caramel?" He hoped it was still her usual Starbucks order.

She sighed. "What am I going to do with you?" she finally said, shaking her head in droll surrender.

"AND YOU BELIEVE her?" Jennifer asked Nate, with more curiosity than judgment.

"I know it sounds crazy, but I think I'm actually starting to," he answered as he took a sip of his tangy Moscow mule.

They'd decided they needed cocktails more than coffee and ended up on the patio at Café Marmalade, a crowded restaurant at the Grove shopping mall, a few blocks from Jennifer's dance studio. Cody lay curled up under their table, chewing on slices of an Opal apple Jennifer had tucked away in her dance bag. Nate felt guilty about making the dog late for dinner but Cody seemed unfazed. And Nate had a bridge to rebuild.

Once they had placed their drink orders, Nate launched into the Amy saga from the beginning. What had been so difficult to put into words only a few days before came tumbling out with ease.

"I mean, why else would someone move to a whole new city, rent a place, get a job, and pay me all this money to landscape what's not even her house?" Nate asked as he speared a forkful of the veggie quesadilla they were splitting.

Jennifer considered that a moment, the mojito she was drinking loosening her lips. "Okay, but … holy fuck! How could your father not have told you all these years? The two of you were like best friends." She stared at Nate. "I mean, weren't you?"

"Look, like I've said, he kept some things inside. The man knew he had cancer for six months before telling his own son. That says something." Nate's hand shook a bit as he lifted his mug for another sip. What he'd just said out loud unnerved him. It made something that had been quietly gnawing at his guts startlingly real; a piece that finally found its place in the puzzle.

Jennifer could sense his shift. "Are you all right?"

"No, not really," he admitted, gazing into his drink. The eclectic sights and sounds around him—the others on the café patio, the passing shoppers and tourists and meanderers—were overlapping in Nate's head, creating a kind of kaleidoscopic effect. If he'd been standing he might have fallen. He gripped his mug, held his breath, and … as quickly as it had arrived, the dizzy feeling passed, leaving just a prickle of sweat across his forehead.

Jennifer, who'd been under the table, feeding the last of the apple to Cody, popped back up. "So what are you going to do?" It took Nate a second to refocus and realize she was talking about his Amy dilemma.

"I'm not sure," he answered, because he really wasn't. "But I'll tell you one thing—she's not going away." He took another chunk of the quesadilla, chewing pensively.

"Why couldn't *my* real mother turn out to be someone else?" Jennifer asked with a wry look, her first thing approaching a smile since they'd sat down.

"C'mon, you love Rhonda." It sounded sarcastic, but he meant it seriously. Sure, Jennifer's mom could be a pill and a snob sometimes, launched into French when she got pissed (even though she was born in the Bronx), and maybe liked her Chablis a bit too much. But she was always nice to Nate (mothers liked Nate—sometimes more than their daughters did), worked hard, and adored Jennifer, even if she had strange ways of showing it.

"Love and like are two different things," Jennifer told Nate, as she downed the last of her mojito.

"All I'm saying is, be careful what you wish for."

"Oh, I always do," she answered, breaking another mysterious half-smile.

The dual meaning of her words, her implication—his inference—flustered Nate. He wondered if he should just quit while he was ahead. It was hard to tell exactly what was going on between them right now. He watched as Jennifer stuck her fork in the cheesy appetizer and took a healthy bite. She gazed back at Nate as she slowly chewed her food. It was kind of turning him on, which, on one hand, seemed like a good sign and, on the other, completely beside the point. He was at a loss for how to act with her and, to prove it, reached across the table for her hand. She looked as surprised as he did and let him hold it for a moment, then gently pulled away.

"Thank you for telling me about Amy," Jennifer said conclusively. She might as well have said, "Let's get the check." Still, why shouldn't she feel that way? What was he offering her? What did she even want? And what Nate wanted from her she was unable to give him. Sitting there, he realized it was something no one could give him: certainty. That is, the certainty that Amy was his birth mother—and the certainty that he should accept her as such. The certainty that it would be worth the long road ahead that leap would require of them.

"Thank you for listening," Nate finally answered. "I appreciate it."

Jennifer narrowed her gaze. "Look at us," she said, "all formal and self-conscious and polite. We're like strangers." She paused. "It fucking kills me."

Sometimes having a dog around can truly be a godsend; think a four-legged version of being saved by the bell. This was one of those times. Cody chose that very awkward moment—Nate's tongue was so cat-caught he could barely breathe—to shimmy out from under the table, shake himself out like he'd just had a swim, and let loose a big, noisy yawn right in Nate and Jennifer's startled faces. The couple sitting next to them, a genial-looking pair of seniors perched over plates of pasta, couldn't help but guffaw at the pooch's outsize presence on the tight patio. Nate and Jennifer joined in, laughing loudly, as if their child had just done something adorable.

NINETEEN

IT WAS ONE thing telling Jennifer about Amy, but it was another letting Danny in on this particular turn of events. Nate knew he'd tell his partner eventually—hopefully sooner than that—but Nate wasn't ready. Nor did he think it was appropriate given the work-related overlap to the whole thing. (Not that he didn't trust Danny with sensitive information about a client, and yet.)

Then again, maybe Nate only opened up to Jennifer as an excuse to see her, as a way back into her good graces—even if her issue with him was his lack of commitment rather than his verbal reticence. But weren't those two things related? No, Nate decided as he drove back to Eagle Rock that night after seeing Jennifer: He'd wanted—needed—to talk, she was who he wanted to talk with, and he was finally able to get the words out. Simple as that. As if any of this was simple.

Nate did, however, call Danny to let him know they'd be back working at Amy's the next day and to meet him there with Butch and Luis if they hadn't already jumped into another gig. Danny, in the middle of giving his kid a bath, sounded only mildly surprised, asked for no details, and told Nate he'd see him at the job. Nate predicted Danny would pepper him with questions in the morning.

Danny didn't disappoint. "You and the boss kiss and make up?" he asked the next day, as they unloaded plants, tools, and big sacks of decorative rocks from Nate's truck. They'd arrived a bit late, and Amy had already left for work.

For a split second, Nate was about to erase Danny's silly fantasy for good, then, once again, the urge passed. "It's all good, okay? I even started digging a dry creek bed yesterday." He indicated the heavy bags: "Hence, the rocks."

Danny, hauling the last of the day's materials off the truck, shot Nate a look that he'd rarely seen: one of hurt. "Wait, so you were here without me?" asked Danny, as if Nate had spent the day at Disneyland.

"Yeah, I stopped by and did a little work. I didn't plan it, I just … ended up here." Nate didn't know why he felt guilty or defensive, but his partner looked weirdly betrayed. "Anyway, even if I did need your help, you had the day off. I didn't want to get in the way of that."

Nate locked the truck and crossed to Amy's lawn, dragging a sack of rocks behind him. Danny, power tools in hand, followed. "Dude, something's going on here," he called, "and I'm gonna get to the bottom of that shit."

Nate pretended to ignore that, though knew there was just so long he could hold back the truth from his friend. He, too, needed to "get to the bottom of that shit." But how, exactly?

Stopping at the ditch he'd begun yesterday, Nate turned to Danny and said, "Help me dig out the rest of the creek bed, would you? I'd like to get it all done before Amy gets home."

Danny studied Nate, more suspiciously this time, and with a mysterious half-smile said, "Okay, but I'm watching you, buddy." He pointed at his eyes with a backward V-sign, then aimed those fingers at Nate.

Nate waved him off with a dismissive grin and they got to work. He couldn't even begin to guess what Danny's reaction would be if—when—he let him in on the strange tale of Amy Lucas Shields.

Amy returned early that day, around three, as Nate was putting the finishing touches on the dry creek bed. The winding trench, which spanned about twelve feet along the far right side of the yard, was filled with a cascade of small rocks of various shapes and colors. A variety of perennials—agapanthus, sea lavender, flax—lined the creek, with clumps of lemon thyme planted between the rocks themselves. As the minutes ticked by, Nate could feel himself getting carried away with his project, almost as if he were trying to prove something. What that was exactly—and whether it was to himself or his employer—he had no idea.

"How much extra is she paying for this masterpiece?" Danny threw out to Nate like a grenade. He didn't even bother to lower his voice in front of Luis, who was hacking away at a massive—and massively overgrown—bird of paradise.

"What difference does it make?" asked Nate, gazing at the formation of mixed rocks snaking through the creek bed. "It won't affect what you get paid." The words were harsh but Nate's tone was mild. He was too busy wondering if he should extend his "masterpiece" another few feet. When he finally looked up he was face to face with Danny, whose dark, deep-set eyes were boring holes into his.

"What?" Nate asked, returning to the planet.

"Number one: fuck you for saying that about my pay. And two: since when do you slap a thousand-dollar project onto a job for nothing? What are *you* getting out of it?" There wasn't a trace of Danny's sideways geniality in sight. He was pissed.

Nate walked away, pretending to inspect Luis's work shaping the bird of paradise. Danny followed Nate like a shadow. "I've never seen you try to impress someone this bad," he told Nate, getting in his face. "You're way cooler than that and that's why I fucking love you, dude."

That threw Nate for a loop. He didn't consider himself particularly cool—at all. Detached or discreet, maybe, but someone to look up to or emulate? That was news to Nate. And maybe Danny was right—not about being a chill guy but about trying too hard, playing his hand, giving away his most valuable asset: his creative ability.

And it made Nate realize something for the first time: that he wanted Amy to be his mother. And that he wanted to be worthy of her. How fucked up was that?

Nate thanked Danny for looking out for him, apologized if he'd sounded snide, and assured him he was in complete control of his landscaping senses. Danny looked dubious but went back to work, mollified for now.

"When you talked about a dry creek bed, I had no idea it would be so beautiful," said Amy when she laid eyes on Nate's striking work. "It just sounded … dry." She was walking the length of the creek bed examining the colorful plantings and artfully arranged spread of rocks.

"Well, it is 'dry.' But it's also a great way to add some hardscape to your landscape. Mix things up." Nate found himself bursting with pride, like a kid showing his parent his straight-A report card. It was not how he wanted to feel at thirty years old, but there it was.

He tried to hide his satisfied expression from Danny, who, out of Amy's eyeline, pumped his fist in a jerk-off motion, tongue hanging naughtily out of his mouth.

"I want to pay you for this," Amy finally said, "and I won't take no for an answer." She pivoted to face Nate, causing Danny, he of the excellent reflexes, to stop his rude gesturing on a dime. He beamed at her with the face of an angel.

Meantime, it didn't escape Danny that Amy had just spilled the beans about the landscaping freebie Nate had—unsuccessfully—been elusive about earlier. Danny's expression read: "No giveaways on my watch, pal" as if it were his name on the truck and not Nate's. No matter, Nate knew his friend had his back.

Exhibit A: "Know what would look amazing here?" asked Danny, eyes slyly aglow. "A footbridge. Maybe in cedar—or teak. Whaddya think, Nate?"

Before Nate could react, Amy, intrigued though she may have appeared, stepped on the brakes. "Can I think about it?" she asked. She stared at the dry creek bed, seemingly calculating how much it was going to set her back.

"Of course, it's just an idea," Nate answered and, with a deadpan glance at his partner added, "Danny's just full of 'em."

Danny took that as his cue, flashed his winning smile, and went to help Luis wrangle the unwieldy bird of paradise leaves. It left Nate and Amy standing there alone with a gap of awkward silence until Amy melted into a warm smile.

"I meant it, Nate, this really is gorgeous," she said, gesturing at the impressive creek bed. "You're an incredibly talented man."

Nate didn't quite know what to say except: "Thank you." Self-conscious, he kneeled down to hand-sweep some wayward rocks back into the creek bed.

Amy's face, lit by a bright slice of late-afternoon sun, turned wistful. "I wish I could take even an ounce of credit for it but, well …" She looked away from Nate as he rose to face her. He could hear her, feel her, swallowing her tears. It brought a lump to his throat, which he struggled to fight back.

No, you can't take any credit for me whatsoever, Nate wanted to say. And yet he didn't have the heart at that tenuous moment to go there. He felt sad for them both that they hadn't had each other all these years. Amy may have been wrong—his father had definitely been wrong—but they'd all lost out. What it meant now, though, was still a question mark.

Amy turned to Nate, composed, bright again. She smiled and Nate saw his own smile in her face. Or did he?

"That dinner invitation still holds. Anytime you'd like," Amy offered, her voice low. "You have no way of knowing this, but I'm a pretty good cook." She watched Nate's face for a reaction, maybe sensed a softening that wasn't there when she'd last suggested it.

"Can I think about it?" he asked.

"Of course, it's just an idea," she echoed him. They traded grins.

And with that, Amy raised her hand in a little wave. As Nate watched her go, he wondered what she might make him for dinner, but dismissed the thought. He was suddenly afraid: not of her cooking, but of taking that first small step—which wasn't so small at all.

TWENTY

WHEN NATE WAS a kid, he never thought all that much about not having a mom. Maybe it was precisely *because* he'd never had one that he'd always accepted his one-parent existence, which, at least as he remembered it as an adult, was fairly exceptional. Jim was a fine dad: concerned, present, and loving, but never hovering. As a result, Nate grew up feeling supported and valued, but also developed an independent streak that helped make him his own person.

Sure, he'd see other kids' mothers picking them up from school or rooting on their soccer matches or weaving with them around the supermarket and wonder what life would be like with one of those seemingly devoted women rounding out his little family. But the thought—and the mood—would pass and Nate would simply go about his business.

Besides, by the time Nate was old enough to know which end was up, he was familiar with all kinds of families—ones with single parents, divorced parents, stepparents, two moms, two dads, grandparent-run—so his situation didn't seem that extraordinary. It also didn't hurt that Jim was such a relaxed, fun, charismatic guy; Nate was envied for the parent he *did* have rather than pitied for the one he didn't.

It wasn't until Nate was older, maybe in his early teens, that he truly registered the absence of a mom, and started to wonder more about his own mother. Coincidentally, it happened around the time he started to date girls and found himself enveloped by their physical and emotional presence in all new ways. He wasn't unprepared for the female sensibility per se; Jim had filled him in, with his usual candor and intelligence, about the opposite sex: what to expect, how to do right by them, the sexual component ("Dad, c'mon!" Nate would moan. "I know all about that part!" Which, at fourteen, he really didn't). Still, he began to ponder what a mother's take might have been about her son's romantic inklings; suddenly a woman's point of view seemed essential, especially if she was someone as invested in his success as his father was.

Nate became fascinated, in an almost scientific way, with the moms of his high school girlfriends, and the duality of thought and process they brought to their children's lives—as well as to their husbands. Whereas most of his guy friends were intimidated by their girlfriends' fathers, it was the opposite for Nate: He found himself trying harder with the moms than with the dads, whose XY energy was more familiar, more clear-cut to him. And in turn, these women took an almost proprietary interest in Nate, something he came to find as compelling as his girlfriends' attention. And when he went out with a classmate who had two mothers, it was double the thrill.

Yet Nate never walked away thinking kids with mothers were luckier, more complete than he was—and it wasn't like his peers didn't gripe their asses off about their moms *and* dads. If anything, he came to realize just how blessed he was to have the father he did, and, though having a mother might have been a great thing, everyone was on their own life journey and so be it. Needless to say, Nate was a lot more self-possessed back then than he was now. Shouldn't it have been the other way around? What happened?

Maybe Nate was looking for the answer to that exact question—or maybe just a sign—when he wandered into the home of a psychic near the Los Feliz intersection of Franklin and Vermont Avenues.

It was the day they'd finished Amy's job (her front yard looked even better than the back—and *that* looked pretty great), and Nate thought he'd treat himself with a pizza from Palermo, one of his favorite Italian joints, where he and Jim had shared many a meal. The popular restaurant had been a staple in the area forever, and made, in Nate's humble opinion, one of the best pepperoni pies in town.

He had half an hour to kill after placing his takeout order (he should've called ahead but it was a last-minute impulse) so he took a walk around the eclectic neighborhood. After paying tribute to his father with a wave at Skylight Books—they'd always stop into the welcoming shop for a look-see after dinner at Palermo—Nate turned onto a residential side street off Vermont and stopped cold at the first house in: a small, slightly dilapidated, white-clapboard bungalow with a neon sign in the window that read "Psychic Reader and Advisor." If he'd ever passed it before he was unaware—it looked like it had been around long before Nate—but, at that moment, it intrigued him.

Nate was not the "psychic readings" type. He wasn't the psychic type at all, never had much interest in knowing the future or hearing about his past; he didn't need someone telling him what he already knew. Nate never read his horoscope, still thought it was a silly concept (his vague interest in them as an eighth-grade conversation starter with girls sealed that deal), and knew little about astrology beyond his sign (Virgo) and its attributes (practical, organized, realistic, observant—blah, blah, blah). Jennifer was into it, had tried to interest Nate in all things Zodiac, but it didn't take. She didn't live her life by astrology by any means, but said she used it to better understand people; said it helped her get along with others if she knew how they operated. (She was a Pisces: dreamy, creative, romantic; that much Nate learned). Apparently, it didn't help her get a handle on Nate—or maybe it did and that's why she ended things.

Nate gazed at the psychic's colorful, blinking window sign and found himself mesmerized. There were many like it all over L.A.—in homes, on storefronts, and at beach piers—and whenever Nate would pass one he'd think they should add "Suckers welcome" to the neon lettering. But not that day. That day, Nate did something startlingly uncharacteristic, and, checking to make sure no one was watching, he went up and rang the psychic's doorbell. It sounded like a Chinese gong.

Her name was Lena and she was a compact, sturdy little woman with bright blue eyes and a neat gray bob. Nate guessed her to be around 70; she could have been anyone's mother or grandmother. They sat across from each other on upholstered straight-back chairs in the house's small, lovingly cluttered living room, which was lit by only one small table lamp and the remains of the day streaming in through the front window. Her enticing neon sign cast an eerie glow over the walls and furnishings.

Nate looked around for a crystal ball or a deck of tarot cards, but the room was disappointingly generic in that regard. That is, if, like Nate, you needed some extra convincing that this seemingly genial, unassuming woman was anything but the charlatan he was expecting. Yet, there he was, anxiously wondering what she might have to say about his life at this uncertain moment.

To her credit—and Nate's surprise—Lena didn't want his money yet: she waved him away when he took out his wallet.

"No, no. You pay after," she said in a vaguely Teutonic accent. "Just give me your watch."

"Wait, hold on," said a startled Nate. "What for?" *What kind of racket* was *this?* he thought, ready to bolt.

"You'll see." She extended her small, lightly veined hand. Her eyes seemed kind and, yes, knowing.

Nate slowly unstrapped his watch—a Swiss Army he'd worn for ages—and handed it to Lena. She held it snugly between her hands as if trying to warm it up, then tightly shut her eyes. Nate could feel his pulse race, his throat constrict. What the fuck was he even doing there?

Then, Lena's eyes snapped open. Her silent, steady gaze unnerved Nate but he was locked into it. The seconds ticked by like minutes. Lena's stare deepened, darkened; her hands tensed around Nate's watch. His head pounded.

Finally, a string of words tumbled from her mouth with a kind of robotic flatness. "Someone has come into your life. Someone you don't trust … but somehow need."

She looked at Nate as if for confirmation but he didn't let on; what she said could have applied to almost anyone. Couldn't it? "Keep going," was all he said.

"You're caught between two worlds—an old one that's safe and a new one with risk."

Nate shifted in his chair. "Can you tell me about this person? This … someone?" His voice sounded far away, detached. The room turned a shade darker.

Lena considered his question, cocking her head as if listening to something only she could hear. "She—it's a *she*—is part of this new world …" Lena rubbed Nate's watch between her hands, concentrating. "And yet, she's not a stranger to your own life."

Nate could feel himself resisting her reading; his arms weren't crossed but they might as well have been. *She's still too general*, he thought, *her words still too interchangeable*. Did he even want her to be right?

"Young man, is your mother still alive?" Lena's voice relaxed. She assessed the stony Nate, perhaps could tell he was refusing to accept what she was "seeing;" he wouldn't have been the first.

And then, as if a tiny door creaked open for Nate, he said, "That's not an easy answer." His eyes softened. He became aware of the simple gold cross hanging from her neck. Nate had no religious ardor whatsoever, but the symbol's presence soothed him.

"No, she's very much here—your mother. Just not in the traditional sense." She loosened her grip on Nate's watch, flexing her fingers.

"What does that mean?" Nate asked, impatience creeping into his voice.

Lena paused, gathered her thoughts, and cagily answered, "I think you already know."

Nate had had enough. He snapped his watch back on and pulled out a handful of twenties. Lena put up two fingers, took Nate's forty dollars, and dropped it in a small carved wooden box on a nearby table.

As Nate left, Lena took his arm with urgency. "It doesn't have to be so hard," she said.

He left without another word, floated back to his car in a daze, and didn't realize until he turned onto Escarpa Drive that he'd forgotten to pick up the pizza.

TWENTY-ONE

ALL THAT WEEKEND, Nate was haunted by his brief session with Lena. For as much as he didn't want to believe she knew any more than he did about his life—even if, these days, he was admittedly fuzzier about more parts of it than usual—he did suppose there was some guidance from her words. And he *did* tend to make things harder than they needed to be. Someone else would have joyously accepted the reappearance of a mother figure after living an entire life without one—especially after they were left essentially orphaned. Thirty was far too young to be without at least one parent. Nate had already spent way too many hours thinking about all the things Jim would never be around to experience—in Nate's life as well as in his own—and it struck him as egregiously unfair.

For better, but really worse, Nate had too much time to mull all this over as he spent Saturday and Sunday finishing the paint job on the Escarpa house, which had begun to speed up after he moved on from the trim to the wood-and-stucco walls. He tirelessly motored over the two days, painting well into the twilight hours until the darkness sent him and Cody—who'd kept him company almost nonstop—back inside.

He didn't speak to anyone all weekend (he thought of texting Jennifer hello but didn't know what to say beyond that) except for Max and Carter, who stopped by while he was out front to tell him again how great the house was looking. Nate self-consciously took the compliment but found he was happy for human interaction. To that end, he kept the guys talking and even offered to help them with some landscaping needs in their side yard—no charge. They couldn't say no.

But Nate's thoughts kept ricocheting back to Lena and Amy and his strange conundrum. It seemed as if he had two choices: ignore Amy, end whatever it was they'd started, and hope she'd move back to Fresno and out of his life; or nurture the relationship she seemed so eager to have and see where it led. That Nate still believed what he'd said to Jennifer about Amy "not going away" kind of made up his mind for him. At least for the time being.

That Monday morning, Nate and Danny started work on the Russos' yard. Corey and Brooke—he was in tech sales, she was a TV development executive—hung out for a while answering Nate's questions and coming up with a few of their own until their offices beckoned. The couple was almost as lively then as they were that first night when they were so happily cocktailed up. Maybe they were amped on early morning caffeine or maybe they were just naturally cheerful, but Nate liked being around them and Danny found them kindred spirits (meaning they laughed at his corny jokes). They all agreed on a dry creek bed—Corey and Brooke had seen Amy's and were knocked out by it—but would wait on the proposed gazebo to see how the yard came together.

The morning went smoothly enough. Nate and Danny, with the help of Butch and a new assistant, Edgardo (Luis was back in Guatemala visiting family), did a major tree and shrub trim, took out any dead or dying plants, and began enlarging the flower beds. Building the dry creek bed would start later in the week.

Meantime, Danny, after his initial joviality with the Russos, was strangely low-key the rest of the day. At lunch, Nate got him to reveal that he'd had a big fight with Alicia and now she wasn't speaking to him. It had something to do with him flirting with their waitress while they were out for a family dinner the night before. Danny denied paying any special attention to his server; Alicia accused him of flirting with everyone. "I'm a friendly guy!" he countered, to which Alicia apparently said, "Aha! So you admit to sweet-talking our waitress!" It was downhill from there and Danny slept on the living room couch.

"Danny, c'mon, you know how you can be," Nate said. It surprised Nate that it had taken Alicia this long to call out her husband on his "friendliness."

"Okay, but you know I'd never *do* anything," Danny assured him between bites of a BBQ chicken sandwich, and Nate believed it.

"So tell her, talk it out, and make some grand gesture to let her know how you feel about her—and only her."

"Y'mean like you did with Jen?"

Danny might as well have said "What the fuck do you know about communicating?" and he'd be right. Nate realized he needed to lay some cards on the table with Jennifer—and with Amy.

And that's just what he did, at least with Amy, after they'd wrapped up for the day at the Russos'. He parked in front of her house, spent a few minutes admiring her yard, and rang Amy's doorbell, but there was no answer. Though it was past five thirty, she apparently wasn't home from work yet. As he turned from the door to wait in his truck, Amy's Camry eased into the driveway. She honked brightly at him, parked before she reached the garage, and bounded out of the car.

"Nate! What a lovely surprise!"

"We started on the job around the corner, so ..." His voice trailed off as he studied Amy's hopeful face. He was there to do what he told Danny to do: communicate. Yet he wasn't sure where or how to begin. Unlike their past conversations, this one felt like it would have—would *have* to have—a more defined result. Or what was the point?

Before Nate could twist his head into a knot any further, Amy took the lead and invited him in for a drink. He needed one and likely so did she. He followed her into the house but not before they stopped to take in the beauty of her front yard together.

Though he wanted a beer, Nate said yes to a glass of the Malbec Amy offered. They sat in her backyard and drank, which was both soothing for Nate—to bask in his and his team's hard work—and unsettling, as he spotted things that needed tending. Amy rested her wine glass on the small teak table between them.

"Not that I'm not happy to see you, because I am, but what made you come by today? Really."

Nate took a long sip of his wine and carefully considered the answer he was about to give. "I think I believe you," he finally announced. It came out like a weary cop exonerating a would-be criminal.

Amy's mouth slowly curled into a warm smile. "I'm glad," she said, then added, "Are you?"

Nate stared out at the colorful row of snapdragons he'd planted, amazed by how fast they'd grown and how rich their colors still looked in the vanishing light. Was he "glad" about Amy and the thoughts that had been coalescing in his head? He wasn't entirely sure.

"You must have *some* feelings," Amy said. She seemed more curious than offended.

"Well, part of me feels guilty," Nate answered, realizing this as he said it.

Amy's eyes widened in surprise. "Guilty? About what?" She swallowed the rest of her wine, then cradled the empty glass in her palms.

He tried to figure out exactly what he'd meant. He searched the bottom of his wine glass for a clue. It hit him. "Guilty … like I'm cheating on my mother with another mother."

Amy poured herself another glass of Malbec. She tipped the neck of the bottle in Nate's direction. He set his now-empty glass on the table as a "yes," and watched Amy refill it.

"Then part of me feels stupid," Nate continued, his thoughts evolving. "Like I've spent my whole life loving someone—okay, theoretically loving someone—who never existed." He took a swig of the wine, then added, because he needed to say it out loud, "Stupid that I believed my father all those years—and maybe stupid that I miss him so much." His eyes misted up and his chest felt tense. He was pissed at his dad and yet there was a gaping hole in his life without him. One that he wasn't sure could be filled by another parent—literal or figurative. He wiped at his eyes with the back of his hand.

Amy left her chair and hugged Nate, tentatively at first and then, when she saw he wasn't resisting, more tightly. "Oh, Nate. You have nothing to feel guilty *or* stupid about. If anyone should feel guilty, it's me." She held Nate another few seconds, then, as if she didn't want to press her luck with him, let go and returned to her seat.

They were both silent until Nate, with a slight challenge in his voice, asked, "How guilty *do* you feel?"

Amy looked jarred by his tone, if not the question itself. Either way, she seemed fully prepared to answer. "I wouldn't wish what I've felt on anyone," she said, the words cracking in her throat. "And I couldn't even begin to apologize to you for what I've done."

Nate was moved and even a bit overwhelmed by her confession. It was more than he expected, even if, in truth, it was Jim he wanted an apology from, not Amy. In some ways, she was as much a victim of circumstance as Nate. He wanted to tell her that, assuage her sadness in some small way, but chose to keep it inside. He realized he wasn't quite ready to give Amy the full benefit of the doubt—it was something she'd have to earn.

Wine glass in hand, he crossed to the rose bushes he'd planted in a pair of large terracotta pots. He was happy to see how healthy and vibrant they were looking. He was also glad to be diverted, if only momentarily, from the emotional whirl of conversation. Nate leaned into a silky white and coral-red rose, inhaling its perfumy scent.

"You know what this is called?" he asked Amy, staring at the striking flower.

"A rose?" There was a shrug in her voice as if answering a riddle.

"Sure, but what kind of rose?"

Amy joined him at the colorful plants. "I don't know. 'A rose is a rose is a rose.' Isn't that what they say?" She smiled at Nate, but he looked lost in thought.

"I don't know, but no—they're all different, all unique, all have their own traits, their own stories. Like people." He met Amy's gaze, and then relaxed into a half-smile. "Don't mind me, I get geeky around plants—if you haven't already noticed."

"Things are what they are."

Nate put on a mock offended face. "Oh, so you *have* noticed. Gee, thanks."

"What? No, that's what that phrase means: 'A rose is a rose is a rose.' That most things are just what they seem—no more, no less." She watched as Nate took that in. "It's from a poem from the 1920s, by Gertrude Stein." She sipped her wine, then gently added, "Your father read it to us in class one day. That's how I know it."

Nate turned back to the rose bushes. "Ah," he said, pinching a yellowing leaf off a thorny stem. Jim was never far away for either of them, was he? "Well, I don't think I ever heard that poem. But I get Gertrude's point: Don't make more of something than it is."

She offered a wistful smile. "Not always that easy to do, though, is it?"

Nate wasn't sure if she meant "not easy" for him or her but appreciated the thought. And how come Jim never showed him that poem? Or had Nate just lumped it in with all the other books and stories and poems Jim had tried, with varying degrees of success, to share with his son—and had forgotten all about it? What Nate wouldn't give for one of those literature lessons now. He took a slug of the Malbec, enjoyed how each hit instantly went to his head.

"Double Delight," Nate finally said, brightening. "The rose. It's called Double Delight. Because it's two colors."

"And they're … delightful?"

He aimed a thumb at the rose. "You tell me." It occurred to Nate that they'd just had a simple, everyday exchange and it felt good. Like he was talking to someone he'd known a long time. The feeling was short-lived.

"Do you know that I've celebrated every one of your birthdays?" Amy asked, crossing back to the patio chairs.

"*My* birthdays?"

She cautiously chose her words. "Every September second, I've lit a candle, tried to picture you, and prayed that if we ever met, you'd find even the tiniest place in your heart to forgive me."

He took that in, surprised by such an act and moved by its tenderness. Yet somehow, it left him with an ache inside. "That's really nice," he finally said, "but a card might have been more personal." He looked away, knowing it was a stupid, kneejerk response; she wasn't allowed to ever contact him—that was the deal. And yet.

Amy took a long pull from her wine glass. Nate thought maybe he should go; escape was so easy. How often had he chosen that route? He preferred not to think about that. Instead, he sat next to her again, knowing she still had more to say. And maybe so did he.

"I told you," Amy reminded him, "when Jim left Fresno, no one knew where he went. No one. And by the time social media became a thing, I'd stopped looking. Until the day I read his obituary, I had no idea you were living in L.A." She put down her wine glass and recited as if reading from the newspaper: "Survived by one son, Nathaniel, a Los Angeles landscape designer."

"So, if Dad lived another thirty years, does that mean I would have been sixty before you tried to find me?" He didn't know what was more jarring, that Jim could have been around so much longer or the thought that Nate would be sixty one day—if he was lucky.

Amy shifted around in the chair to face Nate head-on, daring him to look away. "For years, I would fantasize that Jim would call me. Ask me to break our 'pact.' Ask me to come and visit our son. Come and live with the two of you." She stopped short, swallowed hard, and choked back a tear. "Of course, that never happened. And, well ... I finally had to let go." She let a tear escape, then another, but didn't break from Nate's somber, pensive gaze.

What she didn't know—couldn't know—was that the empty ache he'd been feeling had been replaced by something fuller, more hopeful ... even merciful. Nate couldn't pinpoint his sudden swing of emotion—maybe all the wine had kicked in—but he had an urge to reach out to Amy, take her hand, tell her it was okay, that no matter what, they'd survived the trauma, that maybe she *had* earned his trust. That they had a world of tomorrows to share.

But he didn't do or say any of that because he was still not ready to fully open the door to this relationship—whatever it may hold. Better to quit while he was inching ahead.

There was one more question he had for Amy before he took off, and it surprised them both. "What's a good night for that home-cooked dinner you promised me?" Nate asked as he finished what was left of his wine and realized he'd be driving home with a little buzz. Like everything, he'd have to take it slow.

TWENTY-TWO

AT FIRST, JENNIFER didn't agree to join Nate for dinner at Amy's that Friday night. It hadn't even crossed his mind to ask her until Amy suggested he bring along a date or a friend or "whoever" (who or what might fall into the latter category Nate was unsure, but it was good to have options). He figured he'd go alone, alone being his default mode these days, until the thought of having the equitable Jen around to help buffer any potential landmines suddenly seemed like a good idea.

They hadn't communicated at all since their bumpy get-together at Café Marmalade, so this at least gave Nate a reasonable excuse to reach out. Jennifer had been right: they *were* acting like strangers around each other now. It was unfortunate and unnecessary, but was it fixable?

"Thanks for asking, Nate, really, but … I don't know," Jennifer said when Nate called the next day during his lunch break, sitting in his truck, away from Danny's hyper-alert ears. Jennifer was between classes at the studio and sounded in a bit of a rush.

"She said I should bring someone. I'd like you to meet her," he replied.

"So it was *her* idea?"

"Well, yeah, but asking you was my idea." Nate already regretted calling her, and wondered how he so quickly ended up on the defensive. He gazed out the passenger-side window: it was covered in thick streaks. What the hell did Cody try licking off it and why hadn't Nate noticed?

"Why?" Jennifer countered. "You're not even sure what *you* think about her." Nate could hear the jangling of keys, a whoosh of movement on her end. He knew she often jumped out for a quick walk when she had a break. She was devoted to hitting 10,000 steps every day (for all Nate knew she could be up to 15K), a pattern that started when he bought her a Fitbit tracker for their one-month anniversary. She was so happy with the gift you'd think it was a sleek gold bracelet. Nate always found it one of Jennifer's most endearing qualities: She was all about the little things.

"That's why I'd like your opinion," Nate said. "You're good with this stuff. You're objective, you're smart. Which, of course, is why you dumped me." He gave a small laugh in case she didn't know he was joking—even if it wasn't far from the truth.

"I didn't dump you," Jennifer answered, traffic sounds in the background (yeah, she was walking). "I let you off the hook. There's a difference."

He thought it best not to comment on that. "Would you just think about it?" The sun beat through the driver's side window. He shut his eyes awaiting her response; it suddenly felt so important.

"Okay."

"Okay … what?" Nate asked, eyes still closed, the warmth on his face.

"I'll think about it!"

He popped open his eyes and said, "Okay. Thanks, I appreciate it."

There was a beat of silence, then: "I know you do, Nate." Through the phone, he heard a car horn honk and then the click of Jennifer hanging up.

It could have been worse: she could have said no on the spot—

and Nate would have understood. For now, though, he was thinking there was a 50-50 shot things would swing his way.

JENNIFER WAITED UNTIL more or less the last minute to say yes to accompanying Nate to Amy's. She texted him Friday morning at ten: "Does the invite still stand?"

Nate had all but given up on her, so was thrilled that she came through. His mood perked up significantly

"Why all smiley, dude?" Danny asked as he looked up from shoveling the trench for the Russos' dry creek bed. He and Nate had started working on it that morning

"Can't a guy just be happy?" Nate grabbed his shovel, dug out a pile of grass and dirt, and tossed it to the side.

"A guy, yeah. You? An explanation is usually in order."

What the hell, Nate thought. He'd been elusive with his friend long enough lately; he owed him some truth. At least about this. "I was just talking to Jen, no big deal," Nate said, then returned to shoveling.

"Wait, what? Are you two …?" Danny made the "screwing" sign with his fingers and lewdly raised an eyebrow. It prompted an eye roll from Nate. "Hey, haven't I told you every little freakin' thing that went down with me and Leesh?" asked Danny with mock indignance.

It was true—Danny had filled Nate in on every step of his mea culpa tour with Alicia after their fight about his supposed roving eye. He'd worn his wife down with such a gusher of charm and love that she finally accepted his apology and now they were trying to have another baby—which may have been Alicia's plan all along.

"We're just talking, that's all," Nate told him. "And … maybe getting together tonight." Nate turned away to end the discussion, pretending to be more absorbed in his ditch-digging than he actually was.

It apparently worked because Danny reacted with a simple "Alright! Cool!" and then, flashing his goofy grin, started competing with Nate for who could dig faster. It was one game Nate would be glad to lose.

Even though he was working around the corner from Amy's, after they knocked off at four thirty, Nate drove all the way home to clean up, change clothes, feed Cody, and bring the pup back with him—in case some neutral diversion was needed. He then bucked Friday evening traffic to make his way back to Toluca Woods, stopping en route at a Trader Joe's to pick up a couple of good bottles of wine.

Jennifer, who'd arrived early, was sitting curbside in her electric-blue Prius, passing the time with a heated game of Candy Crush, when Nate drove up and parked in front of Amy's. They shared a half-hug—one could say like the strangers they were trying not to be—and Nate took in her familiar scent of apples and vanilla. He thanked her for showing up; she offered a silent nod in response, then leaned down and gave Cody a slew of kisses all over his head and snout. The dog licked her back ecstatically, tail going a mile a minute. He was showing Jennifer the kind of attention Nate once did, sans tail.

Amy and Jennifer had an instant rapport, which made Nate feel like a bit of a third wheel (how much could he contribute to their chatter about fashion and skincare?) despite his relief that the women seemed to approve of each other. On the upside, it gave him the chance to sit back, observe them both, and allow his conflicted thoughts to reconfigure—perhaps to everyone's benefit. As they visited in the well-appointed living room, which felt more welcoming and less formal now, the smells coming from Amy's kitchen were intoxicating, suggesting a special effort was being made to ensure the evening's success. Nate could feel himself relaxing as Cody sprawled vigilantly at his side, providing his person with moral support. (He could very well have just been waiting for a spiced cocktail nut to fly out of Nate's hand.)

Once they were seated at the dining room table—candles, linen napkins, and crystal glassware showed Amy's extra-mile attention—the conversation tapered off and the three found themselves eating in silence. Nate scrambled for something to say, but Jennifer beat him to it.

"This is amazing lasagna, Amy," she enthused.

"Thank you. It's an old family recipe."

"Is your family Italian?" Jennifer glanced at Nate as if to say: Did you know you were part Italian?

Amy laughed. "Not that I know of," she answered. "My parents were both born in Oklahoma and moved out west in their twenties."

That was news to Nate but, of course, virtually everything about Amy was. It made him realize how much he didn't know, how much he hadn't thought to ask, and how much he may not even want the answers to. The silence returned. Amy, maybe sensing a shift in the air, a point of access, lowered her fork and looked at Jennifer.

"Jennifer, you must think this whole thing is, well … strange."

"I'm just here to support Nate and eat dinner," she answered between bites of arugula and tomato salad. "What I think is irrelevant."

Nate knew Jennifer was trying to stay neutral but had formed plenty of opinions since she walked through the door. Amy apparently thought the same.

"No, it's very relevant," she told Jennifer. "As soon as you two leave, you're going to give Nate your impression. And from the way I see him looking at you—I know he's going to listen." Amy set her gaze upon them both and watched them blush.

"Really, it's none of my business," Jennifer said.

But Amy was insistent: "You have my permission."

At this point, all eating had stopped and Jennifer snuck him a look. He shrugged "go ahead," as curious as Amy was about what she might say.

"Well, okay," Jennifer began. She took a sip of chardonnay, then, without putting down her glass, said, "My mother and I have never had a very good relationship, so I'm sitting here thinking: What if I found out she wasn't really my mom and that my *real* mom was this beautiful, bright, warm woman who made great lasagna and seemed so desperate to finally love the child she never knew?" She swallowed more wine as she let her words hover over Nate and Amy. Their faces were unreadable, each lost in their own thoughts.

"And if that were true?" Amy finally asked, with a whiff of trepidation.

Jennifer couldn't help but turn to Nate as she answered, "I'd be petrified to love her for fear she'd leave me again."

Nate, startled by her honesty, gave an imperceptible nod of approval. It was a tense, unpredictable moment. That is, until Amy visibly relaxed and offered a gentle smile.

"I'd probably feel the exact same way," she said and returned to her food.

Nate felt, if not vindicated by Amy's reply, then certainly "seen" by her. It was as if he'd just been given a kind of permission—a justification—for being so unsure, so conflicted about Amy and their situation. Jennifer's words, too, helped put things into perspective in a way he hadn't quite considered, and he was grateful for her presence—and not just at Amy's dinner table.

They spent the rest of the meal, including superb wedges of home-baked blueberry pie, chatting about TV shows and favorite desserts and Cody's funniest habits, avoiding anything else too personal because, at some level, they all seemed to know the night could so easily go south. And who needed to dodge another bullet just then?

Still, it unnerved Nate when Jennifer spent a good twenty minutes alone with Amy helping with the dishes while he sat on a cushy leather couch in Amy's cozy den as Cody snored at his side. He went in once to see if he could lend the women a hand—though really to hear what they were saying—but they shooed him out and laughed as the swinging door closed behind him.

"OKAY, WHAT WERE you talking about in there?" Nate asked the second they reached Jennifer's car. They were each holding a wrapped piece of leftover pie. Cody stood there eyeing the desserts.

"A little paranoid?" Her smile brightened the darkness.

"No, a lot paranoid. Come on, tell me."

"Basically, she thinks you're God's gift. And I don't mean it in, like, a religious way."

"Okay … what did *you* say?"

"Y'mean, did I agree that you're God's gift? No, but I did ask her for her lasagna recipe. Did you know that she used *four* kinds of cheese? It was pretty decadent." Jennifer opened her car door, placed the pie on the passenger seat, and popped back out.

"And that's all?" Cody sidled up to Nate. He was ready to go. Nate wasn't.

Jennifer eyed him as if weighing how much more to say. "She also thinks I'd be 'good' for you."

That wasn't what Nate was expecting, though, in truth, he didn't know what to expect. Still, he had to ask: "Did she say if I'd be 'good' for *you*?"

"I think it was implied."

"What do you think?" Nate glanced at Amy's house. He thought he saw her shadow in the living room window, but his mind was playing tricks. He looked back at Jennifer who was staring off beyond him, assembling an appropriate answer.

"I think being with you doesn't work and being without you doesn't work," she said.

"For me, only one thing doesn't work—being apart." Nate felt as surprised by his response as Jennifer looked when he said it, considering his previous level of commitment.

She leaned against the Prius. Cody got the hint—they weren't leaving yet—and sat like the good dog that he was. Nate waited for Jennifer to say something, anything. When she didn't, he went with his gut and leaned in to kiss her. She resisted at first, then relaxed, and slowly, warily, returned his kiss. It didn't last long but felt wonderfully familiar. Nate pulled back and studied Jennifer—and she, him. The lush scent of the night-blooming jasmine Nate had planted in Amy's yard filled the silence between them.

"You look so much like her, you know that?" Jennifer said at last.

He didn't know about "so much." If he looked like anyone it was

Jim, everyone said so, even Amy. Still, he had about zero objectivity about any of this, so why get into a debate over it? "That doesn't prove anything," Nate heard himself say, despite himself.

Jennifer looked at him, unfazed. "No … but a DNA test might."

Ah, the DNA test. It wasn't as if Nate hadn't thought about that, of course. He'd even done his share of Googling about its accuracy (99.99 percent seemed pretty darned accurate—and pretty darned eternal). "That still won't answer the biggest question," Nate replied.

"Which is what?"

"Do I *want* her to be my mother?"

She paused, taking in Nate's anxious expression. "Why wouldn't you?"

"You said it yourself in there: What if it doesn't last?"

Jennifer reopened her car door and turned to face him. "Newsflash, Nate: Relationships are complicated. Even at their best." She kissed his cheek and let her lips linger a provocative extra second. "Some things are worth the risk."

TWENTY-THREE

MAYBE NATE ACTUALLY remembered this or maybe he just remembered Jim telling him the story about it. Either way, he was reminded of one of his earliest memories involving his mother: the mother he was told he had and not the one who was kept a secret. (On that front: Nate thought a lot about the DNA test driving home from Amy's and decided it wasn't necessary; if he wanted to believe her—and it seemed he did—that would suffice.)

The rattling double-hung window in his bedroom, one of many things around the house Nate still hadn't gotten around to fixing, brought him back to the one in his childhood bedroom (which, surprisingly, *had* been fixed somewhere along the line). Whenever the winds would whip up, particularly those blustery Santa Anas, the window's loose frame would clatter, making the glass vibrate along with it. The sound may not have seemed like much to an adult, more annoying than frightening. But to a little boy who had his share of bad dreams and scary thoughts (what kid didn't?), his bedroom window took on a life of its own; Nate had pretty much empowered it with supernatural ability.

One winter night, a wicked combination of driving rain and

fierce gusts wreaked havoc with Nate's dreaded window, creating a terrifying symphony of creaks, clanks, and squeaks that nearly made the six-year-old levitate out of his *Power Rangers*-sheeted bed. True to form, Nate had kept his fear of his bedroom window to himself, trying to be strong. But this time, the storm got the better of him and he called out for his dad—loudly.

Jim frantically rushed in, not used to being summoned by his son in the middle of the night. He held his panicked boy. "It's okay, pal. It's just the wind," Jim told him.

"I thought it might be a ghost," Nate admitted, his sobs subsiding.

"If that ever happens again, and you get scared, just pretend it's your mom, trying to tell you how much she loves you," Jim said gently as he tucked Nate back into his blanket (yes, there was even a *Power Rangers* duvet cover).

Nate tried to square his dad's advice with what little he knew of his mother. It could be said he knew more about ghosts, so he put the two together and asked, "Is my mom a ghost?"

"She's more like … a guardian angel—always there, even if you can't see her."

The recollection brought a wistful smile as Nate lay in bed some twenty-five years later listening to the wind tangle with his window. Sure, the "guardian angel" bit was just a story—Jim *was* well-versed in fiction, after all—but it got him through a few other noisy nights in his childhood bedroom until he grew out of his fear. It also reminded Nate how seldom Jim brought up his mother back then—and how little Nate asked about her. That should have been a sign of, well, something, but it wasn't. Until recently.

Nate woke up the next day feeling energized and encouraged. And, after a big bowl of oatmeal topped with bananas and walnuts and two mugs of coffee, he snapped on Cody's leash, and off they went for a long walk on the Occidental campus, their first time in a while.

There were quite a few people around for eight thirty on a summer Saturday, though, on closer inspection, Nate realized the eager hikers traversing the leafy campus looked more like his neighbors than students. It always surprised him what a popular walking spot the site was for Eagle Rock residents and beyond, despite the "No Trespassing" and "Must Show Oxy I.D." signs posted at every entrance. (Had he ever been asked for I.D.? Had anyone?)

Speaking of neighbors, as Nate hung a right onto a new walking path, he ran into Max and Carter. Or rather, they ran into him—literally. They were in serious jogging mode and didn't see Nate and Cody turning the corner. Nate quickly regained his balance, and Max and Carter said they felt like dopes.

"We totally zone out when we run," said Max, the bigger of the two men, though both looked super-fit in their tank tops and gym shorts. Nate felt scrawny in comparison and wondered if he shouldn't work out more but knew the mood would pass once his neighbors did.

"Yeah, and we usually don't train this early," Carter said almost apologetically, "but it's my mom's seventieth and we're cooking for, like, twenty, so … busy Saturday."

Nate tried to remember if he'd ever met Carter's mother but came up blank. Jim would have remembered; he remembered all that kind of stuff. "Big party, then, huh?" Nate asked. "Lotta work."

"Not every day my mom turns the big seven-oh," Carter said, stretching an arm out over his head. "Gotta celebrate while they're still here, y'know?" The words were barely out of his mouth when he looked horrified. "Oh, fuck, I'm so sorry, Nate, I didn't mean—"

"Jesus, Carter," Max said, eyes wide, teeth clenched. He shot his husband a withering look.

It had taken Nate a moment to realize the faux pas. And when he did, he was unfazed. Jim was dead, Carter's mom was alive and well and having a birthday. Good for her. Nate hoped she had many, many more. And he told Carter as much, though both he and Max apologized so profusely you'd think they'd just set Nate's house on fire. The guys jogged away with clearly less spirit than before they'd all collided.

Walking off again, Nate felt unsettled—geez, the day had started so well!—and had a sudden urge to talk to Amy. Before he could overthink it, he pulled out his phone and punched in her number, hoping as it rang that he wasn't calling too early.

"Not at all," Amy assured him, a happy lilt in her voice. "I'm up by seven every day, no matter how late I go to sleep. Can't seem to get off my work clock."

"Yeah, I know what you mean. Though Cody's got his own clock—it's called his stomach—so when he's up, I'm up. When he lets me sleep past six, it's a good day." Nate was feeling better, lighter, just talking to Amy. It reminded him of calling Jim for their daily check-ins. There was something grounding about it, something comfortingly predictable.

Instead of reacting to that, Amy paused. Nate wondered if he should continue talking—but she jumped back in. "Look, I know it probably wasn't easy for you, but I really appreciate you coming over last night," she said. "It meant the world to me."

Now Nate was the one to pause, searching for an appropriate response, his heart leaping one way, his head another. As usual, he erred on the side of caution. "You're very welcome. We had a good time." A trio of joggers was hurtling Nate's way. He reflexively jumped off the path and onto the adjacent grass, taking Cody with him. They stood waiting for the runners to zip past.

"Jennifer seems like a really special woman," Amy said.

"She is."

"But you're not walking down the aisle just yet?"

With the joggers gone, Nate and Cody started off again, the dog's nose pressed to the ground. "I'm not ready to get married. But I also don't want to lose her," Nate told Amy, startled by his sudden candor. Had he even verbalized that yet to himself? He yanked Cody back from a suspicious mound he'd pulled away to sniff.

Amy let out a regretful sigh. "Take it from someone who knows," she said. "If you don't want to lose someone, don't ever let them go. No matter what." Nate didn't know if she was talking about Jim or him. Either way, it struck something deep in Nate.

He stopped in his tracks, startling Cody, who swung his big head around to see what was up. A thought crossed Nate's mind and bub-bled out before he could even think to censor it. "You've never seen the inside of *my* house, have you?"

"No, but I'd like to," came the inevitable response.

"How's … tomorrow?"

NATE SPENT MOST of the rest of his Saturday cleaning the house he realized not another living soul, save Danny and Mateo on painting days, had set foot in since Jim's post-funeral lunch. Now *that* was crazy, maybe in more ways than one.

Although he'd started many indoor renovation projects since moving in, most had yet to be finished, leaving much of the house topsy-turvy and, in places, hard to navigate. The only room that re-mained completely functional was the office, which Nate had taken all that extra care with early on—and it showed. At least the outside of the house was looking good.

By around dinner time—or at least Cody's dinner time, the one that counted—Nate had gotten things into reasonable order: floors swept and polished, rugs vacuumed, dust collected, and tools and random building materials stashed away. As for the holes in the walls, exposed wiring, missing molding, dislodged floorboards, and any other evidence of Nate's ongoing ambitions, he tidied them up as best he could, which is to say he probably should have held back asking Amy over for at least another month. Too late now.

Adding insult to injury, that night, Nate stopped in next door for birthday cake with Carter's mom and her family and friends (a still-contrite Max had invited Nate that afternoon) and saw, in comparison to his own chaotic living situation, what a well-tended home looked like: warm and ordered and attentively decorated. But also personal—so there was no question as to who lived there; two full and rich lives under one roof. Unlike, say, Amy's house, which, although neat and well-furnished, felt more generic, temporary: like the rental it was. It made Nate wonder what Amy's home in Fresno had looked like. What kind of home she even had.

Sure, Max and Carter were both a decade or so older than Nate and likely had more money than he did (not to mention they were both architects, so there was that). But looking around their house made Nate want to rush home and not stop working until every wall, floor, and ceiling, every nook and cranny, was perfect. He'd done pretty well, at least in his own estimation, building his landscaping business. He needed to put that same kind of drive, passion, and creativity into other corners of his life.

Gee, Nate thought with a grin, *all of that because of a little piece of birthday cake.*

He didn't have to worry about what Amy thought of his house—he could have been living in an empty tool shed for all she seemed to care. Still, once she arrived, Nate felt proud that he'd made the effort he did on her behalf. It was also the kick in the ass he needed to make a real plan to finish all the inside work, even if it meant bringing on some help to do so. He was proving nothing to anyone, least of all himself, by going it alone.

Amy listened attentively as he showed her around the house, describing in detail what he'd been trying to accomplish. He was also careful not to throw his dad under the bus, as if the much-needed renovations implied decades of sloth by its former tenant. Nate knew that Amy was likely visualizing the late father of her child in every room they entered, especially at the end of the tour when they landed in his old office.

Nate didn't mention how much he'd shored up the room, deciding to let Amy think the spot was museum-quality intact. Why he felt such a strong need to protect his father Nate couldn't say, but Amy was quite taken with its comfy, library vibe ("My God, look at all the books!") and general throwback feel. He was glad he'd kept the floral couch; it added an authentic touch. So much so that Nate plopped onto it for effect; Cody jumped up next to him and nestled in. They were a picture. It made Amy smile.

But not as much as when, perusing the bookshelves, she came upon a copy of *Wuthering Heights*. She pulled it out, thumbing through it, and practically beamed from ear to ear. "Oh, my God!"

exclaimed Amy. "We read this in your father's class. He said it was one of his all-time favorite books. It became one of mine, too."

"Not exactly the happiest ending, though, was it?"

She thought for a second and then said, a bit enigmatically, "Depends on how you look at it, I guess."

Nate wasn't sure she was talking about the book but let it go. He watched her gazing at its forgotten passages, catapulted back to the Moors. He never recalled his father singling out the book in any special way, though he did remember Jim helping him with a high school paper when it was his turn to read the overheated classic. Amy looked a thousand miles away.

"When we were alone, he'd read to me from it," she said. "Like it was poetry. Maybe it was corny but, at the time, I thought I'd died and gone to heaven." Amy stood there as if frozen by the memory, caught short by an ancient emotional tug. It was a moment so painfully intimate that Nate had to look away, had to try not to overthink the image of his dad beguiling a teenage girl with the haunting words of Emily Brontë.

A tear snaked down Amy's cheek as she closed the book. Nate stood, worried. "Maybe we shouldn't have done this."

Amy brushed away the tear, her shoulders sinking. "I know it sounds crazy," she said quietly, almost reverently, "but I never loved any man more than your father. Certainly not in the same way."

"How can you be so sure?" Nate asked, maybe more surprised than he should have been. "You were only, what—sixteen?"

Cody leaped off the couch. Amy, looking a tad woozy, took his spot. "I was married twice," she explained. "Once soon after college, then once when I was about your age. Both ended after a few years." She smoothed out her cotton shorts with her long, slender fingers. "Consciously or not, I married men who reminded me of your father—sexy, sensitive, intellectual. But neither of them really knew how to love. Not in the way I needed."

Nate didn't know how to respond to that. Or if he even should.

Amy's tone was hushed, cautious. "My first husband—Evan—and I had a daughter. Her name is Robin."

Nate was, to put it mildly, stunned. "You have a daughter? Why didn't you tell me?"

"I think it's safe to say there's still a lot we don't know about each other." She met his fraught gaze without accusation or apology. It just was.

Amy was right, of course. Didn't Nate have almost that exact thought at dinner Friday night? The reality: the more he opened the door to Amy, the more he let her in—the more she let *him* in—and a lifetime's worth of information would come crashing out. And that had to be okay. Still, Amy's last reveal had some pretty astonishing implications.

Amy slid to the end of the couch to make room for Nate. They both watched as Cody trotted off in search of a more interesting spot. "Does this mean I have a sister now, too?" Nate asked, sounding like a little boy on Christmas morning.

She nodded, a startled smile on her face, as if also just realizing that life-changing fact. "She just graduated from Fresno State. Got a degree in finance. She's working in mortgage banking up there." There was pride in Amy's voice but also vigilance as if she didn't want to overwhelm Nate any further. That didn't stop Nate's wheels from spinning.

"And you moved away from her?"

Amy shifted on the uneven cushion. "Well, I raised her for twenty-two years. Did a good job, too. Maybe too good. Robin's always relied on me a little too much." She paused, waiting for a reaction. When there was none, she continued. "Anyway, I had the chance to make up for lost time with another child, so I took it."

Nate studied Amy as he processed this. It was the first time he'd seen her this casually dressed, with only a bit of makeup, hair pulled back and up; laid barer, as it were. It felt comforting somehow. He tried to picture what his half-sister might look like; would they resemble each other in any way?

"She's subletting my condo," Amy said by way of further explanation. With a slightly anxious smile, she tacked on, "Might as well keep it in the family."

"She's lucky she had you," Nate finally said, breaking his silence. And, in case Amy had any doubt, added, "I mean that."

Another thought struck Nate: "Does Robin know about me?"

Amy's face turned bright, hopeful. "She does. And she wants to meet you."

Robin's looks were becoming clearer in Nate's mind, but he realized he was just conjuring up a younger Amy. "Do you have a photo?" he asked before he was at all ready to make this part real.

Amy pulled her phone from her shorts pocket and scrolled through her photos with purpose. When she found the one she wanted, she handed the phone to Nate with a proud maternal grin. He studied the snapshot of Robin, a casual pose taken at a restaurant table.

"We were having breakfast at a place in Fresno called the Patio Cafe," Amy explained. "We were sitting outside and the light was nice, so …"

"She's really pretty," Nate said, though frankly saw little of himself or even Amy in Robin, with her sandy blonde hair, fairer skin, and more angular features. He was slightly disappointed, though didn't know what he was expecting. He was now curious to see a picture of Robin's father (Ethan? Evan?) but doubted Amy kept her first ex-husband's face on her phone—and certainly didn't want to ask. It didn't matter, anyway. Nate had a sister, whatever she looked like, and that was huge. And something else to reconcile.

Nate was starting to feel … not claustrophobic exactly but like it wouldn't hurt to be outside for a bit. He asked Amy if she wanted to see the backyard and she looked as eager as he did for a change of scenery.

The diffused late afternoon sun showed off the replanted yard to fine effect. Nate hadn't spent much time out there since he'd finished working on it a few weeks back—yet another project he'd jammed in during his free time. Unlike the indoor renovations, once he got going on the backyard he found himself unable to stop until it was done. In truth, after the initial digging, weeding, and pruning were history, he was able to knock the rest out in a day. (Nate wouldn't let Danny help, even though he'd offered; his assistance on the front yard had already been above and beyond.)

Amy looked around at the artfully placed collection of perennials and succulents and flowering plants, at the decorative grasses and paths and cozy pockets, and smiled. "I'm not just saying this because you're my son: you really have a gift. You should be getting more recognition for your work."

"As long as my clients recognize what I do, I'm happy. The rest I just do for me and my sanity." He wasn't being coy; it was truly how he felt. Still, he appreciated the praise.

"I've been thinking about something else that might make you happy," said Amy as she inspected a violet amaryllis in rare full bloom. She turned to Nate with an expectant look and asked, "How would you like to take a drive with me up to Fresno? Meet your sister and your grandparents?"

"You mean the grandparents who thought having me would ruin your life?" He could see Amy wince. "I'm sorry," Nate said quickly, "I didn't mean that or … not that way, anyway." He really didn't.

Amy recovered, stood tall, and said, "It's okay. But we've started this journey and I think we need to continue it. One foot in front of the other—just like this."

They reflexively looked up as an enormous red-tailed hawk soared above them, bisecting the sky with such grace and confidence it was impossible to turn away. When the bird had vanished from sight, Nate picked up where they'd left off. "What are your parents like?"

"They're flawed," she answered, not skipping a beat. "How does that sound?"

"Generous."

They started back across the yard. "They're your family, Nate. You should meet them." She stopped to face him. "From where I stand, you're a little too alone in the world."

Nate would never admit it, not yet anyway, but she was right. He had retreated from others since Jim's death, maybe even before that, playing approach-avoidance with Jennifer and keeping Danny at a distance outside the workday (he'd turned down three dinner invitations from him and Alisha, and racked up as many rain checks). As for his other friends, the few he'd kept over the years hadn't called or texted in ages—maybe because Nate had stopped returning their messages. He didn't mean to, it just happened. Whatever the case, he had some room in his life to spare.

TWENTY-FOUR

Nate insisted that he do the driving up to Fresno, despite Amy's offer to take her car. It wasn't that he was being gracious or dutiful about it, even if it came across that way. He was being protective of himself. He was going to be a stranger in a strange land, so to speak, and his impulse was to add familiarity (some might say control, and they wouldn't be entirely wrong) to the unfamiliar, potentially unsettling situation. He loved his Silverado, it felt like home—okay, his second home—and he knew having it along would provide a kind of escape hatch.

Nate and Amy did go back and forth about it until, in the end, Nate suggested his way would be better for co-passenger Cody, who was used to the truck. Amy gave in, seemed appreciative, and said she would share driving duties, no ifs, ands, or buts.

Still, it wasn't as if Nate immediately agreed to the trip when Amy floated it that day in his backyard. It was a big ask and a bigger step, and she told him to take his time and think about it. Frankly, the idea scared the shit out of him—the phrase "Pandora's box" kept coming to mind—and he was unsure what would finally get him to decide whether to go. As the week went on, he realized he needed outside input, so he turned to Jennifer—again.

But unlike the last time he had reached out for an opinion, he and Jennifer had been in more frequent touch, either by text or phone, since the dinner at Amy's. So, when he asked if she wanted to get together for a drink and she mentioned she'd just picked up a tasty red blend from Pavillions, he found himself sitting on one of the loveseats in her cottage after work on a Thursday night. (He didn't have to rush home to feed Cody: the automatic pet feeder had arrived earlier that week and worked like a charm.)

She had greeted Nate with a kiss and seemed happier to see him than he expected. He didn't ask why, didn't want to ruin the moment. But he could feel the gradual shift in their dynamic back to something more relaxed and natural; no longer strangers but not quite lovers. They chatted about their work (he was almost finished at the Russos'; she had added a second modern dance class), the weather, and the new vegetable garden her landlords had planted (Swiss chard and Japanese eggplant) until halfway into their glasses of wine Nate told Jennifer about the proposed trip north—and his hesitation.

"Look, I get it," she said. "You don't know what you'll be walking into up there. But aren't you even the least bit curious to meet them?"

"Not really, no," he said unconvincingly, dipping a baby carrot into a bowl of hummus.

Jennifer stared wide-eyed over her wine glass. "My God, Nate, you have a sister and grandparents. Who knows who else?"

Nate sighed, chewing the carrot. "Okay, maybe I'm a little curious," he relented.

She sat up straighter. "Then you should go. If it gets too bizarre, you can always leave, right?"

"Yeah, I guess, but … I'm still adjusting to the idea that Amy's my mother. I don't know if I'm ready for a whole new family." As he said that he realized the broader implications, which of course the astute Jennifer picked up on.

"Having a family *can* be a big commitment," she said dryly as she took another sip of wine.

"I can handle commitment," Nate answered emphatically. Jennifer raised an eyebrow. "Well, I can," he persisted. "I'm just not sure I can handle any more secrets and surprises."

She softened. "If it were me, I'd rather know than not know," she said gently. "Whatever it is."

Nate thought about how wise and kind and beautiful she was and how he couldn't—wouldn't—fuck this up again. He put his wine glass on the coffee table and sat next to her. "Y'know what *I* know?" he asked.

"What?" she flashed a suspicious smile, yet didn't back away.

"This." Nate took the glass from her hand, set it down next to his, then kissed her—long and deep and blissfully.

When they finally pulled apart, breathless, Jennifer looked at Nate's earnest, satisfied expression and shook her head. "What am I going to do with you?"

"Kiss me again," Nate answered. And, as it seemed like the most reasonable option right then and there, she did. And then some.

The next morning, Nate texted Amy: "Will we need a hotel in Fresno?"

THEY DIDN'T NEED a hotel—Amy's parents had plenty of room for them as well as for Cody.

"Are they dog people?" Nate had to ask.

"Oh, yeah, they love dogs," she assured him.

"Let me rephrase that," he said. "Are they *big*-dog people?" After all, Cody didn't exactly blend into the woodwork.

"They'll love you *and* Cody. Trust me, they can't wait to meet you both."

Nate decided to do just that—to trust: Amy's confidence, Jennifer's judgment, and even his own growing belief that this was a good thing to do. And early the following Saturday he and Amy— with Cody in tow—were traveling north up the I-5 freeway in Nate's newly washed, vacuumed, and lemony-fresh Silverado to an exotic land known as Fresno.

But not before Nate came clean to Danny about Amy, who'd barely come up in conversation since they'd finished her job. That was Danny. He was totally in the moment—one hundred percent there—until the moment was gone, then it was on to the next. In a way, that seemed to Nate like a healthy way to live: no stewing about the past, no coulda-woulda-shouldas, just shoulders back, forward march. He could take a lesson from his ebullient partner. Though maybe that was another reason Nate had waited so long to tell Danny the truth: he knew that if enough time had passed—like after they'd moved on to their next gig—his pal's reaction would be less fever pitch and more modulated, more what Nate needed to hear. Guess again.

"Dude, are you fucking kidding me?" Danny nearly shouted as they unloaded Nate's truck on their last morning at the Russos'. "All that time and you don't tell your boy here a damn thing?" Danny stopped, realized, grimaced. "Shit, I woulda stopped busting your balls about nailing her. I must've sounded like the biggest freak!"

"Not the biggest, no," Nate said, trying to keep it light. "And, look, don't take it personally, alright? It was complicated. It *is* complicated."

Danny gazed at Nate, still in disbelief. "She's your *mom*?" Nate nodded, the concept still astounding to him as well. "I'll tell you one thing," Danny added, "I wish *my* mama looked that good." He tried to suppress a grin but it was beyond him.

"As long as she's really your 'mama,' that's all that matters," said Nate as he pulled a sack of citrus fertilizer out of the flatbed.

Throughout the rest of the workday, Danny eagerly peppered Nate with questions about Amy—more specifically Jim and Amy: He ate up the quasi-lurid details and even unearthed a memory about his own high school teacher crush, the curvy Mrs. Delgado. (Unlike Amy's, his teen dream had gone predictably—thankfully—nowhere.) Once he loosened up and let 'er rip, Nate found spilling the tea with Danny both liberating and heartening. It not only helped him to frame the jarring tale in his mind, start to finish, but to begin to feel inured to its thorny power over him.

Danny, for all his humor, was kind and supportive about Nate's plight and, like Jennifer, encouraged him to meet Amy's family and give the whole thing a chance. "Life's a crazy train, man," Danny concluded. "And sometimes you gotta just jump the fuck on." The guy was definitely his own kind of poet.

"So you've *never* been to Fresno?" asked Amy as she and Nate made their way past the Angeles National Forest, a vast recreation area known as much for its dumped corpses as its stunning mountains and lakes.

"Nope, never. Whatever family Dad had left there moved out of state years ago. And he wasn't the swinging-down-memory-lane type. Obviously." Nate swallowed some coffee from a thermal mug; thankfully, it was still hot.

"Maybe it was also his way of honoring our agreement," Amy considered, looking out at the passing thickets of oak and pine trees. "Running into each other could've hurt everyone."

"Or forced the issue," Nate said. "But you had your pact, so …" He thought it best to leave it there and apparently so did Amy, since she easily switched the subject to Nate's work ("Can you expand your business? Hire more crews? Oversee more, be less hands-on?"), which led to a discussion of her work and desire to become a paralegal manager, maybe for another, larger law firm. She said moving to L.A. had inspired her to do bigger things and felt it was time to grow her career before it was too late; she'd stayed on one rung, workwise, long enough.

Nate was impressed by her motivation and it made him wonder about his own. He hadn't much thought about expanding his landscaping company, was happy things were going as well as they were. Sure, he could make more money—who couldn't?—but at what cost to his own creative and emotional well-being? Still, it was food for thought and maybe he'd bat it around with Danny when he returned to L.A., see how he felt about coming up with a long-term strategy together, a real partnership: "Cronin/Soto Landscape Design." It made Nate smile; he knew Danny would want his name to go first. *Okay, one thing at a time*, Nate thought—*let's just get through Fresno.*

They stopped midway in Bakersfield for a bathroom break, landing at a Barnes & Noble Amy recommended just off the freeway. Nate let Cody do his thing on a grassy island in the parking lot, locked him back in the truck he'd parked under a shade tree, and then he and Amy entered the bookstore. It was a comfortable shop, more intimate than the chain's tri-level store at the Grove in L.A., yet still roomy enough for a well-stocked Starbucks coffee bar, a good-sized seating area with work tables, and a large counter selling the company's NOOK e-readers. (His purist dad used to call them NOPEs, the rare times he'd set foot in a Barnes & Noble.)

While Amy was standing in line for a latte, Nate perused a table of non-fiction paperbacks and, picking up an anthology of Joan Didion essays, realized it was his first time inside a bookstore since Jim died. A pang of grief shot through him like an arrow and it took Nate a moment to recover. He stood there wondering if he would ever get over his father's death or if the sadness would stay with him forever, attacking him randomly and without warning.

Nate didn't realize he was still holding the Didion collection when Amy returned from the coffee bar.

"Joan Didion," said Amy flatly as she eyed the book in his hands. "I know she's a good writer and all, but a little depressing, don't you think?"

Nate quietly put the book back in its place.

"Hey, are you okay?" she asked, catching the uneasy look on his face.

"Yeah, fine," he answered, feigning interest in the other books on the table.

"You don't look so fine." She took a sip of her latte and waited for a response. "What is it, honey?"

It was the first time Amy had addressed Nate with a term of endearment—like a real mother—and it was all he could do not to lose it again. "My dad was a big Didion fan, so … I don't know, it just hit me is all."

"Yeah, I spotted a few of her books on the shelves in his office—*your* office. Well, to each his own, right?" It was a sensitive moment and Amy tried to keep it light, which helped Nate brighten back up. She extended her coffee cup to him; he shook his head.

"Okay then, we should get back on the road," Amy said, starting for the exit. "My mother's a stickler for noon lunch. I predict deviled eggs, tuna salad, Pillsbury crescent rolls, and pink lemonade." She gave Nate a knowing wink as they crossed out to the parking lot, which had warmed up in the short time they'd been in the air-conditioned shop. Cody, head bobbing out the Silverado window, greeted them like they'd been gone for a year, instantly lifting Nate's spirits. He rubbed Cody's broad head as he and Amy got back in the truck.

Dozens of almond, citrus, and plum groves later (not to mention cotton and cornfields and a series of startlingly symmetrical vineyards), Fresno's downtown skyline loomed ahead of the cruising Silverado. Compared to the endless miles of farmland and stark turnoffs they'd passed since Bakersfield, it was like entering a metropolis.

"Don't get too excited," Amy warned after hearing Nate's observation. "Compared to L.A. it's not much." But from the expectant look on Amy's face as they exited Route 41 into the city, he could tell it was more than "not much" to her. He also knew a whole lot was riding on the next 24 hours—for them both.

TWENTY-FIVE

NATE WASN'T SURE exactly what he was expecting from his father and mother's hometown, but driving down the main drag of Shaw Avenue reminded him of a sprawling suburb—mini-malls, big-box stores, chain restaurants, gas stations, and office buildings. It seemed calm, pleasant, a good harbinger for the weekend.

"I worked so many different jobs in there during high school," Amy said, as they stopped at a light by an upscale-looking, open-air shopping center. A sign read: "Fig Garden Village." Nate was impressed by the colorful floral plantings that flanked the entrance.

"Doing what?" Nate asked, wondering if she meant before or after her pregnancy—or maybe even during part of it.

"Oh, the usual teen gigs: cashiering mostly, a little waitressing. Bagged at the supermarket one summer." And, as if she'd read his thoughts, Amy turned to him and said, "Not *that* summer, of course."

Nate, startled by her intuition, quietly nodded. He tried to say something, anything—a response seemed called for. But just then, the light turned green, a horn honked behind them, and Nate drove off, effectively concluding that part of the chat. Amy looked lost in her own memory.

Gazing out at the road, Nate pictured a teenage Amy, maybe the spring before "that summer," working a cash register at Fig Garden, her barely discernable baby bump cloaked by loose-fitting clothes. When he connected that "bump" to himself he felt yet another weird twinge course through him. Something told Nate he'd better get used to them.

Amy directed Nate to the older, more modest university district near Cal State Fresno and they were soon parked in front of her parents' house. It was an unremarkable, two-story, Cape Cod-style home with front and side dormers, boxy windows, and faded gray shingles. A droopy, ancient-looking Chinese elm tree lorded over a blotchy front lawn.

"I know what you're thinking," said Amy as they got out of the truck and faced the house, "that you could landscape the hell out of this place."

She had him there. "Well, I could suggest a *few* improvements," he said with a sly grin. It wasn't as untended as his father's house had once been, but it was pretty drab. Nate would start by giving the massive elm tree a serious haircut to help open up the yard. Cody darted for the old tree and heartily marked his territory.

"Don't waste your imagination," Amy told Nate as he gazed at the front yard. "Changing even a light bulb sends them into a tizzy."

"Got it," Nate said, glad to take off his landscaper hat for one weekend. "So this is where you grew up?" he asked as he went to grab their overnight bags from the truck. Cody followed him as if it was already time to go home.

"Yep. My parents have owned this place for forty-nine years. Moved in the day after their honeymoon—and never left." She noticed Nate's wary expression as he returned with their gear. "Everything alright?"

"Yeah, sure," he answered, standing stock still. Nate could tell Amy didn't look persuaded. "It's just … the second we walk through that door, I'll have grandparents. And a sister. It's kind of a mind-fuck." As soon as the word came out he was sorry, but Amy looked unfazed.

"Like I said: one foot in front of the other. And remember, it'll be 'kind of a mindfuck' for them, too," Amy said, taking her bag from Nate. He realized she was right: it would be weird for everyone. The thought somehow calmed him down.

Amy crossed to the spider-cracked cement front path. "Ready, Teddy?" she asked, forcing an upbeat smile.

"Let's do it," Nate said, relaxing his shoulders and facing the front door just as it opened, framing a wide-eyed, slightly stooped, gray-haired couple.

"There they are!" Amy enthused as her parents stepped out to greet them. Cody turned uncharacteristically shy, sitting on his haunches at Nate's side. Nate tensed again.

"Hi, Mom! Hi, Daddy!" Amy said, sounding more like an eager child than the measured adult Nate had come to know. He watched as she warmly hugged her parents, whose eyes were fixed, almost in wonder, on their grandson. Amy swung around. "This is Nate." Everyone stood there, unsure what to do, so Amy quickly added, "Nate, meet Gene and Diane Lucas."

As if someone hit the "play" button, Gene and Diane sprung to life. "Look at you!" his grandmother marveled. "You're even more handsome than your pictures!" Nate hadn't considered that Amy had sent them photos, even if that made total sense. She'd shown Nate a picture of them, but it was old and they'd aged dramatically since then.

Gene stepped up, extending a hand. "Hello, son, it's nice to meet you—after all this time," he said with practiced formality. Nate shook his hand, the older man's bony fingers belying a no-nonsense grip. He eyed his grandfather, took in his tall, slender frame (in marked contrast with Diane's shorter, stouter one), slightly protruding ears, Amy's same gray-green eyes, and thought maybe he looked like him—or maybe he didn't. Either way, Nate was encouraged by Gene's full head of straight, neatly cut hair, recalling that baldness was passed down from one's maternal grandfather (or was that a myth?). *Jesus*, he thought, *is that what I'm thinking about? Now?*

Gene looked down at Cody, who was still seated as if awaiting an introduction. "And what's this beauty's name?" he asked, his tone lightening.

"This is Cody. He's very friendly," Nate answered, and watched as Gene bent down to pet his new granddog.

Diane, who Nate had instantly assessed to be the more bashful of Amy's parents, opened her arms. "Come here and hug your old grandma," she said, a tremolo in her kindly voice. He gently embraced her—she held him close; her face and neck were warm, moist—but it felt like too much too soon. He could sense his limbs stiffen—and hers quaver. "Can you feel me?" she asked on cue. "I'm shaking like a leaf."

Nate let go, then awkwardly held onto one arm to calm her. But she burst into tears. Amy went to her mother. "Mom, what is it? What's wrong?"

Diane, clearly mortified by her reaction—as was Gene, if his stricken look was any indication—gazed at Nate, her wide, lined face a map of sorrow. "What have we done? We're terrible people. Look at this beautiful boy we never knew."

It occurred to Nate that they were still standing outside; he was desperate to take this into the house. But no one moved until Gene stepped in, calmly put his arms around his wife, and said, "Now, now, Diane, it's okay. It'll be alright."

Amy sent Nate a beseeching look. Before it could get any weirder, Diane settled down and her tears subsided. She shook back her hair, smoothed her blouse, and took a cleansing breath. "Okay, folks, show's over," she said with a wan smile.

"Let's go on inside," said Gene, crossing to the front door. "Robin's waiting for us." The term "one-two punch" popped into Nate's head as he and Cody followed Amy and his grandparents into the house.

GENE AND DIANE'S home looked more pulled together on the inside than out. Though the furnishings appeared old, and the paint, wallpaper, and paneling unintentionally retro, the rooms were clean and orderly, with a lifetime's worth of framed photos and knick-knacks neatly hung or displayed. A whole world Nate had known nothing about.

Robin came rushing out of the living room to greet Nate and Amy as soon as they'd stepped foot in the house. She was more petite than Amy, but just as attractive in her own way—maybe more so than she'd looked in her picture. Her wide-set eyes were similar to Nate's (which were similar to Amy's) but otherwise, he didn't see much of himself in her. She hugged Amy tightly while sending a warm glance Nate's way, one that said *I'll get to you next.*

"How are you, darling?" Amy asked Robin, pulling back to study her. As far as Nate knew it was the first time she'd seen her daughter in person since moving away.

"I'm good, Mom," she answered, then took in Diane's unsettled expression. "Is … everything alright?"

Diane pushed out a little smile. "Oh, don't mind me, Robin June, I was just having a good cry." She indicated Nate and said, "Say hello to your brother." Nate assumed June was Robin's middle name (he was right) and wondered if they knew *his* middle name. (It was Charles, after Jim's father, who died when Jim was six.)

Robin took a deep breath and charged up to Nate. "I'm Robin. So nice to meet you!" She extended a hand, then, as if feeling silly about such a formal gesture, quickly went in for a hug. "How was your ride? Was there traffic?" she asked into his chest. Nate hoped she couldn't hear his heart hammering. She reached out for the bag he'd forgotten he was still holding. "Can I take your bag?" Robin asked and then, before he could answer, she machine-gunned out: "How long are you here for? This must be so wild for you. You're actually very brave!" She checked herself, and, with a nervous grin, said, "Okay, why don't I shut up now?"

Nate was so overwhelmed by her greeting that all he could think to say was "Nice to meet you, too, Robin!" He hadn't realized they'd all already migrated into the living room. Nate had never given Robin his bag—had no idea where to put it or where in the house he'd be staying. It begged other questions: Would he be sharing a room with Amy? What were they going to do now that they were actually there? And how far away was Amy's—now Robin's—condo? He had to get better at asking questions.

Nate looked around and saw that while he was contemplating the universe, everyone had taken a seat, even Cody, who had curled up on a woven throw rug in front of a walnut-mantled fireplace and made himself at home. They all sat quietly, stiffly still, maybe waiting for the other to speak; they reminded Nate of chess pieces, each bound to their own square. He parked himself in the one empty seat, a creaky armchair covered in nubby beige fabric, placing his bag on the floor beside him.

Like a game of whack-a-mole, the second Nate's butt hit the chair, Diane popped up from the couch and anxiously pressed her hands together. "Where are my manners? Nate, can I make you a nice cup of tea? Or maybe you drink coffee?" She looked desperate for something to get her out of there.

"Unless you could use something a little stronger," Gene offered from his perch in a plaid reclining chair, which he was decidedly not reclining in.

Diane made a tsk-tsk sound and said, "Gene, it's only eleven thirty! And lunch is in thirty minutes!"

But Gene was undaunted. "Know what? I think I'll have a beer. Care for a cold one, Nate?"

Nate was so grateful you'd think the cavalry had just burst in. "Sure, why not?"

Without skipping a beat, both Amy and Robin's hands shot up and, in unison, they chirped, "Me, too!" and giggled.

Diane stood there like a cross schoolmarm waiting for her class to behave. Realizing she was outnumbered, she sighed and started for the kitchen. "Four beers, coming up," she said as she made a noisy exit. Cody leaped off the rug to follow her, sensing she was the key to all things edible around there.

When Diane was gone, the living room crowd burst into an ice-breaking chuckle. "I can hear you!" shouted Diane from points beyond, which only made the group laugh again.

Those pre-noon Budweisers, déclassé as they may have seemed, clearly helped ease everyone—except maybe Diane—into lunch mode, and the group seemed a bit more relaxed by the time they were settled around the dining room table. Nate and Amy sat on one side, Robin across from them, and Gene and Diane at opposite heads. Nate wondered if he should have let Robin sit next to her mother but dismissed the thought; there'd been too much walking on eggshells as it was—and he'd barely been there an hour. Meantime, Cody was sprawled under the table, in prime position for wayward crumbs.

"I made your favorite, Amy Beth"—okay, now Nate knew his mother's middle name—"deviled eggs and my famous tuna salad and I got that pink lemonade you used to like."

"When I was ten, Mom," Amy said lightly, sending Nate a conspiratorial kick under the table: *Did I tell you or what?* The gesture made Nate feel like part of a special club.

Diane looked surprisingly unruffled. "Well, you'll always be ten to me, sweetie," she said as she passed the plate of deviled eggs to Robin to begin its trip around the table.

Nate looked at the mounded platter of tuna in front of Gene as he scooped some onto his plate. He wondered what made it "famous" and asked as much.

"Taste it and you'll find out!" Gene said with a wink, handing the platter to Nate. His grandfather was proving warmer than Nate imagined, even if the guy still looked a bit like a deer in the headlights.

It turned out that chopped green olives were Diane's "secret" ingredient and, when Nate noted that, she turned on herself in a way that he didn't see coming.

"Yeah, I'm really gonna give that Rachael Ray a run for her money, aren't I?" she asked, her lips pursed, eyes darkening.

"Well, it's very good," Nate said, though the tuna was kind of dry and there were too many olives for his liking.

"Absolutely, Grandma! *So* good!" Robin piped in with the kind of overenthusiasm that implied it wasn't her first time boosting Diane's ego.

But seconds later, when Gene asked where the crescent rolls were, Diane realized she'd left them baking in the oven and flew out of the room. She returned from the kitchen holding a basket of blackened bread, hanging her head in shame.

"Sometimes my cooking's a damn disgrace," she said, plopping the rolls on the table, eyes brimming with tears.

"The good news is, it keeps me thin!" Gene kidded, though no one laughed, least of all his wife.

"Fine, embarrass me in front of our grandson," Diane snapped, snorting back tears. She sat back in her chair and gazed at her empty plate. Gene stared at his hands; Amy and Robin traded uh-oh looks.

"Mom, please, just calm down. Dad was only joking. You're a fine cook," Amy said, though there was an unmistakable edge to her voice. She put down her fork, took a breath.

"Actually, Diane—" Nate began.

She looked up from her plate. "Grandma," she emphatically reminded him.

Nate couldn't quite wrap his tongue around that just yet. "Okay, well … I hear you make a great lasagna."

"Truth be told, that one's been passed down from my side of the family," said Gene unhelpfully. Diane bolted up from the table and disappeared back into the kitchen. With a helpless glance at the others, Robin went after her, leaving Gene, Nate, and an embarrassed Amy to contemplate their tuna and eggs.

"Poor thing," Gene finally said, "I think this has all been a little overwhelming for her."

"Well, think about what Nate's gone through!" Amy lashed back.

"Really, Mom, it's okay—" Nate stopped cold, shocked that, without thinking, he'd called Amy "Mom" for the first time. It was doubly startling since, just seconds before, the word "grandma" had been so entirely out of reach. The moment was not lost on Amy, who was wearing a faint smile, nor, it seemed, Gene, who clucked his tongue, then started picking at his tuna salad.

They were all silent for a moment until Gene looked up from his plate and turned to Nate. "Son, I can't explain or justify what happened thirty years ago, so I won't," he said with a catch in his voice.

"I just want you to know I—that is, your grandma and I—are just so happy to know you. You're a fine young man. I wish we could say we had something to do with it, but ..." He faded out, like a radio being turned off, but he kept his gaze fixed on Nate.

Amy's mouth had formed an O as she studied her dad with both pride and regret.

Gene slapped his thigh, stood, and announced, "Well, I'd better go make sure she's alright." He gestured in the direction of the kitchen, then looked at Amy and said, "Thank God you don't have your mother's constitution."

As Gene walked off, it occurred to Nate that he'd been thinking exactly that: how when it came to Amy, vis-à-vis Diane, the apple had fallen far from the tree—and practically rolled into another orchard. Was Amy more like her father? Nate couldn't tell; it didn't seem that way. But he really didn't know any of them well enough to judge. What he did know—or had observed anyway—was that Amy seemed far more stylish and sophisticated than either of her parents. He couldn't yet tell how alike Amy and Robin were; Robin came off shyer and more compliant than her mother, despite her occasional bursts. They loved each other a lot, that was more than evident, and certainly a good sign.

When her dad was out of earshot, Amy turned to Nate and gave a helpless shrug. "Like I said—flawed."

Nate, who was suddenly starving, popped a deviled egg in his mouth—it beat the tuna. As he chewed, he thought, *we're all flawed, every last one of us. Doesn't that just make us human?*

TWENTY-SIX

NATE HAD SPOKEN to Jennifer every day since they'd unofficially resumed their relationship a few weeks earlier—"unofficially" because they'd said nothing about what sleeping together again meant nor what their future as a couple might look like. Even though the lines of communication had happily reopened between them in natural and more satisfying ways, they were still both circumspect enough not to rock the proverbial boat. Jennifer seemed to have regained her trust in Nate and the confidence that he wouldn't disappoint her again. Or maybe she'd just recalibrated her expectations. For Nate's part, he found himself acting with a greater need to attach and, hopefully, commit; to meeting Jennifer more on her own quite reasonable terms and not let fear guide his choices. It felt like a second honeymoon, but Nate knew he had to do his part to keep their momentum going—and growing.

After the Lucas lunch debacle, Nate caught Jennifer between classes for a quick FaceTime call and got her up to speed on the Fresno experience. He had booked out to his truck, still parked at the curb, and speedily related the highlights of the trip up, the jittery introductions, and what went down around the dining room table.

Jennifer told him to hang in there and to remember how difficult it had to be for his grandparents. "After all," she reasoned, "they've been living with this secret a lot longer than you have." He then told her how Diane had pulled herself together, apologized profusely to Nate for her tuna meltdown (her expression, which made everyone laugh), and how, before she could explain herself any further, Nate locked her in a bear hug and called her Grandma, as he should have when he first had the chance.

"I'm proud of you for doing this, you know that?" Jennifer said as her next group of students assembled in the studio behind her. Nate appreciated that and told her so, to which she responded, with a raised eyebrow and a playful purr in her voice, "Keep up the good work and there'll be a reward for you when you get home."

What could he say to an offer like that but: "I'm counting the minutes."

Nate sat in his truck awhile longer, gazing out at the shady street, enjoying the quiet, thinking about Jennifer, and then his father: What would Jim say if he knew that Nate was bonding—okay, trying to bond—with the people he'd spent almost half his life keeping his son away from? Yet Nate didn't feel he was being disloyal to his late father; Jim had handled this badly, irresponsibly, so unlike the man he'd seemingly been. It was never too late to right those wrongs, though, if the last few hours were any sign. Still, it surprised Nate that he was leaning into those difficulties and not trying to escape them.

He looked out at his grandparents' scrubby front lawn and scanty plantings and that overwhelming elm and couldn't help but conjure up an instant redo—so much for "taking the weekend off." As usual, mental landscaping calmed and empowered him; he was ready to jump back into the family fray.

Robin left to spend a few hours in her office; she apparently used weekend afternoons to catch up on the past week's work. "But I'll be back in time for dinner," she assured Nate, giving him a quick side hug as she made her exit. Nate wondered what kind of drama would unfold around *that* meal; if a few charred rolls could trigger Diane, what would serious food do? ("Sorry about the roast! It tastes like an old shoe! I'm such a damn klutz!") Gene must have been thinking ahead, because, as it turned out, he'd made reservations for dinner at a nearby Italian restaurant. Amy looked so relieved you'd think her execution had just been commuted.

The afternoon went thankfully without incident. Diane slapped on a happy face (Nate found her oddly endearing and sometimes funny if you dug self-deprecating humor), which also kept Gene and Amy upbeat. They avoided any even potentially controversial or inflammatory topics and killed an entire hour playing an old French card game called Milles Bornes (the Parker Brothers box had a 1960s copyright) that turned pretty raucous once Nate got the hang of it. Cody slept through it all.

Over coffee and Pepperidge Farm Milanos, Diane showed Nate photo albums from cruises that she and Gene took over the last few years: one to Alaska, the other to Mexico (next winter they were cruising from Florida to the Bahamas). In the pictures, Diane wore a variety of colorful sunhats, Gene had on funny-slogan T-shirts, and both looked frankly adorable. Nate wouldn't have pegged them as travelers, though he admittedly knew little about them beyond the events of thirty years ago. Had they changed much since that complex time—or were they essentially the same, just older and, one would hope, a bit wiser?

What else did Nate learn sitting in their living room? Gene had been a salesman—cars, insurance, medical supplies, office furniture—segueing from job to job until he happily retired the second he turned sixty-five and never looked back. Diane worked on and off over the years, mostly waitressing and odd retail gigs, until landing a full-time job at the phone company, which she left at age sixty-two with a decent pension and a collection of friends she still kept in touch with. She made it clear they lived on a fixed income, using those exact words, though Nate wasn't sure if she was getting at anything in particular.

The topic of careers finally led to questions for Nate, who'd been mostly just nodding and listening since they'd finished playing cards.

"So I hear you're quite the gardener," said Gene, reaching for a fourth cookie until Diane shot him a "Don't you dare" look and he shrunk back.

"Landscape designer, Dad," Amy corrected him. He shrugged at the distinction.

Nate cleared his throat, sat up straighter. "Yeah, things are going well. I have a pretty solid business." He didn't know why, but he sounded more apologetic than proud.

Diane leaned forward in her chair. "Maybe you could take a look at my camellias before you leave. They've been looking kind of depressed lately." Now *she* was the one who sounded apologetic. Nate assumed her sad camellias were somewhere in the backyard, which he'd only seen so far through their kitchen window.

"Sure, I'd be happy to. Or anything else around the garden. Just say the word."

"Nate did the most incredible job landscaping my house in L.A.," Amy gushed. "It looks like something out of a magazine."

While Amy kept an eager smile on her face, there was a distinct energy shift in her parents. They turned silent, their bodies visibly retracting into their seats. They practiced synchronized staring into their coffee cups. Maybe it had something to do with the mention of L.A. and what they saw as their daughter's defection from her hometown—and her family there.

Whatever the case, it caused Diane to force a polite little smile and announce that she was going to take a nap before it was time to leave for dinner. Gene decided to join her and off they went toward their bedroom. Nate shot Amy a curious look.

"Don't take it personally," Amy said, swallowing the last of her coffee. "They nap every afternoon around now."

"No worries. I don't mind a little break," Nate admitted. He went outside to check out Diane's camellias, which were as dreary as advertised. He found a pair of hand clippers in his truck (who doesn't travel with those?) and pruned the droopy bushes to half their original size. In a few weeks, they'd show all new signs of life.

DiCicco's was a friendly and relaxed trattoria filled mostly with young families. It stood a few doors down from the Piccadilly Inn where, as Diane pointed out, she'd had her retirement party on the hotel's large front patio some fifteen years before. "I felt like a queen," she recalled wistfully as Gene drove his sturdy, decade-old Hyundai Sonata past it and into the restaurant parking lot.

Robin was waiting for them by her car; she had driven straight from her office and, though in the same clothes as earlier, looked fresh and shiny. She hugged everyone elatedly as if she hadn't just seen them all a few short hours ago. Nate was slowly adjusting to the idea of having a sibling.

They shared two bottles of cabernet (Diane, not to mention everyone else, was way more fun as a result), a large cheese pizza, two orders of meatballs and spaghetti, and a giant chopped Italian salad. They seemed like any other cross-generational family out for a casual Saturday night dinner—and not one whose odd man out only recently discovered he shared genes with four total strangers.

Nate found himself opening up more than he might have predicted. He told his sister and grandparents all about Jennifer: their brief split, the current upswing in their relationship, her past as a member of a touring ballet company, and her present as a sought-after dance instructor. He explained how he'd rescued Cody at nine months, trained the pup himself, and now couldn't imagine living without a dog. (Nate hoped Cody was doing okay fenced off in the Lucas' kitchen; he hadn't looked too thrilled when they left.)

He talked more about being a landscaper, spoke at length about Danny, and gave Diane a few well-received tips to keep her camellias happy. All before his second glass of wine. The others listened attentively, asked pertinent questions, and seemed to be storing away their newfound knowledge about Nate in the same way he'd been doing with them.

Nate purposely didn't bring up his father and hoped no one else would either; he somehow knew no good would come of it. But by the time dessert rolled around—Nate and Gene split a tiramisu; the women begged off—the conversation hit a lull and Robin, with a solemn look, said, "By the way, Nate, I was sorry to hear about your father."

If Nate's hunched shoulders gave off any signal to please end all discussion of his beloved dad at once, it went straight over Robin's well-meaning head.

"Mom told me what an exceptional teacher he was," Robin pressed on. But when that was also met with a chorus of crickets, she turned to Amy and asked, "Should I not have said anything? I mean … oh, this is weird." Robin needed a lifeline, so Nate sent her one.

"No, really—thanks, Robin," he said. "I appreciate it." And he did, maybe just not that very second. Amy, usually more forthright, drained her water glass instead.

Gene put down his dessert fork and sighed. "World's a strange place, isn't it?" The question may have sounded rhetorical, but it was directed to Nate, who thought it best to nod in agreement. "Had your father lived," Gene continued, "Diane and I would have gone to our graves without ever meeting you." He followed a profound pause with: "Isn't that something?"

"Dad, can we not discuss this now?" Amy asked him with as much kindness as the sentence would allow.

"Why not?" he asked with genuine confusion. "Nate's here and we're all being open with each other. Wasn't that the point of this whole thing?" Nate took "this whole thing" to mean this deeply stressful, highly orchestrated weekend visit whose upside was currently dangling by a thread. His piece spoken, Gene stabbed at his cake and took a final bite, as the others drew mental straws to see who would respond.

It fell to a somber-looking Diane, who addressed Nate instead of her husband. "Sweetheart, you can blame us for what we've done, but please don't blame us for having feelings," she said, twisting the end of her paper napkin. "We were just trying to protect our only child."

"Nate's not blaming anyone, Mom," Amy asserted, maybe a bit too hastily.

"For God's sake, Mom," Robin shot back, "let Nate talk for himself! Is this how you're making up for lost time?" Robin looked immediately mortified by her snappish remark. "Oh, Mom, I'm so—"

But Amy put up a hand, stopping her mid-sentence. "You're right," she said firmly, then swiveled toward Nate. "I'm sorry. I didn't mean to speak for you. Is there anything you'd like to say?"

There wasn't, not really. Yet everyone stared at him as if awaiting the words of a storied sage. He disappointed all but himself with an impromptu sidestep. "You know what this moment calls for?" he announced. "A family picture!" And before anyone could protest, he whipped out his phone and nabbed a passing waiter to take their photo, forcing the group to smoosh together and smile like a bunch of happy clams.

The picture came out so well, Nate texted them each a copy, then fought Gene for the bill—and won. Nothing like a few small victories.

TWENTY-SEVEN

IT HAD BEEN a long, event-filled day, to say the least, and Nate was glad it was over—and he didn't think he was alone. He was staying in the guest room, which was part catch-all space/part sewing center for Diane, with a surprisingly comfortable leatherette pull-out couch. Meanwhile, his mother was across the hall in her old bedroom, which, according to Amy, had been more or less preserved in amber since she moved out after college. All that had changed was her late-1980s-era "artwork"—apparently the Bon Jovi and Nirvana posters had to go—but the frilly twin bed, white lacquer furniture, shaggy area rugs, and pink patchwork curtains remained in all their retro glory.

Nate was in a T-shirt and boxers, getting ready for bed—or actually getting Cody's bed ready—when Amy knocked on the open door. Nate waved her in as he placed a folded-over comforter atop two king-sized down pillows. Amy watched with a smile as the dog blissfully burrowed in.

"Now it's my turn," Nate said, matching Amy's smile, as he went to tuck the sheets into the opened sofa bed.

"Sorry it's a little … busy in here," she said, gesturing around the cluttered room. "My mom's always been a bit of a packrat." She pointed to a spooky, torso-only mannequin perched by an older-model sewing machine. "I mean, that thing? Really? I swear it's been there since I was in, like, first grade."

"It's alright, you don't have to make excuses for your mom—or your dad. Or Robin, for that matter. Everyone's got their shit. We all do." Nate plumped a pair of pillows and stacked them on the left side of the foam mattress. Amy, looking pensive, removed a pile of fabric from Diane's sewing chair and took a seat.

"I told Robin about you when she was in high school," she began. "I'm not sure why, maybe as a cautionary tale for her—or a catharsis for me. But one day, I just wanted her to know." Nate sat on the edge of the mattress across from Amy as she added, "She's a good person, Nate. She's doing the best she can with this."

He stared at a framed needlepoint hanging on the opposite wall. It was of a striped cat playing with an unraveling ball of yarn. Nate assumed Diane sewed it, probably years ago based on its slightly faded colors. "What's fucked up in a way," he said, refocusing on Amy, "is that one of your children knew this big secret for years, while your other child had no idea."

"You know it's not that simple."

"I know. And I'm sorry about that. But there's something else." Nate knew he owed Amy the truth. He swallowed and, voice laden with sadness, said, "It's hard for me to think how much your parents must have hated my father. Because no matter what—I really loved him."

"Oh, Nate …" Amy rose from the chair and sat on the mattress next to her son. She gently put an arm around his shoulder and he tentatively leaned into her.

They stayed like that for several moments until Amy pulled back. "They didn't hate him. They didn't even know him. All they knew was that some strange man got their teenage daughter pregnant. *That's* what they hated. More than that, they hated having to lie— and they hated keeping secrets." She stopped, looking lost in the reverie. "If they hated anyone back then, it was probably me."

"I doubt that. You were still their only child." Nate needed to get up, to move around: his head and legs suddenly ached.

"Whatever, we can't change the past, we can only accept it." She rose to face Nate. "I *need* you to accept it."

Nate met her tender gaze. He'd do what he had to do. He'd find a way. Amy hugged him. "Sleep well, honey," she said as she went for the door.

"You, too … Mom." There was that word again. It just came out. Amy smiled at the sound of it, at the validation, and maybe at the luck that this strange, wish-fulfilling experiment might work out.

THE NEXT MORNING, Amy wanted to show Nate more of Fresno. So after a thankfully calm breakfast of bacon and scrambled eggs, with a crescent roll redux—they were perfectly baked this time (cue Diane's relieved smile)—Nate wrangled Cody and they took off in the Silverado for a guided tour.

It was barely nine o'clock, but it was already hotter than the day before, with the San Joaquin Valley humidity turning the air soupy. Nate cranked up the air conditioning as Amy directed him out of her parents' neighborhood and back onto Shaw Avenue, which he now knew as one of several thoroughfares that linked the city from end to end. After driving by Amy's neat but nondescript condo complex (not that far from her parents' house after all), they hung a left on Palm and drove into Fig Garden, the shopping area they'd passed on the way into town. As they circled the well-maintained loop of shops and restaurants, Amy pointed out every place she'd worked, though most of the businesses—save a jauntily named bar and grill called the Elbow Room—had become something else entirely. A popular movie theater was demolished a few decades earlier; not surprisingly, the specialty market where Amy had once packed groceries was replaced by a Whole Foods.

As Amy narrated her retail experience, Nate wondered if his father ever shopped or ate at this civilized mall. Did he go there with family? Friends? Dates? With Eileen? Did he ever cross paths with Amy—randomly or purposefully—in any of the places she'd worked?

Feeling a sudden need to leave, Nate leaned on the gas pedal, and they were back on Shaw before Amy seemed to realize they'd even exited. If she did notice, she conceded to her driver's pace—if not his emotions—and then, with a mix of excitement and dread, asked if Nate wanted to see her old high school (read: her and Jim's old high school). There was a moth-to-the-flame thing going on: Nate was surely a reluctant moth; the past was the flame. Yet wasn't this whole trip *supposed* to be a kind of exorcism?

In short order, they were parked in front of Fresno High, a majestic, brick and plaster structure that, according to Amy, still looked largely the same as when she was a student. She gazed out the Silverado window at the imposing edifice, clearly lost in a mind's eyeful of memories. Nate could only imagine the thoughts flickering through her head; he knew what *he* was thinking and he'd never even set foot in the place.

This being Sunday, the school was closed, so Amy walked Nate around the perimeter, Cody dutifully following alongside. She told him stories of football games and band practice (she played the flute *and* the French horn) and school plays and sneaking a smoke with her girlfriends ("Just to fit in—which I didn't") until they found themselves at a back entrance as a weathered, late-60ish guy wheeled a garbage pail out of the building.

"You folks lost?" he asked in a raspy, seen-it-all voice.

Amy eyed him, agape. "Eddie?"

"That's my name, don't wear it out." He peered back at Amy, trying to place her. "Wait, do I know you?"

It turned out that Eddie was the school's longtime janitor; he was around even before Amy's time there. He certainly must have known Nate's dad but Amy thankfully didn't bring him up. She simply told him that she and her son were visiting from L.A. and, well, she knew it must be against the rules, especially these days, but could they *ple-e-eze* take a peek inside—for old time's sake? Given that Nate and Amy hardly looked like Bonnie and Clyde, Eddie not only told them they could enter ("Just make it quick, okay?") but that he would watch Cody, because a dog *really* wasn't allowed inside.

Once they were through the doors, it looked and felt like pretty much any other well-kept high school, evoking for Nate his days at Eagle Rock High, a largely happy time of life that, like most adults, he probably appreciated more in retrospect. He found himself smiling at the familiar banners, posters, and trophy cases that filled the vaulted entryway; a vibrant, hand-painted mural promoting inclusivity was sprawled along one entire wall. "Wow, all of a sudden I feel like it's my first day of school again," Nate told Amy, who, from her faraway look, had been catapulted back more than three decades.

"So why do *I* have butterflies?" she turned and asked him with a smile.

Nate stopped, took her arm. "We don't have to do this, y'know."

Amy considered his protective words and decided, "No, I think we do."

They meandered along the echoey hallways, past rows of lockers and bulletin boards and classroom doors until Amy slowed in front of one. She gazed through the window, then took Nate by surprise when she told him that it was his father's classroom. *Her* classroom.

"Room 115," she confirmed. "Third period English."

Nate peered in the window as if Jim might still be in there. He felt weirdly frozen in place, wondering how many times his dad had turned that doorknob and entered room 115. With an expectant look, Amy opened the unlocked door, took a step inside, and waved Nate in. She turned on the overhead lights, illuminating a neat and shiny classroom. The walls looked older but the desks seemed newish, as did the signs of technology that certainly didn't exist when Amy sat in third period English. Algebra problems covered the erasable whiteboard where a dusty blackboard surely once hung.

"Someone's teaching math in the English room," Amy joked, turning from the whiteboard. "Think we should tell them?"

But Nate was silent, pensive as he stood at the head of the classroom, maybe in the exact spot where Jim had addressed his students. He gazed out at the empty, melamine-topped desks and envisioned what his father saw as he talked about, what—*Wuthering Heights, Invisible Man, The Catcher in the Rye*? Nate watched as Amy drifted toward the back of the room and took a seat in the second-to-last row of desks. His eye caught a bright purple poster that read "Never argue with a ninety-degree angle—it's always right." Math humor.

"My old seat," she called to Nate as she ran a hand over the desk's smooth finish.

"How do you remember that?" he asked, crossing toward her.

Amy smiled. "I remember everything about this room. Where I sat, who sat around me ..." She pointed to each neighboring desk as she ticked off names like it was yesterday: "Martina Flores, Brad Hartounian, Tanya Spector, Joey Lee, Lisa DiNapoli." She paused. "The posters on the wall, what the clock looked like." She gestured toward a contemporary clock hanging above the whiteboard. "Not like that."

"And the smell," she continued, "like chalk and old paint ... until your father would walk in and fill the room with his spicy aftershave." She called up the brand: "Polo. Do they still even make that?"

"They must, Dad wore it every day of his life—whether he shaved or not." Nate sat on a desktop (Tanya Spector's?) next to Amy, who was staring vacantly at the busy whiteboard. He pictured what she must be dredging up about her time in that classroom; how her life had changed in such irrevocable ways as a result. If she were being honest—really honest—would she do it all over again if she had the chance? Perhaps more importantly: would Jim have stopped the affair before it even started? And, Nate thought darkly, where would those decisions have left *him*? Talk about a mindfuck.

Then, without moving, her head stone-still, tears began to stream from Amy's eyes. She tried to blink them away, but it was no use. They needed to escape—and she needed to rid herself of whatever their cause. Maybe that was happening right then and there in Room 115 or maybe it would happen months from that sticky Fresno morning. But something told Nate he was witnessing the start of the next phase of their journey.

Amy snapped to, wiped her wet cheeks with her opened hands, and looked rattled.

"Are you okay?" Nate asked as he hopped off the desk.

"I don't know what came over me." She sniffled loudly as she swallowed what was left of her tears.

"The Ghost of Eleventh Grade Past," Nate said lightly.

Amy settled herself and took a deep breath. "And here I was worried about *you*. How *you'd* react being here. How embarrassing."

"Trust me, another five minutes and I would've lost it too." Whether that was true or not, Nate was glad that it seemed to make Amy feel better. Misery loves company and all.

"Let's get the hell out of here, okay, kiddo?" But she was already halfway out the door.

They collected Cody from Eddie, who'd taken the amenable pooch for a walk around the football field. (From the janitor's smoky scent, he'd also snuck in a cigarette or two.) "Superb animal you got there, pal," he told Nate, who couldn't disagree. They said their goodbyes and mother, son, and dog piled back into the Silverado and left Fresno High behind.

Amy wouldn't tell Nate where they were going as she directed him south on Echo Avenue then east onto Olive, but he had a feeling there was another gut punch in store. That was okay, he felt he could handle it (besides: morbid curiosity), but could she? So he asked.

"I'm fine, really," she answered, lighter now. "If I didn't think this was good for us—healing for us—I would've taken you to the zoo and called it a morning." She flashed a warm smile. "Trust me?"

"I'm here, aren't I?" That came out less jaunty than planned, but Amy looked undeterred.

"I'll take that as a yes," she said. "And a sign of progress."

They soon reached an eclectic cluster of shops, eateries, and clubs. They passed a few tattoo parlors and weed dispensaries and a dive bar called, of all things, Goldstein's Mortuary & Delicatessen. There was something both welcoming and funky about the stretch, its sidewalks filled with a younger and more diverse clientele than at the tonier Fig Garden.

"Welcome to the Arts District," Amy said in her best tour guide voice. "It used to be cool. I don't know, maybe it still is." She looked out at the laid-back street trying to decide.

But when they drove past the striking Tower Theatre, with its wraparound, art-deco, neon-etched marquee, Nate immediately recognized it as the spot where Jim and Eileen had taken that old photo—and somehow knew just where Amy was leading him.

A few blocks away, they pulled up to a small, squarish, one-story home with Craftsman-style aspirations. The yard was tidy but spare, save a collection of kids' toys strewn by the front door. Nate stared out the truck window at the house.

"Don't tell me, this is where my Dad and Eileen lived."

Amy eyed him, impressed. "Wow, very good. How did you know?"

Nate shrugged. "I may have seen pictures."

"Well, it may not look like much now, but it was a cute little place back then. Especially on a teacher's salary." She reached for the door handle, then looked at Nate. "Shall we?"

They leaned against the Silverado studying the house as Cody sniffed around a patch of grass. "Did he ever … bring you here?" Nate had to ask.

"Oh, God, no—this was Jim and Eileen's *home*. Even then, I knew I didn't want any part of that. And neither did your father." Amy's expression shifted. "Not that I didn't spend my share of nights hiding behind trees, trying to catch a glimpse of him through the window."

"Okay, that's weird," Nate said, wondering which of the few trees around them she used.

"It didn't seem so at the time." Amy paused. "Later, I'd try to catch glimpses of you through the window."

The movie version of that scene flickered through Nate's head. He couldn't help but be moved by her memory; there was so much he'd had no way of knowing. Then he told Amy something *she* couldn't possibly have known: "That's funny, because when I was a kid I'd sometimes look into people's windows to see if my mother was actually living with another family. Of course, I was looking for Eileen, not you." Cody sat at Nate's side, watching the house along with them.

"You wanted a mother. What child wouldn't?" She reached out to hug Nate. The timing was too perfect, the moment too wanting, for him to refuse.

"I'm so sorry." Amy pulled back and beheld her son. "I feel like I'll be saying that for the rest of my life." Nate couldn't respond except with a small nod that implied: *Maybe you will.* And maybe that was okay.

The front door of the house swung open and a young couple and their two small children barreled out. The kids were in colorful party costumes; the parents held wrapped gifts. Cody jumped up and barked merrily as the family crossed the small lawn to an older model SUV parked in the driveway. Nate pulled the dog back as the quartet turned as one toward their sidewalk observers.

"We should go—before we're arrested for trespassing or something," Nate quietly told Amy, only half-joking.

"Don't worry, you can always play the 'I was born here' card," she said with a wry smile as the family piled into the SUV. She followed Nate and Cody into the Silverado and they made their way across town, passing the impressive estates along Van Ness Boulevard until they were back at Gene and Diane's.

TWENTY-EIGHT

SAYING GOODBYE TO his grandparents and sister was more emotional than Nate expected, though, after the morning's sentimental journey, he shouldn't have been all that shocked. Robin had picked up an assortment of hefty sandwiches from a shop by the catchy name of Mr. Pickles and they all sat around the dining room table chatting about everything and nothing. Amy brought up her and Nate's ride around town but avoided any can-of-worms specifics. Nate tossed in what a pleasant, easy city Fresno seemed to be; Robin guessed that it had to feel "small time" compared to L.A.—not that she'd ever been, except for a class trip in sixth grade en route to Disneyland. The comment begged an open invitation to visit, which Amy immediately offered her daughter (but not her parents, who didn't exactly seem to be chomping at the bit).

After, everyone assembled in the driveway as Nate loaded Cody and their bags into the truck. Amy was unusually quiet; Nate couldn't tell whether she just wanted to get out while the going was good or if she was feeling bad about leaving. He guessed it was a bit of both. Robin and Diane were, not surprisingly, teary, while Gene stoically examined the ground. For Nate's part, there was so much more he wanted to say, ask, and understand but knew he had more than enough to process for now.

Gene was the first to move in to hug Amy. "Take care of my grandson, now," he said, with a warm, proprietary tone that tugged at Nate's heart.

"I will. As long as he'll let me," Amy promised, directing a gentle smile at her son. Robin watched them both with such unbridled love and hope that Nate could feel himself further unraveling. But he stood straight and held it together as Robin hugged him goodbye, unsure why he felt such a pressing need to be a "good soldier."

Diane opened her arms to Nate, seeming warmer and more authentic than the day before. "This was wonderful," she said through misty eyes. "Please come and see us again soon. Okay, honey?" Nate said he would and, at that, Diane pulled him closer and whispered, "And just know, when Gene and I pass, we're leaving all of your father's money to you. It's rightfully yours."

Nate nodded at that strange, out-of-the-blue comment, but had no idea what she meant and wasn't thinking clearly enough to follow up. The covert way Diane delivered that bit of news should have set off a few bells, yet before Nate knew it, she had already turned away so he wouldn't see her cry. By then, Nate was focused on Robin clutching Amy for dear life, a mix of desperation and resignation on her face. Amy's eyes sort of shrugged at Nate, which he found endearing because he knew how much she cared about Robin—and now him.

"It feels so strange to leave," Amy said as they pulled away from the curb. She watched her childhood home vanish behind them.

"You can stay," Nate replied, no harm meant.

She turned away from the window. "Do you want me to stay?"

"Only if you want to."

Amy looked disappointed, as if she was hoping for something more definitive, more positive from her son by now. Eyes half on the road, half on Amy, Nate realized he'd fucked up. "I don't want you to stay here. At all," he finally told her, and she immediately brightened.

They didn't talk for a while. Nate was finding his way out of Fresno and onto the 41 South, while Amy seemed lost in thought. He tried recalling the name of that book on one of Jim's office shelves (would he ever start to call them *his*?) by—oh, who was it? Thomas … somebody? Not that he'd ever read it, but he'd always liked the title. It hit him: *You Can't Go Home Again.* Maybe Amy couldn't. Not that she'd been gone that long but, well, things had changed for her—a lot. Maybe he'd read that book after all; he'd only been staring at its cracked spine for most of his life.

Nate switched on his Pandora, needing some music to fill in the blanks (Cody was already fast asleep so even he was silent), and kept it on his usual go-to: the classic rock channel. He knew the day he removed it from the presets—if he ever did—would be a sad one. Or maybe it wouldn't. Maybe it would simply be a celebration of his dad's memory and Nate's moving on. In the meantime, "Carry On Wayward Son" by Kansas came bursting through the speakers, jolting Amy to attention. Nate turned down the volume.

"Sorry about that," he said.

"Oh, no, that's fine. I like this song. Haven't heard it in forever, though." Amy pulled down the visor to check her look in the mirror, and swept some stray hair off her forehead. "A little before your time, no?"

"Chronologically, yeah, but this is all my dad ever played—and all I heard growing up, so it kinda stuck." Nate didn't know why but he felt the need to add, "I like newer stuff, too."

Amy nodded, then stared out the window as they passed a place called Selma. "God, my parents looked old," she remarked, as much to Nate as to the little town zipping past.

"They looked okay to me, but what do I know?" he said with an imperceptible edge as he replayed Diane's parting words. Meanwhile, Kansas sang about noise and confusion and illusion, which seemed about right just then.

Amy spun back to Nate, about to say something, but seemed to shift gears. "When their time comes, I don't know how I'll handle it. I hope I'll be as strong as you've been."

Nate wasn't sure how "strong" he'd been—this weekend being the most recent case in point—but he was glad if anyone saw it that way. "Do you think I'm in their will?" he blurted out.

"Nate, what kind of question is that?" she asked with a short, annoyed tone—very un-Amy, Nate thought.

"You tell me," he answered tightly, turning down the radio as the song ended: *Don't you cry no more ...*

"Tell you what? What are you talking about?"

Cody rustled behind them, sticking his head between them as if trying to "cute" them into not raising their voices.

A produce transport truck the size of a small train barreled up on their right and soared past. Its weight and speed sent a hurricane of sand and dust across Nate's windshield. "Hey, slow the fuck down!" Amy yelled at the disappearing semi as if the driver could actually hear her.

"Sorry," she apologized to Nate as the windshield cleared and the produce truck's ear-splitting rumble faded.

Nate waved her off. His body tensed. "Your mother told me that when she and Gene die they're leaving me my father's money. What money?" It occurred to Nate that he didn't call them Grandma and Grandpa, the newfound familiarity gone.

Amy took a sharp breath. The question seemed to flatten her. Cody instinctively ducked back into his seat and out of the fray. "Twenty thousand dollars," she eventually replied in a small, discomfited voice.

Nate squinted at Amy. "What are *they* doing with it?"

Amy met his confused stare and struggled for the words. "Your father gave it to them," she said quietly. "In exchange for you."

He set his eyes back on the road, trying to process her response. His head felt like it was slowly detaching from his body. "What are you saying?" he finally asked. "That my dad ... bought me?" It sounded so ridiculous he would have laughed out loud—if not for Amy's undeniably grave look.

"He bought *them*. Bought their cooperation. Bought their silence." Amy bit her lip, studied her hands, clenched them into fists.

The whoosh of the asphalt escaping beneath them provided a dull, thudding soundtrack to their fraught exchange. Nate didn't have to wonder, he could tell Amy's words were true—and slowly, astoundingly, knew what they meant. "Un-fucking-believable" was all he could muster.

"My parents didn't ask for the money, Nate. But they did take it." Her voice turned darker as she dug back in time: "My father had been in a really bad car accident and was out on disability, which wasn't much. He didn't know when he'd be able to work again—if ever. Mom was taking extra shifts waitressing to make ends meet. The bills were piling up. They had nothing."

"Christ, how much could my father have had?" Nate wanted to shout, pound the wheel, wake the dead.

"He had you. That was all he wanted."

Nate went stone silent, knocked out by this unthinkable curveball. He clutched the wheel and stared out at the unfolding freeway. For all the good that came of the weekend—and he couldn't deny its worth—it felt as if he'd taken one step back for every step forward. It was like some ping-ponging poker game where he stayed alive, still had a few chips left to play, but couldn't quite pull ahead. That was okay, he'd thought, he'd eventually land in the black. He had a whole new family and that was a big fucking deal. And big deals take time.

But this—this was a dagger to the heart. If only Jim were still around to answer why: why he'd made these dubious choices, who had he hurt along the way, and maybe who had hurt *him*? How often had he looked back at what he'd done? Did he really think the truth would never be revealed? And at what cost to his son? Nate might as well be asking Cody.

"I never thought my parents would say anything, especially this weekend, or I would've told you myself," said Amy, breaking his trance. "It was so long ago, Nate."

She looked at her son with beseeching eyes: *Let it go, please let it go.* But the news was too fresh, too lurid to stash away, to pretend he hadn't heard. To try to un-hear it. It opened a door to a blaze of thoughts best left unsaid—that were said nonetheless.

"What else do you have to tell me, *Mom*?" Nate asked with a snarl. "What other little fun facts are up your sleeve? Oh, I know—maybe your father is really my father? And maybe my father is really Robin's father? C'mon, might as well get it all out now!"

"Nate, stop it! This isn't you!"

"Yeah? Well, maybe I'm not who *I* am either!" He didn't see the minivan speeding up to pass him on his right and had to slam on the brakes to avoid a collision. Nate reflexively threw his arm across Amy as Cody was launched out of his seat and onto the floor beneath him. Fortunately, there was no vehicle directly behind Nate and the minivan took off like a shot (a minivan!). Nate turned to find Cody scrabbling back onto his seat, then looked over at a shaken Amy.

"Are you alright?" he asked with urgency as she resettled herself. "I'm so sorry! I didn't mean any of that. At least not the way it sounded. Which was terrible, I know."

"I'm fine. It's … fine. And, no—*I'm* sorry." She took a deep, head-clearing breath. "And really, I wasn't trying to keep anything from you. It was just another … shitty piece of the whole story." She took Nate's arm. "There's nothing else, I swear."

He saw the hurt in her eyes, the regret. And at that moment, Nate decided to believe her, to continue to honor the memory of his imperfect father, and to try to do what his mother had tacitly asked: to let go of what was and focus on what is. Could he do it? He could only hope. But he also knew it would mean sealing away all the pesky details of the traumatic tale. Out of sight, out of mind. Or maybe in his case, it was the other way around.

Still, hadn't opening up recently to Jennifer, to Danny, even to Amy, paid some obvious emotional dividends? Brought him closer to them, eased his mind a bit? Yet why didn't candor come more naturally? He flashed back on something his father had said when Nate first started dating: "Women like a little mystery, kiddo, don't show all your cards at once." What a strange and oddly sophisticated thing to tell an impressionable teenager. Nate didn't remember taking the advice to heart—girls were already a mystery to him back then, did he need to add more of it to the equation? Nonetheless, the seed had been planted and it apparently took root somewhere in his subconscious. And here he was.

"Why don't you try and sleep a little?" Nate suggested. "You look exhausted."

Amy nodded, appreciative. "Okay, maybe I will. Truth be told, I didn't sleep too well last night." A smile surfaced. "Also known as the forty-year-old mattress challenge."

"Not to mention some thirty-year-old memories."

"Those, too." Amy leaned back, crossed her arms, and closed her eyes. She was snoozing in seconds.

Nate took his right hand off the wheel, reached behind to scratch Cody's head, then settled in for the rest of the ride back to L.A. To paraphrase one of his dad's classic rock favorites: what a short, strange trip it had been.

TWENTY-NINE

Jennifer was barely able to say hello as Nate bounded into her guest house, gathered her up in his arms, and carried her into her bedroom. Cody pranced after them.

"What are you doing?" she giddily exclaimed, legs dangling in the air.

"Sweeping you off your feet!" he just as giddily answered.

And those were the last words they spoke before engaging in a noisy and unusually athletic session of, call it what it was: a lot of sex.

Afterward, happily spent, Nate and Jennifer were gazing at the ceiling from her tornado-struck bed. She was huddled into his shoulder as he wrapped her in his arms. He glanced around the warm, inviting room, noticing several details as if new: the ever-present blown-glass vase of fresh flowers from her landlord's garden; her late grandma's vintage, brocade settee that rested regally against one wall; the whimsical, art-deco ballet poster simply titled "The Dance;" the soft mauve walls and accordion-shuttered windows. It reminded Nate once again how much was still left to do to make his own house a home. He'd fallen behind on that front and, with the

Fresno trip and the Amy angst now hopefully behind him, he could jump back into it.

Nate had dropped Amy off in Toluca Woods before heading straight over to Jennifer's. Traffic had been surprisingly light on the freeways back into L.A. and he and Amy, after she woke refreshed from her extended nap, listened to music (she admitted to a contradictory love of country and classical; Nate indulged her) and kept their chatter safe and surfacy. It made for a pleasant second half of the drive and Nate could feel his optimism returning to pre-Fresno levels. And, it seemed, so could Amy. They shared an easy hug goodbye and promised to be in touch in the next few days.

"I really missed you," Nate told Jennifer, breaking the post-coital quiet.

"I could tell," she answered with a sly glance and a kiss to his stubbly cheek.

Nate returned the kiss, slowly moving south until she clapped a hand on his roving head.

"Okay, tiger," she said with a smile, "enough fun. I have questions."

"What kind of questions?" he murmured, nose still buried in her chest.

Jennifer pulled herself away and sat up. "C'mon—how did it go?"

Nate lay on his side looking up at her. He'd promised himself he would leave the gory details behind, hadn't he? He wanted the good without the bad, even if he had to pretend to others—and himself—that all was right with the world now. Hadn't he been through enough? Didn't he owe this to himself? Did anyone else really need to hear what his father had done? What his grandparents had accepted? What the mother he was finally coming to terms with had held back for so long?

Jennifer's eyes were locked on Nate. "Nate, did something bad happen since we spoke yesterday?" His silence brought panic to her voice. "Was there a fight?" Jennifer's eyes widened. She pulled the top sheet around her and up to her neck. There was something defensive about her pose, as if shielding herself from whatever may— or may not—be said next.

Nate rolled away and left the bed. She didn't budge as he hunted around for his boxers. Ah—there they were. How did they end up under her grandma's little couch?

"Why are you ignoring me?"

"I'm not ignoring you," he said as he pulled on his underwear. Halfway up, he realized they were backward. "There was no fight," he more or less lied, as he reversed his shorts and tried again. Cody trotted in from the living room.

"Then what?" Jen asked, rising, still wrapped in the sheet.

Nate indicated her covering. "Cody's seen you naked, you know." Poor time for a joke, but he was stalling. Trying to keep his word—to himself.

Jennifer moved in front of Nate as he slipped on his jeans. They'd landed in a corner atop his "Landscapers Make It Better" T-shirt. "What are you hiding from me?"

"I'm not *hiding* anything." He zipped his jeans, then grabbed his shirt.

"Yesterday, on the phone, you told me everything. And now? I'm back to playing guessing games." She dropped onto the settee, the sheet draping around her. Cody sat next to her, head raised for petting. She did something she rarely did: ignored him. Jennifer kept her glare fixed on Nate.

This was a shitty way to end a fantastic few hours and Nate knew it. He had to make it better again and somehow couldn't. "Everything was fine," he finally said. "Like I told you yesterday, it was strange, that's all. I'd really just love to leave it there."

Cody pawed at her. She gave in and absently massaged his scruff but remained focused on Nate.

As open and loving as she'd been just a few short minutes ago, he could now see her shutting down in real time, the light going out in her eyes. Nate knelt on the oval throw rug in front of her and tried to take her free hand, her other one still buried in Cody's fur. But she resisted and Nate backed away. "Please trust me," he said.

"Nate, I will not take two giant steps back," Jennifer insisted. "If something's bothering you, I want you to talk about it." She bolted away from him and Cody, the bedsheet slipping off and trailing behind her. Nate followed as she swiped her bra and panties off the vanity stool, where she'd flung them en route to the bed. Day had since turned to dusk.

"Jen, I swear, it's all good," he said. "There's nothing more to talk about." He knew he shouldn't have sworn, was trying to prove a point—but was probably digging a hole for himself instead.

She turned to face him as she stepped one leg at a time into her lacey undies. Nate could watch her do that all day long, he thought, preferably in slow motion. His appreciative reaction to that simple act seemed to register with Jennifer, whose expression softened a bit. "Fine, have it your way," she said with a sigh as she pulled on her bra. "But I'll be asking again."

"Babe, I think you're overreacting."

"Don't 'babe' me. And please—don't ever tell a woman she's overreacting. My God, haven't you learned anything in thirty years of life?"

Nate flinched. That was harsh, especially for Jennifer. Okay, maybe he'd back down and tell her about the twenty grand—after all, it was only as big a deal as he made it out to be, right? Instead, he decided to switch gears and ask her out for a bite. He hadn't eaten since the Mr. Pickles sandwich, and it seemed like a safer segue. But, poor judge of a moment as he sometimes was, she declined—which Nate figured maybe he deserved. As he left, he said he'd talk to her tomorrow. But her lack of a response spoke volumes.

Gloomily driving back to Eagle Rock, Cody perched regally next to him, Nate thought of the phrase "snatching defeat from the jaws of victory." He'd never fully understood what it meant until now— it's exactly what he'd just done with his beautiful girlfriend. He recalled the parting words of Lena the psychic: "It doesn't have to be so hard." It had sounded so obvious, so simple. At the time.

"So why *is* it so difficult?" Nate asked Cody, half expecting an answer. The dog gazed at him with devotion, his dark eyes inquisitive pools, then turned and stared out at the passing cars.

THAT NIGHT, MIND racing, unable to sleep, Nate padded into the office to grab a book—reading was bound to put him to sleep. He turned on the overhead light and skimmed the shelves, noticing no small amount of dust on the familiar volumes. He needed some help on the cleaning front, that was for sure. He came upon *Wuthering Heights*, pulled it out, and started flicking through the old book. Naturally, it reminded him of Amy and his dad. And, while there might have been something eerily fitting about digging into it, Nate knew it would trigger too many of the thoughts he was trying to forget, at least at this midnight hour. So back it went.

He scanned past a couple of the *Gatsbys*, a Didion he didn't remember being there, a pair of John le Carré thrillers, and a beat-up copy of *The Sun Also Rises*, which had clearly seen its fair share of lecture halls. None of them interested Nate. He then plucked *To Kill a Mockingbird* off the shelf. It was one of the few books he had to read in high school (or was it middle school?) that he liked though he didn't recall this version, a worn, yellowing hardcover with the classic leafy oak tree art on its faded dust jacket. Something about the novel had spoken to Nate back in the day and maybe it would again.

Back in bed, Cody sawing logs on the floor beside him, Nate flipped on his bedside lamp and started to read. *When he was nearly thirteen, my brother Jem got his arm badly broken at the elbow.* Damn if Nate didn't remember those exact words. The memory sent a little shiver through him. He kept going, page after page, the lyrical prose engaging rather than exhausting him.

As he was about to start a new chapter, a matte color snapshot fell out of the book. At first, Nate thought it was just a bookmark of sorts. But when he turned the photo right-side up his eyes bugged open. It was of a teenage Amy at her high school graduation—cap and gown, diploma, joyful smile. Her expression read "Ready to take on the world!" *Without the worry of a baby to hold her back,* Nate thought darkly as he gazed at the old photograph.

Then he realized: What was it doing lodged between the pages of *To Kill a Mockingbird*? And what were the chances that this was the book he'd choose tonight? Nate turned over the snapshot. There was an inscription: *Dear Jim—Wanted to share my graduation with you. You will always be a part of me. Love, Amy.*

"What the fuck?" Nate asked the dark.

He did a quick mental computation: According to Amy, Jim had left Fresno shortly after Nate was born, the semester before she graduated. This meant that when Amy mailed this photo to Jim he was already living in L.A. Yet she also told Nate that his dad had left no forwarding address. *No nothing*, if he remembered correctly. Which, aside from the "pact," was allegedly why Amy never tried to find him. That and the twenty grand—let's not forget about that. Was there a part of her that thought sending Jim that snapshot, however it got there, might inspire him to break the agreement and reunite? And baby makes three?

It was all more than Nate could handle at what was now well past 1 a.m. Especially since he had to be up extra early to stop by the Russos' for a final inspection before meeting Danny to start their new job. He tucked the picture back into the book, shut the light—and his mind—and slept fitfully until his six o'clock alarm.

THIRTY

"WE NEVER DID decide on that gazebo, did we?" asked Corey Russo, fresh off a pre-breakfast bike ride with Brooke. The sunny couple, both still in jerseys and cycling shorts, matching coffee mugs in hand, gazed out appreciatively at their newly finished backyard as Nate gave the plantings a last once-over. Everything looked like it had begun to take root, though he was concerned about some yellowing on a few of the larger California natives, especially a quite beautiful manzanita. He'd have to adjust the sprinklers in case they were getting too much water.

"I decided for you," answered Nate. "You didn't need one. You've got plenty going on back here without it." He cast an approving eye on the dry creek bed, which was even wider, longer, and curvier than Amy's, and if he had to say so himself, pretty damn cool-looking.

"Well, we're in love with what you've done back here, Nate," said Brooke, handing Nate a check for his last payment. "You're a true artist. Has anyone ever told you that?"

Only one person. And she was his next stop that morning.

Part of him wanted to bury the thoughts and questions that had been vexing him in the hours since finding that photo—or rather since it found him. But given that she lived so close to the Russos and he just happened to take along that old copy of *To Kill a Mockingbird*, her picture conveniently still wedged inside, Nate couldn't help but stop by for what he knew would turn into an interrogation. Fortunately, he was meeting Danny at nine—and it was already eight—so he couldn't stay at Amy's long. That is, if she was even there.

She was, answering the door already dressed for work in a smart-looking blue pinstripe dress, but still in stocking feet, wielding a mascara wand. If she was surprised to see Nate, she didn't let on.

"Were you at the Russos'?" Amy asked after inviting him inside.

Nate didn't remember if he'd ever even mentioned his clients' last name to her, but she knew it anyway. He nodded, hovering in the doorway. His feet felt like cement. It prevented him from moving forward—or turning and running.

Amy eyed the book in his hand. "Why are you holding a copy of *To Kill a Mockingbird*?"

Without a word, Nate removed the signed photo. She silently left the doorway and returned minus the makeup brush, reading glasses in hand. She put them on, tilted the snapshot up to the daylight, and turned it over, reading the inscription.

"Where did you get this?" she asked, barely above a whisper.

Nate raised the book. "It was in here. Where my father must've hidden it—or whatever he meant to do—after you sent it." His answer was loaded with accusation and conjecture. He was proud of neither.

She studied Nate, composing herself. "Why are you looking at me that way? It's just a picture. And would you please come inside for a minute?"

Their brief relationship had been such an emotional rollercoaster that it was sometimes hard for Nate to remember where they'd left off. He flashed on hugging her goodbye the day before, so things couldn't have ended too badly. But hadn't it been a kind of calm after the storm? All he felt was the storm at the moment. Still, he put one leaden foot in front of the other and followed her in.

They sat in the living room—Amy on the white couch, Nate in one of the wide wingbacks—as she examined the graduation day photo. Glancing around the precise, well-appointed space, it once again hit Nate how different Amy was from her parents. Maybe it was because of who they were, and the more basic way they seemed to live their lives, that she felt the need to rise above them. To be what they were not. Nate always aspired—successfully or not—to be more like his father, even if only in temperament, in goodness. Did he still feel that way?

"What do you want to know?" Amy finally asked. She sounded defensive, weary.

"Why did you send that picture to him? *How* did you send it?" Nate asked, trying to stay calm. "You said no one knew where he'd moved. You said you never spoke to him again. Yesterday, you also said there was nothing else you were keeping from me—and then I find that." He indicated the photo in her hand. "How can I ever really know what's true?"

Amy rose from the couch and handed the snapshot back to Nate as if she wanted no part of it—no part of the memory. She stood above him looking fragile yet resolved. "I never *did* speak to your father again," she said. "All I ever did was write. And only that one note." She gestured with her chin at the photo. "And, sure, maybe sending it was a little cry for attention. I told you, I never really lost my feelings for him."

Nate, unmoved, gazed at her with anticipation. Amy explained that she mailed the photo to Jim's old address in Fresno hoping it would be forwarded to wherever he was—if he'd even given the post office a location to do so. She had no idea if he ever received it—until now, that is—and she never really expected to hear back from him.

"I promise you," Amy said, reaching for Nate's hand, "I did not know where he was living. I did not know where you were. And if I didn't bring it up yesterday after the whole money thing came out, it was because I'd completely forgotten." She squeezed Nate's hand; he let her, then withdrew it. Amy sighed. "Anyway, it's such a tiny thing in comparison," she concluded. "What difference does it make?"

Nate stood, looming over Amy, looking as sad, as wistful as she now did. "If you have to ask that question," he told her, "then you really don't understand."

Amy got up from her chair. "Look, maybe you're still overwhelmed from the trip north," she said with a tinge of hope. "Maybe it was too much, too soon." When he didn't answer, she gently added, "I thought we could finally have a real relationship. Do you know how lucky that would make us?"

He did. Of course he did. And yet. "I've been trying to trust you—wanting to trust you. I have. But it's … the whole thing … it's just really hard."

"No one ever said it was going to be easy. I mean, talk about an understatement."

"Okay, but do I really want to keep putting out all this emotion, all of this effort, only to ultimately fail? For us to fail?"

Amy turned away from Nate and crossed to the front window. "Every time I look at the yard it gets more beautiful."

"Well, it cost you enough," Nate said, coming up behind her. "I hope the owner appreciates it."

Amy faced him, a trace of a smile forming. "Maybe one day I can deduct it from the purchase price." But when she saw Nate's startled expression, she quickly waved away her comment. "Don't worry, I'm not buying anything yet."

Nate peeked at his watch. It was eight forty. He really needed to leave. And he should have before the blunt thought that came to mind flew out of his mouth. "Honestly? I don't know if you should move here if it's just to be near me. I wouldn't want that pressure. That responsibility."

Amy looked like she had just been slapped with a wet towel. But instead of shirking back, she stood straighter. "What kind of responsibility? I can take care of myself quite well, thank you."

"That's not what I meant."

"If you want me to leave town, I'll quit my job and leave town."

Nate placed the cherry atop the self-sabotage sundae. "I don't want you to leave," he asserted. "But right this very second, I'm not sure I want you to stay."

"Well, that's definitive," Amy hit back. "No wonder you can't commit to Jennifer. You don't really know what you want."

She couldn't have known, of course, how that would sting at this particular moment, but Nate sure did. "Please leave Jennifer out of this," he ordered. "And it's not like you've done so great in the romance department." Before he could register Amy's hurt, he made for the front door. "I've got to go. I have a new job to get to."

Nate spied Amy in his rearview mirror as he drove away. She was standing shoeless on the front lawn, looking helpless and increasingly small.

LAKE HOLLYWOOD WAS an upscale enclave of well-kept homes about ten minutes south of Toluca Woods. The neighborhood gave way to the scenic Hollywood Reservoir, a popular walking spot in the shadow of the famed Hollywood sign. Until signing this new gig, Nate hadn't spent much time in the area—beyond giving estimates on a few jobs that didn't pan out—but he'd always liked its tucked-away privacy and quiet charm.

Driving up hilly La Sombra Drive, Nate noticed how many of the older, Spanish-style houses had been enlarged or knocked down altogether and replaced with the kind of boxy, industrial-looking, glass-and-concrete giants that now dotted Los Angeles. He disliked their flat lines and soaring starkness, enormous picture windows, and sleek walls usually painted in austere whites or grays. They were a personal affront to Nate: their sparseness didn't lend itself to the kind of lush, clustery planting designs that had become his specialty. That's not to say he couldn't warm up the pricey homes a bit with some creative landscaping, but the thought didn't excite him. Maybe he *was* more of an artist than he gave himself credit for.

Danny was waiting for Nate in front of a classic, low-slung stucco ranch with leaded windows, arched doorways, and a red clay tile roof. He'd already unloaded the heap of tools from his truck that they'd need to start tearing up the front yard's shrubbery beds, which were getting a full refresh. It was a smaller job than usual, one that Nate and Danny could handle alone, and shouldn't take more than a few days. Still, the homeowner, a veteran TV soap star named Charla Kent, who'd lived in the house since the late-1970s—or "four husbands ago," as she'd brashly informed Nate—said she was "known to change her mind."

Nate, who was feeling pretty alienated after tangling with both Jen and Amy, was so happy to see the buoyant Danny that he grabbed him in a rowdy bear hug.

"What's got into you, man?" Danny asked with his usual broad grin as he disengaged from Nate. "You find out you got two weeks to live or something?" (If that impulsive remark felt "too soon" after Jim's passing, neither seemed to notice.)

"Nah, just glad to see a friendly face, that's all," said Nate.

Danny raised an eyebrow and gave his head a dubious tilt.

"What?" Nate wanted to know. As if he already didn't.

"Rough times up north?"

Part of Nate wanted to give his friend a full report but the other part wanted to stick to his self-imposed cone of silence. That said, it was feeling iffy whether he and Amy could truly make things work, so maybe, Nate figured, he should just scrap plan A and get Danny's unfiltered opinion. Before Nate could proceed either way, Charla popped out of her front door in a violet velour jogging suit, shrewdly unzipped to expose just enough well-toned cleavage to prove the attractive, seventyish actress still had it going on. The lady clearly liked an audience, especially if it contained young men.

"How are my guys today?" she asked in a slightly come-hither voice.

"Ready to make your yard as beautiful as you," Danny said with a smile that could melt butter. Nate was glad at least one of them was a bit shameless. The thing was, Danny meant what he said and knew how to make folks feel good in the process. That was a gift.

Which reminded Nate: He needed to carve out some time for a serious talk with him about new business goals and revising their partnership. That then reminded Nate: It was Amy who'd first planted the idea for him to grow his company. It made him feel crappy about the way he'd left her earlier—in anger and confusion and distrust. Maybe the situation was simply bigger than the two of them—three if you counted his father—and, despite best efforts, there was no real long-term solution.

"Oh, Danny, if only I were forty years younger," Charla said coyly. She thrust her chest out and moistened her glossy lips, gestures she'd likely employed thousands of times for the TV cameras.

"If only *I* wasn't married," retorted Danny with a wink. "Anyway, age is just a number. Isn't that what they say?" Nate didn't know who said that but it sure wasn't Danny. But damn if Charla wasn't blushing like a schoolgirl.

By the end of their first afternoon, the actress had agreed to build a dry creek bed in her roomy backyard, visibly wowed by pictures Nate showed her from their last two jobs. She also gave an enthusiastic yes to replacing a pair of misshapen old peach trees in front ("I haven't seen fruit on these things since Reagan was president!") with pygmy date palms, which Nate felt would add a tropical touch without overwhelming the garden.

To thank Danny for his stellar performance that day opposite a *real* actor, Nate took him out for beers at a neighborhood bar on Hollywood Way in Burbank called Bailey's, which drew an assortment of workaday folks from the nearby Disney and Warner Bros. studios. Alicia had given Danny the okay to hang out with Nate "for an hour—that's it!" and with a one-drink limit, even though she knew he'd have two. He promised to be home in time to bathe Raffi and put him to bed so Alicia could finish up some work that was facing a tight tax deadline.

Nate wondered aloud how he'd fare having to negotiate his free time with a wife ("It's called *compromise,* dude. Look it up!" super-husband Danny told him), though the way things were going for Nate it was currently a moot worry.

Sitting in a cracked red leather booth as a jukebox shuffled between old disco hits and even older Johnny Cash tunes, Nate toasted Danny and thanked him for all his hard work and friendship. Danny smiled appreciatively, then took a swig of his Heineken. He studied Nate over his beer bottle.

"That it?" he asked.

"What do you mean?" Nate replied. In truth, he still wasn't sure how to approach the partnership idea. Amy's words from that morning echoed: *You don't really know what you want.* At the time, that seemed like an unfair thing to say. But now? Maybe it wasn't so incredibly off-base.

"You still haven't told me anything about Fresno. Was it good? Did it suck? Are you happy? Are you pissed off? Were your grandparents nice? Are they crazytown? What about the sister? Was she chill?"

The clacking of billiard balls from a corner pool table blended with the twangy strains of Cash's "Ring of Fire" (Nate recognized the song from the remake he liked by Social Distortion). A wave of exhaustion came over Nate at the thought of revisiting the events of the weekend, even the better ones. But Danny was eyeballing him with such insistence, the kind that demanded, "Are we friends or not?" that Nate sucked down some beer and was about to fill in the blanks. But he took a sharp, decidedly diversionary U-turn and launched into an impromptu proposal to make Danny a fifty-fifty partner in the future Cronin/Soto Landscaping Inc.

"In exchange for half the responsibility for, well, everything," Nate explained. "But, hopefully, double the business—and profit— for both of us."

Danny was so stunned by Nate's offer that he was, for once in his voluble life, speechless. But so visibly proud and honored, he looked near tears.

Danny bucked up and broke into a wall-to-wall grin. "Leesh is gonna be super stoked!" His face turned sober. "Shit, now I can't use the 'we need more money' excuse to put off kid number two."

"I thought that was already in the works?"

"In the works, yeah. In the oven, no." Danny pointed his beer bottle at Nate. "Whaddya think, I just wave it at her and boom—baby time?"

"Yeah, I know how it works, *papi*." Nate rarely used Spanish with Danny, who spoke so little himself. But third-generation American that he was, Danny wasn't proprietary about his mother tongue. He got a kick out of Nate using it and smiled now at the jab.

Nate had a practical thought. "Well, for what it's worth, you'll have more work to do now—and so will Alicia," he said as a noisy disco song called "Get Down Tonight" blared from the wall speakers. "She'll need to do a full revamp of our accounting and salary distribution system and help us incorporate. And that's just for starters." Nate finished his beer and added, "Anyway, maybe it'll buy you some time. I mean, if that's what you want." It occurred to Nate that this was none of his business and ended it there.

They both watched as an older couple, drinks in hand, danced by the jukebox. "Forty years? That'll be me and Alicia," Danny mused.

"Dancing to better music, I hope."

Danny drained his Heineken, then turned back to Nate. "Don't you want that, man?"

"What?"

Danny nodded toward the dancers. "That. Or what me and Alicia have. Or half the world has, for that matter. You deserve it." He paused. "Jen deserves it."

"Jen." Nate sighed. "Yeah, well that's another story." He vacantly rolled his empty beer bottle in his hands.

Danny studied him. "Wait, I thought you two were good again? What happened? She ask about your trip and you wormed out of it?" Before a surprised Nate could protest, Danny tacked on, "Yeah, don't think I didn't notice, 'cause I did. Twice."

Nate looked away shyly, evasively. The dancing couple boogied away from the jukebox toward the bar to scattered applause.

Danny considered his glum partner. "Hey, I get one more drink. Let's do a shot. Celebrate you and me." As he turned to go: "Patrón okay?"

Nate brightened. "*More* than okay." He pushed a twenty at Danny, who waved it away.

"On me, bro. And then you can talk shit about your mom and Jen—or not. No pressure." Nate nodded with a smile and Danny took off for the bar. He stopped short, turning back to Nate. "Hey, it just hit me. Something like … 'Soto/Cronin Landscape Designs' has a cool ring to it, don't you think?"

Nate grinned. Did he know this joker or what?

THIRTY-ONE

THOUGH LOOSENED UP after their tequila shots, Nate still didn't tell Danny exactly what he'd held back from Jennifer, just that, yeah, she was angry that he didn't want to get into it. Danny didn't press him on details, still flying high about the new partnership, and they ended their little celebration within the prescribed hour time slot. Nate expected Danny to complain about having to leave, but the adoring dad instead gushed about how much fun Raffi had in the bathtub and the stories he'd read to his spirited son after tucking him in. It was a sweet moment that left Nate feeling a bit empty, so he sat at the bar alone and downed another beer—which only made things worse.

Exiting the bar into the mid-August dusk, Nate realized he needed to stop the pity party and take action—any action. Maybe more buzzed than he thought, he leaned against his truck parked in the small lot behind Bailey's and impulsively called Jennifer. If she was smart, she wouldn't answer—but he hoped she would. What he would say then, he had no clue. He knew one thing: Whatever he did end up saying would probably be wrong.

"Nate?"

His mouth went bone dry. He cleared his throat. "I said I'd call you tomorrow. It's tomorrow." Brilliant, Cronin.

"What's going on? You sound strange." Nate could hear the clanking of utensils against metal. She must have been cooking dinner.

"Me? No, I'm good. I'm … awesome. Feel like company later?" It was official: He had no control of what was coming out of his mouth. Nate cringed at his slapdash request. He was met with silence on the other end of the line, followed by more kitchen noise.

"Sorry, I'm making an omelet," Jennifer finally said.

"What kind?" Another cringe. More silence. The dancing couple entered the parking lot hand-in-hand. The woman gave Nate a tipsy little wave.

"Nate, I …" Jennifer trailed off. Nate strained to hear her as the couple's car rumbled out of the lot and onto Hollywood Way. She continued, "Look, I might as well just say it now. I can't keep doing whatever it is we've been doing lately. I thought I could, I wanted to give us another chance, but …"

Nate stood straight. "But what?" he asked, forcing an issue he knew was better left unforced. He heard the clunk of her frying pan landing in the sink.

"I need some time alone to make some decisions," she said, finding her voice. "Some *real* decisions this time. And so do you."

Nate started pacing the lot. "Don't tell me what I need. I want *you*—I don't have to think about it." His words sounded fuzzy but, he hoped, only to him.

"Well, you have a funny way of showing it," Jennifer answered with the impatience Nate had coming to him.

He leaned back against his truck, took a breath, told the truth. "Jen, I'm doing the best I can, okay?"

"No, it's not okay. Not for me. I know this is difficult. I know … things have been difficult, but please … just respect what I'm asking for." When Nate didn't respond—didn't know how to respond— she added, "My food's getting cold. I'd better go."

"Sure, fine," Nate managed. "Whatever you want."

At that very moment, it wouldn't have surprised Nate if they never spoke again.

It was only around eight when Nate returned home, though it felt a whole lot later. Cody obviously felt the same way: He greeted Nate at the door like he hadn't seen him in, well, a dog's age. He jumped up on Nate, slamming his big paws into his chest, causing Nate to fall to the living room floor. Cody covered him in slobbery kisses while Nate tried to regain his bearings. He gave up and leaned back against the wall as the dog continued his buoyant tongue bath. It made Nate smile—Cody so often made him smile—and appreciate once again how utterly loyal a dog could be, whether you'd earned it or not. They were truly love machines. People, not so much, thought Nate. They were too complicated, too unpredictable, too demanding. Why couldn't we just be like dogs?

As Cody settled down, Nate pulled himself up off the floor and crossed into the kitchen. He checked the automatic pet feeder to make sure Cody had eaten (he checked every night as if the dog would ever miss a meal), then stood gazing into the open refrigerator looking for something to eat himself. He decided he wasn't hungry—there wasn't much to choose from anyway; a Trader Joe's run was needed—and went upstairs to shower instead. Climbing the stairs, Cody at his heels, Nate thought about what a long fucking day it had been and how the bright spots—the exciting partnership with Danny; starting the job for a, well, interesting new client—were thoroughly overshadowed by the fissures with Jennifer and Amy. It was like the clouds blocking out the sun. He knew that however you sliced it, he'd seriously gotten in his own way. What would Lena the psychic—or better yet, a mental health professional—say about that? Maybe it was finally time to get ahold of a good shrink and find out. The thought scared the living crap out of him, which was as good a reason as any to do it.

When Nate stepped out of the shower he glanced at his cell glowing on the counter and saw that he'd missed a call. It was from Amy, think of the devil. As he toweled off, he weighed if he wanted to hear what she had to say or if it would be better to close out the day without one more thing to think about. He sighed, hit the speaker button, and played Amy's message.

"Nate, it's your moth—it's Amy," she began. "We have to talk this out. We've come this far—don't let it end now." There was a long, uncomfortable pause. "Please call me. Whenever you're ready." And just when it seemed as if Amy was going to hang up, she added, "I love you."

Did she think those three little words would wallpaper over everything? That love, whatever it meant in a situation like this, would conquer all? It clearly did for Amy—she had always been his mother. But Nate hadn't always been her son, not until the last handful of months. No matter, he could practically hear the ball bouncing into his court.

Nate put down his phone and gazed out at the room that his dad had slept in for so many years. It was now a mix of Jim's older furnishings and Nate's newer stuff, a decidedly eclectic combo of functionality over style. For so much of Nate's life, he'd been a visitor to this space, a kind of friendly interloper. It had been a place to snoop around—looking for what, Nate never knew—when he was a kid and Jim was away at work or out with a friend or on the rare date. Jim never ostensibly hid anything in his room: He always kept his wallet and spare change there for the taking atop his dresser, the occasional *Playboy* magazine—when *Playboy* and magazines were still a thing—on his nightstand in full go-for-it view, and nothing in the shoe and sweater boxes that lived on his closet shelf except, well, shoes and sweaters. Still, to a child, there was magic and mystery in the unknown and, though Nate rarely uncovered anything of consequence, there was the thrill of the hunt.

The flashback made Nate smile, the room he now sat in seeming so much physically larger in his childhood memory than it did in his adult reality. He'd also spent so many sad, emotionally draining hours in it during Jim's last months that it amazed Nate that he was now able to sleep in the room with so little issue. If he couldn't conk out it had more to do with his own day-to-day setbacks than any lingering scenes of his father's stalwart suffering within those same four walls. Though Jim's death was still so fresh in his mind, whenever Nate thought of his father it wasn't as he last saw him—a once vital and handsome man undone by pain and disease—but rather as one of a lifetime's worth of snapshots forever stored in his brain. He conjured up a younger, dynamic, and jaunty Jim, with his wide smile, glowing eyes, and irrepressible charm. The man who taught him how to throw a ball, shave his face, grill a steak, drive a car, unhook a bra (yes, he did), and spot wisdom. The man who was there for him every day of his life—from child to teen to young adult. The man who he missed so terribly that as much as he tried to remember him, he also tried to forget. The man Nate wondered if he could ever truly and completely forgive. Or, more to the point, if he even should.

Nate fell back onto the bed next to Cody, stared at the ceiling, and closed his eyes. He immediately started to dream that Jim was alive and well and married to Amy, but that they lived in Jennifer's guest house—as did Nate and Jennifer. Everyone couldn't have been happier. Nice while it lasted.

NATE FOUND HIMSELF a psychotherapist named Mira, a soft-spoken, super-direct woman in her fifties with a compact, comfortable office in Glendale, a busy L.A. suburb about ten minutes from Eagle Rock. He probably could have saved himself a lot of time and effort by just confronting Amy and Jennifer head-on, opening himself up as much as possible, listening—really listening—to their sides of things, and then reconciling his relationships with them or not, as the case might be. Still, if he could have done that in any kind of meaningful way, he wouldn't need a therapist—which any evolved, proactive, and objective person would agree that he undeniably did.

Nate had spent the better part of his second day working at Charla's thinking about giving in to therapy. That is, when the actress, this time in a bedazzled aqua jogging suit (did she even jog?), wasn't interrupting Danny and him with breathy questions about various plants and unsolicited anecdotes about her years on *Days of Our Lives*. Nate wondered if, for all her seemingly grand self-possession, she wasn't lonely and just happy to have a couple of friendly guys to talk to (make that: talk *at*). The thought made Nate warm to her and wonder if she'd ever had any children—beyond the ones she had on TV. Imagine finding out someone like Charla Kent was actually your mother.

Meantime, Danny peppered Nate with a barrage of practical and creative ideas for their partnership, undoubtedly inspired by input from the business-savvy Alicia, who, Danny confirmed, was thrilled and "one hundred percent onboard" about their new collaboration. Nate could picture Alicia's pretty, heart-shaped face bursting into a grin and the happiness she must have felt at that special moment for her husband. On the other hand, how great it had to have been for Danny to be able to share the news with someone he loved so much. Nate *did* want what his friend had, even if it felt so elusive.

When Nate got home around six, he checked his health insurance website for covered psychotherapists nearest his zip code. Of the dozen or so providers that popped up on the screen, he picked Mira. Not only did she have a warm, maternal face (okay, it didn't take a shrink to explain that one) but she listed later office hours than the others: Tuesday through Thursday until 9 p.m. He left a message on her voicemail and was surprised when she called him back about an hour later. Nate stumbled his way through an introduction, told her a little—very little—about why he wanted to see her, and, heart thumping double-time, waited for Mira to ask *him* some questions.

The one she posed, however, was not what he expected: "I have an opening tomorrow night at seven. Would that be convenient?"

Nate figured he might as well take it before he chickened out. Twenty-four hours later, he found himself sinking warily into a pillowy, royal blue couch while Mira, as reassuring-looking as her picture, sat across from him in a matching club chair. He took in the soothing beachscapes that hung on the wall behind her and the hardy, split-leaf philodendron that stood tall and proud next to the room's single window, and could feel his spine slowly relax.

"Have you ever been to therapy?" Mira asked, pen and notepad in hand.

"No, but I did see a psychic recently, does that count?" For some reason, Nate felt obligated to make her laugh. She broke a faint smile instead.

"Not really," Mira answered. "Was she helpful?"

Nate didn't know if this was a trick question. "I thought maybe a little, but I guess not." He gestured around the office. "I mean, I'm here, so …"

"Is that bad?"

Okay, that was definitely a trick question. "Not yet, no." Nate was still trying to keep it light, though he wasn't sure why. Yes, he did, he was nervous as fuck. He felt like he was in one of those dreams where you suddenly had no clothes—and no one notices.

Mira chuckled. A real, audible chuckle. She had an inviting smile, with large, white teeth and full lips. Her eyes closed almost to slits then burst open again. She straightened a silk scarf that was tied around her neck and crossed her legs. Nate noticed she had on the same kind of pointy black high heels that he'd seen Amy wear to work. They looked painful, yet classy at the same time. Jennifer certainly must have had a pair, too, but Nate couldn't remember. Things were unfolding for him at half speed. He was almost too aware of Mira, of his surroundings. Of how the glossy leaves of the philodendron vaguely shivered, the plant in direct line of the air conditioning vent. Or the way those beachscapes tilted to the right, each frame in need of the tiniest adjustment.

"Alright, Nate," Mira began. "Tell me how I can help you."

He gazed at the therapist, carefully assembling his words, aware that the meter was running. Nate swallowed, cleared his throat, leaned his shoulders against the cushy couch pillows, and began. Not at the beginning, but also not at the very end. He took Mira back to that fateful day on the bench at Occidental when Jim revealed what, until then, Nate had thought was the biggest secret— maybe the only secret—his father had ever kept from him.

"How did it make you feel?" Mira asked, pen poised over her pad.

Nate didn't even have to think. "It was one of the worst moments of my life." Actually, he did have to think. "Maybe the worst." Nate added, "Though it *was* worse for my dad."

She took some notes and looked back up at Nate. "How do you mean?"

How do you mean? How could he mean? Wasn't it worse for the person who was dying than for the person who wasn't? So he asked her just that.

"Well, yes, of course," she answered, smoothing out her scarf again. "But I was talking about the betrayal. That's a pretty significant piece of information to hold back from your only child. The one who would presumably have to take care of you, be responsible for you, at some point."

Nate didn't know what was more painful: the memory of that day on the bench or the bluntness of Mira's words. How dare she? She didn't know Jim. And she just met Nate, what, ten minutes ago? Was this what therapy was going to be like? *Supposed* to be like? Sit there and take it? If it was, he was out. He crossed his arms, silent.

Mira could obviously sense his discomfort. She swept her legs beneath her chair and sat forward. "I'm sorry if I offended you. It wasn't a judgment call, it was an observation." She paused for emphasis. "A factual one, I would say."

Nate unhooked his arms and folded his hands in front of him. He hated to admit it, but he knew she was right. And, after simmering a bit more, he told her so. He told her what else he knew: that he was defensive of his dad, who was no longer here to speak for himself, but also confused and, yeah, sure, a little resentful.

What Nate didn't say was that if anyone was going to throw Jim under the bus, it would be him—his son. But was that what he was there to do? What *was* he there to do?

Mira's expression softened. She sat back in her chair. "This is difficult for you, isn't it?"

"What was your first clue?" Nate shot back, instantly sorry for his tone. But Mira looked unfazed, like someone who'd heard it all before—which she no doubt had.

She took a few more notes, which began to unnerve Nate. *What the hell was she writing?* Mira then closed her notebook, set it on a small side table, and clasped her hands together like she had the greatest gift to share with him. Which maybe, in a way, she had.

"I think we've found a very good place to begin," she said brightly, with probably as much excitement as a shrink was technically allowed to show.

Nate peeked at his watch: thirty more minutes to go. Yikes.

THIRTY-TWO

THE END OF August brought an unwelcome heatwave to L.A. that wreaked havoc on power grids, fire prevention, peoples' patience, and anyone like Nate who was in the business of planting things and trying to keep them alive. He and Danny were finishing the job at Charla's, which had continued to expand thanks to her hair-trigger decision making and a cash infusion from a "ridiculous" (her word) advance she'd received to write her memoir. (An internet search by Danny early on revealed that Charla was a lot bigger star—in her day and even now—than he and Nate had gathered.)

The way their work schedule had laid out, the guys left the dry creek bed construction for last. So they were stuck pushing through the labor-intensive project on the two hottest days L.A. had seen in years: a Thursday and Friday that both hit 106 degrees. Charla told them to come back when it cooled down. But brand-new partner Danny had lined up a major gig relandscaping an office park in South Pasadena and they were contracted to begin that Monday. Nate and Danny worked their sweaty butts off (they decided to tough it out without extra help), kept as covered and hydrated as possible, and created a wide and winding dry creek bed in a thankfully shady corner of Charla's backyard. It was even more beautiful, textured, and colorful than the ones they'd built for Amy and the Russos. And, as a humble Danny was quick to point out, "that was saying a ton."

Charla took selfies of them all posed by Nate and Danny's handiwork and promised to post the pics on her Instagram page, which, she claimed (honestly, as it turned out) had more than three million followers. As a result, Cronin/Soto Landscape Designs, as it was now called (Danny equitably concluded that, as company founder, Nate's name should go first) received hundreds of inquiries for estimates. But only six requests were from the L.A. area and Nate learned about the evil of internet bots.

Meanwhile, Alicia had done a bang-up job reconfiguring the new company's financial structure and came up with an intriguing plan for Nate and Danny to double the company's income, though it might mean adding another full-time employee. They'd hold off for now—neither guy wanted to take any immediate chances—but Nate could tell Danny had a newfound respect for his wife's financial acumen. None of it, however, changed Alicia's mind about trying for a second child, though Danny got her to agree to wait six months before they threw all precaution to the wind.

Nate hadn't communicated with Amy—despite her several voicemails and text messages—nor with Jennifer—who didn't answer *his* several voicemails and texts—since he'd last talked to them both in person. It was going on two weeks and it ate away at Nate every day. Yet, in some ways, he'd begun to feel more sanguine about it all than he might have expected. The whole situation felt like an injury that needed to heal after a car crash or some terrible fall. The thing was: when the broken arm or traumatized knee or herniated disc did mend, would it be good as new or never quite right again? Or would the damage simply prove irrevocable?

Nate didn't come up with those analogies entirely himself. He'd had help from his twice-weekly therapy sessions with Mira, who was cracking him open like a tough-shelled egg, one section at a time. As hard as that chipping away was on Nate—who really wants to face their demons?—talking through his problems with the incisive therapist began to put the puzzle pieces of his life together in new and enlightening ways. He was starting to see the bigger picture with more depth and logic, while also recognizing some of the fears that had long held him back. Nate could practically feel a small weight lifting off his shoulders by the end of each meeting, yet was unsure if he could put the new kind of openness he was learning to work outside the pale yellow walls of Mira's peaceful office.

At the end of his fifth therapy session, Nate had a breakthrough of sorts, not that Mira called it that, but the word seemed right. Mira asked if Nate felt that he'd properly mourned the loss of his father. The answer seemed like an easy one—"yes"—but proved anything but as it opened up a kind of emotional trap door. As Nate talked it through, he discovered he hadn't effectively dealt with Jim's passing—not to mention the baggage that came with it—and that he was also in mourning for Eileen and her metaphorical death. He also realized that if she was still alive, he had no great interest in finding her.

"I mean, to what end?" he asked Mira.

"Closure, perhaps—or not." She thought a moment. "But either way you do need to put her aside. Really and truly and entirely. From what you've told me, she's been a force in your life, even if it was beneath the surface. Though I don't think it was."

Nate thought about this as he gazed across the room at Mira's immersive beachscapes. "Okay, but how do I delete someone who was never really there to begin with?"

"In the same way you *add* someone who was never really there to begin with."

Wait, what? He took a guess: "You mean Amy?"

"That's totally up to you. All I'm suggesting is that if you decide that you want Amy in your life in any significant way, then you have to make room for her."

Sometimes Nate wished Mira would just say what she meant instead of making him dig for it, even though he knew—okay, was learning—that this was sort of the point of psychotherapy.

"By completely eliminating Eileen," he stated flatly, finally seeing where this circular conversation was leading.

Mira smiled at her good student. "Yes, Eileen. Who was never actually there to begin with."

And here's what else he came to understand: By doing this "elimination" thing he would now not only be in mourning for his father, but also for the woman he *thought* was his mother. Oh, and, in a way, for his own life, one that would never be the same—so get used to it. It was intense shit (his exact words to Mira), but it had a sort of near-mathematical logic that was starting to make sense to him.

Nate would come home so drained after his sessions with Mira that he'd take Cody for a short walk, drink two beers in quick succession, and then conk out on the office couch, usually with an open book in hand. After the joy of reading *To Kill a Mockingbird*, he'd started to move through other titles from Jim's collection: first Vonnegut's *Slaughterhouse-Five*, which was trippy and fascinating and not always clear; and, no shocker, *The Great Gatsby*, because when Mira learned of his dad's connection to the book, she suggested that reading it again might help Nate's grieving process. He resisted at first—too painful—but gave in to it and was glad he did. He read it through his father's eyes as best he could and maybe understood Jim's passion for the book: Did his father identify, on some level, with the illusive, yet handsome and charming Gatsby?

On the last day of the month, the heatwave broke. While Nate was hosing down his backyard, he noticed how tall and lush the calla lilies he'd planted shortly after Jim's death had become—despite the recent three-digit temperatures. It was as if the growth had happened overnight, which is so often how it seemed with plants and flowers. It gave Nate a rush of optimism, and he had a thought. About Jennifer. Who loved calla lilies.

Nate clipped an even dozen of the gorgeous and stately yellow flowers, wrapped them in a sheet of red and white polka-dot gift paper he unearthed from the back of the office closet, and pointed his Silverado in the direction of Jennifer's West Hollywood guest house. Whether she was there or not wouldn't matter—he knew she often held Saturday afternoon classes so might very well be at work—it was the thought that counted.

Still, as he drove south on the Glendale Freeway, the Killers' "Just Another Girl" coincidentally playing on his Pandora, Nate wondered if he shouldn't let her know he was on the way, just in case. He hadn't done that great "popping in" in the past and, all things considered, this may not be the best moment for a surprise. Nate grabbed his phone and was about to text her when he reconsidered—some might say chickened out—and decided to let the chips fall where they may. His optimism hadn't waned. Maybe that was the actual surprise.

Whether Nate knew what he was doing was up for grabs but, once he arrived at Jennifer's, it was irrelevant—she wasn't there. Or so said her landlady, Ivy, who Nate ran into as he started up the driveway to the guest house.

"You just missed her," said Ivy, her eyes glued on the mega-bouquet in Nate's hand.

Nate hated to admit it, but he was relieved. "Oh. Well, I was just going to drop these off." He lifted the flowers as if they weren't already obscenely visible.

"Those are absolutely gorgeous," she said. "We've tried to grow them here but they never take." Ivy slid her eyes back to assess Nate. "Maybe you could help us do some planting someday. Jen says you're a landscaping genius."

It struck Nate that he'd never really spoken to Ivy, had maybe seen her and her husband, an exceedingly tall man with a shock of steel-gray hair, twice in all the time he'd been visiting Jennifer. He didn't know what a film editor was supposed to look like, but her short, wash-and-wear hair, owlish glasses, and pale complexion—like someone who spent most of her days inside and maybe in the dark—seemed about right. He placed her at around fifty.

"I'd say the word 'genius' is a little overly generous," Nate finally answered, remembering he'd just received a compliment.

"And I'd say you're just being modest." Ivy shot Nate a puckish look. "Jen's also said you're very … I think the word she used was self-effacing."

Jesus, she might as well have said "boring as shit." "What else has she told you?" Nate asked, trying to sound light. It certainly didn't sound self-effacing.

Ivy considered her answer, looked a bit cagey. She smiled and said, "I hope you two work things out." She nodded at the calla lilies and added, "Who wouldn't love those?" Ivy pushed her glasses up the bridge of her narrow nose, raised her hand in a flat wave, and moved off down the driveway.

"By the way, I'd be happy to help with your garden," Nate called after Ivy. "Anytime!" He knew he was trying to compensate for snapping at her, as if it mattered. She was already out of sight. Anyway, did he think if he acted "nice," she'd tell Jen what a prize he was and that they should get back together? Yeah, probably, Nate admitted to himself as he crossed through the backyard—which was lovely as it was and didn't need his help—and stopped at Jen's door. He knocked just because and when there was, of course, no answer, Nate laid the bouquet on her tufted doormat that read "Dance like no one's watching." (Strangely, it had already been there when Jennifer moved in.) He realized he should leave a note with the flowers.

He dashed to his truck, found a pen and a blank scrap of paper, and returned to Jennifer's door. After trying a few greetings in his head he wrote, "From the heart of my garden. Love, Nate," and slipped the note inside the bouquet wrapping. He didn't know what the response, if any, would be, but it seemed like the kind of grand (okay, grand for Nate) gesture that might move the needle in his direction. He also understood if it didn't; he and Jennifer could be done and he just hadn't accepted what he knew to be the truth.

He then thought of Mira, of what she would say, what she would tell him to expect. They hadn't discussed Jennifer at length in their sessions, not yet anyway, but enough for Nate to know that he had lots of work to do on himself—mostly in the areas of trust and openness—to be worthy of her. Jennifer didn't even know he was in therapy (he certainly wasn't going to leave info like that on a voicemail) but would surely be happy to know he was. Still, would it be anywhere near enough?

Man, optimism could be a fleeting thing.

THERE WAS A huge car accident on Fairfax and Santa Monica that blocked the streets in every direction, particularly the ones Nate would need to take him home via the Glendale Freeway. So at Fountain, he hung a sharp U-turn, took Fairfax back up to Hollywood Boulevard, and wound his way to—and through—the Cahuenga Pass. When he reached Barham Boulevard, where he would pick up the 134 Freeway going east, he stopped at a red light and got his bearings. He had a thought and, as if guided by some otherworldly force over which he had no control, Nate found himself driving north on Barham, past the freeway entrance, past the sprawling Warner Bros. Studios, and onto Riverside Drive until he reached Toluca Woods—and Amy's block.

He slowed as he approached her house, no clue what he was doing there or why, but seemingly unable to turn the Silverado around and make haste for the 134. For the second time that hour, Nate wondered how Mira would interpret his actions and realized he'd turned into one of those people who filtered his every move through the eyes of his shrink. He was becoming a cliché—not that he had any intention of stopping therapy.

Nate slowed at the curb a few houses up from Amy's, put the truck in Park but kept the motor idling in case a quick getaway was needed. *You'd think I was here for a robbery, not a visit*, he thought, but knew he was there for neither. This was as close to Amy as he'd gotten since he left her house in a huff twelve days earlier. Mira— yeah, her again—suggested that maybe Nate had been looking for an exit hatch from Amy and the whole graduation photo thing was just his excuse to jump ship. "The mother ship," Nate joked at the time, though Mira didn't smile. Whether she was right about that he didn't know (it kind of sounded like something a therapist might think up in a pinch), but he didn't dismiss it outright, just stored it for future consideration—and the future, sitting there in his truck, was now. He brushed Mira's theory out of his mind and decided to go home. Nothing to see here, nothing to say.

Nate stepped on the gas and zipped past Amy's house—as if he were inconspicuous in his big truck with his name on the side (the company's new name was going on the doors this week)—and caught a glimpse of her exiting her front door. He kept going, checking his side mirror to see if she'd spotted him, but apparently not. Well, she was still living there, he thought, and wondered if she did decide to move back to Fresno if she'd even tell him. That wasn't fair: She'd been trying to get in touch with him and he was resisting, choosing a passive-aggressive move like this impromptu—and frankly pointless—drive-by instead. What had he hoped to accomplish? Did he want to be seen? Was it his way of answering her calls and texts without actually answering? More questions for his next therapy session.

Nate aimed his truck toward the 134 and put an end to this wholly unsatisfying afternoon.

THIRTY-THREE

NATE HAD GIVEN himself a break for the rest of that weekend, something he rarely did—he of the Busy Hands Are Happy Hands club. Even as a kid, he was never one to park himself in front of a TV for hours on end and watch a sporting event or sitcom reruns or some reality show marathon. These days, even a two-hour movie was too long a sit for him, the itch of unproductiveness or downright sloth creeping into his bones at the thirty-minute mark. If he did finish a film, on streaming or cable (forget theaters), it was usually in three or four sittings, which was strange considering he had infinite patience for his work projects, so often filled with the kind of minutiae and painstaking focus that would drive another person bonkers.

He put aside his latest home task—finally restaining those sallow kitchen cabinets—and spent the day sleeping in (which, for Nate, meant till eight o'clock), eating a big, leisurely breakfast of pancakes and eggs and about a gallon of coffee, walking Cody for an hour or so around the blissfully quiet Occidental campus, and then sprawling on his bed, air conditioning cranked high, and reading the entire first half of another of his dad's favorite books, *The Accidental Tourist* by Anne Tyler. A story of a withdrawn guy haunted by tragedy who finds love with a lively dog trainer, the book was one he might have once found too quirky or melancholy but now connected to in stirring and unexpected ways. Around five o'clock, he conked out mid-page for an unprecedented nap (the last time he slept during the day was a decade ago when he had the flu), awoke at six in time to feed Cody, nuked a Trader Joe's frozen lasagna for himself, then crawled back into bed to finish the book before turning in for the night. It was one of the most relaxing days Nate could remember and, even though it felt a little "lonely old mannish," he didn't care. It was a vacation from life.

That isn't to say he wouldn't have liked his sleepy Sunday to be interrupted by a communiqué from Jennifer, who'd kept radio silent since he'd dropped off the flowers and mushy note. Perhaps he should have rethought them both. Nate had to force himself not to check his phone every five minutes in the event of a missed call, text, or email from his maybe-probably-soon-to-be-officially-ex-girlfriend. He finally had to put two rooms' distance between himself and his cell, leaving it in the kitchen while he read in the bedroom. (He also turned off the ringer and all alert sounds for good measure.)

It once again drove home the truth: that Nate had fucked up his relationship with Jennifer and had only himself to blame. Still, he kept picturing the vibrant calla lilies filling her blown-glass vase, a kind of symbol of Nate's love for her—whether she wanted it or not.

Driving to the South Pasadena office park to begin week two of their latest landscaping job (the extensive redo would easily take another two weeks but it was serious cha-ching), Nate slowed at a construction stop on Fair Oaks Avenue and absently stared out the window at a digital time and temperature sign outside a U.S. Bank: *70 degrees … 8:03 a.m. … September 2.* Holy shit—it was his birthday! *Are you fucking kidding me?* he thought, astounded that the date hadn't registered with him all weekend or even when he woke up that morning. It hit Nate like an anvil just how truly in the ozone he'd been—for so long.

"Happy birthday to me," Nate said aloud in glum astonishment.

He was jogged back to reality by an insistent car horn from behind signaling that the lane had reopened. Nate hit the gas and moved off down Fair Oaks. You'd think at least Cody might have said something birthday-ish when he nudged Nate awake at his ritual 6 a.m.

Was it any coincidence that Nate had forgotten his birthday on the first one he'd be celebrating without his dad? (He didn't need Mira to answer that.) Jim had always been the first to wish him a happy birthday. When Nate was growing up, he would rouse him with a birthday cake breakfast and a pile of presents, goodies based on not-so-subtle hints his son would start dropping in the weeks—sometimes months—before the big day. Jim would pretend not to be registering Nate's gift "suggestions" but secretly kept an ongoing list and tried to fulfill the boy's every earnest request. Once Nate had moved out, his father would call him at exactly 7 a.m. to make sure he'd be his son's first birthday greeting, even if Jennifer—or maybe another sleepover guest—had gotten there first (which Nate never let on, lest he deny Jim his proprietary spot).

It was, of course, a year of firsts—first everything without his dad. Nate had muddled through this past Father's Day without him, but Jim had died so soon before it that the emptiness of the holiday barely seemed real. The true challenges would be here before Nate knew it: Jim's birthday in late October and that awful corridor between Thanksgiving and New Year's Day that could test the fortitude of even the happiest, most complete person.

The fact remained that today was Nate's birthday, that he had no plans to celebrate it and no one to celebrate it with. He didn't mean to be a baby about it, but he wasn't exactly feeling great about the day's prospects. He was also wigged out that it took an electronic sign outside a random bank to remind him of something he should have been thinking about the second he woke up. What was that about?

He decided to file it under "shit happens" and bring it up tomorrow night in therapy. It would doubtlessly take up the entire fifty minutes.

"Happy birthday, partner!" Danny shouted as soon as Nate arrived at the job site.

If Nate didn't feel dazed enough, that was just the icing on the, uh, birthday cake. How the hell did Danny remember when Nate didn't?

"Because it's the day after *my* birthday, stupid," Danny informed him with a cockeyed grin that said: yeah, you screwed up. The guy was nothing if not cool.

"Yikes, sorry about that," Nate said sheepishly, and then told Danny how he'd even forgotten his own natal day.

"Okay, that's kinda fucked up," Danny responded, looking more concerned than amused. It made Nate squirm, so he charged off toward the south side of the sprawling, low-rise office building where he and Danny—and steadfast project assistants Butch, Luis, and Edgardo—were about to plant a row of towering olive trees.

Danny sped after Nate and stopped him in his tracks. "I wasn't done!" Danny said. "I've got questions—birthday questions."

Nate wanted to get to work and leave the birthday stuff behind, at least for now. But Danny wouldn't budge. "So, you and Jen gonna go out tonight, get crazy?" he asked, knowing the answer but testing his friend anyway.

"Yeah, I doubt that," Nate answered. "It might help if we were actually talking."

Danny crossed his arms and planted his feet in the grass where they were standing. "I'm listening," he said, making it clear that he wasn't going anywhere—and neither was Nate.

Nate glanced over at the guys, who had begun digging enormous holes for the new trees. They'd be busy for a while and Danny was intractably in Nate's face, so he filled his friend in on all that had—or hadn't—been going on with Jennifer since he'd last broached the subject the night of their celebratory drinks. In truth, there wasn't so much to tell, with the story of the calla lily fiasco closing out the bleak summary. He took full responsibility for Jennifer's need to separate before Danny could blame him for it: He knew Danny thought Jennifer was pretty near perfect and that Nate was a bonehead.

"How much 'time alone' do you think she'll need?" Danny asked. He'd relaxed his stance and backed away a bit, giving Nate some space.

"I don't know—a lifetime?" Nate managed a dark smile.

Danny did something he didn't often do: He considered his answer. "She'll come around," he finally concluded.

"How do you know?"

"I don't." He shrugged endearingly. "Just seemed like the right thing to say."

Nate smiled and clapped Danny on the shoulder. "Let's get busy, yeah?" That day alone, they had to plant those five massive trees, tear out patches of the front lawn to make way for new flower beds, and refill the planter boxes along the building's east flank with eco-friendly succulents.

"Might be a good time to patch things up with your mom," Danny said, as he fell in next to Nate. "Birthdays put everyone in a good mood." Nate hadn't told Danny anything new about the Amy situation but he'd obviously gotten the point.

"Except me," Nate shot back. It was only like, eight thirty, he thought. The day *could* improve. How, he wasn't sure.

"Hey, you can hang out with me and Leesh and the kid tonight. We'll get pizza from that place you like—what's it called, Pomodoro?"

"Palermo."

"Bottom line, bro, you shouldn't be alone on your forty-first birthday."

Nate shot him a dry look. "*Thirty*-first."

"Just checking," Danny said, grinning.

Nate mulled Danny's offer as they approached the glass-encased building. He decided he didn't want to put anyone out—and wasn't sure he'd be the greatest company. "Appreciate the offer, pal, but I'll be okay."

"Your call. We got you, that's all."

And before Nate could thank him, Butch, Luis, and Edgardo, like a practiced musical act, dropped their shovels in unison and launched into a noisy rendition of "Happy Birthday to You." Meantime, Danny, singing along, produced an immense chocolate layer cake as if from thin air (was it hiding behind a tree?), lit a candle, and presented it to Nate to do the honors.

He was stunned, overwhelmed, and so damn moved that he blew out the candle and burst into messy tears. Danny bear-hugged Nate like he was going off to war and let him unload into his broad shoulder. Butch, Luis, and Edgardo didn't know what to do, say, or think—didn't they just sing "*Happy* Birthday?"—so, one by one, they gingerly picked up their shovels and resumed digging. The cake could wait.

Despite the way it looked, Nate's day had just improved.

DANNY INSISTED THEY call it a day an hour early and Nate gave in without a fight, even though they'd barely gotten past the lawn removal. It was, after all, his birthday, and he still had half a cake to finish. (Once Nate's waterworks display was over, they all shared slices of the superb cake and Luis sweetly joked that his singing could make anyone cry. All discussion of Nate's meltdown thankfully ended then and there.)

When Nate arrived home around five, he found a parcel lodged in his mailbox. It was neatly wrapped in brown postal paper with no return address. He brought it inside along with the leftover cake and set them both on the kitchen counter. He goofed around with Cody a minute, grabbed a Blue Moon from the fridge, took a long swig, and then opened the curious package. It contained a wrapped gift and a card with "Nate" written in tight, angled script across the envelope.

He studied the handwriting: It wasn't Jennifer's—hers was wider and loopier—so he figured this had to be from Amy. Which it was. He pulled out a colorful card with a generic but heartfelt birthday greeting inside. It was signed: *I'll be celebrating tonight with or without you. Love, Amy.* Nate stared at her message, remembering how she said that she'd lit a candle on every one of his birthdays. He wondered if she'd done so today. Or was she waiting for him? *I'll be celebrating tonight with or without you.* Was that an invitation? Was she hoping he'd show up at her house and they could mark his birthday together?

As Nate considered her veiled offer, he unwrapped the gift, tearing away its silver-and-gold embossed paper to reveal an enlarged, brass-framed copy of the family photo they'd taken that night in Fresno: Nate, Amy, Robin, Gene, and Diane all in various stages of slapped-on smiles. They looked momentarily happy—and maybe they were—like any other bunch of tossed-together family members with a patchy history. And what clan doesn't have its skeletons? It still shocked Nate to think he had a "clan." An extended family. If he wanted one. Sadly, he still wasn't so sure. And there it was yet again, Amy's claim: *You don't really know what you want.*

I know what I don't *want,* Nate thought. Didn't that count for something?

Nate took the framed picture and his beer to the kitchen table and sat in one of the old wrought iron chairs, his mind spinning. As he swallowed more beer, he returned to the thought of Amy lighting that birthday candle all those years (*was it on a cake?*), in memory of the son she gave away—and maybe trying to make herself feel a little less awful about what she'd done. It couldn't have been easy for her in any way. She'd said as much and Nate was inclined to believe her.

Even though Jim had proven to be an unreliable source of truth, Nate also couldn't help but think that if his dad saw something good and decent in Amy, young as she was at the time, that she must still be a person of character, of quality. All she wanted now was to love her son—better late than never, some might say—and Nate was not allowing that to happen. She was losing out and so was he. Yet something was stopping Nate from spending his birthday with her—or anyone else for that matter—and he decided he needed to honor that feeling, whatever the reason.

He'd bring it up in therapy, he thought, for the umpteenth time that day. He'd better book a double session.

Nate wondered if the family photo wasn't a kind of manipulative gift on Amy's part: *Here, look at what you're missing.* It was hard to say, and maybe best not to ponder.

Nate strode into the office and went for the bookshelf that had long held that old snapshot of Jim and Eileen. He removed the dusty photo (God, he *had* to start cleaning more) and replaced it with the picture of Amy and company. He stood back and gazed at the shelf, at the jarring change in décor and all that it represented: Mira had told him to "eliminate" Eileen and "make room" for Amy, right? Sure, the action seemed a bit on the nose, but Nate felt strangely satisfied, strangely … liberated by it. He could practically feel a new space ticking open in his heart—and another one closing.

He wasn't ready to toss the picture of Jim and Eileen—maybe never would be—so he slipped it into the bottom of a desk drawer, beneath a stack of old papers, where it could quietly live for now. Nate glanced over at the new family photo once again and realized it was next to a copy of Michael Chabon's *The Mysteries of Pittsburgh*, a book Jim had recommended countless times until Nate finally read it and thought it was pretty great. Stirred by the synchronicity of the moment, Nate slid the book off the shelf, fell onto the couch—Cody instantly curling up next to him—and began to reread the old novel. Unlike much else, it was as good as he remembered. As was the rest of the chocolate birthday cake, which he demolished.

It wasn't the worst birthday after all.

THIRTY-FOUR

THE NEXT DAY, Nate, Danny, and their crew worked an extra hour to make up for the time they lost knocking off early in honor of Nate's birthday. They ended up on a roll and not only finished digging, shaping, and planting all those front-facing flower beds (alternating pink and white azaleas were the centerpieces), and replenishing the building's lengthy row of side planter boxes (pencil trees, jade plants, and nandinas made a formidable trio), but began the Japanese-style garden that would grace the complex's outdoor seating area. Nate and Danny would net a tidy profit on this job and they'd share a nice chunk of it with Luis, Butch, and Edgardo—who were now talking about forming their own landscaping business. They were talented guys, tireless workers, and knew their plants inside and out, so Nate figured it was only a matter of time until they joined forces. Anyway, who couldn't use a little healthy competition?

Jennifer had apparently thought Nate would be home around his usual time since she'd been waiting for him in front of his house for nearly an hour. Or so she told Nate, who was nothing short of shocked to see her parked in his driveway when he pulled up that night. His first thought before getting out of the Silverado was that something must be terribly wrong. Why else would she have driven all the way to Eagle Rock during rush hour—or at all, for that matter—considering they were no longer speaking to each other?

They exited their vehicles in unison and met at the edge of the front lawn, like children forced to apologize for naughty behavior.

Jennifer looked up first. "The place looks fantastic," she said, indicating the new paint job and refreshed landscaping. Nate realized she hadn't been to Escarpa since the day of Jim's non-memorial memorial lunch nearly four months earlier, which, just then, seemed like forever ago.

"Thanks. I finally got to do what I'd been pushing my dad to do with it. Too bad he had to die for it to happen, huh?" Nate didn't mean to smile, it wasn't funny, but he was nervous and confused. Jennifer didn't look like anything was wrong. She looked fine. Better than fine, in her V-neck tank top, skinny cropped jeans, and white Keds. But he asked anyway: "Jen, is everything okay?" She didn't move. "I mean, you're not exactly who I expected to be waiting in my driveway."

"Who *were* you expecting?" She raised an eyebrow.

"Well, no one," Nate answered a bit defensively. "That's not the point."

"I know. I'm sorry, forget it." She kicked at the grass with the toe of her sneaker. "I just … wanted to stop by to thank you for the flowers."

The flowers. Oh, *those* flowers. It had been three days already. They seemed kind of beside the point—or maybe beyond it. "You could have just texted," Nate replied without snark. "Saved a trip." Okay, maybe some snark. And maybe he was feeling more hurt than he was letting on.

Cody started barking from inside the house, right behind the front door. It was snappish, insistent, as if to say: *Why are you out there when I'm in here?*

Nate motioned to the house. "I should probably get inside."

Jennifer reached for his arm. "Can we talk?" She let her hand rest on his for a second and then pulled away.

Nate felt grimy compared to Jennifer, who looked daisy-fresh, all glowing skin, the scent of vanilla oil wafting off her neck and shoulders. Cody's barking quickened. Sometimes he could be the world's most patient dog. This was not one of those times. "Uh, sure. Of course," Nate told Jennifer as he took out his house key and started up the front path. "Come on in."

Cody gleefully barreled into him as he opened the door, then lurched over to greet Jennifer as she followed Nate inside. She crouched and rubbed Cody till he rolled over in utter bliss. The dog looked happier to see Jennifer than Nate did, though, to be fair, their relationship was decidedly less complicated. They all landed in the living room as Cody ran figure eights around the humans.

When the pooch calmed down, Nate directed Jennifer to the couch, which was looking a bit worse for wear these days—or maybe he was just seeing the tweedy old thing through her discriminating eyes. She sat in one corner of the sofa, leaving room for Nate, but he opted for the cushiony armchair next to it. As he sat he noticed the welting around the seat pillow was fraying. He needed to think about new furniture. Maybe Max and Carter next door could give him some ideas. Nate leaned back in the chair and focused on Jennifer, who had one leg tucked under the other. She was biting her lower lip.

"Sorry I missed your birthday," she finally said.

"That's okay, it was just … a day."

"Guess it didn't come at the greatest time."

Was she joking? Just in case, Nate volleyed back. "I tried to postpone it, but they wouldn't let me."

They both managed a small smile but there was a curtain of tension floating between them.

Jennifer sat up straight, both feet on the floor. Nate noticed the light grass stains on her sneakers where she'd toed the lawn. "I've thought a lot about us these last few weeks," she told him.

"I have too," Nate said, though he wondered who'd thought more about whom.

She nibbled at her lip. "And I've decided maybe it's time I just accepted the way you are."

Nate studied Jennifer's face but it looked more troubled than reconciled. "I'm really not such a bad guy," he said, forcing a smile. He didn't even convince himself.

"Of course you're not," she replied, leaning forward, her shoulders tilting toward him. "You're a really *good* guy."

Nate lightened, feeling the pendulum swinging into friendlier territory.

"That's what makes this so much harder," Jennifer said, looking at her hands.

Nate reflexively slumped down in his chair. As if on cue—because who can sense pain and sadness quicker than one's dog?—Cody stood in front of Nate, poked at him with his snout, and raised his neck for a cherished rub. *This'll make my guy feel better*, he seemed to say. *And if not,* I'll *feel better!* Nate could read Cody like a book; far better, apparently, than he could ever read Jennifer.

"So, I gather this isn't about getting back together," Nate said as he kneaded Cody's craned neck.

Jennifer finally looked up from her hands, wiped a tear away with one. "Nate, I want to be with someone who really needs me," she said, gently yet decisively. "Someone who lets me in. Lets me know when they're hurting. And lets me help."

Nate popped up from the chair, bailing on Cody mid-scratch, and sat next to Jennifer. He took her hand, still damp from tears. "I can be that guy," he told her, meeting her moist eyes with every ounce of sincerity he possessed.

She held his gaze. "But what if you can't?"

Nate moved in closer, tightening his hand around hers. That she hadn't let go yet gave him resolve. "I'm not a psychic, Jen," he said, flashing on Lena and her murky living room. "I can't predict how anything's going to turn out. All I can do is try."

She pulled her hand away. "Like you've tried with your mother?" Nate looked like someone had shot him with an arrow, though he shouldn't have been surprised. "I spoke to her," Jennifer continued. "She told me what's been going on. What happened up in Fresno. Which, case in point, is more than you did."

"Wait, you called Amy?" *No, that couldn't be right.* "What did you do that for?"

"She called *me.* At the studio. She was worried about you, you idiot."

Jennifer stood, leaving Nate alone on the couch. Cody's snout found Nate again, but his eyes were locked on Jennifer. She was staring out the front window, arms crossed in front of her.

Nate could feel his blood simmer. He didn't want it to; he wanted to stay calm, rational, contrite. Be the man Jennifer wanted him to be. The man *he* wanted to be. But he was up on his feet and in her face before he could stop himself. "Did she tell you that my father paid off her parents so he could 'own' his baby son?" Nate asked. "That was a heartwarming little surprise."

Jennifer watched Nate warily—his jaw was tense, his eyes flaring. "Yes, she told me," she answered evenly. "And honestly? I think you're blowing the whole thing out of proportion."

Nate swallowed, balling his hands into fists. He hated how he felt, how he knew he was going to sound. And yet: "She shut me out for thirty years. I think almost any reaction I'd have is justified."

"Not if you want to have a mother," Jennifer replied with a near-mystical certainty.

Nate's fists tightened, fingernails digging into his palms. He counted to five in his head. "Sorry, it's just not that black and white," he finally said, his voice wavering. "Anyway, this is between Amy and me. I don't expect you to understand."

Now Jennifer looked like the one shot with an arrow. But she quickly recouped, lifted her chin, and threw her shoulders back. "Well, that's where you're wrong," she asserted. "I do understand how you feel about her. What I *don't* understand is why you think I wouldn't."

Nate gazed at her, unable to respond, to form an even remotely satisfactory answer. It was still so complicated to him, as if those past weeks of psychotherapy had never existed. Why could he talk these things out with Mira but still not with the woman he loved?

"I've got to go," Jennifer finally said. "I'm teaching tonight."

"You are?" Nate didn't mean to question her but, as far as he knew, she rarely held classes past eight o'clock. And it was already seven thirty.

"No—I'm actually not," she replied without apology as she headed for the front door. "But I still have to go."

And she was gone before Nate could think of one more stupid, unconvincing thing to say.

"IT PISSED YOU off that she talked to your mother about you, didn't it?"

The light had changed dramatically in Mira's office in the time that Nate had been seeing her. They were transitioning from summer to fall, it was getting darker earlier, and a pair of floor lamps—one in each corner of the room—was now needed to augment the muted brightness that once filtered in through the single window. The framed beachscapes looked softer, the philodendron leaves a tad less perky, and a cocktail would not have seemed entirely out of order—for the time, if not the place.

Although Nate had been talking about his latest tense encounter with Jennifer, all roads kept leading back to Amy—which he found more annoying than enlightening. But Mira insisted on connecting those dots and it made Nate wonder if he'd been missing even more clues than he'd imagined.

"Well, I guess it would've been worse if Jen reached out to my mom than the other way around," Nate realized. "But I still don't like being talked about behind my back."

"Why? What are you afraid of?" Mira's pen was poised over her writing pad. (At first, he was uneasy when she made notes, and now felt weird when she didn't—did he need to bring that up?)

"What am I afraid of?" he repeated, mulling, unsure. He took a stab: "Not being there to defend myself?" He watched Mira's large, shimmery eyes as she considered this. She'd blown out her dark hair; it looked straighter and fuller than usual, and Nate realized he knew absolutely nothing about this woman beyond what he could intuit from within the four walls of her office. Therapy didn't seem like a particularly level playing field.

"Are you asking me or telling me?" she asked. Nate had decided there was little that his therapist didn't already know—like a teacher with all the test answers—but he still felt she was owed a response.

"Somewhere in the middle, I'd say."

"Do you think you *need* defending?"

"No, but I'm pretty sure I'd need … explaining."

She pinned a wayward lock of hair behind her ear. "You know what I think?"

"That's kind of why I'm here." That made Mira smile. Nate so liked it when she seemed amused. He didn't know why, but he still wanted to entertain her.

"I think you need to start doing some of that explaining—to the people who deserve to hear it."

Nate rearranged himself on the couch but couldn't get comfortable. "What if I can't?" he wanted to know. "Can't explain, can't … go there. Wherever 'there' is?" He dropped his head into his hands. "Fuck, I don't even know what I mean anymore."

"Look, just start somewhere. It's better than nowhere."

"That sounds like an old song lyric," Nate said with a sullen stare.

"Okay, how's this: You don't have to have all the answers about your feelings before you begin to share them—as if they'll somehow be used against you."

Nate raised his head, a chord struck. He was reminded again of his father's "women like a little mystery" theory; Mira's words sounded like a distant cousin.

Mira looked squarely, unequivocally, in his eyes, and said, "Nate, I don't often give my patients direct advice, direct orders—but I'm making an exception."

"I'm listening."

"Call your mother."

THIRTY-FIVE

BUT HIS MOTHER got there first.

The next afternoon, while he and Danny and the crew were rounding third base on the office park job—they'd finish ahead of schedule if the client didn't come up with any late-breaking must-haves—Nate's phone rang. He checked the caller ID and saw Amy's name. He wasn't as surprised as he might have been 24 hours ago before Mira gave him his marching orders. Maybe he'd willed his mother to call so he wouldn't have to make the first move.

Nate considered letting the call go to voicemail, maybe returning it when he was driving home from work. That was the old Nate. The new Nate picked it up on the third ring. "Hello?" he asked as he walked into the shade.

"You answered!" Amy sounded startled, as if she'd been prepared to leave a message—one that, perhaps like all the others lately, would go unreturned.

"Yeah, sorry about that," he said.

"Don't be sorry about answering."

What? "No, I meant sorry about *not* answering. Before. It was just …" He had no good, or at least practiced, explanation so let his voice trail off. He glanced across the lawn at Danny, who seemed to be eyeing him with brotherly concern. Nate waved him on: *Don't worry.* Was there a wave for *Okay, maybe worry just a little?*

"Don't hang up," Amy said. "I'm calling as a client, not a mother."

Nate wasn't planning on hanging up. Then again, he hadn't been planning on picking up. He mentioned neither, just waited for her to continue.

"The gardenias you planted? They're dying. In fact, they're probably already dead. Could you please stop by and take a look? If anyone can bring them back to life, I know it's you."

Nate closed his eyes, listening to the hum of traffic on Fair Oaks; Luis and Edgardo's distant, yet lively Spanish patter; the vague office sounds coming from Amy's side of the call. He thought of Mira and of Jennifer and his dear dead dad who probably deserved the brunt of Nate's ire but still lived atop that pedestal. And how old habits are the hardest to break.

"I can stop by after work," Nate told his mother before he could change his mind.

He'd planted the gardenias in a corner of Amy's backyard beneath a stately old pine tree that provided the flowers with an ideal mix of shade and filtered sunlight. But she was right: they were dying, which was crazy since the rest of the yard had flourished in the past few months. Nate kneeled and examined the once-fragrant flowers that were now brownish and crumbly. Why was the universe picking on them?

"Of everything you planted, I think they were my favorite," said Amy sadly as she stood over Nate. "And, oh my God, the smell. Like the richest perfume." She was still dressed for work and looked quite beautiful, Nate thought. "I tried to water them, trim them, even talk to them," she told him. "But they look worse than ever."

"Gardenias can be kind of temperamental," Nate explained as he snapped dead leaves off the plant. "They don't like too much attention. Sometimes, if you just leave them alone, they come back on their own." He gazed at the rueful gardenias, then at Amy. As pretty as she looked just then, she also looked fragile.

"So, there's nothing you can do?" she asked.

Sure, he could dig them out and plant all new ones. Try again; clean slate. But, when it came to nature, Nate was a bitter-end kinda guy. It wasn't over till it was over. And damn if he hadn't spotted a few new sprouts amid the moribund gardenia stems.

"Give it some time," Nate offered. "You may be surprised at how they respond."

He was surprised by how *he* was responding; how much more composed he was feeling with Amy than he'd expected. Driving over he didn't know what to expect or even think. All he knew was that he was being propelled down the freeway by duty to a client— or maybe his therapist—more than by any pressing need to reunite with his mother. Or so he told himself.

"I can do that," Amy answered. He could see the worry lines across her forehead lighten, her eyes brighten. Was it all because of her beloved gardenias? "Thank you, Nate."

She smiled softly then moved a few steps toward the house. "While you're here, could you come inside? I have something for you."

Nate hesitated. There was something a bit sideways about the request: come for the gardenias, stay for the actual point of the visit. Which was what? The phrase bait-and-switch came to mind but it seemed unfair. After all, those flowers *were* pretty dead …

Amy saw his uncertain look, his fixed stance. "Come on. It'll only take a minute," she assured him. Had she added, "I gave birth to you, for God's sake, would you give me a fucking inch here?" it wouldn't have been out of line.

Nate followed her through the back door and into the kitchen.

"Can I get you something to drink? A beer, maybe?" Amy grabbed the refrigerator door handle, hoping for a yes. Nate nodded, figured it'd help keep him mellow, and she handed him an invitingly cold Corona. Amy pointed to the dining table. "Have a seat, I'll be right back."

Nate leaned against a counter instead and took a long, satisfying swig of beer. As he held the bottle aloft, he realized his fingernails, despite the post-work scrubbing he'd given them, were still a bit dirty. Hazard of the profession. He scanned the kitchen; it seemed fuller since he'd last seen it: more small appliances and knickknacks; a few fliers stuck to the fridge door; a large ceramic bowl filled with ripening melons, avocados, and bananas; a small framed watercolor of a lighthouse hanging to the right of the sink. It looked more lived-in now, not like the kitchen of someone passing through.

Amy swept back in holding a beautifully wrapped gift box, maybe six inches all around. She handed it to a wary Nate. "Happy belated birthday," she announced. She was trying—hard—and he needed to lean into that.

He took the package, studying the intricate bow atop it. "Uh, thank you but this was completely not necessary." Anyway, wasn't that framed family photo his gift?

"No, it wasn't, but … well, open it." She hugged her arms against her chest and watched him in anticipation.

It was a wristwatch. A good one. A Seiko, the kind with the cobalt blue face and stainless-steel band. It wasn't Nate's style exactly. He had a soft spot for his old Swiss Army watch; it was simple and indestructible and had served him well. But he liked the look of this one and had mentioned it on occasion to Jennifer. Not as a gift hint and not as something he would buy for himself (God forbid!), just as an observation. One that had evidently been passed on to Amy.

"Jennifer said you've been wanting one like this," Amy said, reconfirming his suspicions. "And I hope you weren't angry that we spoke to each other," she added carefully. "A few times."

Oh, now it was a few times. When did that happen? Why did that happen? He took a breath, kept calm, and remembered that Mira told him to explain himself. "I was angry," he admitted. "I guess I felt outnumbered, not in control of my own narrative."

They both looked surprised at that choice of word: narrative. But it was perfect. As if he were channeling Jim. Maybe he was.

"You're entitled to feel however you like," Amy said. "Just don't shut us out because of it." *Us.* Okay, what else had she and Jennifer yakked about? Before the conversation could dart anywhere troublesome, Amy waved him to the table. "Come on, sit. Try it on." She nodded at the watch shining up from the gift box like a beacon.

Nate knew he couldn't—wouldn't—keep the watch but took a seat and tried it on anyway. The woman had just bought him a five-hundred-dollar gift; he owed her the effort, the consideration. He snapped the metal band shut and straightened the slightly chunky timepiece over the veins of his left wrist. His forearms had become ropy as Jim's had been; like much else, he hadn't really noticed. The watch rested heavily against his skin, the blue face gleaming beneath its glass dome. It fit Nate perfectly, like it had been assembled just for him. It was, in a word, gorgeous.

Nate told her so—and then told her that he couldn't accept it. He watched her face fall.

"Why not?" Amy asked almost inaudibly.

"It's too much. I … I just can't take it." He should have removed the watch then and there and returned it. But he held back. Amy's hurt was simply too palpable. She needed a moment to breathe. They both did.

She spoke first. "What is it? Do you think I'm trying to bribe you? Hoping you'll say, 'Buy the house, stay in L.A., be my parent'?"

"I don't think you're trying to bribe me," he answered, even though at some level he knew he did. He still didn't move to take off the watch. He loved the way it felt against his wrist, so cool and solid. He was a terrible person.

Amy fiddled with the bowl of produce on the counter, moving the pieces around like it was a puzzle made of fruit. She turned back to him; her expression hardened. "Nate, look, I've done the best I can here. Nothing can ever make up for spending your whole life without a mother and for being lied to. Not one watch—not a hundred watches. But that's in the past. I'm offering you a future. But if you're too angry or resentful or stubborn to accept it, then just say so and I'll quit. And you know I can." She spun back around to face the fruit bowl. An antique shelf clock in the next room ticked loudly.

Nate was shocked by Amy's diatribe, by the stiff set of her jaw, her drained expression. Wasn't he the one who was supposed to be doing the explaining? But it turned out, she wasn't done. She crossed back to the table, sat next to him again, looked him in the eye.

"And I'll tell you something else," Amy began, her voice as clear as a bell. "The sooner you learn to accept love, the sooner you'll be able to grow up. You don't want to accept it from me? Fine. But don't let a woman like Jennifer get away over something *I* did." She punctuated her speech by grabbing Nate's beer and taking a long swallow. She set the bottle back on the table with a thunk. It didn't seem like an Amy move but she *was* in rare form.

He gazed at the beveled glass tabletop, letting her words course through him. "I appreciate that, I do," he finally said. She was right, of course. He and Mira had circled related territory a few sessions ago: his worry that "accepting love" also means accepting its potential loss. "And I *wish* I could just say, 'Sure, buy the house, I'm in! Bring on the rest of our lives!' But I can't. Because, yeah, maybe I *am* angry and resentful and whatever—and getting in my own way. But honestly? It's all so fucking difficult." It was the best answer he had just then and, in its own weird way, it felt good to let it out. To let her in again. Even just a crack. Even if it wasn't exactly what she wanted to hear.

Or maybe it was. She sat back in the chair, assessing her son. "Well, that sounds like some kind of a … I don't know … start, maybe?"

Nate didn't know, couldn't say, had said enough for now. He unsnapped the watch band, removed the Seiko from his wrist, and set it on the table. "I love it, I really do. It was a beautiful thought."

Amy sighed; she had seemingly lost what little momentum she'd just gained. "You're worthy, Nate. Worthy of so much. You could *have* so much. That's all I want for you."

"And what do you want for you?" His tone may have been challenging but the question was sincere. He didn't know enough about her, maybe purposely so—and that was his fault.

Amy picked up the watch as if searching for the answer in its cobalt dial. She looked up at Nate. "I want to feel better about the life I've lived. Is that so much to ask?"

Nate shook his head, wistful. "No, it's not. Not at all." They sat that way for a moment until Nate rose. "Keep an eye on those gardenias, okay? Let me know how they're doing."

Amy stood. "And you're sure there's nothing I can do? To help them along?"

"No, but I have a feeling they may surprise you."

Amy walked him to the front door. As he went for the doorknob, Amy grabbed his arm, gripping it tightly. She looked nervous. Nate could feel his pulse quicken. *What now?*

"Okay, there is … one other thing, though," she said. Nate kept silent, so she took a breath and continued. "My law firm has offered me a full-time job. My boss said I've become 'a real asset,' quote-unquote. Which was lovely." She realized she was still holding onto Nate's arm and gently let go of it.

Nate relaxed. "Wow, that's great. Good for you, Amy." But her cautious stance said otherwise. "I mean, it is great, isn't it?"

"Oh, absolutely. Better salary, health plan, the works." Amy locked eyes with her son and added, "But, of course, only if I stay in L.A."

And there it was, Nate thought, the *real* reason she'd summoned him there. What a loaded visit it had become. He flashed on Amy's more lived-in kitchen, which struck him now as a case of accumulation more than commitment. That was likely because she hadn't wanted to push Nate on the issue any more than she already had—and he certainly hadn't done much to help it along. But the rubber was finally meeting the road. And Nate knew he was at the wheel.

"And that all depends on me?" he asked in confirmation.

"In a way, yes."

He chose his next words carefully. They had been through so much—together and apart—in the relatively short time she'd lived nearby that Nate couldn't deny the empathy he felt for her, for what she'd been attempting, all because of him. But he couldn't be responsible for her life any more than she was responsible for his.

And, as much as he might want to, he still couldn't break down that wall of resistance, lest it crush him in the process.

"I can't make that decision for you," Nate said quietly. He turned and opened the front door. It felt like a punctuation to his statement, but it was simple distraction; he didn't want to watch her reaction.

"No, I suppose you can't," Amy answered.

Nate said goodbye, holding back the hug he might have offered if not for that last exchange, and was out the door before he could change his mind and grab the Seiko.

THIRTY-SIX

WHEN NATE WAS a little boy, he used to ask Jim how he knew how to be a father. "I went to daddy school," Jim would answer as if it was the most obvious thing on earth. As if some people taught literature, like he did, while others taught the fine points of parenting. Nate would picture a classroom with a bunch of men who looked vaguely like Jim being lectured by someone maybe older and wiser about how to tuck your child in at night (and which bedtime stories to read them), how to make grilled cheese sandwiches and SpaghettiOs, or how to act like two parents when there's only one.

"Is there a mommy school, too?" Nate would ask, equitable child that he was.

"Oh, sure. They're everywhere," Jim would reply, doubling down on the baloney he was throwing. "I'll point one out next time we pass it."

Nate would sometimes wade into the "daddy school" weeds: "Do you get a rest period? Are there report cards? Did you like your teacher?"

Jim would muss Nate's hair, tell him he was asking too many questions, and change the subject before he dug too deep a hole for himself. Nate eventually lost interest and found all new things to bug his father about.

Still, as lively and creative and loosey-goosey as Jim could be, he was pretty much a straight shooter. Ask him a question, he'd give you the answer, whether it was appropriate or not. At the very least, his responses were usually true—or as true as he knew them to be. There was whimsy, yes; candy-coating, not so much. Which was why, when Nate got older, he thought to ask his father where that whole "daddy school" business came from; it was kind of unlike the man he came to know.

"Back then, I was scared shitless half the time. I didn't want you to be too," Jim admitted as they were driving to Dodger Stadium to watch the home team clobber the Cardinals. "I figured if you thought I actually studied what to do, wasn't just winging it, you'd feel more secure—even if *I* didn't."

Jim turned down Foreigner's "Long, Long Way From Home," which was playing on KLOS. "For the record, kiddo, I never lied about anything else to you. And I never will."

Nate, who'd just turned thirteen, didn't think much of that comment at the time. He was still too young to know that if you never lied about anything there was no reason to say that you didn't. Much less promise not to ever do so again. He'd also never heard the term "projection," at least the psychological use of it. Nate was just so happy to be going with his dad to a Dodgers game—Jim was about as interested in baseball as Nate was in Victorian literature—that he wasn't about to ponder anything deeper than how many Dodger Dogs he could persuade his father to spring for.

It was extra strange because, as a kid, Nate always felt totally, if subconsciously, protected by Jim, despite—or maybe because of—his dad's largely carefree demeanor. Who would have guessed that, for a time, Jim had been "scared shitless?" It may have been an irrational worry, but Jim loved Nate so much—so much more than he ever thought he could love another person—that the enormity of being responsible for someone else's entire existence was, in those early days anyway, too overwhelming to bear. Nate learned that last part one night maybe a dozen years later when Jim got sloppily confessional after a few too many cocktails.

This all came bubbling up during Nate's next therapy session. It was a few days after his last encounter with Amy, the events of which—save his stubborn refusal to decide her future and, in turn, his own—Nate replayed in detail for Mira, down to the shade of blue of the Seiko watch. Despite his rejection of Amy's generous gift, Mira said his time with his mother seemed "peppered with progress."

That made some sense if, like Mira, you didn't have all the facts. Nate was about to rectify that, thought he'd roused the energy to explore his complex feelings about Amy's job offer—and its greater implications. But at the last split-second, he defaulted to a joke instead.

"As opposed to what?" Nate smirked. "'Salted with setbacks'?" They'd become comfortable enough with each other to give or take the occasional jab. For Nate, it took some of the naval-gazing gravity out of the sessions, which, he knew, was part of why he was able to keep returning. The other part was how he'd come to depend on them, to his continued surprise.

Mira looked amused by his alliteration, then quickly sobered. "Still, what that 'progress' means for your future remains unknowable," she said with sphinxlike authority. It was as if she knew he'd left out a key piece about his last meeting with Amy.

Like the crystal clarity that Nate had learned could near-magically appear in a therapy session, he came to a sudden conclusion. "I don't want it to be," Nate replied. "I want to know what's going to happen with Amy because, right now, this kind of ... parental purgatory? It's not working for me. Or anyone else for that matter."

"Is that your way of saying 'I should have taken the watch'?" Mira eyeballed Nate, then scribbled a few notes, her first all session.

Nate glanced at his Swiss Army watch, noticing how scratched the crystal had become. "I just couldn't bring myself," he said. "It would have been like saying, 'That's okay, no worries. Thirty years of what might have been has been gladly erased with the snap of one stainless steel watchband!'"

"Even though she assured you that wasn't the point of the gift?"

Nate was quiet. He knew he was being as stubborn and resentful as Amy suggested. Didn't he just say he wanted out of parental purgatory?

To that end, he finally revealed what he'd left out earlier about Amy. He felt sheepish and said as much, but Mira seemed nonplussed. Clearly, her patients held back shit all the time.

Mira rearranged herself in her chair. If she'd worn glasses, this is when she would have taken them off, maybe rubbed the bridge of her nose. She scratched the side of her head with her pen cap instead. "Let's switch gears for a minute."

Nate adjusted himself on the couch in anticipation. He saw that the split-leaf philodendron was looking more alert. Had he told her last time to water it more? If he didn't, he should have.

Mira raised her head a bit as if addressing the air. "Do you want children of your own, Nate?"

"Wow, that's a pretty big question for this late in the session, isn't it?"

Mira didn't answer, awaiting his reply. Nate reconfigured his body on the cushions again. The query caught him by surprise. He shrugged. "In theory, sure."

Mira narrowed her gaze. "What does that mean?"

"It means … not now but maybe at some point."

"I see. So, the answer is no." Nate was about to jump in but she put a hand up. "Which is fine, really. I wish more people would say no to that question. It would show they were being honest. Most of my patients shoot me an automatic yes."

Nate had no idea what she was talking about, just that he apparently answered correctly. But had he? "Where's this going?" he finally asked with just a few minutes left to their session.

Mira put her pad aside, scooched to the edge of her chair, and folded her hands atop her skirted knees. "It's curious, that's all." Nate stared at her. "Usually when people are very close to at least one parent, they want to repeat that experience with their own children."

"I didn't say I didn't want kids. I'm sure that I do."

"Doesn't sound so sure. Not that it matters, men change their mind on the subject a lot more than women."

"It might be nice to have someone to actually *have* this imaginary child with before thinking more about it, wouldn't you say?"

Nate didn't mean to sound pissy but there was a needling to Mira's tone that made him defensive. He could feel a thin layer of sweat erupt across his forehead. He glanced at the sleek digital clock perched on Mira's desk: it was ten to the hour. She usually started wrapping up by now, yet she looked like she was hunkering down for the night. Mira caught his drift.

"It's okay, Nate, my seven o'clock canceled, so you're my last one. Let's follow this thread a little longer." She paused. "Is that alright?"

He was starving and eager to get home to Cody, who asked no questions, couldn't care less about Nate's stupid issues, and just wanted to snuggle and get his belly rubbed. *Why can't human life be that simple?* Nate leaned back against the soft sofa pillow.

"Did you and Jennifer ever talk about having a family?"

"Together?" Nate wasn't going for a laugh but Mira rolled her eyes and shot him a sideways smile. It relaxed him. He thought back on his happiest days with Jennifer when they were coasting on a romantic cloud and it sometimes felt like they were the only two people on the planet who'd found love. "We did," Nate admitted. "Even came up with names." He flashed back for a second, trying to recall what they'd zeroed in on. "Two boys and a girl: Spencer, Connor, and Zelda."

"Zelda?"

"It was actually my dad's idea, but Jen kinda dug it."

Mira took a stab. "For Zelda Fitzgerald?"

"The fun part, not the schizophrenic part." Thinking back, Nate hoped Jim had just been joking about the name; it seemed like a loaded choice.

Remembering his and Jennifer's children chat evoked a similar talk they'd had about where they would live if they ever, well, got to the point of having those kiddos. Nate voted to move out of the city, somewhere more bucolic where they could have acreage, a giant garden, and lots of dogs; Jennifer fantasized about moving to Manhattan and opening her own dance academy for Broadway hopefuls. Both were pipe dreams, of course, and complete opposites. Yet neither of them had said no to the other's wishes; it had been more about being together. Mira retrieved her pad and pen, and made what seemed like a string of notes. She looked intent. Nate gazed across as if he could read what she was writing. Did he really even want to?

"What do you do with all those notes?"

She finally looked up from her pad and smiled at Nate. "Wouldn't *you* like to know?" Her eyebrows almost comedically rose and fell. Nate shrugged because he didn't know what he wanted, except to go home. But it still wasn't in the cards.

Mira sat back, turning serious again. "I imagine you're wondering why I'm asking you about children."

Nate didn't have to wonder: most everyone and everything Mira brought up led back to Amy. You could practically see it happening, like one of those real-time virtual maps that tracked your Lyft driver. All that was missing was a countdown clock that showed the minutes it would take for Mira to reach her destination.

And he was right. It was pretty masterful how Mira worked her way—in record time, given the lateness of the hour—from Jennifer and Nate's would-be brood to whether he feared that fully accepting Amy as a mother might, over time, erase Jim's place as Nate's favored parent—and maybe diminish his father's memory altogether. In between, they touched upon whether Nate thought he'd make a good dad, if he felt he could be a good son to Amy, and, in turn, if Amy would be a good mother to him—good enough to change his life to find out.

NATE HAD BEEN given so much food for thought that he literally felt full and, despite his hunger pangs sitting with Mira, didn't feel like a meal when he got home. Instead, he gulped down a beer, snapped a leash on Cody, and walked him over to Occidental.

The fall session had recently started and the campus was abuzz as students crisscrossed in pairs and trios warmly lit by the tall, Victorian-style lampposts that lined the walkways. Cody stopped and lifted his leg on one of these lights, then gave an excited "look at me" bark. Not that too many passersby noticed; they were too wrapped up in their own joyful energy, the kind that came with the promise of starting afresh. They'd lose it by the end of the term—most college kids did, Jim used to say—but there was nothing like a clean slate to make you look and feel ready to take on the immediate world.

Moving through the campus that night, Nate didn't feel his usual nostalgia for his own academic past. He was enjoying the infectious enthusiasm of the younger folks around him, yet had no desire to be one of them. Maybe he was still preoccupied with the torrent of topics that emerged from his therapy session like worms from a newly dug hole. Or maybe it was because he knew he had to keep moving forward and stop looking back, a default which, to say the least, had not been serving him well these last months. Still, something about living in the moment felt good and right just then: a small sign of progress—or maybe a stab at his own clean slate.

Nate had stopped in front of the Mary Norton Clapp Library (the name still killed him) to let a couple of effusive dog lovers make a fuss over Cody when his phone rang. He saw that it was Danny, so he excused himself and moved off to answer the call.

"Cronin/Soto Landscape Design," Nate said in a mock official tone. "You got the cash, we got the flash."

Danny ignored the joke, nearly bursting through the phone. "Yo, Cronin, ready to be an uncle again?"

"What?" Nate stopped so abruptly that Cody banged into his shin. "Wait—*you*?"

"Well, me *and* Leesh—and the Raff-ster. Yep, we found out tonight. It's official, dude!" Danny sounded positively giddy. Before Nate could respond, Danny crowed, "Wait, I'm putting you on speaker. Congratulate your accountant."

"Hey, Nate," Alicia called coyly through the phone. "Big news, huh?"

"Huge! Wow, congrats, you two. This is awesome!" Nate was surprised to feel a lump forming in his throat. He gave a quick cough. "Does Raffi know yet?"

Alicia let loose a deep, joyous chuckle. "Yeah, he asked if we could get a puppy instead. Not sure it totally sunk in. But it will!"

"Not sure it's totally sunk in with me either!" Danny joked.

"It better sink in, mister!" his wife told him with a sweet jab to her voice. Despite their occasional speed bumps, Danny couldn't have picked a better mate than Alicia. She was the tether to his balloon—and, in turn, he gave her flight. The lump in Nate's craw grew just thinking about that.

"Hey, so what's the wish? Girl, or another boy?" Nate asked extra brightly.

"Girl!" Danny and Alicia yelled in unison. Nate guessed Raffi was enough boy for now.

"And if it *is* a girl," Alicia said, "we'd like to name her Natalie."

"Nice!" Nate said, though he completely missed the connection. Danny could tell. "After *you*, dumbass!"

Nate was speechless. He watched as Cody blithely sniffed around a dewy stretch of grass. A skinny guy with earbuds and an orange Oxy cap whipped past on a skateboard. It seemed like an unlikely sight just then, but maybe thirty-one-year-old Nate and his oversized dog were the odd ones.

Nate snapped to. "Wow, I'm incredibly honored. And completely blown away." *And undeserving*, he wanted to add.

"Yeah, don't get all sappy on us, pal. We liked the name, that's all."

"Don't listen to him, Nate," Alicia piped in. "If you didn't make Danny a partner, we couldn't have afforded to do this. Not now, anyway." She paused, maybe for her own tightening throat, and added, "This is 'thank you.'"

It was a good thing Danny and Alicia hopped off the phone as quickly as they did—clearly to call another dozen people before it got too late—because Nate was ready to lose it right there in front of the old Mary Got-the-Clapp Library (that's what he used to call it once he was old enough to know what it meant). He fell onto a bench beneath a lamppost and let the tears flow as Cody quietly curled up on the grass beside him. Nate was glad it was dark—dark enough, anyway—and that no chipper students were looming in either direction. He wanted to be alone but needed to chill out a minute before he and Cody made their way back home.

Nate was happy for Danny and Alicia, of course. And it wasn't as if he wanted what they had … exactly. He always felt there was something a bit prescribed about their life together, that they'd moved ahead with marriage and a family too early for Nate's taste, much less timetable. Yet, as a result, unlike Nate, they had a solid, stable, seemingly long-haul relationship, not to mention a great kid and another on the way. Meanwhile, Nate felt light years away from any of that, the remarkable circumstances of this past year suddenly feeling like more of an excuse than a reason for, as Mira would have it, his inexorably linked romantic and familial struggle.

Nate was aware that you can't have it both ways: freedom and solitude, yet also the warmth and constancy and devotion of one person who is there just for you—and you for them. He'd loved having girlfriends, even if none, except for Jennifer, ever really lasted that long. At the time, each relationship had seemed long enough. They would run their course and Nate didn't remember much consternation on either side, likely because what they had didn't matter enough. It was fun—until it wasn't.

Only with Jennifer did they both care enough about the other to cause pain, or rather for the pain to be the result of their uncertainty. Make that Nate's uncertainty, which only became an issue once faced with a more permanent arrangement. Strangely, it was Jennifer who seemed the uncertain one now, or at least the one unwilling to give in to something less than what she needed, expected, or was worth. He missed her—so much—but they seemed to be at an impasse and Nate wasn't sure if there was any way left for them that was strictly and irreversibly forward.

Still, that Nate should learn that Danny and Alicia were having a second child less than, what, two hours after the subject of kids came up in therapy felt like some kind of message from the universe. It was one without a conclusive answer or direction but maybe a purpose. And if that purpose was for Nate to end up sitting on a college campus bench in the near-dark quietly sobbing as the world spun happily around him, well, it was probably worth listening to.

He dried his eyes, then cocked an ear and tried to hear what the cool night air, the fragrant eucalyptus trees, and the splatter of stars above were trying to tell him. And if he listened very, very, *very* closely, he could make out a small, faint voice telling him, in the most loving tone imaginable, that he had all the power he needed to change the world—or at least the world he'd so tentatively inhabited for far too long. He just needed to trust, to believe, and to forgive. It was the only way.

Cody sat up, gazed at Nate, and let loose a toothy yawn. It was time to go home.

THIRTY-SEVEN

NATE EXPECTED HE'D fall right into bed and pass out after his long and emotional day; he'd earned a dead man's sleep. But sitting on the office couch, polishing off an old bag of pretzels, and watching one of the interchangeable home-makeover shows on HGTV—its only distinguishing feature: it wasn't the one with the twin brothers—he found himself not only still awake but wired. It felt like he'd had a major jolt of caffeine, which he hadn't. Not since breakfast, in fact. Reading usually helped put him to sleep, though he hadn't plucked anything out of Jim's book collection since *The Great Gatsby*. It would mean starting something new, which struck him as too heavy a lift at ten minutes to midnight.

Nonetheless, he scanned the bookshelves on the off chance he'd spot something worth diving into. Just when Nate was thinking he should stop mining Jim's old books and read something written in, say, the last decade, he spied a slim paperback flanked by copies of Thomas Mann's *Death in Venice* and Virginia Woolf's *Mrs. Dallo-way* (Nate yawned just reading those titles). The volume in between was called *The Book of Given Names* and, with its deeply cracked burgundy spine, faded pages, and retro cover art (two lily white infants: a boy in baby blue and a girl in pale pink), looked like a relic from another era. Which it was, as evidenced by the 1962 copyright Nate found a few pages in. He also saw his late grandma's name, Helene Cronin, written in neat script on the inside cover. It was obviously Jim's mom's book, which his father had somehow ended up with.

Intrigued, Nate brought it back to the couch and began thumbing through. It was divided into two parts: common boys' and girls' names of the time and their meanings. Like any good narcissist, Nate immediately went to search for his own name. It was listed after "Nathan" and before "Neal" and read: *Nathaniel: Gift of God.* Just like Amy had said. Not for nothing, there was a little red "X" marked next to it. Had Jim put it there? It made Nate wonder if his father ever thought to change his birth name once Amy, who said she'd chosen it, was out of the picture. Or perhaps Jim actually liked the name and it kept him linked to Amy.

Like so much else, Nate would never know.

He turned to the girls' names and found, near the start of the list, Amy. It meant "beloved." Nate sighed. *You can't make this shit up,* he thought. He flipped through to the N's, found the name of his potential soon-to-be namesake (the idea of which still astounded him): Natalie. It was French for "Born on Christmas Day." Made sense as he considered it, given the word "nativity" and all.

Nate realized he never asked Danny and Alicia if they'd name a boy after him as well. He could already hear Danny's answer: "Nope, only if it's a girl. But you could go have your own son, dude. Name him anything you want!" Then he'd wink and flash that secret-weapon smile of his. Nate would roll his eyes but also feel shitty about being conflicted about the prospect of fatherhood—among other things.

He went back to the A's and hovered over Amy's name. He thought about their trip to Fresno, how much she seemed to genuinely love her new garden, the beautiful watch she bought him. He thought about how truly horrible it must have been to have to give up a child and agree to never see him again. And how utterly astonishing it had to have been—how astonishing it still was—to reunite with that same child a lifetime later. It was a one-in-a-million story and it could no longer be denied.

But another story needed finishing first.

Nate, Danny, and company put the final touches on the office park that Friday, and, at the end of the day, the building manager gave the all-clear. "You fellas did one hell of a job," he told them, and the "fellas" couldn't disagree: the place looked like a million bucks. Danny took about a hundred photos of their gorgeous work, including a dozen or so selfies of himself, Nate, and the guys, before they left for a celebratory tailgate party at Danny's house. Alicia was less than thrilled with the rambunctious revelry unfolding in her driveway. But Nate could tell she was glad to see her Danny so happy—the kind of happiness that comes from accomplishment.

"He's so proud of your partnership," she whispered to Nate on the sly, after she'd stomped outside to rail about the music blaring from Danny's phone. She and Raffi ended up hanging with the group and even dancing with Danny, against her faux protests. Although Alicia always played the responsible one, Nate knew she enjoyed cutting loose with the best of them. He stood back and took in the Soto family's infectious joy. It only reinforced the decision—decisions, actually—that he had made over the last few days.

He was proud to say that he didn't ask for Mira's approval or permission; didn't want any further input, which felt like a big step after all that therapy. Still, he knew he wouldn't have gotten there when he did—maybe wouldn't have gotten there at all—without her. And, whether everything worked out or not, he'd be forever indebted to his savvy and deeply insightful shrink. He'd also be keeping their forthcoming session Tuesday night.

THERE ARE TIMES in Los Angeles when the weather couldn't be any more perfect. When the sky is like a clear sheet of blue topaz, the sun is bright and uplifting, and a gentle, stirring breeze envelops you like the world's gauziest cotton candy. It was something of an autumn phenomenon and it made Angelinos want to live forever. Like anything was possible. For a little while, anyway.

Such was the case that morning as Nate—Cody riding shotgun, the Killers on Pandora—drove into West Hollywood to ask Jennifer to be his wife. He knew she'd be at work; she had a standing 10 a.m. class on Saturdays, which he reconfirmed on the dance studio's new website. And for some reason, Nate wanted to do this at a time when she would least expect it. Or maybe he just didn't want to wait any longer lest he change his mind and fuck everything up again. He also felt it would be good to have other people in the vicinity. (An audience? Strength in numbers?) He wasn't entirely sure of anything; he rarely was (except for his work; that he could swear by). But he did know this: He had one more chance to make things right with Jennifer and, if he couldn't, they would have to call it a day— or, more specifically, two years and five months.

He hadn't talked or even texted with her since their spat about her secretive call to Amy. He had considered reaching out, but there was nothing more to say; his only recourse was full redress and dramatic, unequivocal action. Was it ever too late to become a knight in shining armor? Damn if he wasn't going to try and find out.

Melrose Avenue was crazy busy that morning and Nate had to park a few blocks away from the dance studio on a residential side street. That meant Cody had to come with—he couldn't just wait parked in front of the studio where Nate could keep an eye on him. Maybe that was a good thing. Jennifer could almost never say no to Cody.

Nate made sure the ring he was going to present to her was secured in its case and tucked safely inside his jacket pocket. He jumped out of the Silverado, opened the passenger door for Cody, who leaped out as well, and they made their way up to Melrose and then two blocks down to the dance studio. Nate felt nervous and cautious—but also hopeful and determined. He couldn't even begin to guess how this was going to turn out, but that was okay. If he'd learned anything these last months it was that life was messy and unpredictable. It was filled with risk and uncertainty but hopefully reward. He just had to get out of his own way.

The ring. Nate didn't know a lot—make that anything—about engagement rings, most importantly how to buy one. But, after work Thursday night, armed with two hours' worth of internet research, he stopped at a jewelry store in bustling Old Town Pasadena and made a life-changing purchase. Fortunately, his salesperson, a 50ish blonde with bee-stung (or maybe Botox-stung) lips named Esme, deftly guided Nate to the perfect, one-carat diamond solitaire. Once he gave her his budget—modest but not impossible—and she brought out three options, each lovelier than the next, he chose a pear-shaped stone flanked by two tiny baguettes set on a simple, white gold band.

Esme lauded his choice and exclaimed, as if it were 1965, "No woman in the world could possibly say no to this ring!" Still, Nate made sure it was returnable because he was offering it to a woman who could very possibly say no, though he didn't explain that to Esme. He didn't have to. She sized up Nate and his situation with a single, knowing glance and assured him that he had seven days to bring it back for a full refund.

"You won't though," she said, channeling the psychic Lena. "I have a sixth sense about these things."

Nate handed over his Visa card and walked out with his potential future nestled in a tiny, black velvet box.

When they reached the dance studio, Nate hesitated outside the entrance. He wasn't having qualms about proposing but about just showing up cold like that. Would it seem presumptuous? Yes, absolutely, but he knew that driving over. Would it turn Jennifer off from even considering his offer? If it did, he reasoned, she wasn't going to accept anyway, so what was there to lose? Boosted by that sliver of logic, Nate entered Jennifer's workplace just as her class was breaking up. He panicked, wondering if he should have brought flowers for her as well, then remembered that didn't exactly knock her socks off the last time. Calmed, he and Cody entered the studio—*Shit, were dogs even allowed inside?*—causing an instant hubbub among the dozen or so exiting students because, well, a jumbo, tail-thwacking, tongue-lolling doggo was blocking the doorway.

Nate pulled Cody aside to let the young dancers pass, but each one stopped to pet, fuss over, or otherwise admire the four-legged visitor. A shocked Jennifer appeared behind the group and, out of her students' eyeline, shot Nate a wide-eyed glare, throwing her hands apart in a gesture that read *What the fuck?* He didn't expect a 21-gun salute but … well, he admittedly didn't know what to expect.

She forced cool for appearance's sake and then, as soon as the last student disappeared, brusquely asked, "Nate, what are you doing here? The both of you."

He was going to say something icebreaking like "Cody wanted to see you." But that seemed too cute given Jennifer's stony stare. "I'm sorry for just showing up like this … again," Nate said, "but can we go talk somewhere?" Remembering his manners, which felt long out the window, he added, "If you have a few minutes."

Jennifer studied her surprise guests, her face relaxing just the tiniest bit. "We can talk right here," she answered, folding her arms and straightening her stance.

Despite her obvious annoyance, she looked more beautiful to Nate than ever, with her hair pulled tightly back, a bare hint of makeup, dance leotard outlining her shapely form. Still, he could feel Esme's upbeat prediction slipping away by the second.

Nate took a breath. "Okay, look, I know I've—"

"This is stupid standing here," Jennifer broke in. "Let's go sit in the office."

Nate, his trusty dog at his side, gratefully followed her into the small office at the back of the studio where they opened metal folding chairs and sat facing each other. Cody plopped himself down on a stretch of carpet and licked his paws. The room was cramped, with gray walls, a cluttered desk, a few dance posters for decor, and a small window overlooking the alley behind the building. At least it was private.

"Sorry for the mess," Jennifer said, gesturing around the office. Nate shrugged; it was the least of his problems. "I have another class in half an hour, so …"

"Right. So, I was saying …" He paused. What *did* he want to say exactly? All he had was the truth. *His* truth—as he knew it, as he felt it. And now he had to make her feel it. He started big: "Did you know I've been in therapy?" Nate was surprised at the level of pride in his voice. But it was nothing compared to the surprise on Jennifer's face.

"How would I know that?" she asked, eyes and mouth agape.

"Well, I have been. This therapist in Glendale named Mira. And, you know what? It's been kinda great." He explained, "I mean, yeah, it was a little hard at first, doing all that talking, all that revealing. But I don't know, it's been really … freeing. Does that make sense?"

She thought for a second. "Does it make sense to you?"

"It does now. Honestly, I wish I'd gone sooner. I probably should have gone as soon as Amy entered the picture."

"You *should* have gone when we first broke up. No—*we* should have gone. I should have dragged you kicking and screaming."

"So why didn't you bring it up back then?" he asked. It would have been a reasonable question—coming from someone else. Jennifer cocked her head the way Cody did when he couldn't make heads or tails of something. "I know," Nate admitted, "I wouldn't have gone. I would have shut down. I was scared. I was stupid." He could feel his eyes fill, his stomach clench. He looked away, then quickly turned back, locking eyes with Jennifer. "I'm so sorry. For everything. For fucking so much up between us." Then added, because it was the God's honest truth, "You could do so much better than me."

Jennifer's shoulders slumped; her eyes misted over. Her enveloping anger and resistance seemed to dissolve. "Did Mira tell you to do this?" she asked, more curious than critical.

Nate shook his head. "She doesn't even know I'm here. But I know she would approve."

"That's good to know," she said dryly, and then sniffled, blinking away a tear. "What did she tell you to do about your mother?"

"Not much directly. She kind of gets me to reach my own conclusions. About most things."

"What else have you concluded?" Jennifer crossed her arms

again, shifting in the stiff chair. "Aside from the idea that I'm too good for you." There was the faintest hint of a smile on her face, but it vanished as quickly as it had appeared.

Nate wanted to launch into a whole laundry list of things—it felt like all he'd done was "conclude" lately. But he was eager to get to the main event; the ring box was burning a hole in his pocket. He looked around the drab room. It was not where he wanted to propose to Jennifer, though he still had more to say before doing so.

He stood. "Hey, can we go in the studio? It's a little brighter in there." Which was his way of saying "less depressing." Jennifer shrugged, seemed to agree, and led him and Cody out of the office and into the studio, with its skylight and high, narrow windows lending the space a kind of camera-ready glow. There were no chairs, so the humans sat facing each other, cross-legged on the worn hardwood floor, in front of a mirrored wall. Meanwhile, Cody nosed around the wide, spare space; if he was lucky, a student left half a granola bar somewhere.

"Okay," Nate began again, "so you asked what else I've concluded." Jennifer watched him attentively, if skeptically. From her look, Nate felt the clock ticking. And not because she had another class about to start. He wished she'd say something, anything; ask more questions, feed him his lines. But no, she just waited. So he cleared his throat and went for it.

With what seemed like the speed of light, he went chapter and verse on his discussions with Mira. He apologized—profusely, poetically—for saying that Jennifer wouldn't understand how he felt about Amy; it was *he* who didn't understand, and maybe still didn't completely. But, he said, he wanted to try—he was *committed* to trying. He wanted Amy in his life. He wanted his sister and grandparents in his life. He wanted a *life*. And he wanted that life to include the phenomenal woman sitting across from him. If she would forgive him, if she would have him.

And before another word could be uttered, Nate rearranged himself to a kneeling position. "Jennifer, I love you so much and I want to make you the happiest woman alive. I want to be everything you need, everything you want me to be. I want us to be together forever and ever." And, with Jennifer frozen in stunned silence, he took the velvet box out of his jacket pocket, opened it to reveal the gleaming diamond ring, and said, "Will you marry me?"

Nate felt it was safe to say Jennifer was not expecting anything even remotely close to this when he and Cody appeared in her workplace a mere half an hour before. Still, her face held such a singular air of astonishment that for a fleeting second Nate barely recognized her. She gazed at the ring as if it was some magical talisman, then looked up at Nate with a mix of confusion, uncertainty, and heart-bursting elation.

"Try it on," Nate urged her. "See if it fits." When she didn't budge, Nate gently removed the ring from its berth and held it in front of her. She slowly extended her left hand, which, like Nate's right hand, was trembling imperceptibly. He carefully slipped the solitaire on her fourth finger. It fit perfectly.

Jennifer studied her bejeweled hand, still in a daze, then slowly regained her composure. The joy he'd sensed amid her doubt seemed less discernible now.

She took a breath. "Nate, it's beautiful but … I really don't know what to say."

He rose. "Well, I was hoping you'd say yes, but I'll also accept 'I'll think about it.'"

She stared at the solitaire again. It caught the sunlight filtering in just so; for a flash, it looked five times its size. "I can't believe you did this," Jennifer said. "Here. Now."

"I should have done it a while ago. I was an idiot. I still may be, but at least now I'm an idiot who proposed marriage to an amazing woman." He wanted to take her hand, draw her in close, kiss her slowly, deeply, eternally. But he decided to take his cues from her. She didn't reach out to him, didn't speak, didn't burst into tears or a full-blown smile. What she did do was shake her head in bemusement.

"What?" Nate asked. "What are you thinking?"

"I'm thinking that maybe you're actually a little crazy. That maybe we both are."

This time, Nate took her hand. She didn't flinch or retract it. Just watched him. "Is that so bad?" he asked.

She smiled. "I don't really know. I don't really know much of anything right now." She glanced back at the diamond. "Except that somehow you chose the exact ring I would have. So, there's that."

And before Nate could give a shoutout to the pillow-lipped Esme, Jennifer's eyes swung toward the window looking out to the hallway. That's where a handful of students waited, watching the scene unfolding with rapt attention.

Jennifer shook herself clear, threw back her shoulders, and gestured toward her inquisitive pupils. "I need to go." She glimpsed the solitaire. "We'll talk." It was hardly your typical response to a marriage proposal but, even Nate had to admit, it wasn't a typical proposal.

"I'll be waiting by the phone," said Nate, like the hopeful lover in some old movie, the kind Jim would sometimes watch on TCM and Nate would get sucked into against his—and even his father's—better judgment.

Jennifer made no motion to return the ring, so that struck him as at least one positive sign. He gave her a quick kiss and led Cody out of the studio, locking eyes with the curious students as he passed. Nate shrugged at them innocently—what could he say?—then exited into the intoxicating, late morning air.

THIRTY-EIGHT

"**W**AIT, **DUDE**—**ARE** you shitting me?" asked an astonished Danny.

"Nope. I shit you not," Nate replied. "I asked her to marry me." Nate had called Danny as he drove away from his parking spot a few blocks from the dance studio. Though it was hardly a done deal with Jennifer, he felt elated, wired, excited. He had taken a giant life step and, though he knew the road that got him there was twisty and filled with potholes—many of his own making—it was an overwhelming sense of accomplishment, one that he needed to immediately share. Which was also something startlingly new for Nate. He could feel himself beaming through the phone.

"Was she, like, blown away? I mean ..." Danny took a breath to figure this out. "When was the last time you two even talked?"

Nate realized he'd never told Danny about that last fraught meet-up with Jennifer at his house, hadn't told anyone but Mira, and needed to backtrack. So, he quickly filled him in on the bit about Jennifer talking to Amy, how shitty it made him feel, and the big stink he made over it, which might have sent any woman running for the door. Which it did. And yet.

"That's 'cause she loves you, man," Danny said conclusively, then yelled some wits'-end threat at Raffi who was clearly testing the limits of the terrible twos. "And I'm having another kid, why?" Danny asked, more to himself than to Nate.

Nate turned off Melrose onto La Brea and headed north toward the Hollywood Freeway. Cody's head was stuck out the passenger window, eyes closed, basking in the warming breeze.

"So, what happens next?" Danny wanted to know. "With the future Mrs. Cronin?"

"Well, the future Mrs. Cronin has to decide if she wants to even *be* the future Mrs. Cronin." Nate stopped at a light across from Pink's famous hot dog stand. His stomach rumbled. Was it too early for a foot-long with chili? Apparently not—the lunch line was already snaking out along the sidewalk.

Danny wondered, "Hey, so what happened to the ring?"

"When I left, it was still on her finger."

"Suh-weet," Danny practically sang. "You're in, my brother."

"Yeah, I thought it was encouraging, too, but ... I think it's been firmly established that I don't know what the hell I'm doing."

"Screw that, you did great. I'm proud of you, partner."

Nate grinned, appreciating the vote of confidence. "The good news is, I have a week to return the ring—full refund. So."

"In a week you'll be planning your honeymoon, you'll see."

"I wish I had your confidence," Nate said. And he meant it. The light turned green; he left hot dog haven behind. Cody gave up his perch at the window and curled up in the passenger seat.

"I'd put Leesh on so she could congratulate you but she's out shopping. Wait'll I tell her, she's gonna be super happy."

Nate heard a two-year-old's screech come wailing through the phone. "Is everything okay?" Nate yelled over the noise.

"Yeah, yeah, it's cool. The kid just saw a squirrel. He's trying to catch it but the fucker's just too fast." He realized: "The squirrel—not Raffi."

They laughed. Raffi piped down, and Nate and Danny made a plan to meet at Starlight Nursery Monday morning before heading over to start their latest job: tiering and planting a steep hillside behind a house in Bronson Canyon, a tucked-away spot in the Hollywood Hills. ("I'm gonna wear me some golf shoes for traction!" Danny had joked when they first saw the precipitous property, though there were worse ideas.)

Nate hung up and, his enthusiasm still in high gear, decided another phone call was in order. Amy answered on the first ring and sounded both excited and wary to hear from him. They'd kept their distance since The Day of the Blue Seiko (he wondered, like with Jennifer's diamond ring, if Amy had a week to return the watch—and if he should have taken it after all).

Her words that last time about him learning to accept love had resonated and, in their way, helped bring him back to Jennifer. And now he could return the favor. Amy had said that she wanted to feel better about the life she'd lived; by being her son—really and truly—Nate could give that to her. He was ready. He was willing. And, he thought, finally able.

Besides, there just might be a wedding to help plan.

Still, the hesitation he heard in Amy's voice when he asked if he and Cody could stop by for a visit gave him pause. Until, in a lighter, brighter voice she told Nate, "Of course, honey, we'd love to see you."

We? It turned out that Robin was down from Fresno for the weekend. "Really? That's great!" Nate enthused, because he had a mother and a sister and it was time to appreciate the inconceivable turn of events in his life and start putting the darker parts of the past—Jim's past, to be exact—behind him. "Be there in fifteen," he told Amy as he swung away from the Hollywood Freeway entrance and toward the Cahuenga Pass en route to Toluca Woods.

Nate parked at the curb in front of Amy's house, pulling up behind Robin's bright red Kia Soul. He admired the sun-drenched front yard that he and the guys had planted; it was looking lush, rich, lasting. As he exited the truck, leaving Cody inside for now, he wondered how Amy's gardenias were doing and reminded himself to be sure to take a look. Nate rang the doorbell, eying a pair of empty cartons sitting beside the front door. He figured maybe Robin had brought Amy more of her things from up north. He smiled to himself: *might be a good sign.*

His mother opened the door looking less kempt than usual. She wore old jeans and a stained white T-shirt, taupe canvas slip-ons, and not a trace of makeup; her hair was tucked under a Fresno State Bulldogs cap. Nate wondered if she and Robin were cleaning the house or repainting a room, though he wasn't sure why they'd be doing either.

Amy hugged Nate hello as if their last meeting had ended on a far brighter note, which continued Nate's new wave of optimistic resolve. Robin, looking a bit scruffy in shorts, a halter top, and flip-flops, greeted him warmly, yet there was also something guarded about her. Given how anxious she was much of the time Nate was in Fresno, he assumed it was just more of the same. It's not like he was all cucumber-cool either; in a way, he was starting over with the both of them. And he wanted it to go well.

While they were still in the foyer, Nate beamed. "I have some, well, maybe—*could be*—exciting news to tell you," he said, starting for the living room. He didn't want to share his proposal story in the cramped mud hall, wanted to see Amy's face full-on when he told her. But Robin stepped in front of her brother, blocking him from going any further, catching Amy's eye as she did so.

It still didn't dawn on Nate what mother and daughter were up to, though it did register how quiet Amy had become. Then, just as Amy said, "Nate, I have something I need to tell you first," he glanced over Robin's shoulder and into the living room. He spied a row of open, packed cartons on the floor and several pieces of furniture turned this way and that.

"Let's all sit down for a minute, okay?" Amy finally said, gesturing for Robin to step aside and let them pass. Robin, a worried look on her face, backed away and followed Amy and Nate into the living room. "Sorry for the mess," said Amy, straightening one of the wayward wingbacks, "we're kind of in the middle of something."

"A little redecorating?" Nate asked brightly, though as the words came out, he knew his guess was wrong. His instinct was confirmed by the women's stiff silence.

Just then, Nate realized some of Amy's personal items—framed photos, pottery pieces, a stack of art books—were missing from their usual spots around the room. Like one of those bolts of lightning that sometimes hit him during therapy, it struck Nate that the missing items must be what were wrapped in newspaper and sticking out of the unsealed cartons a few feet away. He glanced back at Amy and then locked eyes with Robin, who didn't wait for her mother to explain what he now knew.

"Nate, Mom's moving back to Fresno," Robin confirmed, her voice thick, quavery. She turned away from her brother as if she'd just confessed to a crime.

Amy jumped in. "I wanted to tell you, but it all happened so fast. And, after that last visit—honestly, I didn't know what to think." She was on the verge of tears.

"I know. I handled it weirdly—badly," Nate admitted. "But even you said that conversation was, what did you call it? Kind of a start?"

"Until it wasn't," Amy reminded him, more direct now.

The watch. "I should have taken the watch. I loved the watch. You were right, I was just being stubborn. I apologize."

"Honey, it wasn't the watch," Amy said quietly. "And I think you know that."

He did. He did at the time. He couldn't help himself. Any more than he could help himself now. He eyed Robin taking in this exchange, her head down and tilted away, like someone trying-not-trying to watch a car roll off a cliff. Nate could feel his heart hammering in his chest, prickles of sweat breaking out under his shirt. How stupid, how cavalier, to think he could waltz into his mother's house and think she'd stay just because he asked. Like she didn't have a mind of her own, a life of her own, a shred of dignity. He forgot how happy he'd been just a few short minutes ago.

Nate jumped off the couch. "I don't want you to go!" he said loudly, urgently, startling Amy and Robin.

"What?" Amy asked, eyes narrowing, flummoxed.

Nate crouched in front of her. "I missed having a mother for thirty years, I can't miss thirty more." Just then, Cody began barking from the truck. Nate had forgotten all about him.

"It's too late," Robin told her brother. "She's made up her mind."

"Robin, please!" said Amy. Robin shrunk back, her face a mask of anxiety. It looked as if Amy was about to speak again, but nothing came out.

Nate stood, assembling his thoughts. "I know I said I couldn't decide for you: about taking the job, about staying here. But I was wrong. I *can* decide. You should stay." His voice cracked; his eyes filled. "You should stay and be the mother I never had."

Amy looked overwhelmed by Nate's passion, his commitment to her—to them. "Oh, Nate," was all she could muster. Meantime, Robin appeared shaken, like she was losing her grasp on an already tenuous situation. Cody barked again in the distance.

Nate sat back down on the couch, staring out at a spot somewhere between his mother and sister. "I spent my whole life thinking my mother died so *I* could live," he began. "That in the most innocent and unexpected way possible, I was responsible for another person's death." He shifted his gaze to Amy, hunched forward on the couch. "Then you came along and, suddenly, we both had the chance to erase a lifetime's worth of pain and guilt. Only I wasn't ready to give all that up. Until now."

"Oh, my God," exhaled Amy. She crossed to the couch, sat next to Nate, and hugged him tightly, desperately. He started to cry, resting his head on her shoulder. Robin watched them cleaving to each other, seemingly not quite sure how to react. The antique clock on the mantle delivered a series of mournful clangs heralding the new hour.

Amy pulled away from Nate, composing herself. She tucked a few stray wisps of hair back behind her ears and smoothed out her wrinkled T-shirt. Nate was on the verge of a smile, the kind that came from the relief of unburdening one's soul. But, somehow, Amy's expression was more subdued, even troubled. Any thought of a smile vanished from Nate's face.

"I'm sorry, Nate. I'm so, so sorry," Amy said. The pain in her voice was palpable.

Nate looked from Amy to Robin and back. "You're leaving, aren't you?" he asked. By then, he knew the question was rhetorical.

"It doesn't mean I don't love you. Won't always love you …" Amy's voice drifted off. She glanced nervously at Robin, who looked calmer now that her mother had spoken her piece, difficult as it was.

"Mom will come visit," Robin assured Nate. "*We'll* come visit. And you'll come see us. It'll be great, you'll see." Nate's expression was so obviously dubious that Robin seemed forced to add: "We're going to be a real family. We promise. We love you, Nate." It sounded convincing enough and maybe she believed it. Maybe even Nate believed it. But, just then, it all seemed awfully beside the point.

Amy took Nate's hand. "Please understand, my darling."

He understood. He understood all too well. He'd made it too difficult for Amy, spent too much time on the fence—sometimes completely on the other side of that fence. Thinking, overthinking, waffling: *Should she stay or should she go?* And the other day, when she needed his answer most, the love he was holding back most, he disappointed her. Maybe for the last time. She was packing up her toys and going home—with the child who needed her for real, not in theory. Maybe it was the path of least resistance. Or maybe Amy just wanted her old life back.

He suddenly had so many questions, mostly of the practical kind: *Don't you have a lease? What about all this furniture? What about your job promotion? Will you move back into your condo? What do Gene and Diane think?* He could have asked her all that and more, stayed there and fought for her. But he didn't. Cody started barking again, more insistently now, like he was yapping out a code. Nate decided to leave before he did or said something he'd regret, and quickly hugged Amy and Robin goodbye.

"Wait!" Amy called, as Nate grabbed for the doorknob. "What was it you came to tell me?" she asked, genuinely curious.

Nate thought about Jennifer, looking so radiant in the dance studio, the diamond ring glinting off her hand. But the undeniable thrill he had felt in that moment with her—its potential, its faith in something good and true—had all but evaporated.

"It's not important," Nate answered, his hand still stuck to the doorknob as if it were going to twist itself.

Amy studied him. "Are you sure?"

He didn't have the energy to even begin the story much less finish it.

"Okay, look, just … wait here for a second, would you?" Amy asked, already halfway out of the living room. For a few seconds, time stopped, and then Amy returned with the Seiko box in hand.

"I want you to have this. No debate," she ordered Nate as she thrust the gift at him. He reflexively took the watch, holding it to his chest. "Wear it, don't wear it. Sell it if you want. But please—just take it."

So, he did. And with one final look at Amy and Robin, Nate left to reunite with his barking dog. Because Cody needed him.

THIRTY-NINE

AROUND SIX THAT night, while Nate was lying on the living room floor, stroking Cody's thick coat and in major life assessment mode—*Should I have fought for Amy to stay? What if Jennifer says she doesn't want to marry me? What if I moved to Fresno?*—Max and Carter knocked on his front door. They stood there bearing two bottles of wine, one red, one white, both smiling toothily. If Nate didn't know better, he'd think they were a little stoned. Maybe he didn't know better and they were.

It was their tenth wedding anniversary—or rather yesterday was—and they'd been sent a case of assorted wine from Max's sisters in Tucson as a celebration gift. As the guys explained it, they were never at a loss for wine, and now was no exception, so they thought they'd share the surplus with their neighbor and, if he had a corkscrew, maybe they could all enjoy a glass and visit. Carter said it had been too long since they'd just sat and talked, though Nate honestly couldn't remember any time they'd actually done that. Their conversations were usually in passing, unplanned, bumping into each other as they rolled out their trash bins for garbage day, or like that morning they'd almost collided on the Occidental campus.

Maybe Carter was confusing it with the times they'd spent talking with Jim, who found the guys not only considerate neighbors but interesting and eclectic, which probably meant they'd read a lot of books.

Before Nate knew it, he and his visitors, lounging around the living room, had polished off the bottle of red—a tart but, Nate had to admit, tasty Italian Barolo—and were opening up a pale pinot grigio. A loose-lipped Max and Carter (they admitted they'd each popped an edible before coming by—aha!) recounted the highlights of their ten-year marital history for Nate, who learned far more about their lives than he'd ever think to ask a pair of, at best, casual friends. Acquaintances, really.

Turned out the couple had had their share of ups and downs—infidelities, commitment-phobia, competitiveness, crossed wires—during their dating years. But all that seemed to fade away once they tied the knot and got past the attendant anxieties and doubts. Their stories reminded Nate so much—too much—of the kinds of things that had plagued him and Jennifer (save the infidelities part, as far as he knew) and the new hope he found once he finally proposed, even if the outcome was still up in the air. Two men, man and woman, it didn't seem to matter; human nature was human nature.

The guys' openness—and the wine—made Nate unusually gabby and he told them the entire Jennifer saga right up to that morning's exhilarating, bended-knee entreaty. Max and Carter, who'd met Jennifer briefly several times, couldn't believe she didn't immediately accept Nate's proposal given how "spontaneously romantic" they thought it sounded. Nate didn't agree or disagree—his neighbors were just being nice (and a bit happy-drunk)—although he'd be lying if he said he didn't try to sneak a peek at his phone every few minutes to see if Jennifer had called or texted with an enthusiastic "Yes!" She hadn't.

Watching Max and Carter, who seemed so in sync as partners and people, with their good-natured digs, finishing of each other's sentences, and generally shared warmth, Nate pictured where he and Jennifer could be a decade down the road—if married, that is.

Yet unlike Max and Carter, who had chosen not to become dads ("We never say never!" Max declared, though from the look on Carter's face, that particular train had left the station), Nate and Jennifer might have a few little ones racing around the living room. Which made him wonder: *Would they even be living in this house in ten years? Would their old relocation fantasy become a reality? More importantly, would there be a "they?"*

Despite—or maybe because of—Nate's increasingly fuzzy head, he realized he should be banging down Jennifer's guest house door for an answer instead of sitting in the safety of his living room getting soused with his neighbors, well-meaning as they were. But before he could make a move toward that goal, or even determine whether it was the sanest or most effective gesture at that very moment, Max launched into a discussion of Jim that kept Nate bolted to his cushion.

It seemed that Max and Carter spent many an early and sometimes later evening sharing a bottle of vino with their professorial neighbor accompanied by much deep discussion—and not just about great literature as Nate had predicted. If their chats often started off debating favorite authors (and, yes, they got an earful about Joan Didion), the trio would invariably segue into more personal matters. Not surprising, thought Nate: How much could even Jim talk about books? What *was* surprising, aside from the apparent frequency of these get-togethers, which Jim had rarely mentioned to Nate, was how revealing his father was to his neighbors—to hear them tell it, anyway.

"When we first moved in and got to know your dad," Max recalled, "he seemed like the type who'd gotten by on looks and charm and an ability to talk to anyone about almost anything. I swear I said to Carter, 'I really like that guy but I'll bet he's got a hella flip side."

"You didn't say 'hella,'" countered Carter. "He never says 'hella,'" he confirmed to Nate.

Max shot his husband a jaunty eye roll and continued: "Anyway, so this one night, I'm pouring us our first glass—your dad brought over a Grenache, I remember because we'd never had one before—and he bursts into tears."

"I mean, big, sobby, end-of-the-world tears," said Carter, draining his wine glass. "It was so unlike him. At least as far as *we* knew."

"And then he hits us with 'I have six months to live,'" Max revealed to Nate, who was dumbstruck to discover that his dad had told two relative strangers about his fatal condition long before he'd ever informed his own son. The guys could see how rankled Nate looked by that—and maybe why.

"Wait, when did he tell *you*?" Carter asked carefully.

"When he thought he had two months to live. So, y'know, do the math." Nate felt a headache rolling into his skull. He put his drink down on the coffee table and slumped back in his chair. Cody, who'd been curled up in a corner of the living room since the first bottle was uncorked, trotted over to Nate and sat attentively at his side.

Max and Carter traded a look as Nate simmered. "If it's any consolation," Max offered, "he was terrified to tell you."

"So, he told you and Carter first? Like, what, as a trial run?" Nate grabbed his glass and took a hit of the pinot. It didn't help. Cody parked his head on Nate's lap. That helped. Nate massaged the hound's ears.

Carter continued in his measured tone. "Okay, look, we stepped in it here and we're really sorry—"

"*Really* sorry," added Max. "We weren't thinking. We always just assumed he must have told you right after—like *right* after—he spilled it to us."

"And it's none of our business but, well, your dad loved the shit outta you," said Carter. "The last thing he wanted to do was hurt you. In any way."

Nate softened, resting a hand atop Cody's head. "Did he tell you that, too?"

"He didn't have to," answered Max. "The way he used to talk about you? Like you hung the moon." He leaned back on the couch pillow. Carter took his hand.

The gesture moved Nate. His eyes filled. "Did my dad mention that he lied about who my real mother was? For my entire life?"

It occurred to Nate that Max and Carter knew nothing about Amy, certainly not from him. And why would they? It was too big a story to simply drop in passing, and they'd never run into her on Escarpa. Hell, she'd only been there a few times—and once never left her car.

Max and Carter took in that thunderbolt of news silently, poker-faced, as if deciding how—or if—to respond. Their awkward reserve made Nate think maybe Jim *had* let it slip about Amy during some drunken meet-up with the boys next door. Some dark night of the soul thing. And revealing that to Nate now, on top of their last admission, would be too much for him to handle.

"Holy crap. Seriously?" Carter finally asked, eyes widening, mouth agape. If he was faking his reaction, he was doing a pretty decent acting job.

"This sounds kind of juicy," Max said, as he topped off their wine glasses, emptying the second bottle in the process. "Who is—was—your mother, anyway?"

"Is," Nate answered. And, convinced that his dad hadn't disclosed that explosive piece of family history to his neighbors, he felt an urgent, uncharacteristic need to share the facts with Max and Carter. So he did, chapter and verse, in even greater detail than the recount he'd given them of his relationship with Jennifer. It felt especially important and timely: it helped Nate frame his wildly disparate feelings about his mother, which had been tested and torpedoed earlier that day when he discovered she was leaving L.A.

Max and Carter, well-oiled as they may have been, were excellent listeners and, based on their startled questions and seemingly spontaneous comments, reconfirmed Nate's sense that this story was falling on virgin ears. Replaying the tale start to finish like that, to people he knew relatively little about and vice versa, made Nate feel guilty that he'd held back confiding in Jennifer and Danny as soon as he'd found out about his mother. That it took another stranger—his therapist, Mira—to get it out of his head and off his chest wasn't something Nate was proud of, though, sitting there with his neighbors, he *was* proud of the progress he knew he'd made. If only his maybe fiancée-to-be felt the same.

Turnabout being fair play, Max told Nate about his own mother, who died in a car crash when he was in college. "You've been handed a fucking gift, man," Max said, a catch in his voice. "I'd give anything to have my mom back—to *have* a mom. And here it happened to you, just like that." Nate shot him a dubious look. "Okay, not 'just like that,' but look, it happened. And you like her, right? You said she's a good person?"

Nate nodded. He understood where Max was coming from; he couldn't argue with him, even though their circumstances, vis-à-vis mothers, were totally different.

"And did you know that I was adopted?" asked Carter, as if not to be outdone. Nate shook his head; how could he have known? "She raised me practically on her own. She and my father split when I was a kid and, well, he tried, but he was a pretty absentee dad for a lot of my life. I owe everything to her." Carter held back a tear and took a long slug of his pinot. "I don't care how old we are, we need a parent."

In one graceful move, Cody slid from a seated to a prone position on the hardwood floor. It freed up Nate's hand to retrieve his wine glass for a final gulp as Carter's words hit home. Nate had had the chance to have a parent nearby, to offset some of the crucial years they'd lost, to bond as mother and son on a day-to-day basis. But he'd let it slip away. He'd let anger and confusion, instead of logic and wisdom—and let's not forget maturity—rule his choices and actions. Nate didn't need Mira to tell him that, in the end, he hadn't wanted it to work with Amy. And now, instead of a mother, he was left with a self-fulfilling prophecy.

Max and Carter could tell how wrecked Nate seemed and they apologized again for opening any floodgates. Nate took a deep and cleansing breath and invited the guys on a tour of all the work he'd done on the inside of the house, partly inspired, he told them, by the pristine state of their home. Max and Carter were surprised and flattered.

Nate brightened considerably as he showed his neighbors all he'd repainted, refaced, refinished, and reconfigured. They were especially impressed by his efforts in the kitchen—Nate had eventually regrouted and polished the backsplash tile, making it look good as new.

Revisiting all his renovations in one fell swoop made Nate feel the same sense of accomplishment as when he finished a big landscaping job. He'd done good; even Jim, for all his blasé neglect of home and hearth, would have heartily approved. But Nate knew one thing for sure: a bigger sense of accomplishment was waiting for him outside that door, and first thing in the morning, he was going to tie up two super important loose ends.

FORTY

NATE WOKE UP Sunday morning at seven fifteen, only to realize he couldn't remember much of anything since he'd climbed into bed some eight hours before. The long, loaded, and exhausting day had clearly overtaken Nate's system and he didn't even stir when Cody, who'd begun the night dozing on the floor, jumped onto the bed and snuggled up next to him. If it wasn't for the dog's wet snout butting his face, Nate might have slept another few hours.

It didn't take more than a few seconds, though, for Nate to remember the day's dual mission: get Jennifer to marry him and convince Amy to unpack her boxes and stay in L.A. He had no idea which would be the harder sell or how either defining moment would pan out, but he was ready to rock—and didn't plan to take no for an answer.

Nate grabbed his phone from the bedstand and was disappointed, but not surprised, to see that no overnight texts or emails had arrived from the two most important women in his life. A simple "yes" from each would have made everything so much easier, but he didn't deserve easy—he deserved to fight. Or rather, they deserved to be fought for, given the erratic and exasperating ride he'd taken them both on. But that was over. It was time for a new beginning.

He took Cody out in the back for his morning "evacuation," fed him breakfast (Nate tossed in a handful of blueberries, which always sent the pooch into a paroxysm of joy), and made himself a spinach and cheddar cheese omelet and a pot of extra-strong coffee to fortify him for the events to come.

Nate then took a long shower, shampooed twice, shaved carefully, and neatened his hair with a squeeze of styling product he honestly didn't remember buying. He ironed a sky-blue short-sleeve cotton shirt of his dad's that he'd always liked, threw on a pair of nice jeans, then traded them for pressed tan khakis, laced up his new white Pumas, and stared at himself in a full-length wall mirror. He looked like a nervous kid going on his first date with a girl he was trying to impress, which wasn't that far from the truth.

He considered taking Cody with him to Jennifer's but decided to go solo. He'd used the dog as a kind of buffer—and charm magnet—too many times with her and knew it was time to face the woman he loved without any distractions. Cody seemed to instinctively understand and trotted off to the kitchen for his morning nap before Nate had even reached the front door.

Nate checked his look in the foyer mirror one last time and seemed satisfied with who was staring back: someone serious, respectful, and hopeful. He grabbed his truck keys and opened the front door, but nearly hit the ceiling when he found himself facing Jennifer, who was standing there about to knock, her raised fist frozen in mid-air. It took them both a few moments to manage their shock before either could speak. Meanwhile, Cody spoke for them as he raced to the door, happily yapping and wagging at the sight of Jennifer. Who could blame him?

The two stared at each other, waiting for someone to make the next move, until Jennifer said, "Can I come in?"

Nate leaped away from the doorway and allowed her to pass, swallowing her up with his appreciative eyes: paisley-print cinched dress, low-heeled leather sandals, the turquoise necklace he'd gifted her last Valentine's Day, her hair in a sexy upsweep. Like Nate, she had clearly put an effort into looking extra-presentable, though succeeded him by a mile because, well, just look at her.

"Would you believe I was just coming to see you?" Nate asked.

She gave him the once-over. "Is that why you're dressed like you're going for a job interview?"

He laughed. "So, you *do* believe me."

Jennifer smiled and gingerly sat on the couch, Nate in a chair across. Cody stood in front of her, antsy for some love. She freely complied by kissing his snout and rubbing his ears with both hands. Watching, Nate felt a little guilty that he wasn't planning to take Cody with him to Jennifer's. He belonged with them. But did Nate and Jennifer belong with each other? It didn't take long for Nate to find out.

"Do you still want to marry me?" she blurted out, restraint or caution be damned.

Nate wasn't sure he'd heard right. Was it a trick question? The eager, wide-eyed look on her face said otherwise. As did the pear-shaped diamond still perched on her ring finger. It glistened in a shard of light.

"More than anything in the world," he answered. "Do you?"

There was a long beat of silence, and Nate thought maybe he *had* misread her. It wouldn't have been the first time. Then she broke into a radiant smile.

"Yes. Yes, I do."

They sprang out of their respective seats and wrapped each other in hugs and kisses as Cody pranced wildly around them, infected by their joy. You'd think they'd just won the lottery. In a way, maybe they had. It'd just taken a little longer than expected to collect the prize.

On the flip side, you'd never think that as recently as last week they weren't exactly speaking to each other.

Nate pulled back from Jennifer and looked squarely at her. "Why?" he asked, infusing so much purpose in that one simple word.

"Why what?" she answered, still all smiles.

"Why did you finally say yes?" They were standing nearly nose-to-nose as Cody panted at their shins.

Jennifer considered Nate's question, feet still planted in place. "Why did you finally propose?"

"I couldn't not." He realized how that may have sounded given the amount of waffling he'd done for far too long. And yet, it was the first thing that came to mind; brief though it was, he decided not to qualify it.

In the movie version of Nate's life, Jennifer might have borrowed his answer and repeated it back to him. It would have made for good dialogue and, in some respects, made perfect—and perfectly symmetrical—sense. But for all her newfound exuberance, she was still nothing if not forthright and didn't let Nate off the hook. That is, since he asked.

Jennifer sat back on the couch, traces of her smile still flickering. "Well, number one, I love you. I always have, even when we've been apart. But just because you love someone doesn't mean you have to spend the rest of your life with that person. Or that you're even supposed to."

She gazed at Nate, who wasn't sure where this was going but expected—well, hoped—it would end well. She had, after all, agreed to marry him. Jennifer studied her engagement ring for a few seconds before looking back up at Nate.

"I always felt like you and I were—are—supposed to spend our lives together. But I was never really sure how we would get there. For all that we shared, you kept so much bottled up inside that it sometimes felt like I was in love with half a person. And I'm talking way before your dad died ... and everything that came after."

Nate felt a lump form in his throat. "Oh, Jen, I'm so sorry. You know that, right? But I feel whole now—more than I ever have. And I'm going to be there for you, one hundred percent. I swear it. I'm going to tell you so much of what's going on in this thick head of mine you're gonna want me to shut up already."

She smiled. "I'll take my chances." Then, with a knowing wink, "Oh, and thank Mira for me, would you?"

Nate beamed back at her. "Absolutely." He paused, turning serious. "And look—I also want to hear everything *you're* thinking, everything *you're* feeling, everything *you* have to say. I want to be the best husband and partner and, hopefully, one day, dad, I can possibly be." Nate paused, letting the lump slide down his throat and vanish. He leaned across, taking her hand; she squeezed back.

"Dad? Really?" she asked, a tear returning to her eye.

It occurred to Nate that Jennifer had agreed to marry him without being sure he still wanted kids. He was suddenly sure. "Remember Spencer, Connor, and Zelda?" he asked.

She smiled wistfully. "Let's rethink Zelda, okay?"

Nate joined her on the couch, and they sat quietly in each other's embrace. Jennifer looked at her fiancé.

"I may not have always understood why you've done certain things, but I've always trusted you. No matter what—and not to sound corny—you've always felt like home to me."

"You *are* home." Nate gestured around the living room. "If you want it to be."

She cocked her head, raising an eyebrow. "Fine, but we need to have a serious discussion about redecorating. All due respect to the former owner."

"Agreed!" Nate answered happily. There was so much to do, so much ahead of them. He felt a surge of optimism like never before.

Jennifer sat up, enthused. "Let's go tell your mother, then we can tell my parents."

His mother. Right.

Nate quickly updated Jennifer on Amy's imminent departure. He related how he'd gone to her house to tell her about proposing to Jennifer and was met with packing boxes, apologies, and a warily anxious half-sister who had come to reclaim their mom. Nate didn't fault Robin—or Amy, for that matter—but couldn't have been more disappointed.

"For all I know, she may have already left," Nate said. "Just when I was finally ready for her to stay."

"Oh, baby, I'm so sorry. And I'll bet she is too."

He told her he was planning to go see Amy one last time that morning. See if he could convince her not to move.

"Want company?" Jennifer asked with an eager smile.

"I was hoping you'd ask."

FORTY-ONE

AMY'S HOUSE LOOKED deserted when Nate and Jennifer pulled up in front, Cody's head out the back seat window, checking out the action—or lack thereof. Robin's Kia was gone and Amy's car was not in the driveway. Unlike yesterday, the shrubs and flowers looked a bit dry, wilted, forsaken. Or maybe that was all in Nate's head. His mother was evidently gone, and he felt like a fool for missing the opportunity of, let's face it, a lifetime.

"I think we're too late," said Nate. "Correction: I'm too late." He reflexively glanced at his Seiko watch (Jennifer had dubbed it "handsome"), which he'd put on before they'd left Eagle Rock.

"You don't know that for sure," Jennifer replied, halfway out the Silverado door.

Nate and Cody followed and met Jennifer on the stoop as she rang the doorbell. Nate felt a sense of futility, though it was mitigated in part by the joy he felt about his and Jennifer's engagement. They stared at the front door as if willing it to open by sheer focus. There might as well have been crickets chirping.

And then they heard a lock unbolting and saw Amy framed in the doorway. She looked surprised to see Jennifer and Nate staring back at her. She was dressed casually but smartly, hair and makeup in place, and looked far more herself than yesterday. Nate didn't know if that boded well for his mission, but there she was and it was now or never.

"You're still here," Nate said, stating the obvious.

"I am." Amy eyed her visitors with uncertainty. "It's nice to see you, Jen." She bent down to pet Cody. "You too, mister."

"We have some news for you," he told his mother, taking Jennifer's hand.

Amy shifted her gaze from Nate to Jennifer and took in their clasped hands and promising looks. "Was it what you wanted to tell me yesterday?" she asked with a raised eyebrow, her eyes making contact with Jennifer's tasteful solitaire.

"Can we come in?" Much as Nate didn't want to see Amy's packed-up house again, he didn't want to have this important conversation in the doorway.

"Okay, but it's kind of a mess."

Nate flashed on the chaotic living room from the day before and could feel his heart sink. Did he really think she'd changed her mind about moving? That Robin would have left town already if her mother wasn't following behind? No, she would have stayed and talked Amy into returning home. Talked until she was blue in the face. It's why she'd come down to begin with, wasn't it? Still, Nate had a persuasive speech prepared—he wasn't letting his mother go without a fight. Not this time.

Nate, Jennifer, and Cody trailed Amy into the house but stopped short as they entered the living room. Everything was back in its place: every stick of furniture, piece of art, throw rug, and knick-knack. It was neat as a pin. Not a carton in sight. A telltale upright vacuum stood in a corner. For a second, Nate thought he was hallucinating. Jennifer looked confused.

Nate, still dazed, swept a hand around the room as Cody began sniffing a couch leg. "What is all this? You said the place was a mess." He locked eyes with Amy, a smile spreading across her face. "Wait—you're staying?"

Amy nodded, a bit sheepishly. "Is that okay?"

He took a second to let it sink in. "Yes, absolutely! Of course! I mean … wow." He and Jennifer traded shocked looks. "I was all ready to try to talk you out of leaving. Which I should have done yesterday, but …"

Amy sighed. "I know. Robin."

"What *about* Robin?" came a voice from behind them. They turned to see Robin standing in the living room entry, grocery bag in one hand, a tall, potted white orchid in the other. "Hi, Nate," she said sprightly, a marked change from the day before. "And you're the famous Jennifer!" She'd clearly seen pictures. "Oh, and Cody!" That produced an enthusiastic tail wag in Robin's honor.

"Jen, this is Robin. My sister," Nate said, wondering how Robin fit into Amy's change of heart about moving. He was still reeling from the sudden turnaround.

"Great to meet you," Jennifer said, extending a hand, even though Robin's were full.

Robin put down the bag, gestured "one second" to Jennifer, and handed the flowerpot to Amy. "Consider this an official house-warming gift," she told her mother. "Nate will know how to keep it alive, I'm sure."

"Oh, thank you, honey, that's so sweet." She scanned the room. "I'll put it on the table by the window. It'll get lots of light." Amy looked at Nate for confirmation.

He glanced at the rays flooding in through the designated window. "Orchids do best in *indirect* sunlight, so ..."

Amy eyed Nate with pride, like a mom whose kid just won the science fair. "Well, we'll have plenty of time to find the perfect spot," she said, and Nate couldn't help but smile.

"Oh, and I picked up snacks for the drive home," Robin said, pointing to the market bag. "Got an extra package of that dried mango you love, don't let me forget to leave it for you."

If Nate had any doubt that Amy was staying in L.A. and Robin was leaving without her, that last sentence settled it. He could feel a slight lift in his chest, but also a pang for Robin who he knew, whatever her reasoning, had to be taking one for their newly expanded team.

Robin turned back to Jennifer with a smile, extending her hand. "Okay—now!" The women shook hands. "Wonderful to meet you, too," Robin said as they folded into an inevitable hug.

"Let's sit down, we'll tell you what happened," Amy said to Nate and Jennifer, moving toward one of the wingbacks. "Then you can tell us about you two—and when the wedding is," she added with a grin.

"Wait a second. What wedding?" Robin eyeballed her brother and future sister-in-law. "Oh, my God, really?"

Nate looked at Amy in surprise. "How did you—?"

Amy smiled, indicating Jennifer's diamond ring.

"Right," Nate realized.

"Some messengers *we* are," Jennifer joked.

"I'm thrilled for you both," Amy said, as she took a seat. "And Gene and Diane will be too."

"Well, I'm over the moon about it," Robin agreed, dropping into the second wing chair. "And Jennifer, we need to become very close, very fast, so I can be a bridesmaid."

Jennifer didn't even flinch. "Consider it done."

Nate and Jennifer settled in on the white couch, held hands, and listened as Amy picked up the story from the time Nate left her house the day before. It turned out that, despite Robin laying the groundwork for her mother's return to Fresno, she was intensely—and unexpectedly—moved by Nate's candid and heartfelt appeal to Amy.

"She realized just then how much you needed me—and knew you'd finally realized it too," Amy explained.

"You kind of blew me away," recalled Robin. "Even if I didn't react that way while it was happening." She paused for a moment before adding, "It hit me how much you'd lost in life and how much I've had. And that seemed unbearably unfair."

Cody dropped his head on Nate's knee, gazing up at his dad with those irresistible, big brown eyes. Nate scratched him behind the ears as he considered what was shaping up to be a whole new way of life—of living. It was thrilling and frightening and made him feel blessed and triumphant. And, as he'd hoped, totally worthy.

"Are you okay?" Nate thought to ask Robin. He was impressed by her selflessness and decided right then to make that relationship work to its fullest extent. He'd never had a sibling and now he did. And he was going to cherish that.

"I actually am," said Robin. "I may be tougher—or at least more resilient—than I thought." She added with a warm smile, "Don't let this marshmallow exterior fool you."

"Who knows, maybe you'll want to move down here someday," said Jennifer.

Robin shrugged. "Maybe. But for now, I think it'll be good to continue to be on my own up north."

"Though she may not exactly be 'on her own' for long," Amy offered with a sly smile.

Robin met Nate and Jennifer's curious gaze. "I've just started seeing this guy. His name's Trey. We met shopping at Whole Foods." She added, with a self-deprecating eye roll, "We bonded over a pack of flaxseed muffins."

"Well, if it works out, you can say it was love at first bite," quipped Nate, which elicited a round of groans. "What? I thought that was pretty clever."

Amy smiled. "In any case, I think your sister will be just fine."

The mantle clock rang twelve times, heralding the noon hour. Today the chimes sounded stately, welcoming, momentous. Cody's ears twitched at the noise.

Amy went on to inform Nate and Jennifer that she'd texted her boss at the law firm that morning to see if her promotion was still on the table. It was and he was happy she'd changed her mind. As for her living situation, Amy planned to stay in the rental until she could maybe swing a place of her own in high-priced L.A. Her new and improved salary would help on that front.

"And you're sure you want to do this?" Nate asked. Glad as he was at the outcome, he didn't want Amy to have any regrets or misgivings. It was fresh-start time.

"I've never been surer in my life," Amy answered with a smile so wide and authentic that it laid all further questions to rest.

Jennifer sent Nate a look that said "Don't just sit there." He went to the couch and hugged Amy, who burst into happy tears and Nate did the same. Not to be left out, Jennifer was also an emotional puddle before it was all said and done, especially when Amy waved her over for an embrace. The future in-laws squeezed each other tightly. Robin then joined the circle, spreading her arms around Nate and Jennifer and resting her head on Amy's shoulder. Cody barked, wanting in on the wave of warmth. There was plenty of love to go around.

When they returned to their seats, Amy gazed at her son and his fiancée. "Now it's my turn to ask: Are you two sure you want to do this?" She wiggled her finger in the direction of Jennifer's diamond ring.

"I've never been surer in my life," Nate and Jennifer answered in unison, laughing at their unplanned duet.

Just then, Nate had the urge to bring up his father. He didn't quite know how or why, but it felt like Jim was inordinately missing at this watershed moment. Then again, Nate thought, Amy wouldn't be here if his dad was, so maybe things were exactly where they were supposed to be. Life being what it was and all.

Then Nate had an idea.

FORTY-TWO

JIM'S WORDS "AT least you'll know where to find me" rang in Nate's ears as he parked the Silverado above the beach at Portuguese Bend and gazed out at the Pacific. It looked more silvery than blue as the late afternoon sun reflected off its gentle waves. Nate knew his dad's ashes had swept out to sea and vanished long ago along with Jim's heart and soul. But not his memory, which had continued to loom large in Nate's mind for so many reasons—some good, some not so good. Nate knew that time had a way of softening the sharper edges and that he would ultimately remember Jim not for the way he reinvented such a singularly important truth but for the love and devotion he'd otherwise shown his precious son.

Still, Nate knew what he had to do to move on from the pain of the past months and the disappointment he'd felt about the man who had gone from hero to a kind of knight in tarnished armor. It didn't seem fair or right that things with Jim had ended up as they did, but really who's to say? For all Nate knew, their path had been preordained and life had turned out better than it had any right to. He'd never know.

He was thankful that Jennifer and Amy agreed to accompany

him out to the Palos Verdes Peninsula for the emotional postscript he had in mind. (Robin opted to get on the road so she wouldn't be driving home in the dark.) Nate had said goodbye to Jim all by himself that first time at Portuguese Bend (okay, Cody had been there, as he was again), but this time he needed people around him, other people who loved him and he loved back. His lone-wolf days were disappearing behind him.

It wasn't lost on Nate that three very different women, with three very different agendas, had brought him out of himself and back into the world again. And, no matter what the future held in store—because clearly, who could ever really predict?—he'd be forever grateful to Amy, Jennifer, and Mira for the parts they played that had led him to this moment.

With Cody traipsing alongside them, Nate, Amy, and Jennifer made their way down from the bluffs onto the beach and, shoes off, crossed the coarse sand to the water's edge. They stood staring out at the infinite Pacific as the salty breeze and encroaching clouds lent a chill to the air and reaffirmed autumn's arrival. Nate found the coolness a bracing, evocative reminder of L.A.'s subtle way of creeping up and forcing change, sometimes when it was least expected.

From his perch on the sand, Nate thought about Jim's literary love, Joan Didion, and wondered how often she'd taken in this exact view during her days at Portuguese Bend. What coursed through her fertile mind as she watched the tide ebb and flow, the random swimmer glide across the waves, and the seagulls and pelicans soar above the water and against the sweeping sky? Was it the famed author's contemplative, enigmatic qualities that drew Jim to her work? In the end, wasn't his father just as inscrutable? How much did Nate choose to see and how much did he choose to ignore for the thirty years he spent with his beloved dad? How clearly would he see his mother the more he got to know her? How clearly would he see himself?

But today wasn't so much about questions or answers as it was about actions. So Nate took out a vial of Jim's leftover ashes, which he'd kept for reasons he couldn't explain at the time but now made perfect sense, and slowly unscrewed the cap. As Amy and Jennifer looked on (Cody was already doing laps along the shoreline), Nate raised the vial into the air and said, almost as an incantation, "I love you, Dad. I forgive you, Dad. You'll always be with me, with *us*." He paused and added, "I won't pretend to understand everything that happened, but I'd like to believe that somehow it was for my benefit. That you acted out of love to protect me—maybe even from yourself."

Nate was silent for a moment, arm still reaching for the sky. He traded a look with Amy and Jennifer, who returned gentle, loving, understanding smiles. "Do either of you want to say anything before I say goodbye to Dad for good?" He lowered the vial back to his side to give the women a minute to think. Parting words could not be rushed.

"I'd like to say something," Jennifer said, moving a few steps closer to the ocean.

"Please," Nate said, waving his hand at the expanse.

"Jim, I just want to thank you for helping to make Nate the man he is today: good, strong, thoughtful, capable, loyal," she said, staring at the horizon. Nate could feel his face redden at the compliments; it brought another warm smile to Jennifer's face. She continued, "You were always so kind to me and I loved you for how much you loved Nate. Maybe that's what's most important. So … if Nate can forgive you, I can too." She took another step toward the water. "Rest easy, Professor."

Nate took Jennifer's hand. "That was beautiful." He grinned. "No wonder I wanted to marry you." She squeezed his hand, then moved in and kissed him tenderly on the lips.

Nate turned to Amy. "Mom?"

She sighed, then: "Well, considering I haven't spoken to the man in thirty years, I suppose I might as well say something."

"That's the spirit, Amy!" Jennifer joked as Cody found his way back to the trio, panting happily, his paws caked in wet sand.

Amy looked out at the waves and composed her words. "Jim, I'm sorry you're gone and that you went through so much pain at the end. You had so many years left to do so much more. But if your life *did* have to be cut short, at least it gave me the chance to finally know our son and, hopefully, make up for at least some of the time we missed." She paused, holding back her tears. "I know I'll never replace you, but I'll watch over Nate—and now Jennifer, too—with as much love and care as you might have." She glanced wistfully at the marrieds-to-be. "Oh, and, Jim, in case you're wondering, I forgave you a long time ago, though I'm still not sure I've completely forgiven myself. But I'll keep working on it."

Jennifer put an arm around Amy, who was still staring out at the Pacific. "How did that feel?" she asked.

"I don't know. Better late than never?" she replied with a smile.

"I'm sure he would have been happy to hear that. I know I am," Nate said, tightly clutching the vial of ashes, ready to set them free. He looked at Amy and Jennifer and raised the container in the air. "Are we ready?" The women both nodded.

Nate faced the water. "Don't worry, Dad. We're gonna be okay." And with that, Nate flung the ashes into the air. He watched them get swept up in the breeze until they flew off every which way as the sun began its descent into the glimmering sea.

ACKNOWLEDGMENTS

Like Nate when he lost his father, I was thirty years old when my mother, Natalie, died. It was decades too soon for her, but a lifetime too soon for me. She was a wonderful mother and a perpetual guiding light, as well as a great friend. Not a day goes by when I don't think about her and what it might be like to still have a mother—or at least to have had one much longer than I did.

Those kinds of thoughts about my own long-gone parent laid the groundwork for *The Mother I Never Had*, which I then spun into a wholly fictional "What if?" tale. That is, what if you never had a mother and suddenly found yourself with one at a particularly vulnerable and susceptible time in your life? In this case, right after the death of the one parent you *did* have? How would it change you and how would you incorporate that virtual stranger into your life? How fortuitous would a scenario like that be? How complicated?

So first and foremost, I'd like to thank my mother, to whom this book is dedicated, for everything she was and all that she did for her children. Mom, you are sorely missed.

To my family and friends: My deepest thanks for your ongoing love, support, and enthusiasm throughout all of my creative endeavors. Especially my better half, Bill, who after all these years never ceases to laugh at my corny jokes and mistakenly thinks I'm far more talented than I am. You're the best. And to my sister, Lynn, a late-blooming writer, who is always there with a ready ear, an encouraging word, and a well of emotional insight.

To everyone who read, talked up, recommended, posted about, promoted, interviewed me for, and maybe found a little bit of themselves in my last novel, *The Last Birthday Party*: You were the candles on its cake. Or to use a more tried-and-true phrase, the wind beneath its wings. (Yeah, I know, but it's really a great lyric at times like this.) You spoiled me with your attention and, just so you're aware, I'm expecting it again.

Enormous thanks, kudos, and hugs to the doyennes of Hadleigh House. Every author should be lucky enough to have the likes of Allison, Alisha, and Anna in their corner for the long and painstaking journey of publishing their work. I'm thrilled that we've been able to enjoy an encore to our relationship with this second book.

To my editor, Kate, who has once again proven to be a wonderfully astute and insightful force for making my words and thoughts make as much sense as intended. I love her note upon reading the first draft of *Mother*, that it had "a layer of humor in even the darkest moments." Who knew?

I'd also like to give a shoutout to Renee Weiss Weingarten, who founded the vibrant Facebook community known as Renee's Reading Club. Your devotion to books, authors, and readers is second to none and this writer greatly appreciates the kindness you've shown him and *The Last Birthday Party*.

And finally, to all the mothers and fathers we've ever had, who've done the profound, challenging, and hopefully gratifying work of raising their children the best way they knew how: My hat is eternally off to you.

ABOUT GARY GOLDSTEIN

Gary Goldstein is an award-winning writer for film, TV, and the theatre with more than thirty produced screen and stage credits. His first novel, the romantic comedy *The Last Birthday Party*, won a 2022 IBPA Benjamin Franklin Award for Excellence in Fiction. The New York native and longtime L.A. resident is also a contributing film reviewer and arts feature writer for the *Los Angeles Times*.

Read more about Gary at www.GaryGoldsteinLA.com
or follow him @GaryGoldsteinLA.

The Mother I Never Had
Book Club Questions

1. Nate is shocked and overwhelmed, of course, when he finds out who Amy actually is. What was the biggest secret you ever learned about a relative? How did the news affect your life?

2. Jim had his reasons for not being honest with Nate about his mother, but was an otherwise great father. Had he lived, do you think Jim would have ever told Nate the truth about Eileen and Amy? If so, when would Jim have been most likely to do so ?

3. Nate initially wanted to follow in his father's footsteps and become a teacher, but decided to go into landscape design instead. Did you ever study for one career only to shift gears into another? Where did you begin and where did you end up?

4. Amy doesn't reveal her true identity to Nate until she mostly has no choice. Did you think less of her for her initial pretense and think she should have come clean from the start? What would you have done in her situation?

5. Nate didn't have an inherent love of literature but incorporated books into his life out of devotion to his father. Was there an activity or interest essential to one of your parents that you took on to be closer to them? Was it short-lived or did it continue?

6. It's been said that you can tell a lot about a man—and how he may treat his romantic partner—based on how he treats his mother. How do you think Nate's dynamic with Amy helped or hindered his relationship with Jennifer?

7. Based on how Amy's parents handled her pregnancy, how did you feel about the way they acted toward their grandson, Nate, thirty years later? Did you find them sympathetic or at least relatable? Should Amy have forgiven them? Should Nate?

8. Was there any point where you felt Nate was too hard on Amy? How much of his overall response do you think was based on his anger at her versus his disappointment in the father he idolized?

9. Landscaping plays a major role in Nate's daily life—it's both his vocation and avocation. Did you find any specific symbolism in his work as it related to his personal or family life or the story's theme?

10. When it came to Jennifer and Nate's relationship, ultimately love—and patience—conquered all, but it was certainly touch and go for a while. What are some of the issues that you and your spouse or partner—or another couple you may know—had to surmount before finally being able to commit to each other?

11. Discuss Nate's relationship with his business partner, Danny. They're two very different men yet find a special kinship. How do they complement each other's personalities? In what ways are they more alike than they may realize?

12. Robin is caught between her love for and reliance on her mother and her excitement about having a brother. In the end, she takes the high road and encourages Amy to stay in L.A. with Nate. What kind of future do you think Robin and Nate will have as siblings?

www.ingramcontent.com/pod-product-compliance
Lightning Source LLC
Chambersburg PA
CBHW020130310726
48970CB00006B/1811